CRITICS RAVE ABOUT *USA TODAY* BESTSELLING AUTHOR JADE LEE!

BURNING TIGRESS

"The latest in Lee's *Tigress* series...offers a more humorous tone, but have no fear: Lee's deft eroticism hasn't lost any of its power. With her latest variant on the Tigress practice, Lee's star continues to burn bright."

—*Booklist*

"Lee brilliantly utilizes the m ntasy, drawing on ancient Taoist s and the belief that by each nirvana.... With a neets strong plotline that West in a mesmeriz s sensual and spiritual and displays he fullest."

—*RT BOOKreviews*

SEDUCED BY CRIMSON

"Up-and-comer Lee showcases her talent for the paranormal as she deftly blends action and romance with the eerie. Brava!"

—*RT BOOKreviews* (Top Pick)

DESPERATE TIGRESS

"Elegant complexity and beautifully rendered flaws in Shi Po and Kui Yu elevate the latest novel in Lee's series to a new plane of accomplishment. If Lee's skills continue to grow at this rate, it will be she who becomes an Immortal."

—*Booklist*

"Her story transports readers onto another plane of erotic romance."

—*RT BOOKreviews*

"If you long for a fresh reading experience, *Desperate Tigress* is just the ticket."

—*Romance Reviews Today*

MORE PRAISE FOR JADE LEE!

HUNGRY TIGRESS

"A highly sensual, titillating read."

—*RT BOOKreviews*

"*Hungry Tigress* is unusual and provocative...[and it] delivers a love story that all romance readers can appreciate."

—*Romance Reviews Today*

"Jade Lee is quickly on her way to becoming a unique and powerful voice in this industry."

—A Romance Review

WHITE TIGRESS

"An erotic romance for those seeking a heated love story."

—*RT BOOKreviews*

"Jade Lee has written a complex, highly erotic story... extremely sensual."

—*Affaire de Coeur*

"This exotic, erotic and spiritual historical romance is unique."

—Harriet Klausner

DEVIL'S BARGAIN

"Jade Lee has written a dark and smoldering story...full of sensuality and heart-pounding sex scenes."

—*Affaire de Coeur*

"A luscious bonbon of a sensual read—the education of an innocent: hot, sensual, romantic, and fun!"

—Thea Devine, *USA Today* bestselling author

"A spicy new debut...."

—*RT BOOKreviews*

CORNERED

"Say you love me. Admit it."

Her mouth went dry. She opened her mouth to speak, but no sound came out. She couldn't lie to him. Not now, not with him planted so deeply within her and his eyes so intense on her.

"Say it," he whispered. "Please."

She swallowed. If she said it to him, she would have to mean it. She tried to move her hips, tried to distract him, but his fingers bore down hard to keep her still.

"Do you?" he rasped. "Do you love me?"

Did she? Could she?

There was only one way to find out....

Cornered Tigress

JADE LEE

LEISURE BOOKS NEW YORK CITY

A LEISURE BOOK®

January 2007

Published by

Dorchester Publishing Co., Inc.
200 Madison Avenue
New York, NY 10016

If you purchased this book without a cover you should be aware that this book is stolen property. It was reported as "unsold and destroyed" to the publisher and neither the author nor the publisher has received any payment for this "stripped book."

Copyright © 2007 by Katherine Grill

All rights reserved. No part of this book may be reproduced or transmitted in any form or by any electronic or mechanical means, including photocopying, recording or by any information storage and retrieval system, without the written permission of the publisher, except where permitted by law.

ISBN 0-8439-5689-5

The name "Leisure Books" and the stylized "L" with design are trademarks of Dorchester Publishing Co., Inc.

Printed in the United States of America.

Visit us on the web at www.dorchesterpub.com.

Cornered
Tigress

AUTHOR'S NOTE

The opening chapter quotes come from an excellent cookbook titled *The Wisdom of the Chinese Kitchen, Classic Family Recipes for Celebration and Healing* by Grace Young. They are not always direct quotes due to space considerations, but I tried to keep the meaning the same. Although I am a terrible cook myself, I found this book to be a joy to read and highly recommend it.

A lively fish is a good omen. Its tenaciousness symbolizes the fish's immortality. Thus, to eat a fish that fights to the very end is to ingest the ultimate in long life and good fortune.

Chapter One

Number One Slave paused outside the doorway. Without moving a muscle, he took visual stock of his clothing and his thoughts, even ran a hand over his shaved head. All was in order, and yet he could not stop the rising panic in his chest. Rather than fight it, he nurtured it. He allowed fear to tremble in his hands and narrow his vision. In this manner, he stayed alive in his master's presence.

He entered Su Jian Lie's eating chamber on his knees. Master Su did not require such acts of his top slave, but Number One had seen many others before him become overconfident in their status. Even his older brother had succumbed and it had eventually cost him his life. So Number One remained on his knees before his master to remind himself that for all his wealth and status, he was still a slave.

Master Su's eyes did not even flicker as Number One entered the chamber. The morning ritual was well established, and so the master finished his tea in silence while the breakfast congee was removed and sweet leaves were thrown in the brazier to chase away the smell. Sparks momentarily flashed on the master's jade bracelet: a five-toed dragon, an obviously imperial gift to the most well-connected businessman in all of Shanghai. Then, with a twitch of his finger, Master Su commanded his first slave to speak.

"The day dawns bright, plum blossoms open to the sun, and a branch trembles in the wind. Mayhap it will fall. The dog whimpers in fear and awe." The poem was not his best, but the meaning was clear. It had nothing to do with the actual weather. In truth the sun was middling today, the sky gray even in this most exclusive neighborhood of Chinese Shanghai. Winter was fast approaching and no early spring blossoms appeared anywhere. The poem was about various people his master controlled. Or soon would control.

"Speak of this branch," Master Su said.

"Farmer Luk has an ill crop. His debt is only three quarters paid."

"Daughters?"

"Already sold and not very pretty." Barely enough to pay the interest.

"Sons?"

"Three."

"Pretty?"

"The eldest."

Master Su tightened his lips. It was a grave thing to sell a man's eldest son. "Speak of the dog."

Number One hesitated, weighing his words as was appropriate when passing judgment on a man and his family. "Farmer Luk acknowledges your power and trembles in all humility. The dog acts as a dog should."

Master Su's eyes flickered. He would be merciful, not because he was a forgiving man but because, on this day, he appeared bored. Whipping a beaten dog would not entertain. "Sell the youngest to the emperor as a eunuch.

Then sell the ox. Let the other boys pull the plow. He shall have an extra month."

Not so merciful, then. Number One dipped his head in obedience. No farmer could pay the debt in one month when the harvest was already counted and sold. And the loss of the ox would make even that a hardship. But another month as a free man was no small thing.

Master Su poured himself more tea. "Speak of the blossoms."

"Two grow upon the branch. One is dark and ready to wither, the other small and barely begun."

Master Su's eyes did not rise as he drank with reverence, but Number One had seen the twitch in his fingertips. Master Su was surprised that two blossoms had appeared. As was his custom, he dispensed with the dullest first. "Mr. Wang does not pay his tax?"

"He lied about the receipts as you predicted." The smallest touch of admiration colored Number One's tone. It was not feigned and it helped to hide the anticipation that quickened his heartbeat. Master Su was innovative in his murders, especially when bored.

But the expected death was not to be. Instead, Master Su raised his eyes to the calligraphy on the wall. It was a Confucian adage about the timely use of all resources, including people. "Then opportunity is given to the dog."

Number One acknowledged the statement with a nod. Farmer Luk would be allowed to force Mr. Wang to confess his lies and pay appropriate recompense. Whatever money the farmer could threaten or force or torture out of Mr. Wang above the initial debt would be applied to his own payments. In this way, Master Su received the money due and a new slave as well, all without expending any effort at all. Of course, neither Wang nor Luk would understand their enslavement. No one did until it was much too late. Always debt brought them within reach, then greed kept them inside while Master Su feasted on the profits. In the end, all served to their best ability while Master Su's coffers grew.

"And the second blossom?"

"Tan Kui Yu and his wife, the Tigress of Shanghai, were taken last night. They are imprisoned by General Kang and questioned regarding a missing son." Number One delivered the news in the same even tone as he used for everything else, but inside, his belly quivered with excitement. He had gone to great effort and expense to cultivate the spy network that had brought him the news. Now he would know if his efforts were worthwhile.

Master Su took a long time thinking. While his gaze remained abstract, his right forefinger stroked each of the dragon's toes on his imperial-gift bracelet. Such was his way when presented with a fresh blossom. But this possibility had everything the master searched for: chance for great gain in wealth and power, revenge against a family that had opposed him, and best of all, a challenge to relieve the ache of boredom.

"Who knows of this?"

Number One swallowed. Here was the most dangerous part. He had acted with initiative. If he had guessed wrong, then he would be killed for his impertinence. "None who still live," he answered as smoothly as possible. "Save General Kang, who has left for Peking, and the guards who watch the forgotten prisoners."

Master Su's brows lowered in dark fury. "You would kill soldiers of General Kang in my name?"

"Never!" Number One rushed to answer. "Drunken brawls are common among soldiers, and no general values a man with a loose tongue. General Kang will not miss his men." Number One said the words and prayed they were true. More vital, he prayed that his master believed them to be true.

With horror, Number One saw his master reach beneath the table to finger the white man's gun. It was an ignoble weapon, hidden so a man could not see death coming, and Master Su was lethal with it. His breath in his throat, Number One considered his options. There were none. No way to run without being shot, and no way to talk his way free. Master Su had been known to shoot babblers on principle. Number One could only press his forehead to the floor and pray the end would be swift.

Finally, the master made his pronouncement. "A gift of a dog to the hawk who saw this blossom."

Number One lifted his head, his mouth gaping. Had he heard true? As the hawk who brought this opportunity to light, was he to be given a reward? He saw the truth in Master Su's profile as the man stared at the Confucian adage. His reward was Farmer Luk and the farmer's charge, Mr. Wang. The terms would be as usual: a premium to Master Su on all receipts from the farmer's land and Wang's gem store, but the rest would be his own. With prudent management, Number One could be very, very rich soon.

Number One banged his forehead three times on the floor in gratitude and then scurried backward on all fours, out of the room. He did this in thanks and in remembrance, knowing that Master Su would understand the significance. For all that Number One had just gained the wealth of the elite, he was still a cockroach before his master.

A man's high-pitched scream cut through the coolie a-ho chant that droned in the distance. Captain Jonas Storm cursed as he spun around, his gaze immediately finding his sailor dangling from the rigging. Beside him, the Chinese customs official peered as well, but his eyes would be less able to discern form and function in the early morning glare.

Lester dangled upside down, halfway up the sail. One leg was clearly snapped, but Jonas couldn't tell if the man was unconscious from the pain or something much worse.

"Dead?" asked the official in badly accented English.

Jonas narrowed his eyes as he watched the half-Chinese boy Adam scamper up the ropes. That child was quick and agile as a monkey. And, more important, he wasn't thinking about drinking and whoring like the rest of his suddenly careless crew. Even better, he was a calm boy, levelheaded in a pinch and smart as a whip. But for all that, the child was still young and would react badly at the sight of his first dead body.

Jonas waited, his fingers idly toying with a small brass key in his pocket, as Adam checked the sailor. Suddenly, the boy audibly cursed and punched Lester. Jonas sent a silent prayer of thanks to Mother Mary. Obviously Lester wasn't dead, just stupid. Of course, the customs official beside him didn't know that. So Jonas began his own set of fluid curses, half in English, half in Shanghai dialect.

The official turned stunned eyes back to Jonas. "Man dead?"

"I am cursed!" he said in English. Then he repeated it in Chinese just to make sure the man understood. "His mother will hex me when she finds out. Me and all I commerce with."

The official shied sideways. "What is 'hex'?"

"A magical curse. Very evil and very powerful." Then he groaned and spat into the greasy Shanghai mud. "Ill winds surround me like flies," he said, irritated to realize that for today, at least, it was true. Then he pretended to gather his thoughts to focus on the paperwork. "You say that Tan Kui Yu has not taken care of this? He has always sorted through the papers as we dock." It wasn't a lie. Kui Yu should be there with all the customs work already completed. He swore again. "Bloody hell, the curse is spreading to my associates."

As expected, the customs man looked terribly alarmed. By nature, sailors were a superstitious lot, but the Chinese made his crew look like pragmatic bean counters. Mention a curse, and their yellow skin turned almost white.

"I suppose you'll have to inspect the cargo, too," Jonas continued. "We'll be hours together."

That was all that was needed to completely terrify the official. No one wanted a white man's curse polluting their luck. "No, no!" the man stammered, obviously anxious to be gone. He pulled out his tiny box of red seals called chops and began stamping with a vengeance. "I'm sure Mr. Tan had everything in order. No need to trouble you anymore, especially on a day like today." One last uneasy glance at the unconscious Lester, currently being lowered from the rigging, and the official fled.

Jonas allowed his grimace to ease. Really, he ought to thank Lester for pissing up this morning. Instead, the horny bastard would be nursing a busted leg and a neglected dick. Well, experience was the best teacher. Meanwhile, Jonas had his own pile of problems to be sorted. He'd spoken the truth when he'd said this morning had an ill stench to it. Since the very beginning of their association, Kui Yu had never failed to meet him at the pier. The man always came well ahead of the customs official with plenty of time to direct the storage of the more sensitive goods.

So where was he? And where was Frank? The *Auspicious Wind* should have arrived a week ago, but he hadn't seen it or her ship's captain anywhere. No Frank, no Kui Yu, and now Lester had taken a tumble. He did not like the smell of that.

A bellow from the ship caught his attention. The men were wondering what to do with the injured Lester. Jonas bit off a curse as he trudged up the gangplank, his tasks already itemized in his head. First, he would square away Lester and the cargo. He would use Kui

Yu's usual warehouse for the regular shipment. The sensitive cargo would have to wait until later.

Second, he would find Frank and get an accounting from him for *The Auspicious Wind*'s cargo. Truthfully, he needed the cash more than an accounting, but he would demand both.

Third, he would find Kui Yu even if it meant traveling to the man's home. He'd already named the Tan compound The House of Beautiful and Angry Women. Not a place he wished to visit on an unlucky day. But with a hold filled with rapidly spoiling cargo, he had to move his shipment now. And that meant finding Kui Yu.

Assuming, of course, no other witch chose to spit on his day.

"What trickery is this, you diseased son of a monkey? These aren't fish! They're foul minnows." Little Pearl straightened away from the market stall with a sneer of disgust. In truth, the air tasted of dying fish not yet spoiled, but she didn't say that.

"Aie, aie! What abuse you spew!" returned Mr. Gui. "This is the thanks I get for saving the best of the catch for you? All morning long, shoppers come to me and ask to pay exorbitant amounts for my fish. No! I cry. They are saved for Little Pearl of the Tan household."

"Then they must have switched fish when you weren't looking, you blind old fool. What is here is not fit for a dog."

Mr. Gui threw up his hands. "A dog! General Kang's chef was just here, praising my fish to the skies. Said the general wanted more for His Honor's table. That he had a distinguished—"

"Bah!" Little Pearl said, cutting him off. "What do soldiers know of cooking? Mr. Tan, however, has an excellent palate. He knows a lively fish when he tastes it, and Mrs. Tan feels the qi in every bite. She told me if I bought from you again, I would be thrown out on the street!" She peered down at the bucket by his feet containing three fat steelheads squirming in the tiny space. There were the fish he had saved for her, and after a moment's study, she judged them acceptable. "You have nothing I want," she said as she hefted her market sack.

"Wait, wait!" Mr. Gui called. "You have not seen the best yet." Then he brought out the bucket.

Little Pearl made a show of sneering. She and Mr. Gui both relished their daily squabble. She would not shorten it too soon. "Average," she groused. "Nothing more than average."

"What! Are you sick as well as stupid?" Mr. Gui went on, pouring his yang into defending his fish and insulting her senses. She let him rant, a part of her appreciating his fire. In truth, Mr. Gui was in rare form today and she should enjoy the display. But the morning was advancing fast and she was anxious to be in her kitchen cooking for the afternoon meal.

"Very well," she finally sighed, cutting him off midsentence. "I will take your diseased fish at your ridiculous price, but I will have those shrimp as well."

"You are crazy!" he cried.

"You are stupid!" she retorted.

Then they got down to serious bargaining. In the end, Little Pearl had her steelhead fish, her shrimp, and a small squid. Mr. Gui had the last of her purse and a happy wave as she left. They would both eat well tonight.

But Little Pearl's smile faded long before her tiny, bound feet made it out of the market. It was a sad day indeed when a riotous session with Mr. Gui could not make her happy. Her store of male yang energy was obviously depleted. It lasted less and less time lately, and she had no understanding of why. Female yin, she had in abundance. It kept her skin fresh, her step light, and her body amazingly youthful. Indeed, no one would guess her at nearly thirty years of age. She looked and dressed more like a mature sixteen.

But the yang energy, the power willingly surrendered by men in their sexual emission, this energy she could not seem to retain. She harvested as much as she could. She daily sat in contemplation and purification of that yang. But bit by bit, her fire faded, her assertive power and male strength withered long before she could use it. Once she could retain the fire for weeks on end. Now, she was lucky if it lasted a few days before listlessness returned.

What was happening to her? Without enough male yang, she would never be able to attain Heaven and become a Tigress Immortal.

A few months ago, a white woman—Lydia Smith— had reached the highest level a tigress could and became an Immortal. Such a thing had shocked and revitalized the entire school, Little Pearl included. Little Pearl had devoted what extra time she had to increased study and meditation. But without yang, she would be unable to reach even the antechamber to Heaven, the mystical Chamber of a Thousand Swinging Lanterns.

She passed a group of cripples and beggars that congregated on the Tan side of the market. Her gaze expertly scanned the group, picking the men who would be good sources of yang for herself and her fellow students. The women she disdained, her stomach churning at the scent of dirty women. There were some who would appreciate the added yin, but Little Pearl was not one of them.

By the time she made it to the Tan household, her feet were numb and her calves burned. If she hadn't spent the last of her purse on the squid, she could have taken a rickshaw, but she counted the excellent food well worth the pain in her legs. The mistress had a fondness for squid made with just the right amounts of ginger and plum, and Little Pearl would suffer much for the great

Tigress Shi Po. Without Mrs. Tan, Little Pearl would still be a drugged prostitute spreading her legs for whatever dog paid Madame Ting. Instead, she was creating culinary feasts and teaching the pathway to Immortality to China's discarded women. It was a good life, and one she valued greatly.

With that happy thought in mind, she entered the front courtyard. She stopped dead, her sacks of fresh food slipping in her grip, but not tumbling to the ground. Even a destroyed courtyard, even horse dung and smashed roof tiles could not make her spill good squid in the dirt. Something terrible had happened last night, and Little Pearl choked on her fear for the Tans.

Swallowing down the bitter taste, Little Pearl ran through the main gate. "Mistress Tan! Mistress Tan!" she screamed as she rushed past the receiving hall. The scent of torn herb pillows lay heavy on the air. Even the family garden was in disarray, the lovely fountains smashed beyond repair. "Mistress Tan! Mistress Tan!"

Her words echoed back to her in the empty courtyard. She could tell by the way the sound fell like stones that no one was about: no students, no servants, no family. Only Little Pearl and her dying fish that still squirmed faintly in her sack.

Biting back tears, Little Pearl went to the kitchen first. She quickly disposed of her marketing, and then went in search of the Tans. She went through every room and secret hiding place. Everywhere she looked she saw disaster. Broken pots, churned mud, torn tapestries, but no blood and no bodies. Blood and death had their own smell, and she could taste nothing like that in the air.

Not dead then, only captured. And with no Mrs. Tan to tell them all was safe, the servants had disappeared. Such was the nature of Mrs. Tan's work that she had ordered all who worked or studied here to disappear should something appear amiss.

Little Pearl stepped into the Tans' bedchamber and struggled against her tears when she saw the broken bedframe and shattered perfume vials. She cursed the Manchurians who ruled over China. She cursed the Qin and most of all she cursed General Kang, who no doubt was the one who'd abducted the Tans in the middle of the night. Only Kang's soldiers had horses to break the courtyard stones and foul the ornamental shrubs. And only the most powerful general in all of China would dare abduct the wealthy Tans from their bed.

Little Pearl felt her hands clench. She was a small woman with bound feet. She had little money and no status. But still she thought of punching the horrible General Kang in his face. She would beat his arrogant brow and rip off his privates. Then she would tear open the cell door and bring the Tans home where they belonged. She would personally supervise the drawing of the perfumed baths, and she would make them such a feast that the hateful Manchus would be completely forgotten.

That was what she would do if she could. Frustration filled her with a surge of rancid yang. It coiled in her breast and found escape in vicious curses and violent fantasies. But soon even that yang depleted, leaving her weak and trembly amid the debris of an emptied home.

The Tans were not here. She had walked the compound twice, mentally cataloguing all the damage. It did not take long for her to form an idea of what had happened. The soldiers arrived in the dead of night. Neither the master nor the mistress had been in bed. They had been in the main exercise chamber and teaching room. She had no idea what they'd been doing. She had found a poisoned dagger, discarded clothing, and a message to herself. This she had quickly torn open, praying for a different explanation, but what was written there only added to her confusion.

Little Pearl, Shi Po had written, *allow Kui Yu to manage all funeral arrangements. He will wish to do so himself. To you, I entrust my most precious Tigress school. I know you will run it well for I have seen your great yin heart and vital yang force. I also ask that you take charge of my husband. He will need a strong woman at his side and I know you will make an excellent wife for him. May your qi ever flow strong and clear, my dear friend and fellow cub. Knowing you are here lightens my passing.—Shi Po*

Little Pearl read the missive three times and still had no idea what it meant. Obviously, her mistress had expected to die. Did that mean she'd known General Kang would come for her? But Kui Yu was gone, too. Or was he? None of it made any sense.

Without conscious thought, she wended her way through the compound back to the kitchen. She would make soup for herself and the servants, something that could be eaten whenever whoever eventually appeared. It would boil in the back courtyard fire, the aroma an enticement to servant and student alike. Since no worker was around to start the fire, Little Pearl abused her feet more as she gathered charcoal and wood. The fire lit quickly, her hands moving at lightning speed. She poured water into the pot, then added the leftover stock from last night's chicken. One of the steelheads would go squirming into the pot as soon as the water boiled. In the meantime, she would chop vegetables while she thought.

She harvested the last of the green onion, chopping it quickly while the unnerving silence ate into her calm. The Tan household was marked by noise and movement of servants, students, even animals. All were absent, and so she doubled the noise of knife against wood to drown out the stillness.

Eventually the women appeared. By ones and twos, the students slipped into the kitchen, their eyes wide, their shoulders hunched in fear. Little Pearl acted as she always did. She pointed to the food, and as they ate, she gave them their instructions. No class today. Instead, they would clean and take stock of what had survived the night and what had not. All this would be reported back to Little Pearl in the kitchen. And in this manner, she survived the bulk of the day.

The first visitor appeared just before noon: Mrs. Sing with the laundry. Little Pearl paid from the kitchen money and made no answer to the woman's probing questions. Everything was as it should be, she lied. Why do you ask?

Then came the usual parade of beggars, cripples, and the curious. Despite her lies to the laundry woman, anyone who peered into the front courtyard would see the disaster. To these outsiders, she maintained a steady stream of small talk as if nothing were wrong, no one was missing, all was normal.

Ken Jin appeared just after midday, Ken Jin and his newest white pet. She dispensed with them as quickly as possible. She was ill-tempered with her former dragon partner, but she had no time for his games. They had once cared for one another, but he had grown too attached. Now she allowed her anger to pollute the air between them as a reminder to them both that a dragon and tigress might share yin and yang in their sexual congress, but they never loved one another. Nevertheless, when he left, she found herself stripping vegetables with more calm. If anyone could find out the truth about the Tans, it would be Ken Jin. She trusted him that much.

Time to steam the dumplings for the prostitutes' evening meal. Many of the students practiced their craft at the nearby pleasure gardens. None would receive dinner despite the exorbitant prices the madams charged for their services. So Little Pearl gave them dumplings filled with vegetables and herbs to aid in yang energy retention. They would eat between clients and gather much yang.

She had set the first dumplings in the steaming pot

when another caller appeared: an associate of Master Tan requesting an audience. Little Pearl sighed. These interruptions did not make for balanced food.

She wiped the moisture off her face and hurried to the reception hallway. Two steps outside of the kitchen and she had to turn back around. She could not appear before a businessman as a cook. She quickly stripped out of her food-stained tunic and pulled on a respectable gown. She had only one—a well-worn black silk tunic with gold embroidery to bring brightness to her dark eyes. It was designed for seduction, the clasps pulling the fabric tight to her small hips and pert breasts. The skirt was slit all the way up her thigh. It was a respectable *chong san* for a respectable woman, though rather elaborate for midafternoon. It also made the men salivate and their yang surge, especially since it gave full view of her tiny bound feet.

She'd taken too much time changing her clothing, so now she had to rush to the receiving chamber. She used the handholds placed throughout the compound to ease the ache in her legs and to speed her progress, but she still appeared inappropriately breathless when she stepped into the reception room.

"My deepest apologies for the delay," she whispered, her voice automatically taking on the husky tones of a seductress. She never consciously changed her mannerisms, they simply shifted as she donned one outfit or another.

The man turned to greet her, his black Manchurian queue barely shifting with his body. She smiled and bowed to him, belatedly realizing that she had erred. Not only had she forgotten to order tea, but she was not hidden behind the women's screen. Only a prostitute or the clumsiest servant would appear before a visitor like this.

She felt her shoulders hunch in shame and her gaze dropped to the floor. Too late to slip behind the screen now. At best, she would have to act as exactly what she was: a stupid, ignorant servant awkwardly thrust into a role too elevated for her training.

"Master Tan not home today," she said in a coarse accent. "Best come back tomorrow."

The man didn't answer but studied her with unnerving intensity. She reciprocated the inspection, but through lowered eyelashes. He was of average height for a Han Chinese and had a fastidious appearance. His tunic was made of the best silk and excellently tailored, but his tone was modest, his entire impression . . . inconsequential. All except for a nearly hidden jade bracelet on his right wrist: an imperial dragon which marked him as a very well-connected man in Shanghai.

He dressed to be unnoticed, but Little Pearl had been trained to evaluate a man's qi in a heartbeat. This man had enough yang power to overwhelm a woman. He was not insignificant. If anything, he had the power of a governor or viceroy running through his veins. That he would hide such strength beneath modest tailoring made him doubly dangerous. The deadliest snakes hid in the most common grass.

"Greetings, Tan mistress," he said formally, his friendly tone completely at odds with his suppressed energy.

"No, no," she responded with pretend embarrassment. "I am not the mistress here. I am merely—"

"The cook. Yes, I know."

She blinked, momentarily stunned. His lips curled in a friendly smile that clashed with his energies. She could not define how, only that she did not trust his false openness.

"You are Little Pearl," he said. "Kui Yu spoke of you often. He praised your cooking. . . ." His voice dropped in tone. "And your beauty."

Was she supposed to be flattered? What kind of woman would be pleased that she distracted her mistress's husband? She straightened and folded her hands demurely before her. "You are correct, sir. I am the cook. Please return tomorrow to speak with Mr. Tan."

"But he is not coming back. Nor is Shanghai's most famous Tigress. Surely you know this."

It took all her training not to leap upon his news and demand answers. She lifted her gaze to his open expression and pretended complete stupidity. "I don't understand."

"The Tans have been taken by General Kang. You will most likely never see them again."

"You are mistaken," she said coldly, but her muscles trembled with the strain of remaining upright. His yang power was overwhelming, and she was rapidly failing beneath the onslaught. Her yin urged her to soften and yield. "I have served all the Tan guests, and you have never been one of them."

His smile widened at her words, and too late she realized their double meaning. She meant that she'd served them food. He obviously knew she did other tasks as well. Too late she remembered that he'd called Shi Po the famous Tigress of Shanghai. He knew, then. He knew what was taught here and was titillated by it.

Except once again, his energies did not feel sexually excited. They felt . . .

"I apologize," he said with a sudden burst of laughter. Her thoughts scattered at the sound, and she found her gaze pulled back to him. He looked like a stick pretending to be the happy Buddha. "I am Mr. Su, but you should call me Jian Lie. I believe that we shall become fast friends, you and I, as we weather this storm."

He was trying to seduce her, she abruptly realized. First he complimented her looks, then he offered her information, and lastly, he extended an equal friendship to her, a lowly cook. Add to that the heated pulse of his yang energy, and most women would collapse in gratitude without even knowing the cause.

Truly, he had the skill of a dragon, and yet such a focused campaign left her angry. She had no time for seductive games. The dumplings were probably rotting in the steamer right now. Still, she had responsibilities to Shi Po's students, if nothing else.

She straightened. "If you return tomorrow, I will find a student for you. Your yang runs too strong. It must be very uncomfortable." Then she bowed deeply before him. "My apologies, but my duties call me."

She turned to leave, but he stopped her with words that cut like cold iron. "Mr. Tan and I had business together. With him in prison, I must take on his tasks just as you must become mistress here. Do not think to gainsay me on this. I must see his papers."

"Mr. Tan is not here," she retorted firmly, part of her wondering where she found the strength. "Please return tomorrow. Perhaps he will see you then."

He released a hiss of frustration, a hot breath that fouled the air between them. Truly his yang was poisoning him. "The Tans will not return. How will you teach her students, feed their servants, and pay their taxes without money? How will you honor your mistress without my help?"

"By locking Mr. Tan's office door against all who would rob him."

"I am not a thief!" he spat. "I am trying to help!"

She almost believed him. But experience taught that a man of strong yang could make a woman believe almost anything. And yet she felt abused by him rather than persuaded. His yang cut tiny rivulets into her as surely as a knife scoured the scales off a fish. To hide the pain, she dropped into a respectful bow. "Apologies, sir, but I must attend to my duties."

He relaxed then. He smiled and ran a hand over his face as if in exhaustion while his bracelet winked in the sunlight; casual gestures that appeared too polished to be true. "Soon the money will be gone and creditors will break down the door. Only I, Su Jian Lie, can help you." He paused and his gaze burned with yang intensity. "All depends on you now. The Tans' fortune is under your control to strengthen or waste. Think of how you will be rewarded should you make the right choices. I will return for your answer tomorrow."

She had no answer for that and no time to ask; he spun on his heel and left while she remained frozen with indecision. Could he be right? She cared nothing for a reward, but what if the Tan money did depend on her? How could she manage? The kitchen money would not last long. Fortunately, she knew the location of the other cache: a large sum of money for emergencies. But how much was there? The Tan household required much cash to support both home and school. What if the Tans returned to find that their home had been lost, the students scattered to the wind, and nothing remained of all that had once been?

Was it truly Little Pearl's task to see that all remained as it once was? The thought was horrifying. And yet who else could bear this burden?

Jan. 11, 1878

Dear Albert,

How is it at home? Are you well? And Mum? Is she the same? Life on ship was really exciting for about an hour. Then it became completely awful. All my books were stolen. I found one of them later, half the pages ripped out. They were used to light lanterns, I think. The rest were probably thrown overboard for spite.

My blanket was taken too while I was sick. First day was sun and work, but I didn't mind because it was different. Then there wasn't much sun. Then it was wet, everything wet all the time with no way to get dry or warm. Then I was sick—puking into a bowl and still wet. I missed you and Mum so much.

It's better now. I'm not sick anymore. And I've learned how to hide things so they don't get stolen. Captain Brown is teaching me and calls me a right smart boy, which is why the others hate me. They're older and don't like it when I understand the calculations. I still can't touch the sextant, but someday I will. Someday I'll be charting courses all over the world.

It's not so bad now. I've even gotten used to the worms in the food. But there's either a lot to do or nothing, so I think about you a lot. The first days out of port are the worst. Everyone's nasty and missing their drink, Hory worst of all. But he makes sure everything's right so we won't sink. And if you're fast on your feet, you don't get cuffed that much.

Sam's got a friend on a boat that's going back to London. He's taking this letter and a shawl for Mum. I daren't trust them with my share, so you'll have to wait for the money. Probably the shawl, too, but you can tell her I tried.

—Jonas

The main purpose of slow-simmering vegetable-based yun *soups is to correct and restore proper yin-yang balance. A bowl of* yun *soup is often served at the beginning and end of a meal.*

Chapter Two

The white man came before sundown. Though he arrived at a decent hour, the clouds had thickened, darkening the sky to pitch and making the man appear like an ugly baboon growling at the coming rain. A maid saw him trudging past the front gate and screamed in terror, thinking him a dark ghost come to eat her.

Little Pearl cursed the silly woman and set her to washing vegetables; she did not trust the girl with the squid. Then once again, Little Pearl changed her clothes and stomped to the receiving hall. Her legs had long since gone numb from all the coming and going, but there was no help for it. As Mr. Su had said, she was mistress of the Tan home today. She'd just never realized how hard it was on the feet.

She stood behind the women's screen and spoke her apology. "Mr. Tan not home," she said. "Please come back tomorrow." She spoke in Shanghai dialect, knowing he understood. Even so, her words were slow and clearly enunciated so the ape would understand. She knew a little English, which she practiced when she could, but today was not the day to encourage a baboon to stay.

He answered in kind, his Shanghai words excellently spoken, but slow and clear as if he spoke to a child. "Where is Mr. Tan?"

"Not home today. Come back—"

"Where did he go this morning?" His voice had the low rumble of disturbed yang, but it did not boil over.

"I do not know," she lied.

"He was supposed to come to the dock today. I have his cargo. Did he leave a message?"

Little Pearl frowned. This white captain was well-known to her. He disliked fish, but enjoyed crab. He relished steamed bao, but disdained fried pork dumplings. It was the oil he disliked, she guessed, because when she dropped the pork into soup, he praised her to the skies.

"But where is he?" the man grumbled, his words directed to no one in particular.

Little Pearl peered around the corner. His hair held water in its twisting coils, and his face was shadowed with dirt and evening beard. His eyes were a strange changeable color of blue and green and brown, and they seemed to shift darker with his frustration. He cursed and took an agitated turn about the room.

Little Pearl watched the display with interest. It was like seeing a storm roll and pitch in the sky, except he was inside the house and the taste in the air was of the sour docks. Was he angry? She had never seen this man in a fit before. Drunken, yes. Happy and content, often. But angry? Never.

He turned back to the screen. "Can you tell me anything? Don't you worry about him? Where is his wife? Are you still there?"

She stared at him in shock. She heard true concern in this white man's voice, read the worry on his face. He cared for the Tans, and her heart softened for this lost animal.

She looked down at her attire. Dressed in this gown, he might mistake her meaning if she stepped free of the screen. But she had long since learned how to deal with overamorous men. This one was large—very large in the way of white men—but she had manservants nearby. She had no fear for her safety. It was only propriety that she challenged if she showed herself.

"Hello? Are you still there?"

She stepped out from behind the screen. It wasn't a conscious decision, merely an instinctive response to the anxiety in his voice. "Greetings, Captain Jonas," she said as she bowed formally before him.

He smiled. "You are Little Pearl, the cook."

She looked up in surprise. "You remember me?"

"Of course." He leaned forward in a friendly manner. "All men remember an excellent cook."

"You are too kind." She bowed again, pleased by his compliment even though she felt awkward with the familiarity in his manner.

His smile faded as she straightened. Though she kept her head canted down, as was proper for a woman talking to a man, she watched him closely. She knew when his thoughts returned to the situation at hand. He rubbed a hand over his jaw and his expression grew serious. "Can you tell me what happened? When was the last time you saw Mr. Tan?"

How much to reveal? Could a white man be trusted to remain discreet? She could not risk creditors throughout the city learning of the Tans' disappearance. They would be banging on the door in a moment's notice and she did not have near enough coin to hold them off.

"Where have you looked for him?" she asked, ducking his question.

"At the docks, of course. And at the office he keeps to manage his new buildings. No one has seen him today. When did he leave this morning?"

She shook her head, as if she didn't know. "Where will you look now?"

He grimaced. Amazing, how mobile his weathered face appeared. Chinese faces were smooth and flat, and children were taught from birth to hide their thoughts behind a placid exterior. But this man was all hard lines and hair: bushy eyebrows, large nose, and a chin slightly reddened from beard. These things should have distracted from the man's expression, but instead they combined to reveal his every emotion.

"I could ask at the tea houses. . . ." His voice trailed away as he frowned. He clearly didn't like the idea. Neither did she. Every merchant in Shanghai would know of their difficulties within an hour.

"You will not find him there," she said softly.

His attention riveted on her and she nearly stumbled as his yang force hit her. Primal male energy, focused and refined, surrounded her as if she suddenly stood in the center of a storm. It buffeted her from all sides, and for a moment she simply stood still to better appreciate the churning power.

"What do you mean?" he asked in a quiet tone. Another woman would have been deceived, might have thought he barely cared about the answer. But she could feel his yang intensity and knew she had all of his attention. She knew, too, that once begun, she would have to tell him all. He would settle for nothing less.

"I believe the Tans were taken by General Kang." She paused to quiet her emotions. This was the first time she had said the words aloud to someone not in the Tigress community. Though the fear was never far from her mind, she had spent most of the day praying that it wasn't true. Saying it aloud now, to this white stranger,

made it too real for her to deny and emotions churned
sourly in her gut.

"Would you like to sit down?" he asked.

She blinked, confused by this white man's courtesy.
Chinese women did not sit before men. Certainly a cook
would never sit. But his hand cupped her elbow and
steered her to the guest couch. She went without demur,
all the while wondering at her compliance.

"Tell me all from the beginning."

"The general came yesterday during the afternoon. He
searched for something, did not find it, then left. Mrs.
Tan thought they were safe."

"And Kui Yu? What did he think?"

Little Pearl looked at her hands. It was not a servant's
place to comment on her master. Even worse, it was not a
woman's place to make such judgments. And yet, she
stumbled into an answer despite her training. "He
thought to leave, but . . ."

"But his wife convinced him all was safe." Though he
kept his tone neutral, she felt the shift in his yang. He did
not approve of Shi Po, and she stiffened at the insult.

"There was no reason to fear. The general had come
and gone." He didn't contradict her, but then again, he
didn't need to. Obviously, something had gone wrong.

"Tell me the rest," he urged as he knelt before her. The
sight was bizarre. No man kneeled to her unless in the
throes of sexual ecstasy. That he did so now without embarrassment disconcerted her. And still she felt compelled to talk.

"I brought the marketing as usual this morning but
the home was deserted, the garden churned from horse
hooves. Later, Mr. Su told me General Kang imprisons
the Tans."

"Who is Mr. Su?" Though his voice remained level,
she felt a sharpening in his energy.

She shrugged. "A man who claims joint business with

Mr. Tan." She dared to raise her gaze level with his. "You do not know him?"

Far from stiffening at her visual challenge, the man met her gaze frankly. "Never heard of him, but that means nothing. Kui Yu has many associates."

She did not respond, too confused by a man who allowed her to stare directly at him. Was he so sure in his power that he could allow a servant to challenge him without punishment? Truly, the whites were barbarians with no idea of place.

Meanwhile, the man sighed with his whole body. He seemed to slump before her as if in the midst of yang release, but this man was not reacting sexually. He was thinking and planning, or so she guessed. She waited in silence until her curiosity won out. With a Chinese man, she wouldn't dare ask, but this was a barbarian who had allowed her to look directly at his eyes. "What will you do now?"

He shrugged. "That depends on you."

She flinched. She had no understanding of why, only that her body recoiled as if from a blow. His eyes narrowed at her movement, and she cursed herself for her unnatural reaction. Fortunately, he made no comment. He simply waited for her to compose herself. All in all, it was very Chinese of him, and she felt her mind reel once again. How did one behave around a barbarian? Finally, she nodded. "What do you want?"

"I have a cargo. Kui Yu's cargo, actually, that I have to move before it spoils. But I don't know who it's supposed to go to."

"Mr. Tan's stores."

He nodded, but his eyes remained narrowed. "The lace has already been delivered. But he had other clients for the other cargo."

She shook her head. She understood none of this.

"He has a list somewhere of who gets what." His expression firmed as he peered at her. "I would like to see his papers. That list is somewhere."

She shook her head. She didn't dare let a white man see her master's papers. "Mr. Tan is very resourceful. He will return."

"God willing. I'll make some inquiries, but I don't know that pressure from a white ship captain will help."

True enough.

"In the meantime, I need that list."

"No." She abruptly pushed to her feet, tottering slightly before she found her balance. Where she discovered the yang to deny him, she had no idea. No woman or servant would dare do such a thing, not so forcefully, and certainly not to a man. But such was her discomfort with this white barbarian that she couldn't wait to escape his disturbing presence. "No," she repeated. "Mr. Tan will return soon."

Then she fled for the kitchen. Minutes later, a servant told her that he departed without anger or violence. She could only shake her head at the bizarre white behavior. What would it take for Captain Jonas to release his fury? Her hands stopped untying her skirt. What of this mysterious list? Would it be obvious? Did she dare look for it? Did she dare not?

She turned slowly around and headed for the master's office. She did not feel right going into this room. It was a man's place. Its energy was male; its contents the things of business. What did she understand of such things? Nothing. And yet, she would feel safer if she had this list in her control. Mr. Su also had wanted to see Kui Yu's papers, therefore this list must be very valuable. She had to find it to protect it.

She stepped into this most forbidden of rooms and went slowly to Master Tan's desk. How similar it appeared to her scholarly father's desk. Ink stone and brushes sat neatly to the right. She smelled parchment from the white barbarian books along the wall and stale tea from a forgotten teacup. A dirty plate and chopsticks lay beside it. Papers did indeed litter the desktop, but all were stacked and shoved to one side as if the master had been working on something else that was now put away. A letter, perhaps, or notations in a book that was now stored.

She dared not touch the stack of papers. Her father had bellowed in rage whenever she looked at his writings. She had no idea why she thought his work fascinating. Confucian dictates and her father's failed political treatises were of no value to anyone. But as a child, she had been endlessly drawn to his scribbles. Not since she'd been sold at the age of eight had she looked at a man's work.

Yet now she had to. Of all the people attached to the Tan household, she was the only servant who could read. She could ask one of the wealthier students to assist her, but she did not trust some of these bored wives not to betray the Tans to their husbands. Immortality was of value to all, but when it came to commerce— what woman did not wish to gain advantage for their family?

She touched a bamboo scroll, furious to see that her fingers shook. She would do this thing. For the Tans, for the students and people who toiled here, she would read the master's writing. She peered through the gloom at the rushed scribbling.

It was an unfinished letter to the master's brother-in-law, hastily scrawled, and just as quickly discarded. It asked for help against General Kang should disaster fall. Apparently, the master had not liked his phrasing. He had scratched out words and stroked others on top. This was not what the captain wanted.

She touched the papers next, seeing lists of expenses for the silk factory. She noted a column discussing mulberry trees; another itemized workers and their pay. She saw a full list of dyes and bolts along with a discussion of donkey carts.

Then came the things she feared to touch. Written on yellowing barbarian paper, the things were flat, flesh colored, and carried a strange smell. A newspaper, the master had called it. On it, she saw small black shapes that she could not read. She had no knowledge of barbarian magic or their things. She did not know if she would hurt it if she unfolded the page or if it would explode like their weapons if not respected.

She would have turned away then. She would have fled the room in failure if she had not seen more barbarian paper beneath the larger folded item. She could see the master's writing on it—some in Chinese, some in barbarian notation. She had to see this paper. She had to understand it if she could.

But she couldn't force herself to touch the paper. Her fear was too great. She knew she was being foolish. The master daily worked in here without damage. Why would he endanger himself? And yet, he had forbidden the servants to clean in here. He said he had barbarian weapons in here. A gun, he called it, and he had no wish for a foolish servant to accidentally blow his head off.

But a paper was not a gun, she told herself, so she compromised. She snatched up the chopsticks from the master's discarded dishes, using them to lift the newspaper away. Beneath it was indeed a list of sorts. Could this be what the white captain wanted?

She didn't know. But just in case, she took the paper and coiled it into a tight roll no larger than three chopsticks. She would hide it in Master Tan's secret cache of money. Then it would be safe.

She crossed to the floor directly beneath the painting of a dozen wild horses leaping across a stream. The floorboards looked no different here than anywhere else, but she knew how to lift them away. Shi Po had showed her the box of money kept in secret there for emergencies. Once, she'd said, it had held all Kui Yu's wealth, and such was his great love for his future wife that he had given it all to Shi Po. Now it contained gold and jade to last them for months. Little Pearl would put the paper there.

She knelt on the floor and carefully pried up the board. She smiled at the plain box that sat amid the inevitable dust. The rolled paper would just barely fit inside, assuming it wasn't already filled with money. Leaning down, she opened the box. She knew the truth even before the cry escaped her lips. From the very first moment this morning, she knew disaster lurked if only she had the strength to look. But she had been too afraid and too hopeful for the Tans' quick release from prison. And she had wanted to cling to the belief that there was lots of money for her use. But it was all gone. The box was empty.

Biting her lip to hold back the tears, Little Pearl carefully placed the rolled paper into the box. It looked small there as it slowly unfurled, and she worried at the dust that would mark the page. With an amazingly steady hand, she shut the lid and replaced the floorboards. Then she rose and walked calmly back to the kitchen.

Without money for food or gold to pay the bill collectors, she would have to look for other means to support the compound. She would have to demand payment in advance for classes. She would have to sell furniture or jewelry or services to survive. Or she could sell the list to the white captain, take the money and run away. She could disappear into the Shanghai slums and ply her first trade to survive, leaving the Tan fortune to wither or prosper without her.

Should she run? Or should she stay?

She made her decision in the time it took to walk to the kitchen. The Tan fortune would not benefit from her help. She had no understanding of it. Even with the best of intentions, she would likely destroy all she touched. She could do nothing for them.

Which meant she had to think of herself. She would wait two more days. The Tans' disappearance would not stay secret longer than that. Then there would be bill collectors barging through the door. She would be unable to protect the things they would take, unable to stop them from rampaging through the house destroying what little was left.

She would run then, but not right away. She would take two days to prepare herself. She would gather what money she could, keep a satchel of her clothing at hand, all the while searching for a new position, new possibilities. Could she find a job as someone else's cook? Probably not. No woman wanted a former prostitute in her home.

Little Pearl sighed, too afraid to think of the future. For the moment, she would finish the prostitutes' dinners. Very shortly, she would be one of them.

Jonas terrified his rickshaw driver. He hadn't done anything more than step into the seat and direct the man—in Chinese—to the docks. The skeletal-thin runner had gasped, showed the whites of his eyes, then whipped through the streets as if a demon sat behind him. At least he hadn't run away. Jonas had picked the man for his obvious near-starvation appearance. Hunger drove a man to risk even a white barbarian passenger.

Jonas eased his bulk back against the hard bamboo bench just as the rickshaw hit a large stone. The jolt was so hard he lost hold of the tiny iron pick lock in his pocket, and he grunted in dismay as it slid from his trousers to fall on the floorboards. A moment later it was lost forever as it slid between the bamboo slats to the gravel below.

"Damn," he muttered, though he had no particular

fondness for the instrument. Meanwhile the rickshaw runner nearly choked on his terror as he surged faster.

"Slow down," Jonas urged in Chinese. "I am not going to eat you." Or breathe fire. Or spook your children, your fortune, or your luck. Well, he thought dryly, perhaps he might taint the man's luck. His own had been severely tarnished of late.

Kui Yu in jail? Of all the people to run afoul of the government, he would never have guessed Tan Kui Yu. The man was moderate in temperament, shrewd without malice, cunning without evil, and he had a kindhearted streak a mile wide once you got past all that Chinese politeness. The man's only fault was that he loved his wife.

And that, obviously, was what had gotten him in trouble. The Tigress Shi Po and her unnatural religion had caused many an ill in her husband's life. She'd tortured him with unfaithfulness, taught her deviant ways to a cult of followers, and generally destroyed the efforts of a good man.

Years ago, Jonas had urged Kui Yu to abandon his wife. At a minimum, he should have severely curtailed the witch's activities before disaster struck. Always, Kui Yu had resisted. And so, with a valuable business partnership at stake—and a good friendship—Jonas had held his tongue. Now, Kui Yu was in jail and Jonas tottered on the edge of financial ruin. All because of a single evil tigress woman.

At least the cook had not tried her seductress ways. Beyond appearing before him in a dress meant to make a man's eyes pop out of his head, she had acted respectfully and with surprising gentility. He did not blame her for keeping Kui Yu's office closed to him. Suspicion was natural among the Chinese, and even more so when one served as cook to a cult.

But that did not help him. He had to move his cargo now. It was much too sensitive to sit in his hold. Hell, it had been dangerous enough having the stuff on board during the long voyage from San Francisco. Was that what happened to Frank and *The Auspicious Wind*? he wondered. Had his crew discovered the cargo and mutinied? Or got so drunk that they were completely ineffective during rough seas or pirate attack or any of the million things that could go wrong during an ocean voyage?

He didn't know. All he'd been able to discover was that *The Auspicious Wind* was overdue. Tomorrow he would dispatch inquiries to other ports of call, but it would take months for even vague answers. In short, *The Auspicious Wind* was presumed gone and all his money, cargo, and some very good friends were likely dead on the ocean floor. His friends he would mourn, the cargo loss he would absorb, and even the destruction of one half his fleet could be dealt with. But only if he could sell this current cargo, only if he could pay his crew from the proceeds, and only if he found Kui Yu's list of buyers before his goods spoiled, were destroyed, or worse yet, discovered by the authorities.

God, he hated Shanghai. The yellow mud stench pervaded everything and the noise cut through a man's thoughts like angry hornets. The laborers chanted, the hawkers called, and the fishwives dickered all in a high-pitched whine that set his teeth on edge. And yet, the city burned through his thoughts when he wasn't here. He ached for the commerce that thrived here. He loved the bustle of growth and the excitement of endless opportunities. And best of all, Shanghai housed his best friend in the world, save his brother.

He and Kui Yu had made their fortunes together. They'd met when both were lowly apprentices making side deals of their own. They'd relied on each other for over a decade now, and both had prospered. To have it all end now because of a woman made him sick to the point of violence. But he had no outlet for his fury, no focus for his hatred. Only shit at every turn and a suspicious cook who wouldn't let him mitigate the disaster.

He couldn't let her stop him. He understood Little Pearl's caution, even applauded her for it, but too much was at stake for her to stop him; he needed that list of buyers, but how to get it? Reason hadn't worked, and he couldn't wait for her to come around to his way of thinking. Other options included theft, but the compound was heavily guarded and he had no desire to spark an international incident. Threats or blackmail worked with some of the people he dealt with, but he had no desire to threaten a servant, much less a woman, and he had no blackmail material on her anyway.

He had the most bizarre urge to seduce her into cooperation. Ridiculous, really, since he had no skill at the business and no time for such a lengthy process. He was merely reacting to her beauty and months at sea. And yet, the thought would not leave him. His longjohn had been a thick, hungry annoyance since the moment she'd stepped out from behind that screen. He'd seen her legs first. Her skirt had slit open to reveal creamy skin the color of old ivory. They were muscular, too, with strength enough to grip a man just how he liked. He'd noticed the bound feet as well, and thought it a crime, but that was the way in China. He had the sudden image of unwrapping the tiny toes to kiss their pain away.

He jerked his thoughts back to the present with a vicious curse. He had no time for this. And yet, what were his options? The rickshaw was slowing as they neared the docks. He would unload his sensitive cargo tonight. He knew a warehouse he could use; a quiet one, small and secretive, and run by a man Kui Yu trusted. With luck, the owner would not object to working directly with a white captain. Then in the morning, he would make inquiries into freeing Kui Yu. Failing that, perhaps he could visit his friend in jail and learn the names he needed. Then he wouldn't have to deal with Little Pearl at all.

Odd, how the thought depressed him. He climbed the gangplank with heavy steps, his thoughts already turned to his bunk, only to discover that disaster had already struck.

March 25, 1886

First mate! Albert, I'm a first mate now! Old Tom died of a fever. The captain spoke beautifully and a number of the crew even cried. Then he told me. I went into his quarters—the captain's—and he showed me the log book. Said I was first mate now and to do him proud. We had an extra grog ration to celebrate. And as soon as we make port, we're going to celebrate in style.

—Jonas

People who know mushrooms can judge their quality just by looking at the caps. Fa qwoo *caps have deep cracks and are said to resemble flowers. In presenting Braised Mushrooms, always place the caps on the platter stem-side down. Cooking* fa qwoo *is reserved for special occasions.*

Chapter Three

Little Pearl's jaw ached as she deepened her suction, drawing Jian Lie's dragon farther into her throat. His dragon pearl expanded across her tongue and she was pleasantly surprised by the exquisite power in his pre-emission. She tasted tangy salt without excessive water or unnatural sweetness. Truly, this man had rare and pu-rified yang. She ought to be salivating in anticipation of his release.

She was salivating, and yet she was also bored, her yin rain restricted, her body tight from aches. Yesterday's ac-tivities had kept her running well beyond normal, and her bound feet had not been up to the task. Despite all she did to remain youthful, tigress bodies were not im-mortal. She was aging, and her legs burned from yester-day's strain.

She shifted her caress, feathering her fingertips down the shaft as one would play the lute. There was more length than typical, so she had ample room to stroke and excite, but her mind continued to drift. She was kneeling on the hardwood floor and the knobby bump of bone just below her kneecap cut painfully whenever she shifted. She longed for the sweet cushion a tigress usually used, but Jian Lie had thrown the thing away. He claimed that the herbs nauseated him and the added height made her angle wrong.

She recognized the lie for what it was. He was not the first yang supplier who enjoyed the sight of a submissive woman. Whatever little sleights he could administer, he would. Normally, she did not care. So long as he donated his yang to her vastly depleted stock, then she would suffer petty annoyances at his direction. But after yesterday, her legs protested the insult and the pain distracted her focus. If her situation weren't so dire, she would have refused Mr. Su's request for tigress service. But she could not afford to make him an enemy, and she did have desperate need for both his money and his yang.

If only there were a better way to gather male energy. She could be done with men altogether. But this was the only way to gather male power, and therefore the only way to attain Heaven. She would do what was required and be paid for her efforts.

Fortunately, she had been a tigress for years. She could bring a man's dragon to release without a tenth of the concentration she normally lavished on an evening's meal preparation. And yet despite all her skill, her fingering the lute and tongue-stoking of the dragon fire, the man had yet to give her what she needed. Why would he not release?

She redoubled her efforts. She narrowed her thoughts to the texture of his dragon pearls as she cupped them. She began coordinating suction with the beat of his heart felt along the dragon belly. The man was unusually still, his body absolutely controlled. She glanced at his face. His eyes were closed and his breathing completely hidden by his tunic. Even his bare legs were locked solid like cold metal. If she did not know better, she would think she practiced with a jade dragon—a man well versed in the control and use of his yang. But that couldn't be possible. All the male practitioners in Shanghai had come through the school at one time or another. All wished to learn from the famous Tigress Shi Po. Jian Lie had never been one of them.

And yet, his unnatural control betrayed him. He obviously understood the practices taught here. Indeed, she abruptly realized, he had begun a yin/yang battle with her! He had no intention of releasing his yang to her. He merely used her stimulation to excite his yang without giving her any of the energy she so desperately needed. It startled her to realize that this man—any man—could value qi power over sexual release. None but a dragon would do such a thing. And none but a misguided, misinformed man would think to engage in a power struggle with her. She had the reputation of a woman able to take qi from any man alive.

Little Pearl narrowed her attention even further. She shifted her right fingers around his pearls and began to pinch tiny bits of his skin—not enough to hurt the pearls, but more than enough to stimulate his release.

No change in sound or movement. Jian Lie could have been made of stone for all the reaction he gave. She was discouraged—until she tasted another yang drop seeping from his dragon's mouth. The man was flesh and blood, and he was prey to the same vulnerabilities. She would win in this contest.

She tightened her left-hand grip along the shaft, drawing his dragon's skin down while she shortened the play of her lips and tongue. The dragon's neck was most sensitive in this way, especially with the judicious use of teeth. She abraded him slowly, then quickly, then slowly. Then she extended her smallest finger to the *jen-mo* point, the place where a woman's womb would open were he female. She drew tight circles there and nearly grinned when his flesh began to tighten. His dragon was compressing, preparing to roar. And when it did, she would be there, ready to catch all his expended yang. She would take his power and grow stronger from his most purified essence. This was the path of the tigress, and she relished it, especially as she brought an image of her ancestors to her mind.

In her mind's eye, she turned to her most hallowed family spirits, those who guided and protected her entire family. Somewhere back in Jiangsu there was an altar built to these ghosts, a revered place of worship and devotion. She spat upon it and them as she sucked upon this cold man's dragon. *This is what I do*, she hissed at them. *This is what you made me do.*

It was time. She could feel the yang energy gather. Mentally, she pictured a cloud of yang seeping out of his dragon, exhaling from his pores, infusing her face and body with his strength. She closed her eyes to better take his power, but the energy did not tingle along her lips as usual. The yang did not flood her senses as it should, and so she increased her efforts.

No effect.

What was wrong? She analyzed her technique. Her motions were flawless, her timing exquisite, and yet still she could not take his yang. She searched his body for clues. His pearls were lifted, his dragon engorged with fluid. He should have released long ago, and yet he remained locked in place without movement or even deep breath. That was wrong. Without air, the fire was lessened, the release would be less than full potency. And once again, his actions betrayed him. Strict management of airflow was a technique practiced by jade dragons. Clearly, this man had training, but from whom? And how to subvert it?

She extended her right fingers. Now her third finger massaged the *jen-mo* point while her littlest slid even farther back. She pressed it upward, wiggling slightly as she found the opening. The timing would have to be perfect. Another breath and then . . .

Heavy hands landed on her shoulders and shoved her backward. She was unprepared for such a thing. His hands had been tight to his sides, his fingers frozen in half extension until they suddenly threw her down to the floor. She landed hard, the impact jarring her spine from tailbone all the way up to the base of her skull.

"You are worthless," he spat as she stared into his glittering eyes. He kicked at her feet, obviously trying to spread her legs. But she was a tigress and no man ventured there. She allowed his force to push her leg to the right, but she continued the motion, rotating her entire lower body around. In the next heartbeat, she was able to settle back on her knees, her head bowed in false submission.

"My gravest apologies, Mr. Su. I shall try again." After all, she had found the key to his release. Why else would he have thrown her away so violently? She only needed a few moments more. A few well-practiced strokes and penetration from her tiniest finger, and she would gain his most precious yang.

"You are too vile to touch me again," he growled. He reached down and drew up his trousers, closing them with efficient movements. Then he unhooked his purse and pulled out half what she had been promised. He dropped the coins on the floor before her, his sneer twisting his face such that he resembled a man in full release. It was an odd thought to have of a man reviling her, and yet she could not shake the image. The glee in his energy was too strong to miss. He enjoyed humiliating her. It was, in fact, his yang release. Twisted, verbal, and ugly, it flowed from him with as much ecstasy as a dragon roar. And as such, she drew it in, absorbing it with triumph. *Humiliate me*, she silently urged, *revile and abuse me*. All this energy, she would use to reach Heaven and Immortality. She bowed her head to hide her smile.

"Thank you, Mr. Su, for your forgiveness," she murmured as she quickly picked up his coins. It was enough to pay for the week's food.

"I shall visit the nail shacks in the future," he continued. "They are cheaper and better than you." His hand abruptly cupped her chin to draw her face up while his nails sliced tiny cuts in her skin. "They are prettier, too."

She let her eyes water because he obviously enjoyed it, and because it would prolong his yang release. "I am sorry, Mr. Su. Please let me try again."

He spit on her face. She didn't wipe it away. The yang it contained was too powerful to waste. "You will not touch me again. If you wish money, you will have to look for a different way."

"But I know no other!" She wasn't lying. This was the only way she could obtain the money to support herself. With feet barely larger than a lychee nut, she could not labor as others did. Teaching classes only brought a tiny fraction of what she needed. All that remained was yang accumulation from paying customers.

He knelt before her, his eyes gentling as he came level with her. The sight was false, of course, and her yin energies hardened automatically at the lie. "The creditors will come soon. Surely you know this."

She did, but she did not answer.

"They will come with lies and false claims. They will barge down your door and take everything they can, even your purity." He grimaced. "Such as it is."

"You need not fear for me," she said.

"I do not," he snapped. "You are as mud beneath my dog. I fear for me. My fortune hangs on a knife's edge all because I trusted Kui Yu."

"The master has not abandoned you!" Her cry was automatic, her defense of Kui Yu a natural response she would need to suppress, especially since it was exactly what Mr. Su wanted. His eyes glittered.

"He *has* abandoned me," he shot back. "Perhaps not by his design, but that does not change the facts. We are defenseless, little cook, and unless we work together, we shall both suffer and die."

She could not help that his words terrified her. For all that they might be cleverly shaded lies, she knew what happened to defenseless women. She saw the aged hags every day when she came from the market. She would die before being reduced to that. "What do you want?" she asked, her voice trembling despite her best efforts.

"I must see Kui Yu's papers. He—"

"He has many papers all over the desk. Private letters as well as business. I cannot—"

"A list, then. Names of people to receive a shipment from a white captain. He has come to see you, I believe?"

She nodded, her energies suddenly too chaotic to risk speech.

He grimaced in sympathy. "A strange breed, these whites. Frightening and evil, they kill our children, violate our women, and poison the men with opium. I never risk meeting one of them without guards." His gaze abruptly sharpened. "Do you still have strong male servants? If he should become violent, can they protect you?"

"I . . ." She couldn't think. What he said was true, and yet, it was also not true. Captain Jonas had been to the house many times. He had never been violent or dangerous. But then again, she had never been this vulnerable before.

"I will send my guards to help you."

"No!" She did not want his spies in her kitchen, but she could not say that. She lifted her gaze to him, allowing her fear to shimmer in her false tears. "Others would notice. They would wonder why Mr. Tan does not hire his own servants. I cannot risk such a thing."

He nodded. "True, true. But what if the white man kills you?"

She had no response, only questions and fear.

"If the captain appears, you must send a message to me. Offer your services in exchange for money. I will know what you mean."

She frowned. "You will send guards then?"

"Yes, of course. It will be like a code between us. A secret communication."

"But what if you want . . ." She frowned as she struggled to find the words. "What if I simply wish to help you release your excess male energy?"

His body abruptly stiffened, and his expression grew hard and cold. "Make no mistake, Tan cook, I will never, ever want that from you again."

She dipped her head, accepting his rebuff. "We have other girls—"

"No." There was no compromise in his tone, no room for her to tempt him.

"As you wish," she said.

"I wish you to accept my guards," he growled. "For your own safety."

"My safety resides in secrecy," she returned.

He stood, straightening his garments before he stepped to the door. "It will not last long," he said. "Then you must accept my protection."

She watched him leave, feeling strangely empty despite the yang she had taken. Still, she counted this morning's work well done, her plan executed with only minimal discomfort. She had absorbed much-needed yang, gathered some money, and most important, she now knew Mr. Su's plan. He wanted the mysterious list, and he would play upon her fears to get it. She had no doubt that his "guards" would be experts at discovering hidden boxes and the papers contained within. She would have to make sure that the household remained closed to all strangers in case he sent the "gift" of a guard despite her refusal.

Meanwhile, her next step was clear. She straightened, heading to the kitchen to prepare the afternoon meal. She would send a message to the white captain. Mr. Su had made his offer this day. It was time to learn what the white barbarian would give. She licked her lips, disquiet eating at her small store of energy.

Would a white man's yang taste barbaric?

The guns were gone. Jonas stared at the empty compartment and felt his breath go deadly quiet. The guns were gone. He'd thought no one knew of the secret hold. He'd thought it the safest place to store Winchester rifles. He'd thought . . .

The guns were gone. Why would his mind not move on from that one fact?

"Confiscated by whom?" he demanded, his voice a low rumble barely pushed from his frozen chest.

His first mate shuffled his feet. "I didn't tell anyone, Cap'n. I didn't tell 'em this was here."

Jonas barely moved. His gaze didn't even flicker from the empty storage space. But in his mind's eyes he saw every broken board, every smashed panel and ripped wall in his beautiful clipper ship. No, the customs official hadn't known where the storage space was, but he had known that secret storage places existed. He had known and had sent his men to find it. He could well imagine the glee the Chinese bastards had taken in destroying a white barbarian's ship. They'd probably laughed as they took hooks and axes to every hatch, every wall, every . . .

"We tried to find you, but they wouldn't wait and they had men, Cap'n. A whole battalion. I couldn't stop—"

"Who, Seth?" Jonas wrenched his gaze from the empty hold to his first mate's face. Seth was lanky in the way of a rolled sail—lumpy in odd places, strangely skinny for a twenty-four-year-old, but with an inner strength that defied his looks. Right now, the boy's gaze was steady despite the fact that he had just allowed the Chinese government to confiscate their entire livelihood.

"Gave his name as Chen, sir. Customs Official Chen."

Jonas growled. It was a low rumbling in his belly that gathered force and momentum with every second it continued. He meant to end it. He was not a beast to growl in front of his first mate, but the sound would not be contained. It built within him, churning in his gut until he abruptly pivoted and planted a single fist in the wall beside the hatch. The door had been ripped off its hinges anyway, the wall boards gouged and broken. The entire panel would have to be torn down and rebuilt. In short, it was a useful destruction, a purposeful movement, and as such it gave him no relief from his fury.

"Chen who?" he growled through clenched teeth.

"Customs Official Chen, sir. He wouldn't give me more than that. And without speaking more of their heathen language, Cap'n, I couldn't..." His voice trailed away.

"The whole cargo, Seth? They took everything?"

"Aye, sir. An' not just the cargo. Ropes, sails, foodstuffs. Even the chickens cook bought this morning."

Jonas closed his eyes. His hand throbbed and he knew his knuckles bled. What a pansy he was becoming, annoyed at the tiny pulse of pain that beat in his hand. And yet, better to think of that than how he would search through Shanghai for Customs Official Chen. Sweet Jesus, there were probably a thousand Chens just on the docks. How would he find one man?

Bloody hell, he needed Kui Yu. None of this would have happened if the man hadn't been arrested. If his wife had been a good, faithful Christian woman. If ... A thousand ifs crowded into his thoughts. He allowed them to churn, knowing that in time, the quiet place deep inside would speak. That place of God or inspiration or just dumb luck would eventually whisper a solution.

"How 'bout *The Auspicious Wind*, Cap'n?" Seth asked in a tentative voice. "Was her haul good?"

Jonas found his eyes turning back to the empty hold. "Never arrived, Seth. Never—"

"But that's the fleet, Cap'n! You just got the two boats."

"I know, Seth."

"Without the cargo—"

"I know, Seth."

"But what 'er we to do? Have you the blunt to repair the ship? What about a new cargo?"

"I know, Seth."

"We ain't seaworthy, Cap'n. Not without our stores an' some of the holes. They took it all, Cap'n. And what they didn't take they destroyed. They—"

"Will you shut the bloody hell up?"

The boy snapped his jaw shut, proving that he wasn't completely stupid. Jonas sighed, feeling weariness pull his entire body down—toward the empty hold. "You got an account of everything they took?"

Seth nodded, handing over the tally in silence.

Jonas didn't even fully look at it. He merely saw the length of the list and let his gaze slip back to the empty space beneath his feet. He was ruined, dead broke, his only asset an outdated clipper that wasn't even seaworthy anymore. He rubbed a hand over his face, letting the scrape of his beard pull at a long cut on the side of his hand. Jesus, he was tired. He'd barely slept any of the last three days. Bad weather and an ill-tempered crew had kept him at the wheel in the freezing rain. Then a day spent gadding about Shanghai looking for Kui Yu had put him one foot into the grave. He couldn't think. He couldn't act. "They got my whiskey, too, didn't they?"

"Aye."

Jonas turned slowly to his bunk, his one luxury on the ship: a real bed with a feather mattress. It was in a thousand tiny pieces. Wouldn't even make good kindling, and the down was scattered in gray tufts about the floor.

"Get me a hammock," he ordered. Then he took four steps to the wall before slamming his fist into the paneling beside his bed. Leaning forward, he looked into the hole he had just created. Sure enough, a support beam stood a bare inch off of his impact point. He could tie one end of the hammock to the beam there, then anchor the other half on the broken beam beside the hatch. "I'm going to bed."

"Cap'n?" Seth gasped.

Jonas turned, arching a single brow at his first mate. "Bring me a hammock," he repeated calmly. "I'm going to bed."

"But—"

"Then you will have a choice, Seth."

"I ain't leaving, Cap'n. I'll serve you to death."

Jonas barely restrained a groan. Lord, the young could be so earnest. "Not yet, Seth. Not to the death just yet."

The man looked crestfallen. "Oh. Then . . ."

"Find the official, Seth, this customs man Chen. If you find him and the cargo, then you'll sail my next ship. You'll captain it and take your appropriate cut of the next—"

"Captain! Thank you, Captain! But what about . . . You aren't going to . . . But you mean another ship? Have you found Mr. Tan Kui Yu, then? So you have . . ."

Jonas held up his hand. In time, Seth understood and sputtered into silence. "Find me a hammock, Seth. Then find the cargo. I'm going to bed."

"Aye-aye, sir! Right away, sir!" The man hesitated halfway through his turn. "But the choice, sir. What was my choice?"

"Think hard, son. Think if you want to continue in this

life. Risking everything on Neptune's whim, never settling in one port for more 'n a month, never seeing your girl or your kin, year in and year out. The cold, the wormy food, and the constant grumbling of crew and merchant and officials alike."

"It ain't that bad, Cap—"

"It is that bad, and you know it. Think if you want to do it, son. I'll do right by you if you want to leave. I'll get you cash somehow, set you up at an accounting house. You're good at figures and smart as a whip. You'll do fine—"

"I ain't leaving, Cap'n. I told you that."

Jonas sighed. He knew that would be the answer. The young were invincible in their own minds, and the world was like pearls before their feet. "Then you've chosen, boy. Find the customs official and the cargo, and you'll have a boat to captain out of port."

Excitement flashed in the man's eyes. Excitement mixed with a dash of greed and the steely flint of determination. "I'll find Chen, sir, and I'll get that cargo." His body was quivering with energy, and Jonas knew the man was already thinking and planning—not only how to get the cargo back, but how to manage his first command. And then Seth surprised him. He didn't rush out the door, didn't even turn. Instead, he frowned. "But what about you, sir? What are you—"

"As I said, I'm going to bed." Jonas sighed, once again rubbing his hand over his face, irritating the cuts on his hand. The burn kept him awake for a moment longer. As for what would happen when he woke, he wasn't sure. Finding the cargo was only half the problem. He still needed to get Kui Yu's list of buyers. That wasn't something he could trust to a subordinate. It wasn't something he would trust to God Himself, not with the Chinese government now involved and Winchester rifles at stake.

"I'll get you the hammock, sir. And then I'll get that cargo. You'll see. You can trust in me. I'll work night and—"

"Good night, Seth."

"Aye, sir."

The boy was gone in a flash, then back moments later with the hammock. Jonas would have taken the rope netting then shut the door on Seth's earnest maneuvering, but there wasn't a door anymore. There wasn't even a full wall. So he suffered in silence as his first mate fussed and hurried about setting up the bed.

Mercifully, the boy made quick work of it. Barely fifteen minutes later Jonas was able to settle back and close his eyes. Immediately, the empty hold appeared in his thoughts. Empty space. Missing rifles. Bad, bad luck.

"Messenger from the Tan house," came a call from above deck. "Some cook is offering the captain something."

"The cap'n's sleeping," Seth answered from much too close. "What's he offering?"

"Heathen gibberish. Yang relief or some such."

Jonas felt his eyes pop open. That couldn't be right. Yang was male energy, released during . . . Jonas groaned. At least he wasn't thinking about his empty hold anymore.

March 28, 1886

Dear Albert—

Forgot that it's your birthday. Damn, you're old now. Sixteen! A real man. When I get home, I'll take you to Madame Mysterious to celebrate like men do. Don't go spoiling the fun early, now. Hold off till I can go with you. Just a couple months, I swear. Wait and I'll make sure it'll be a night you never forget, little brother.

And after you're a man, you can sign up with us. It

*won't be like my first voyage. As first mate, I can show
you things. It'll be us two together again. Mum will understand, and besides, you're a man now. She can't keep
you in her skirts forever. And guess where we're going?
Captain told me yesterday. Told me to start studying the
maps and the like.*

*China! We're going to sail lace and whiskey to
China, and we'll all be rich, rich, rich! Mum's kept you
home long enough. It's time to take hold of your future
like a man.*

—Jonas

Stir-frying is full of life and energy, and requires quick reactions. Garlic, ginger, and vegetables require immediate stir-frying, but poultry, meat, and seafood should cook undisturbed for a minute or two so that the ingredients sear slightly beforehand. If you immediately start stirring, the meat will surely stick and tear, yet too much hesitation will result in food that is overcooked.

Chapter Four

Jonas slept, though not well. He dreamed of his dead friends on *The Auspicious Wind* and his horrific finances and rising debts. Still, when he woke, he breathed deeply into his chest, looked out the broken hatch to the equally damaged hallway and thanked God he was alive. Morning brought light and wind and new challenges. What man wouldn't feel his pulse quicken at the thought?

Seth, apparently. The first mate was stumbling up the gangplank as Jonas hit topside. The young man's black hair pointed every which way, and his eyes were bloodshot with drunkenness. Jonas would have been angry if he didn't see the slight lift in the boy's gait. Something good had happened last night.

Jonas didn't speak, just stood leaning against the rail. Seth would tell him soon enough. Indeed, the man half tripped, half hopped onto the deck, coming to a stop right before him. "Mornin', Cap'n." Definitely drunk.

"Good morning, Seth. Anything interesting in Shanghai?"

Seth grinned. "Good mornin'. Good women. Good . . ." He paused for a belch that fouled the air between them. "Good grog."

"Aye," Jonas answered. Something was in the wind, but he couldn't guess what.

Seth's face fell. "Didn't get the cargo back. Not yet."

Jonas felt his hopes sink. He hadn't even realized how much faith he had placed in his first mate until disappointment curdled in his stomach. Still, something had made the man happy. Thankfully, he didn't have to wait long to find out what. Seth's smile curved upward again.

"Found a woman," he said. Blinking, he straightened his spine. "Er, not what you think. The woman knows all the customs officials—Li, Wong, Wang, Chu." He lifted his hands, gave a litany of names. "Chiang, Chin, Tong, Lu." Then he grinned. "Chen."

Jonas straightened. "Customs Official Chen?"

Seth nodded. "All seven of them. Plus Chan and Cheng."

Progress then, but not success. Not yet. "Get some sleep, Seth."

"I'll find 'im, Cap. I pretend to be drunk and hear more than they think."

"I don't think it's much of a pretense."

"But it was, Cap. Well, not at the end. Then I had to drink for real. That's how I found the woman. She serves the drink, Cap. Had to keep ordering to keep her talkin'."

"Go to bed, Seth. You'll need a clear head for tonight."

"Aye, Cap." The boy wove his way to the ladder. Jonas watched to make sure he didn't fall headfirst to the lower decks, but Seth was surefooted even when drunk; he made it down the ladder only to pop his head back up a moment later. "Don't forget the yang thing. Cook. Messenger. Important."

"I remember," Jonas assured him. It had been high on his list of things he wanted to forget last night but couldn't. In truth, it had taken all his resolve not to answer the call right then. But only a fool visited the House of Angry and Beautiful Women without a clear head. This morning was a different story. Seeing Little Pearl was at the top of his list—right below beginning his ship's repairs.

Jonas had only a skeleton crew on board, and his only carpenter was currently drunker than Seth. He needed to oversee the work. A clipper was a good ship, but it was quickly being replaced by the faster, uglier steamships. He couldn't afford to have ill-done work. And yet, he barely sipped his coffee before he headed to his cabin. He needed a shave and clean clothes before venturing to the Tan household.

Little Pearl's summons yesterday could be exactly what it seemed: an invitation to dally in the way a man dallied at a whorehouse. Without Kui Yu to manage things, money would be very tight. The household would have to earn their keep some way. On the other hand, her message could conceal something a great deal more important. That's why he'd waited last night though the desire to rush to her side had been like lightning bolts to his system.

It made no sense, the intensity of his desire. Every time he'd shut his eyes and begun to drift to sleep, he'd jolted awake with the desperate need to find Little Pearl. Kui Yu would claim it was a tigress summons, that Little Pearl's female yin was calling out to Jonas's yang. Jonas saw it as something simpler. His longjohn was crying out for the sweet oblivion that waited between a woman's thighs. But either way, he couldn't respond. Not if this was about dalliance—simple, expensive dalliance.

Thus, he'd waited. He'd refused the call, allowed his cock to shrivel up from neglect, and tried to sleep. If Little Pearl wanted something more, she would send another messenger.

The servant arrived while he was still looking for a shirt suitable for a lady's presence. What clothing wasn't bleached by the sun or mended a dozen times over had been stabbed by the customs men.

"Sorry to disturb, Cap'n, but a heathen's here wanting to speak with you."

Jonas silently cursed his tie as he pulled it tight around his neck. "They're called Chinese, Wilson," he grumbled at his newest sailor. "To them, we're the heathens."

"Of course, sir. There's a Chinaman here to see you. Don't speak a lick of English except to say your name."

"Thank you, Wilson."

"Don't know how you understand their honking and grunting. Sound like—"

"Thank you, Wilson. Make sure to keep that pitch boiling hot. If it don't set well, I'll be coming to you."

Wilson blinked. "Me, sir?"

"You." Stirring the pitch was the dirtiest, smelliest, most dangerous job on a ship repair. Aside from the obvious problems of handling boiling tar, the stirman smelled for days. Burns were common. It was no wonder the man balked at the command. But someone had to do it. Wilson's ignorant comments had just earned him the job. Besides, he was one of the few men on board without a hangover.

"I'll be at the Tan household," he added, then he left.

Jonas and the messenger traveled by carriage. Kui Yu had a white man's understanding of horseflesh and kept a carriage for times when he wished to be ostentatious. That Little Pearl had roused the vehicle spoke to her need to see him again; Jonas couldn't suppress a smile of anticipation.

They made good time into Chinese Shanghai. The carriage was well marked, so the guard waved them through without comment despite the fact that Jonas was sitting there clear as day and white men weren't allowed outside of their given territory. In truth, Kui Yu had made arrangements for Jonas to move freely. Bribery thrived in Shanghai. To that effect, Jonas "accidentally" spilled some coin as they passed.

Twenty minutes more and they pulled into the carriage house at the back of the Tan compound. The driver maneuvered with an expert hand, driving quickly down side streets that avoided the front gate, but even his skill couldn't prevent Jonas from seeing down the usually quiet main road where men of various ilks now crowded. Most were bill collectors by their looks, men none too happy to cool their heels at the front gate. Apparently the news had gotten out. Tan Kui Yu was in jail, and it was time to get what they could.

"How many?" Jonas asked his driver.

The man shrugged, not answering. But the rigid cast to his body revealed an anger and a fear that hadn't been there an hour ago.

Ten minutes later, Jonas was sitting down to the most delicious plum wine and dumplings in the world. The brew was hot, the chicken delicately spiced, and from the first bite, his stomach fought a war with his mouth. One wanted to be filled while the other wanted to taste. Ah, a good chef was a blessing, a miracle from God above.

But where was Little Pearl? Given the repeated summons, he had expected the woman to appear the moment he arrived. But the Chinese had their own timing, and she was softening him up with good food and sweet wine. It would be rude for him not to enjoy her delicate offerings.

So he ate with delight. And as much as he tried not to drink the wine, she had neglected to send tea and he was thirsty. The room was pleasantly warm and the perfumed cushions teased his mind with exotic Chinese smells—ginger, sandalwood, lemongrass. Other words drifted through his thoughts, but his mind was fogged, his stomach pleasantly full.

Drugged? Had he been drugged? He shifted on the couch, trying to wake his body and spirit. No drug. He knew the feel of opium, the hunger of hashish, even the bite of coca. What he experienced now was simply a full belly and a shortened night's sleep.

Where was the woman? Cooking, most likely. Or practicing her unnatural religion. The Chinese had a strange concept of time, unusual rhythms and no understanding of a man's business needs. He had a ship to repair, a bed to reconstruct—and a woman to enjoy? Warm. Welcoming. God, it had been so long. Little Pearl would have a spicy taste, he'd bet; sweet as the heavens above, but with a bite to whet a man's appetite.

His longjohn stretched and grew, though not enough to be painful. His imagination was fired by the thought of Little Pearl's legs braced along his ribs, her sweet weight sliding down him from above, a long, wet heat.

She had nice breasts. He would love to watch them jiggle. They wouldn't at first. She favored the tight silk sheaths that all Chinese women wore, that harsh fabric that pulled taut and held flesh immobile like a sail in a stiff wind. But let the winds relax the tiniest bit, let those clasps slip open and the fabric peel away; that's when her flesh would appear. Old-ivory white and as tender as a ripe mango. They'd jiggle then. And they'd taste like spiced wine.

His longjohn ached now with the image. What he wouldn't give for the whisper of fingers along its length, pressure dancing in the most unexpected ways. The torment had him sighing like the wind through the rigging. It was a good sound of full speed and a bulging hold. China would be on the horizon and he would be coming home.

Lightning flashed through his body. Danger simmered there, excitement and promise, as the wind picked up. Along his belly, hot moist air stirred as his hips rolled forward with the shifting skies. His longjohn surged upward into the hot cavern—was sucked in, was drawn in just a little further. More. More. Small teeth abraded and a tongue soothed.

Ahhhhhhh. . . . rgggah!

Jonas came awake with a choking gasp. He surged forward without conscious thought, his hands reaching out and connecting with soft shoulders encased in old silk as soft as down. He shoved away even as his grip tightened, sinking his fingers into sweet female flesh. He smelled soy sauce and spiced fish, and he saw Little Pearl's sleek black hair knotted into a low bun at the base of her head. She was bent over him, her face hidden. And her mouth . . . sweet Jesus, what she was doing to him!

He pushed her away. Her suction broke with a pull and a pop that took all the strength from his legs. He meant to hurl her away from him, but his hands would not release. He gripped the hard ridge of her shoulders and felt the old silk tear beneath his hands. He immediately gentled his grip, or he tried, but his heart was pounding in his chest and his skin was slick with sweat. And he couldn't think. God, he couldn't think!

Cold air tickled his balls and the wet along his cock felt like ice. He nearly pulled her back toward him— anything to chase the chill, anything to finish what she'd started. But no. At the moment, there really wasn't any thought beyond that: *No.* He mustn't sink his hand into her hair. Mustn't throw her down on the floor. Mustn't spread her legs and push himself inside her. Must not . . .

His trousers were unbuttoned. Well, of course they were unbuttoned. They were open! Everything was open and pushing free and cold and wet, and Jesus she smelled good. She raised her face to look at him and her mouth was glistening red. Her lips were slightly parted and curved into a welcoming smile.

His belly tightened, his cock twitched. His fingers

tightened, and he felt muscle, bone, and strength beneath her softness. God, she was beautiful.

"Hello, Captain Jonas," she said in a breathy whisper. She spoke in badly accented English, but he understood. It was her tone more than the words. She wanted him. She welcomed him. She . . .

He shoved her away. He pushed her harder than he'd intended, and she abruptly tumbled backward. He watched in horror as her bottom hit the floor and she continued back, dropping until her head . . . But her head didn't strike the hard wood. She moved with lithe grace, twisting as she rolled, her belly and hips agile as any cat's. Within seconds she was back on her knees looking at him as if he were the one who had just . . . Who had started . . . Who had . . .

He scrambled to button his pants. Oh hell, just touching his longjohn was torture. The maneuvering it took to tuck it away, to button up, to . . . His hands were shaking and his thoughts would not coalesce.

Little Pearl folded her hands before her. She was on her knees, her head slightly bent, but her gaze remained fixed on his face. She was watching him as a startled animal would, in absolute stillness. But she was no animal and he had not surprised her. She had . . .

"*Why?*" There were a thousand questions churning in his mind, but that word was the only one to escape. At her blank look, he repeated it, this time in Chinese. "Why?"

She arched her eyebrow at him. It wasn't a calculated movement, as it was on so many whites. Little Pearl was Chinese, and the dark curve of her brow was a thin measure of her expression. But in this case, it was natural, unschooled, and very subtle. She raised her eyebrow as an animal might sniff the air: in wary curiosity. She could not understand why he was so appalled by her actions.

"Do you always seduce men while they sleep?" he asked. His trousers were closed, his clothing back in order, but his body still hummed and his skin felt prickly with an edgy kind of energy. Lust, anger, and disgust all warred for supremacy in his soul.

"My deepest regrets, sir. I misunderstood." A formal apology such as could be heard throughout China whenever white and yellow clashed. For some reason, it made him all the more furious.

"Don't lie to me, you—" He bit off his words before he called her a whore. She was no whore. She was a cook. Something must have driven her to do such a thing. He took a deep breath, trying to cool his temper. Unfortunately, this only pressed his johnson hard against his trousers. The pleasure and pain of the movement ate further into his control. "Answer the question," he said firmly. "Do you always seduce men while they sleep?"

She lifted her chin and defiance sparked in her bright black eyes. "Did you not expect that when you came here? A release of your yang—"

"Yes, yes. I remember." He waved her to silence, then finished the gesture by rubbing a hand over his beard. He knew what she had offered in her message, but that had been a cover for something else. Hadn't it? She had needed to see him, and this was the most unremarkable way to bring him. He had known she would offer her tigress services. Hell, his entire ship had known. He simply had not expected her to be so forward as to take him when he was sleeping. What could she possibly gain from such a thing? "Is it the money?" he pressed. "Do you need money so desperately that you would force . . . ? That you would . . ."

"Perhaps I do not please you," she responded with a gentle smile. "There are other girls, all tigresses—"

"No! No!" The very thought soured his stomach. In the shifting currents of this conversation, one fact was a solid anchor of certainty. He wanted her. No one else. He sighed, wondering what to do. "Why?" he repeated.

Her gaze slipped to the floor, and she was the picture of modesty and subservience. "How may I serve you, Captain Jonas?"

"By answering the damn question! Why did you call me here? Was it for money?"

"Yes." She did not look up.

It was part of the answer, he was sure, but there was more. He'd stake his ship on it. "You can get dozens of men if that were your wish. Why me? And why do it while I was sleeping?"

Her head lifted slightly, and he caught a flash of confusion in her expression. She said, "You have never availed yourself of our services, here or at Madame Ting's house."

He frowned, half-pleased that she'd noticed and half-frightened by her knowledge of him. "White men are different. We do not casually—"

"Your sailors do. Your crew does. But you—"

"Not all whites behave like rutting beasts!" He grimaced, trying to get to the heart of the matter. "Why me, Little Pearl? Why did you pick me for this?"

"I wish to honor your association with Master Tan Kui Yu." Her body dipped lower in a partial bow. "I apologize if I misunderstood."

He pushed up from his seat, pacing in agitation. "You understood. You knew—"

"Perhaps some tea would be helpful. Or more wine. I shall—"

"Stop right there." He didn't yell the words; he didn't need to. She froze in a half crouch. Then, as he kept his gaze hard on her, she slowly lowered herself back down.

"How may I serve your honor?" she whispered.

He grunted, not in the least bit fooled. After all, he'd seen his mother pull the same act a thousand times. False subservience that hid an ulterior motive. Money had been his mother's ultimate goal. Little Pearl, though . . . He settled on his knees before her. He was taller than she, larger and more substantial—or so she made it appear as she shrunk down to the tiniest space she could. He reached out and touched her chin.

God, her skin was soft. Old cotton, ripe peach, baby kitten—all these images flashed through his mind at the single caress of his thumb across her cheek. His groin tightened and he clamped his jaw shut to prevent the act he knew she would welcome. He would not kiss her, though need drove him hard.

"What do you want, Little Pearl? I will honor your request if I can. In this way, I give respect to my friend Tan Kui Yu."

She blinked, obviously thrown by his offer. He didn't blame her. It was a rash act. With all his responsibilities, an open-ended promise like this was ludicrously impossible to fulfill. And yet he had every intention of fulfilling it.

"Lie back," she said, her voice a siren song of temptation. "Let me taste your essence."

He gulped, and his longjohn roared in response. "And what will this tell you?"

She didn't answer, at least not in words. Her eyes blazed and her body swayed forward. Her lips parted and her fingers twitched. He was quick to grab her hand. He had no wish for her caress to distract him while he searched her face for clues.

He found his answer in the oddest place: her feet. Her poor, bound feet. He had not even been looking there; his gaze had been on her face, but he was taller than she, so he had been looking down. He saw her tuck her tiny embroidered shoes beneath her bottom, out of sight. And then the answer blew into his mind with all the force of a gale wind. Little Pearl was an aristocrat. Only the wealthy bound their daughter's feet. Only the elite could cripple their girls such that they would be carried everywhere they went. So, Little Pearl had begun life as a rich girl, and as such she had been taught rich girl values:

money and sex. No matter what the country, wealthy girls were used to barter power, their only assets in their sexual allure or their dowry.

Whatever had happened to Little Pearl to make her into a cook for a cult hadn't changed her education. Power for her came from her body. So she'd tempted him with her skills in order to obtain power over him. Did she even think sex should have a basis in the heart? He doubted it. For her, sex meant power, nothing more.

He dropped back onto his heels with disgust. He didn't understand why he felt such crushing disappointment; he only knew that Little Pearl and her manipulations no longer interested him. He pushed to his feet. "I need that list, Little Pearl. Find it and I will give you Kui Yu's share. You can use it to"—he waved vaguely at the compound—"do whatever it is you do here." He knew what she did, but he had no wish to call her a whore to her face. "Without it, you and I have nothing to discuss." He grabbed his hat and headed for the door.

"The creditors become more aggressive." Her words were rushed, a hurried attempt to keep him nearby. "Soon they will break through the gate."

Jonas shrugged. "Offer to pay them in trade. I am sure you will have enough takers to survive." He glanced back at her. It was weakness, a last need to see her beauty. He paid for it with an ache. Her eyes appeared tragic, her body curved in supplication. He could almost believe her completely vulnerable, adrift in stormy seas. But this was a lie, an expression perfected by the most common of prostitutes, and so he hardened his heart to the sight, much though it hurt him to deny her. He said only, "Thank you for the meal. It was excellent."

"Kui Yu would thank you for helping me."

He nearly laughed. Not because it wasn't true or that he was unwilling; he owed his friend a great deal. "You have not yet said what it is you want," he said. "Beyond sex, of course." He turned his body toward her, but did not look at her. He'd already made that mistake.

She didn't answer, and in time his curiosity overcame him. He looked at her face only to see anxiety, fear, and even confusion flit across her features.

"You don't know, do you?" he wondered softly. "You don't really know what you need, and so are looking for someone to tell you." Then he bit his lip, understanding coming slowly and painfully to his consciousness. After all, wasn't that what his mother had done, time after time with all her johns? She'd just wanted someone to take care of her while she did what she had been trained to do. "You want to be my mistress." He grimaced. "I'm not interested."

"What about a cook? You like my cooking. I can make dishes fit for the emperor himself."

Tempting. Exceedingly tempting. But . . . "The list, Little Pearl. I need the list."

"I will burn the list if you do not help me." She glanced out the window to the front courtyard. Even here, he could hear the sounds of the creditors just beyond the front gate. "Make them go away or I will destroy the thing you want."

"I thought you said you didn't have it."

"I will burn all the master's papers. All his books, too."

A bluff if he'd ever heard one. She respected Kui Yu too much to destroy his office. Still, she was finally open to negotiations. "Let me search for the list," he suggested. "You can be with me when I look—"

"No."

"Kui Yu trusts me. I would not harm him or any in this house."

"No."

He opened his mouth to argue further, then shut it on a sigh. She would not budge, and he would not force her . . . yet. "Very well," he said. "Good day."

He turned and left. She said nothing more to stop him, and he damned himself for slowing his steps in hope. She had nothing he wanted except that list. Damn, he had to find a way to speak with Kui Yu. But how?

He was deep in thought as he passed through the receiving gate into the front garden. His steps slowed as he neared the exit. The clamor of bill collectors was loud. At the moment, the men were laughing with each other, talking politics and trading lies. They might have been sitting in a pub. But the congenial mood would not last. Time would make them more desperate. Right now, none had been paid and the debts were only a day or so old. But wait another couple days and the atmosphere would change. More collectors would come. Worse, if one was paid, then the others would riot. All knew that they were here as scavengers picking at bones. Only the most aggressive and vicious would get paid.

He ought to warn Little Pearl. He should tell her to have strong guards with her when she accepted any inside. And to negotiate shrewdly for both a smaller bill and the promise of silence. Each bill collector had to leave with a little money and a great show of anger, otherwise the rest would descend as a mob. He ought to know. He'd learned very young how to juggle creditors.

He glanced behind him, then steeled his spine. This was just his longjohn talking, urging him to go back inside. Little Pearl could handle creditors. And if she couldn't, that would merely increase the pressure on her to accept his help. It was to his benefit to see her mobbed.

He rounded the stone wall and stepped through the front gate. He would visit the prison again. Perhaps he could bribe— His steps didn't falter, but his mind did. There were a good deal more bill collectors out here than he'd expected. All of them stared at him in shock. While all knew that Kui Yu had dealings with the whites, they probably hadn't expected to see one walking out of the compound free as he pleased.

Jonas smiled genially as he moved, making sure his hands were free. He thought he might recognize one or two faces in the crowd. He was Kui Yu's business associate; surely they'd seen him before. Surely they thought—

"White devil!" one man spat.

"Not a devil," Jonas replied in Shanghai dialect. "Just a businessman." He picked up his pace, but the crowd was moving with him. Others rushed to stand directly in front of him.

"Why are you here?" demanded one. Apparently, they weren't spooked by a white man speaking Chinese.

"Just business," he answered quickly. "Looking for Mr. Tan—"

"He was paid! Why else would he be smiling?"

"I have no money," he said as he scanned the street for a means of escape. Nothing. Just high walls and angry merchants.

"You!" bellowed another. "You're why Mr. Tan was imprisoned."

"You poison our city!"

"You rape our women!"

"Devil!"

He tried to run, but was blocked on all sides. He tried to maneuver to freedom, but there were too many hands reaching for him, pulling at his clothing, grabbing for his hair. He didn't want to fight. Though his hands curled into fists, he kept them tight to his sides; he had no desire to escalate matters.

Then a rock came at his head—a small stone, badly thrown. He didn't see it until it flew right in front of his face. He reared back and saw the stone hit another man in the cheek. And as the unintended victim fell back a step and blood welled up on his face, Jonas had an instant to realize he was doomed.

The crowd seemed to draw breath in shock, pulling up short. If there had been an opening, Jonas would have taken it; he would have ducked or dived or crawled away if he could, but he was surrounded on all sides. There was only one chance. Tucking his head down, he rammed forward. He shoved one man out of his way, then another backward as he picked up speed.

With one breath, the crowd roared in fury. Something hit Jonas on his shoulder. He didn't register the pain; only the shift in balance as his body absorbed the impact. He was nearly free. He pushed another man aside, then stumbled over a leg or a stone. He tried to leap free. He was crouched low enough to spring, but was unstable after the stumble. His jump was rushed and off of one foot.

He meant to leap between two men, but failed in his aim. He impacted one of his attackers nearly full force in the chest. The man grunted and went down, but he had strong arms and gripping hands, and Jonas had no footing to stop his fall. They both tumbled to the ground.

Even with the man beneath him, Jonas still suffered from the impact. His right hand took the worst of it as he tried to brace himself on the stone street; then his head dropped hard, and his chin dug into the man's shoulder, slamming his jaw shut but thankfully halting downward movement. He tried to push away, but his right arm wouldn't work—too numb from the impact—and his left was pinned beneath him. All he could do was roll sideways off his attacker as he tried to regain his feet.

He didn't make it. There were legs in the way, and fists rained down on him. He kicked out, he punched, he even used his head as a club, but for every blow he landed, seven more struck him. Every inch of space he gained was lost on another front.

The end was inevitable, though he delayed it as long

as possible. All too soon, someone managed a blow to his ribs. He lost his air. His fists stopped swinging and protected his head instead. And though his spirit raged, his mind lurched.

He surrendered to unconsciousness.

October 1, 1886

Dear Albert,

I don't understand why you won't come sailing with me. It is a much better life than tending to Mum's demands. She is a whore, Albert, and she will always be a rum-sot whore. Despite everything you do, one day the wrong man will use her or she will drink too much and choke on her own vomit. You know I speak the truth.

If you had a girl, I could understand. No man wants to leave a good woman behind. But I watched what happened. Girls looked at you—you're passable enough—and you looked back. But never did you touch them, not until you were drunker than a cabin boy and could barely perform.

Has Mum twisted you up so much that you cannot even soberly think of whoring? She would be the first to laugh at you for that. Men diddle, Albert, and you are a man now.

Oh damn. I'm late for watch.

—Jonas

October 3, 1886

Albert—

I have had a great deal of time to think. Night watches do that for a man. And the captain pointed out that as a man you must chart your own course. Not everyone is cut out for a sailor's life. Very well, brother. What do you intend to do? Do you really wish to be a dock worker? Is there nothing else that your heart longs for?

I met a woman, Albert. A girl in Dover, the daughter of the captain's friend. Her name is Annie and she smiles in a way to make a man give up the sea. Is there a girl like that at home? I could understand that, Albert. But you spoke of no one except Mum, and a couple nuns with Father Simon.

I will be back in summer. Think hard, little brother. Think of your life and what will be your lot.

—Jonas

Rice is one of the seven necessities of life. Along with oil,
wood for cooking, salt, soy sauce, vinegar, and tea, it is all one
needs in order to begin a home.

Chapter Five

Little Pearl watched Captain Jonas leave. She kept her eyes down and her posture defeated. Many men needed to believe they had broken their women so that they could be the big, generous male and relent. But Captain Jonas did not even look back, and before long, she heard his steps as he headed through the front garden to the main gate.

Apparently, the man had no need to humiliate a woman to feel powerful. She wasn't surprised. His yang energy was strong. It was also very barbaric, though not in the way she expected. His energy was primal—a swirling, chaotic storm—but it was locked in a box, raging in silence, carefully closed away. Nothing she did could release it. Not her carefully planned seduction, not her abasement or even her threats. She knew this was not true of all white men. China was rife with stories of their debaucheries. But Captain Jonas was different. He would not be easily managed or manipulated to her will.

She sighed, and with the breath she released all linger-

ing hope for a solution. She had no skills for the running
of a school or the management of Master Tan's affairs.
And with the creditors already at the door, time had run
out. She would need to leave. She would take what valu-
ables she could carry: tigress scrolls, jade balls for the
women's practice. If the Tans returned from prison, she
would give the items back. If not, then she would keep
them and count them as payment for her long service.

She slowly gained her feet, a bone-deep weariness
keeping her head bowed even as she walked back to the
kitchen. She never made it. The sound of an angry mob
reached her clearly. So soon? She had expected another
day at least.

"Aie! Come, come! Quickly. Everyone!" she cried.
There were too few in the compound, but what servants
and students remained, she organized as fast as she
could They had few weapons: a shovel, a few brooms,
and her excellent kitchen knives. "Outside!" she ordered.
"Chase them away! Chase them away!"

The women moaned and the men cowered, but she
had been born in a family that knew how to give orders.
She slapped the nearest man and pinched the cringing
woman beside him.

"Go! You fight for your lives, you idiots!" She grabbed
a broom and led the charge.

No villain had breached the front courtyard, but she
could hear the angry cries just outside. She had a bare
moment's thought to stop. After all, the violence hadn't
reached them yet—but it would. Best to stop it now
while the courtyard still remained protected. Besides,
momentum had already pushed her through the gate
and fear had her swinging in wild arcs. She may have
bound feet, but she could still crack skulls with a broom.

"Aie! Aie!" she screamed, and was pleased to hear an
echoing cry from the servants behind her. "Get away!
Get away!"

She knocked over people left and right, banging them on the head and pushing them away. They turned to stare at her, their eyes wide with terror. She bared her teeth and kept swinging, and most ran from her fury.

She grinned. This fighting was easy! It was a moment more before she realized the truth. She was knocking people over easily because their backs were turned to her. They weren't gasping in terror at her, but in surprise. In fact, this mob wasn't aimed at the Tan household at all, but at something a few more steps down the street.

She kept moving, kept swinging. She had no choice now that she'd begun. Some of the mob was turning on her now. Still, she would not stop until the crowd dispersed, until they knew the Tans were not so easily destroyed.

"Get out! Get away!" she screamed as she tottered on her feet.

A man reared up before her. He was angry, his fists large, and he hit her twice—once in the face and once in her ribs, throwing her sideways. She kept hold of her broom, but it was no use in breaking her fall.

She cried out and softened her body, adjusting so she would roll when she hit the ground, but she never landed on the hard stone. Instead, she flailed into another man. When he shoved her away, she lost her broom. She curled into a tight little ball just as another man stumbled into her. No blow landed, but the impact jarred her shoulder and spine where they collided. Her bound feet gave her no purchase, but at least the attackers had slowed her fall. She landed hard on one knee, then rolled to her side, fury and pain making her scream curses.

Her bottom hit stone and she reacted immediately. Something large was behind her back. She used it for balance as she kicked and hit and cursed whatever came near. She invoked the goddess Kwan Yin to shrivel the men's balls and their luck. She cursed descendants and livestock, then prayed that whatever flesh she touched shriveled into black pus.

And when her breath ran out and her yang fire faded, she collapsed back on the ground and glared at the surrounding men. They had pulled back into a rough circle. She searched for her servants and students only to realize they couldn't be seen. Either they'd run, the damned cowards, or they had fallen as well. She was alone, in the middle of a mob, with nothing to save her but . . .

They weren't staring at her. Or rather, they weren't all staring at her. Some looked to the heavy thing behind her. She twisted, only now realizing she leaned against the dead body of Captain Jonas. He was beaten bloody, his near arm looked broken, and his glorious churning energies were completely silenced. She gaped and stared, then drew another breath and began to curse them all again.

"You damned idiots! You have killed him! You have killed him!"

"Death to the white devils," a man growled, but not too loudly.

She rounded on him with fury. "He was going to help me! He was getting me money!" She had no idea where the lie came from, but once said, she could not change it. "You have killed a white man outside my door! The devil gunboats will hunt you down. They will blow up your homes and your businesses! They will kill us all for this!"

A man near the captain squatted, shoving Jonas onto his side, then spat in the dirt. "He is not a rich white." He pocketed the captain's meager purse as he spoke. "No one will care—"

"Are you stupid? He is white! All whites are rich!" She glared at the faces of everyone surrounding her. "I know you, Chin. And Sung and Wang. I know you all!" She pushed to her feet, changing a cry of pain into a grimace as she put weight on an injured leg. "When the whites come, I will tell them. I will tell them who you are! And then—"

She hadn't even seen the blow coming, but one exploded across her face. The force threw her to the ground. She landed on the captain's legs, his bulk saving her from spilling her brains on the stone.

"You will tell them nothing!"

Too late she realized her mistake. They would have to kill her now, or fear white retribution. She scrambled for another way out. "The ghost people haunt their murderers. Killing me won't stop that. His spirit will find you and curse your luck—"

"He's alive."

The voice came from behind her, from near Jonas's body. Little Pearl twisted to see, hope sparking within her heart. Could it be true?

Mr. Gao knelt by Jonas's head. He had a hand pressed to the captain's chest. "He breathes. He lives."

"Carry him into the courtyard!" Little Pearl bellowed. "I have herbs that will save his life." She looked up when the crowd hesitated. "Do you want a white man's ghost at your door? I can keep him alive and then there will be no gunboats, no white man's curse. Do it!" She glared at Mr. Chin, a small man who transported cottons for Kui Yu. "Do it or I will curse you with my dying breath. I am a tigress, Chin Wo Han. Your balls will burn, your dragon will leak black pus, your qi will—"

"Carry him inside! Now!"

They were not careful, but they were fast. Mr. Gao helped her stand and promised to send special tea to ease her rapidly swelling face. She grunted in acknowledgment, then hurried after the men carrying Jonas. On the way, she saw her servants and students. They had not run; merely been overcome, and she smiled in gratitude. Then she turned her attention back to the men carrying

Captain Jonas. "Touch one item in the Tan household, and I will see that my curses come swiftly."

"Where should we take him?" Mr. Chin gasped as they maneuvered through the front gate.

"The rooms for practice," she answered. "Out of my way, out of my way."

She hobbled unsteadily, pain slicing up her calves with every step, but still she moved faster than the men. They seemed to be afraid to touch the captain now that they were trying to save him. She snorted as she opened the receiving door for them.

"You do not fear to hit him, but now you shake as you save his life? Hypocrites," she spat. "Idiot cowards." She continued to curse them, watching carefully to make sure they took her abuse without complaint. If she stopped, if she let them think for even the slightest moment, then they might change their minds. They might find courage and decide to kill them all.

She continued to spew, thinking out loud of all the curses that tigresses knew. She stayed inventive and graphic all the way to the side building with many bedrooms. That was the house of practice, easily accessed from the back gate, safely removed from the family quarters, and well furnished with bed and dressers and—

It *had* been well furnished, before the soldiers came. Did any have an adequate bed now? The men were getting weary and irritable. They would not help much longer. Besides, she was running out of ways to curse a man's dragon. As they climbed the stairs to the bedrooms, she began mentally reviewing the contents. Would any room be acceptable?

None. But at least the third room had a solid bed. Ten thousand thanks to Buddha! Captain Jonas was deposited with jarring haste. And as his head bounced lightly on the mattress, the white man let out a low moan.

"That is his spirit groaning!" Little Pearl cried. "It is

ready to leave his body. Run! Before it escapes and follows you! Go!"

The men flew out the door, the last of their courage deserting them. And only when the sound of stomping feet faded did Little Pearl finally allow herself to lean backward against the wall. Damn, her feet were in agony! Her legs ached, her face burned, and myriad other complaints filtered into her consciousness. Yet none were lethal. In truth, she had suffered much worse at one time or another.

Now, to deal with the white barbarian's wounds. She pushed herself off the wall, her hands shaking as she approached. She had not been able to see the extent of the damage before. Now she catalogued them with the precision Tan Shi Po had taught her.

Bad shoulder, bad arm, but not broken as she'd before feared. Cuts and blood everywhere. His face was discolored and swollen. Fortunately, his breath was steady, his skin not flushed with fever . . . yet. Turning to the door, she called for water, bandages, and salve. Some bottles had escaped the soldier's rampage. "And scissors!" she added. She had to cut away his clothing.

All arrived eventually, none fast enough to keep her from thinking nor slow enough for her to lose her nerve. She could do this. She could touch and bind a white man's wounds without stealing his yang or disrupting his qi. She only hoped his dragon was undamaged. If he had lost his male organ, then she doubted he had the strength to survive. Preparing for the worst, she hobbled to his side and pulled at the fabric of his pants. Then she began to cut.

His yang center was damaged. No wonder he had passed out. His dragon pearls were swollen and hot, and the dragon itself was discolored from bruising. She adjusted its position and clucked in sympathy. The pain must have been excruciating.

Her eyes traveled back to his arm and shoulder. First

things first. He could have a dozen or more pressing injuries, and she would have to care for them all. At a minimum, he required cold compresses for his head and bindings for his arm and shoulder. Best to do that while he slept. Then, after the most urgent problems were addressed, she would turn her attention to his dragon.

It took a long time. His ribs were broken, and he had ugly bruises up and down his legs. But he was a strong man, large and vital and not nearly as physically ugly as she'd expected. Indeed, the hair that covered much of his body was surprisingly soft. She'd even run her fingers through the mat along his chest just to experience the sensation. To her shock, her yin had begun to flow, moistening her mouth and softening her belly.

She stumbled backward, dropping uneasily into a chair brought to ease her feet. She had touched this man, she had stroked his dragon and teased his pearls. She had done this not more than a few hours ago, and she had not reacted with such yin dew. She had, in fact, had to steel herself to touch a white man; she had brought her ancestors into her thoughts and made them watch what she did for their shame. She had done all these things, and her body's reaction had not been one tenth of what she felt now.

Had she been injured in the fight? Had she experienced a blow to the head that disordered her natural rhythms? It must be so. Why else would she react so strongly to a shriveled, hurt body when she'd had nothing but disdain for the strong, healthy one?

Grimacing in disgust, she began to check herself for damage. Her feet were the most pressing problem. They pulsed with an agony similar to when her mother had first broken them. But it was a familiar pain, one brought on for beauty and maintained for modesty, or so her mother had often said. Little Pearl had long since discarded such notions. Her bound feet were her greatest asset—no less and no more. They guaranteed a livelihood outside of these walls. Men came far and wide to lie with a woman of tiny feet.

She would check their bindings later, but experience told her they were simply bruised and overworked. No great damage there.

Farther up, her legs were bruised but not broken. Her right knee was the worst. It was swollen and would not bear much weight, but it was not hot to the touch and would eventually heal. Beyond that she had only bruises and scrapes, nothing frightening. Mostly, it was her yin center that alarmed her. It was hot and moist and throbbing as had not happened in many years—perhaps not ever—and the very thought alarmed her.

She heard a low murmur of sound from the inner courtyard. Stepping out of the room to the hallway, she looked over the railing at the yard below. She saw three servants—two men and one woman—standing aimlessly in the middle, clearly wondering what to do. Looking at the overcast sky, she was startled to realize how much time had passed. It was well past the afternoon meal and would soon be time to begin evening preparations.

Sighing, she turned to descend to the first floor. The servants quieted at her sound and followed her movements with anxious eyes.

"The ghost man—," one began, only to be interrupted by his companion.

"Hss! He is no ghost. At least . . ." All three glanced fearfully to the room above.

Little Pearl dredged up a reassuring smile. "He still lives, but word must be sent to his ship. And someone must sit with him while I cook."

One of the men immediately bowed. "I will go to the ship. I will tell them."

"No. I will go!" cried the other man. "I went before."

But the first was already on his way. He was chased by the second.

Little Pearl stared, shocked by their sudden willingness to work. She opened her mouth, intending to question what had just happened, only to have the girl interrupt her.

"I will go cook, mistress. I can make excellent rice. You yourself praised it. Most excellent rice, you said. I can—"

Little Pearl raised her hand, silencing the woman. "Why do you wish to cook?"

"I am most excellent—"

"Why?" she pressed again.

The girl did not answer except to look anxiously up to where Captain Jonas rested.

"You are afraid?" Little Pearl asked, though it was more of a statement than a question.

"If he becomes a ghost, he will haunt—"

"He will not die." In truth, she had no reason to believe Captain Jonas would live. He could have any of a dozen injuries that would kill him at any moment. But she had to cook, and someone had to stay with the patient. "It is perfectly safe to stay with—"

"I cannot, mistress! I cannot!" Then the girl glanced slyly at Little Pearl's bound feet. "I will make the rice," she said, and she ran off to the kitchen.

Little Pearl let her go. What choice did she have? She could not give chase, not with her feet in such pain. And she hadn't the strength to force a terrified girl to sit with the captain. What if the man began to cough or needed to urinate? The silly girl would run screaming for her life. And if the men's scramble to leave was any indication, all the other servants would be equally useless.

So Little Pearl resigned herself to suffer barely tolerable rice seasoned badly. At least this would be easier on her feet. With a sigh, she turned back to the stairs, climbing slowly. She had no excuse now. She could strengthen the captain's yang without fear of interruption. His only chance of survival was if his qi remained strong enough to heal his body. And the only way to keep a man's qi strong was to keep his yang center stimulated and powerful. She would have to put her hand and her mouth on his dragon and stroke it into fullness, praying that his yang would then strengthen every other part of his body. She would have to be very careful and it would take a long, long time as he was very ill.

What if he woke during the process? He had been angry before, but this was for his very life. Would he understand that?

She doubted it. Grimacing, she realized she would have to tie him to the bed. How else would she be able to minister to him in the way he needed? Barbarians did not understand the workings of qi or yin and yang.

Fortunately, when she was not a cook, she was a tigress teacher. She would explain to him what was happening. And if he did not understand, then his returned health would quiet his complaints. On the other hand, if he was very compliant and his health very strong, then she would at last have a partner on whom to practice. Because for some bizarre reason, her yin responded to his yang. Perhaps experimentation would be possible. But first she had to find a rope strong enough to hold him.

Black. Quiet. No waves.

Jonas stirred in the darkness, feeling unsettled. Something was out there. Something was nearly within reach . . . or nearly not. Something must exist, and yet nothing did. He was alone.

Where was it?

Sensations filtered into his consciousness. Pain. Pleasure. Breath. Pain.

He searched restlessly, not focusing on the sensations.

They were too many and too confusing to follow. Besides, he had questions, a million questions.

Pleasure. Pain.

Where was it? Why couldn't he find it?

Pleasure. Pain.

Sensations crowded out his questions. His heartbeat was accelerated, his body was waking. Pleasure. Pain. Yes. No.

Why?

He opened his eyes. He was not on his ship. He smelled ginger and soy, and his every breath burned like a fire too hot to localize. His stomach rolled and he fought nausea, breathing in shallow pants as he closed his eyes again.

Where was he?

Pleasure curled in his thoughts. Like a kitten hiding from a storm, it tucked into his lap and burrowed deep—warm and sweet—the purring vibration was a pleasure in the midst of turmoil. He smiled and in his mind stroked the animal, giving as much comfort as he received.

What was a cat doing here? Where was here?

Gritting his teeth against the pain, he opened his eyes again. Wood ceiling, small chamber, predawn light. He heard birds in a nearby courtyard and tasted too little salt in the air. He was on land then, in a house. What happened? The fire in his chest and arm had not abated. It continued to coil inside him searching for an outlet. And still the kitten continued to purr, the light hum of vibration too high for a cat.

He frowned. The pain was luring him away, demanding attention, distracting him from his questions. But something felt very right and very wrong at the same time. Did he want to know what?

He opened his eyes again. It took a conscious decision to do it. The realm of the physical was so overwhelming, he was not sure he could swim in those seas. But he had to know what was right and what was wrong. Without that knowledge, he was lost.

He saw again the narrow room, recognized the architecture as Chinese, and began to remember. He had gone to see Little Pearl. She had tried to seduce him, and he had stormed off. He needed to speak with Kui Yu. And then . . .

The mob. The fury. Too many . . .

He gasped as memories flooded back. He jerked only to have pain flood his body and mind. Even so, he had lifted up enough to see. Little Pearl at his . . . doing . . . Bolts of fire exploded throughout his system, and he roared in fury.

"Get away! Get away from my—!"

Pleasure. Pain. Right. Wrong. It all made sense now. And yet, it made no sense at all.

"Get away," he gasped as he fell back, pain and despair drowning him.

The purring stopped. Or rather, Little Pearl quit that faint hum she made as she pressed her mouth to his exposed longjohn. But her tiny hand continued to cup his balls with warmth, and her downy soft cheek still rested so gently on his penis. Then it started again.

"Stop. Please stop." He made his voice as firm as he could with what little breath he had.

"I am not stealing," she said. "Your yang center has been injured. It must be strengthened or your whole body will wither and die."

He meant to argue with her, but the stimulation of her words, the shifting vibration of her speech stopped him. Not because it felt good. On the contrary, her sounds were discordant and irritating, and he longed for the steady hum to return. And when he did not object, she began again, the note a low soothing vibration that quieted his fire.

Pleasure. Pain. Right. Wrong.

Wrong.

He tried to move to stop her, but the smallest tensing of muscles brought renewed agony to his chest and arm. Besides, he now realized, the woman had him trussed like a Christmas goose. She needn't have bothered. The pain in his body prevented him from striking out. So he stilled and focused on speaking rationally.

"Stop." His voice sounded weary and indecisive, so he repeated himself, speaking with more power. "Stop now." She did. "Please, cover me up."

He had only just realized he was naked beneath layers of blankets expertly draped to expose only his . . . what had she called it? His yang center. As if all he was to her was a set of balls and a cock.

"Cover me now!" he snapped. She didn't move, and he opened his eyes to glare at her. She looked at him from her position against his longjohn. Her eyes were filled with confusion, and her expression revealed a wounded hurt. "Damn it," he growled.

She quickly straightened and did as he'd bade her. He kept his jaw stoically shut as she worked, mourning the loss of her heat, her touch, and her damned humming. So he focused on other things. He could see now that she knelt on a cushion beside his bed, and when she finished her task, she folded her hands neatly before her and kept her face and head bowed in silence.

Lord, he felt like he'd just kicked a kitten. Why the image persisted, he hadn't a clue. She was a woman, not a pet. And what she'd been doing was wrong. Didn't she know that? Apparently not. So he sighed and tried to explain. "You can't go around touching . . . sucking . . ." He released a frustrated moan. "It's wrong."

"I stole nothing," she said to her knees. "It was only humming—a healing. Yang responds to certain sounds."

He growled. "I am white. A God-fearing Christian man. I don't believe in your Chinese mumbo jumbo."

She lifted her head, irritation making her words curt. "Healing does not require you to believe. Only to accept."

"Well, I don't accept."

She tilted her head, obviously stunned. "Then you wish to die?"

"Of course not!"

"They why do you refuse—"

"Because I'm Christian!"

She stared at him, then finally shook her head. "I do not understand this word."

Speaking caused a great deal of pain, so Jonas tried to economize his conversation. He also tried to take stock of his situation. He'd obviously broken his ribs. Wrenched his shoulder, too, though it was not broken. Other aches and pains, probably, but they were all lost amid the general misery.

"How long has it been?" he asked.

She tilted her head, clearly confused by his question.

"How long was I unconscious? From the mob, right?"

She nodded. "You were attacked yesterday midday. I fought off the mob and brought you here. For healing."

He felt his lips curve at the emphasis she put on her last two words. Odd, that he found humor in her pique, but there was nothing normal about this situation. "You fought them off? How?"

"I was not alone. And I thought you were dead." She shrugged. "They were frightened of your ghost."

He blinked. He must be more hurt than he thought. Her words made sense. "Are they gone? Will they—"

"They will not come back for a few days at least. As I said, they are frightened of your ghost."

The Chinese were frightened of a lot of things. Might as well take advantage of their terror of spirits. "Get a message to my ship. Have them send men—"

"It has already been done. Your men protect this house." She dipped her head. "My thanks."

He stared at her. He'd done nothing but get beaten within an inch of his life at her front door. "I should leave. Release you from this trouble."

Panic flared in her eyes before she quickly lowered her gaze. "You are not well enough to move."

"My men can carry me."

"Through Chinese Shanghai? You will bring doom upon us both. The authorities have turned a blind eye to your coming and going so far. Do not think to push them too far."

He frowned. Kui Yu had kept a steady flow of bribes to someone. Jonas had never been stopped at the crossing into Chinese Shanghai. "If I could look at his papers, I would know who to bribe."

She shook her head. "Such things would never be written down."

Probably true. "I could go hidden in a palanquin. Pretend to be—"

"You would surely die. You are not strong enough—"

"You do not wish me to leave."

She said nothing, merely pressed her lips together and stared at her knees. He looked at her, wondering how to proceed. Then a noise startled her. Someone had entered the courtyard below. He heard footsteps on stone and a strange nasal music that silenced the birds. Little Pearl tilted her head to hear better, and in this way the light fell for the first time on the right side of her face.

"You're hurt!" he said. Her skin was discolored, her flesh swollen. She had taken a blow to the face and the sight infuriated him.

Her gaze returned to him. "Are you in pain?" she asked, ignoring his comment.

"No. I mean . . . your cheek. It's swollen."

She nodded. "I am aware of this."

"But doesn't it hurt?"

"*I* have adequate qi to heal this injury." Her gaze slipped down to his longjohn. Clearly she thought his power was severely compromised.

He closed his eyes on a sigh. Then he felt her hand, a tentative weight on his thigh. He tensed immediately but did not open his eyes. "No, thank you, Little Pearl."

The weight disappeared. "So it is true. Barbarians know no moderation."

His eyes popped open. "What?"

"You whites are either driven solely by your appetites or stop them up completely so that you wither in a bitter, slow death."

"What?" He didn't dare raise his head for fear of jostling his ribs, but he did manage to twist his head slightly. "Don't be ridiculous! We don't die bitter, slow . . . We don't!"

She nodded, her expression both sad and wise, and he found himself resenting her attitude. "Such is the way with many men in China as well. You do not understand your own genitals."

Heat coiled into his face. This was not a polite conversation. And yet he could not help but argue. "We know how to use . . . What to . . . We know."

"You know how to have sex and urinate, but your energies are squandered, your life force wasted or stopped up completely." She leaned forward and patted his hand. "If you wish, I will teach you. I will show you how yang can bring you a long and healthy life." She frowned. "Unless your 'Christian' is a kind of monk. You are forbidden to touch your dragon?"

"What?" Why was it so hard to follow her conversation? "No! I'm no monk. I can touch . . . If I want . . . Well, I shouldn't, but . . ." He grimaced as he reordered his thoughts. "Only my wife may touch me."

She pulled back onto her heels. "You are married, then. I understand—"

"No. No! If I were married, then she would be allowed. But until then—"

"So your Christian is like most Chinese men. You should not engage in sex outside of marriage. And yet you do. You have not learned how to manage your yang, and so you daily fight to suppress it or to find a woman to release it." She shook her head sadly. "Such ignorance. All over the world." Then she pushed upward. She moved slowly, forced to lean on the mattress as she struggled onto her tiny feet. "Ling Su has returned from the market. I must begin cooking."

At the mention of food, his stomach rumbled in hunger. Odd, that he could be both ravenous and nauseous at the same time, but pain created many inconsistencies. Fortunately, he was familiar with the progress of broken bones. He would only be in agony for a week. Then he would merely be miserable.

"I will send one of your men with rice, then you must rest."

"When will you return?" He wasn't sure why he asked, but he wanted to know.

She sighed. "The others fear your ghost and will not come." She shrugged. "But I cannot stay by your side all day. I have other responsibilities." He heard a strange note in her voice—both weariness and fear colored her tone, but there was pride as well. He smiled. The burden of command was familiar to him.

"I do not wish to add to your problems," he said.

She bowed. "I will be back as often as I can." She paused at the door. "Stroke your dragon as often as possible, but do not release your seed. That will kill you for sure." She frowned. "You don't know how, do you?" Before he could answer, she waved a hand. "Never mind. I will send pictures with your man." Then she was gone.

Jonas watched her go and tried to suppress his disappointment. Her conversation was bizarre and her morals made her no better than a common whore, or so he told himself. But he had been raised by a whore, and he knew that there was nothing common about Little Pearl. Had she truly fought off a mob to save him? He didn't believe it. He couldn't believe it. And yet he was obviously here, apparently safe and healing.

He fought back through his memories to the attack. He remembered the faces and the blows. Those damned bill collectors had intended to kill him. At a minimum, he would have been left to die in the middle of the street. Someone had stopped the mob. Someone had carried him here and tended his wounds. Could it be Little Pearl? But why? And how?

He struggled with the questions and spent a great deal of time comparing his hostess to all the other whores he had known. None of them would have braved a mob to rescue him. Not even his own mum. Certainly none of them would have sided with a foreigner over her own people.

Thankfully, Seth arrived quickly to address some more pressing problems. While his first mate cut his bonds and carried him to the pot, Jonas heard a steady litany of distracting reports beginning with the state of the missing cargo—still missing—continuing through the state of the damaged ship—still damaged—and finishing with the mood throughout Shanghai—still ugly.

The Boxers were gaining strength and support. And though none thought the antiwhite bastards would ever make it out of the north, the rabble had now begun creating problems all the way down to southern Shanghai. The attack on him personally had been quickly hushed, but Seth offered to report it to the British authorities.

"No!" Jonas was breathless after his return to the bed, breathless and light-headed from pain. But he still retained enough of his senses to instruct the young man. "Then we'd have to say how I got into Chinese Shanghai. We'd get a whole lot of attention—"

"Could help with the cargo."

"Yeah, it'll force it so far into hiding, we'll never find it. Quiet is best, Seth." Then he closed his eyes, taking a moment to regain his breath before he asked his next question. "Where are the men?"

"Got a few just inside the courtyard—out of sight, but still available if needed."

"Good."

"Makes the ladies squeal if they come inside. Something about ghosts."

"No squealing." Lord, his whole body was clenched from the pain; screaming women were the last thing he needed. "The bill collectors?"

"No mob. At least not right now. I think they're afraid of spirits, too."

"Your idea?" Jonas probed. Seth was clever. Maybe he'd thought of the ruse.

"No, sir. Was all set up afore I got here. By Little Pearl, I think. Want me to ask?"

"No. No."

"She told me to bring you this scroll. Said I should help you understand the pictures. It's right—"

"No!" Jonas didn't have the strength to grab the parchment-bound bamboo sticks. Fortunately he didn't need to move to distract his first mate. "I'm too tired. I'll look at it later," he lied. "Now quit dawdling here and go find me Customs Official Chen."

"Yes, Cap'n! Right away." Thank God, the boy took the hint and disappeared. Unfortunately, that left Jonas with nothing but more questions and a pain strong enough to drive a man insane. He closed his eyes, keeping his breaths shallow as he struggled some more with his thoughts on Little Pearl. Had she really . . . ?

He slept. And when he woke, there was a naked woman in his room.

April 5, 1887

Dearest brother Jonas,

I don't know when you will receive this letter. Perhaps it will come long after you have made port and received the news from someone else. Mum passed today. She died in the manner we always expected: beaten by a customer then festering in rum. It took a week, and she spoke of you often. She was very proud of you.

There is no money. The furniture and clothing have all been sold. You already knew she pawned the jewels you brought. Even the pearls lasted barely a week after you left. I leave now to live for a week with Father Simon, to study and then take orders. You have daily challenged me to step away from our mother's skirts, to become a man, to do as men—to do as you do. I have done so, my brother. With you and with others. And at the time, I enjoyed it. But no more.

Believe me when I say this is my choice.

Look for Father Simon when you return. He will know where I am. And I pray that you embrace me then as Father Bert.

—Albert

The Chinese believe walnuts resemble the shape of the brain and, thus, are good for nourishing the brain. Any foods that resemble the shape of a body organ are said to be good for that organ.

Chapter Six

Done. Dinner was finished and the kitchen set to rights. The compound set to rights. White sailors were set to guard. All was exactly as it should be, thought Little Pearl. Or exactly as well as it could be given the Tans' absence. Even Captain Jonas had slept all day in a healing rest without fever. And now she had one last task before she could sleep. It was a ritual she performed every night without fail, no matter how exhausted or sick she might feel. It was the core of her practice and the only way to remind herself of who she was and what she did. She was not a whore; she was a tigress. And so she would perform her nightly exercises to calm and center herself such that she would remain beautiful and never again face the horror of a night on the street.

She made her way slowly, climbing the stairs with care. When her feet went numb like this, she was prone to falls. She climbed by finger touch, embedding her nails in the walls as she hauled herself up. Her first practice room had been up here nearly a decade ago. She and Ken Jin had climbed in the dark many a long night.

This time, a different man awaited her: a lanky white man named Seth. He held a lantern for her and smirked in the way of all arrogant men who think with their dragons. "He still sleeps."

"Fever?"

"None."

"Then go to your ship, First Mate Seth. I will tend to him now."

First Mate Seth hesitated, his eyes narrowing in suspicion. She applauded his prudence, but she hadn't the patience to gently allay his fears. "If I intended to kill him, I would have left him on the street. You have his clothing and his purse—"

"He is too sick for rutting."

Her eyes widened with an abrupt surge of fury. It faded as quickly as it hit, thrown at the feet of her ancestors as yet one more humiliation she had to endure because of their betrayal. She waited for the anger to pass, feeling it fade less quickly than usual. Truly, she was tired if she could not ignore the slights of a young man. "I would not think to tell you how to sail your boat," she snapped. He blinked, obviously not understanding her meaning. "I have spent a lifetime studying 'rutting.'" She spit out his crude word. "Do not seek to instruct the teacher."

"But why else would you—"

"Go home, First Mate Seth," she growled. "Your captain is safe here. I have no intention of touching him except for healing." It was no lie. She had spent much of the day thinking over her two encounters with Captain Jonas. She had never heard of a white man who refused yang stimulation, but was not surprised they existed. That a man so strong in yang stopped his energies, however, did shock her.

It also impressed her. Never would she have believed a white man could be so disciplined. Given his powerful qi, he would need the intelligence and control of a jade dragon. How startling, especially given the wild barbarian energy within him! If she hadn't seen it with her own eyes, she would never have believed it possible. And yet, Captain Jonas had indeed stopped her—twice—from stimulating his male organ.

The question, of course, was how to turn such a situation to her advantage. The creditors would stay away for a couple more days. She had already whispered pretend fears to her best gossipmonger, worrying aloud that the captain's spirit, dark and powerful, furious at his injuries, would surely haunt whomever it happened to find. No one would brave the compound under such circumstances. Indeed, all of the servants avoided the practice rooms, if they showed up at all. Little Pearl didn't mind. Fewer mouths to feed, fewer expenses. She needed only to keep Jonas apparently teetering between life and death while she waited for the Tans' return.

It was enough, and yet she wanted more. She wanted his yang strength for herself, as a bulwark against the future. She wanted to see him become a refined and steady source of yang power for his own health as well. What a magician he could become if he only knew what he had!

She entered the captain's room and stared at his pale form, slack-jawed in sleep. He was a handsome figure for a white man. She was even becoming accustomed to his hair enough to notice the lean strength in his body. His arms were thrown open and his legs were slightly spread. He looked dominating even in sleep. And as a captain, he was used to controlling his men, ordering their time and efforts. All those things helped refine yang. Ah, what power he could have if only he opened his mind. What a wonder it would be to rest safe and protected in his arms.

She sighed. No point in wishing. She crossed to his side and sniffed the air. His bandages would have to be changed soon, but she had no wish to disturb him now. So she settled on the blankets she'd arranged on the floor. There was no place in this tiny room for another bed. She would sleep here on the floor, ready to help him when he woke.

She wore her cooking clothing, so it was no hardship to strip them off. And though she enjoyed the scents of her work, she murmured in pleasure when she tossed aside her blouse and allowed the smokey scent of soy and ginger, burning oil and searing pork to fade from her consciousness. Her breasts bobbed free as she also untied the diamond-shaped undercloth. The tassels had long since worn away and the embroidery was faded, but the cloth was soft and comfortable—a sensuous pleasure—as she pulled it away. Since the autumn bite in the air kept the room cold, she untied her skirt but kept it pooled about her legs. She would strip it off later, after the yin river warmed her.

Lastly, she unbound her feet. Water and cloth were always kept in the practice rooms, so she was able to gingerly wash some feeling back into her feet and legs. The pinpricks of pain were familiar and therefore welcome, and soon she was able to tuck her right leg tight to her yin center with her heel and toes pressed hard against her cinnabar cave.

She spared a moment to look at her patient. He was deeply asleep. Many tigresses worked in partially public places. They said the fear of discovery added to their yin stores. What few experiments she had made in this arena told her that discovery was not one of her fears. She cared not who watched nor when. The act was all that mattered, so she closed her eyes and tried to concentrate. Normally she would already be wet by this time. Her mind and her body were well trained in this process. It was a measure of her exhaustion that she was bone dry.

She began with a low hum. Shi Po had not taught her this, but Little Pearl had learned that her yin responded better to a vibration—a hum. The tone was higher than the one used for yang, it fluttered in her chest until her body began to vibrate. Eventually, the sound lowered from her throat to her chest until it finally centered deep within her womb.

She pressed her fingers to her breasts. The placement was exact, the four fingers of each hand against the side of each nipple. Then she began spiraling outward, performing the dispersing circles as she threw off both age and clogging energies. When her fingers reached the outmost area of her breast, she reset, returning to the center to begin again. In this way she smoothed and cleansed her yin. Then she reversed her strokes. Instead of releasing qi, she now actively energized it. Her spirals narrowed, her hands pushed up and in. Up and in. Up and . . .

Nothing. Even her mouth was dry.

She opened her eyes in disgust only to see Captain Jonas's dark eyes staring back at her. She froze. Her hum stopped, while her hands remained suspended just above her breasts. As she watched, his gaze dropped to her large, dusky nipples. She did not move, but she felt his gaze like a caress. To her amazement, her nipples tightened. She felt the slow contraction above and the sweet moistening below.

She didn't move for fear of disrupting the spell. Her breath shortened to a shallow pant and her nipples tightened to hard peaks tighter than she'd experienced in years.

Captain Jonas swallowed. She saw the convulsive movement even in the dim light of her single lantern. Her gaze dropped to his yang center. She watched as the blankets shifted infinitesimally. His dragon was stirring, his yang recovering. If she wished him to heal, then she need only continue her nightly exercises. He would watch and his yang would strengthen.

But she couldn't move her hands. No one since Ken Jin had ever watched her evening work. It was a time reserved for her alone. And yet the way he looked at her—not just her breasts, but at her—as if she were the sum of everything he had ever wanted or needed. Nothing would distract him from her, nothing would keep him from her side. It made no sense. He was merely a man too long denied the sight of a woman's breasts. And yet, his yang energy reached across the room and her yin responded with sweet rain after a great drought.

Never, not even with Ken Jin, had she hungered for a man as she did now. And he wanted her just as desperately.

Without conscious decision, she began the energizing strokes. His gaze followed her hands as they spiraled inward, closer and closer to her yin buds. She heard his breath catch as she touched her nipples, thumbing a single time across them. It was not part of the exercise, but she couldn't resist, especially as the motion made his nostrils flare. Her neck stretched. She was arching her back into her hands, not because she wanted a deeper touch but because she wanted him to see her body at its fullest.

Her breasts were large for a Chinese, but not as bulbous as a white woman's. She wondered what he thought of them. Then she wondered no more as the crease in his blanket grew thicker and higher. His dragon was lifting its head to see.

She began the next spiral, starting again at the outside of her breasts and narrowing in. Her breath was supposed to be timed with her strokes: outward on the down stroke, in on the up, but her air would not sync with her movements. Instead she matched his breath, flowing with the lift and lowering of his chest. To be so in sync with a man not her partner was unusual. That he was white made it all the more bizarre. And yet she would not stop.

"Touch yourself," she murmured, her voice the low hum of seduction. "Stroke your dragon along with me."

"I . . ." He swallowed.

"It is healing."

"It is perversion."

She smiled. "Only the ignorant call it that. Will you not try?" He had no response, clearly undecided. So while he struggled with his white man's values, she switched her position. She straightened her right leg, now wet with her rain. She could smell her scent in the air and smiled as she saw his nose twitch.

She extended her right leg outward, then pulled her left in tight. Once again, her heel and toes pressed hard against the cinnabar cave. There was so much yin, her flesh felt hot and her body supple. Her back and her hips would not stabilize and she wiggled to find the best position.

Though she looked down, she knew the captain was watching. She heard his breath rasp and felt his yang energy surge toward her. She was not surprised to look up and find another bulge had joined the lump formed by his dragon. It was his hand slowly closing around his organ. She could not see what he did beneath the blanket, but she imagined his long calloused fingers surrounding and holding. His touch would be firm—masterful even—but there would be a reluctance in his stroke, a hesitation that would tremble along the skin and make his body stretch toward completion.

She looked to his face and noted his grimace of distaste even as his eyes drooped in the languor that comes with stimulation. He hated himself for what he did. His conscience pricked him, and that struggle added an extra energy in the room—an anger that spiced their hunger.

She licked her lips in appreciation and set her hands to the outside of her breasts. She would time her stroke with his. As he pulled the dragon belly down, she would stroke her breasts to fullness, tweaking her peaked nipple at the same moment his dragon mouth opened for a taste.

The bulge beneath the cover moved. She began her circles, spreading her fingers to encompass more of her breasts as she spiraled inward. His hips shifted on the mattress, pushing forward into his hand. She pursed her lips, sucking slightly as her fingers narrowed to her nipples. She pinched and a streak of fire shot like hot oil through her body.

Then the stroking began again. Circle, pinch, then a streak of heat that coalesced into an oil fire in her womb. The tempo was slow at first to accommodate her spirals and his wounds. But soon his hand began to move faster and her breath became shorter. She breathed quickly now, licking her lips to spread moisture to her mouth. Below, her heel ground in a circle that only became unconscious after much practice. She heard Jonas's breath in the silent room, low and heavy but with a power that throbbed in her blood. Like ginger in oil, it hissed and spat at her, adding flavor to all she did. Then he began to speak.

His words were in English, so she understood barely half of it. But the vibration he made, the pitch and roll of his voice touched something deep inside her.

Her yang stores, she realized. His words stimulated her flagging male energies. She felt a surge of power in the form of lust. Her hips rocked forward of their own accord and she wished for a partner. Her gaze immediately leaped to his face though the thought was ridiculous.

She could not have a white dragon partner. Such a

thing had never been done. And yet, Chinese men had recently taken white women as their tigresses and with great success. What if his white yang could do such a thing for her?

She pinched her nipples, taking a moment to elongate them toward Captain Jonas. His nostrils flared, his gaze was dark like a stormy sea, but he had stopped speaking.

"What did you say to me?" she asked. In truth, she didn't really care about his meaning. She just wanted to hear his voice again. He blinked as his gaze fastened on her face.

"I called you a whore and a witch," he answered in Chinese. "I called you every ugly thing I could think of." Anger throbbed in his voice, but she saw no hatred in his face or body. Even his disgust was aimed inward, at himself.

"You are strengthening your yang."

"I am a damned sinner! I should not . . . I . . . I . . ." His hand still moved beneath the blanket, but his eyes were tortured, and his breath shortened. He was nearing his release.

"Stop stroking yourself. You must not release your seed." She froze as well, knowing that he would still when she did.

He did, but reluctantly and with an embarrassment that set fire to his cheeks.

"How do you feel?" she asked.

"Like a fool."

She stared at him, waiting for his yang fire to recede. In her experience, men were simple creatures capable of only a single emotion at a time. But perhaps that was Chinese men because this white captain was more complicated. This man reviled himself even as his hand continued to stroke his dragon. He insulted her in a language she couldn't understand, then seemed apologetic for his opinion.

"I have been a whore," she answered, unsure why she was speaking. Words were rare in this type of encounter. "Many call this magic, but I cannot force any action of you. What you do—"

"Is my own choice." His words were a defiant growl, and she bowed in agreement. But as she dipped her head she saw that he had begun to stroke himself again. Unbidden her hands moved as well, circling her breasts and lifting them toward him.

"You strengthen yourself," she said. "A man cannot live long without a strong yang center."

He arched a brow at her. "And a woman?"

"My yin centers are here," she flattened her hands to encompass her breasts. Then she let a hand slip lower to her belly above her womb. "And here."

His eyes seemed to glitter. "Not there. Lower." His tone deepened and took on the force of a command. "Lower."

Her littlest finger extended and dipped down beneath the band of her skirt. It was untied and so opened easily, but not so far that he could see what she did.

"Let me see," he whispered.

"It will be too much for you. You will release your seed."

His face hardened. "Let me see!" It was an order given by a man used to command. And yet when she refused to move, his expression crumpled. It did not collapse as so often happened with men unused to power. It shifted into an angry desperation, as if he needed to see her touch herself and yet reviled himself for so basic a desire. "Please." Not a whisper nor a command. She could not categorize his motivations and so was caught in hesitation.

"Why?"

"It will aid my healing."

Her lips shifted a demure smile. "You do not believe that."

"My dragon wants it." He stumbled with the Chinese words, but his meaning was clear.

She shook her head. "Your dragon does not rule your head."

His hand started moving faster. "Yes," he gasped. "Yes, it does."

"Stop stroking. You cannot afford—"

"Take off your skirt." His hand moved faster and his face began to flush.

"Stop!"

"No!"

She abruptly stood and her skirt slid down one hip, but caught on the other. She stepped to his side and whipped the cover off his body, quickly grabbing hold of his wrist. His hand was large, his wrist corded and strong—a fitting match to his thick dragon. Her tiny hand was no match for his strength.

"You will harm yourself," she cried.

He had stopped his stroke, but did not release himself. "Show me," he said.

"Then you will stop?"

"Take off your skirt."

He had not promised, but what did she care? She had told him the truth. In his state, releasing his seed could kill him. If he chose to disregard that, she could not stop him.

She shimmied out of her skirt. His gaze riveted on her tattoo—a tigress that coiled over her pleasure grotto. Its head roared from her shaved mound, its spine twisted along her lotus petals, and its tail danced up her tailbone.

"Let go of your dragon," she ordered. He did. His hand opened and lifted to hover uncertainly just above the dragon's mouth. She leaned over, acutely aware of how her breasts jiggled as she moved. She didn't have to see his face to know he watched their every shift and sway.

She firmly set his hand down beside his thigh. His other hand began to lift—headed for her breasts probably—but she stopped that as well. Then she stood there, leaning over him, her breasts dangling between them as she held him still. She looked at his face. Amusement shimmered there and she wondered a moment if she had been tricked. Had he pretended desperation so she would come over? One glance at his dragon told him his yang hunger was no illusion.

"You wish to see?" she asked.

"Yes."

"Then remember that you see a tigress. Many pay large sums for what I give you tonight."

His lip curled in disdain. "You wish for money?"

No. "Of course," she said. "But your men even the tally between us. They protect this compound from bill collectors."

"Then let me see what my men have bought." Anger sharpened his tone, and she wondered why. She might have asked, but he gave her no time. His hands had lifted again, so she stopped them. She climbed up on the bed and pinned his wrists with her feet. Or at least she tried. But on her tiny, unbound feet, the sensations were too intense, her footing too uncertain and his wrists simply too large to hold. So she dropped to her knees.

He was a large man in all respects, but she was flexible and strong. Still, she had not straddled a man like this since . . . since she had been a whore. The vulnerability of this position was too risky for a tigress. Men could not be trusted to remain immobile. But Captain Jonas was injured. Even if he could not control himself, a single punch to his ribs would drop him like a rock. She was entirely safe.

And yet, she was horribly exposed. The air hit her wet cinnabar cave with icy clarity, and her thighs tensed in instinctive withdrawal. But there was nowhere for her to go. She had promised, and he was watching with a dark intensity that momentarily distracted her.

"You have never seen a tigress tattoo, so I will explain. To become a tigress requires many hours of study, years of practice."

He curled his lip, his gaze still on her lifted tigress face. "I understand your practice. My mother was a master."

She stilled, surprised. His mother was a prostitute? "Anyone can spread their legs. A tigress trains to strengthen her body and her mind."

His gaze hopped to her face. "Why?"

"Because we are not whores."

His expression stilled and she had the sense he was waiting. But for what?

"The exercises tone our muscles, make our skin soft and youthful, and create waists as supple as a willow reed." She demonstrated the easiest move, shifting her hips forward as if pushed by the wind, then allowing the rest of her body to follow in a slow, sensuous wave. The sway was easy from long practice, and yet it was also difficult to perform spread open like this above his hips.

"You are beautiful," he murmured.

"I am more than beautiful," she said without vanity. "I am strong and flexible, my skin cups breasts tight with a girl's first blush, and my mouth is red and moist."

He didn't answer, but she felt his hands tense beneath her shins. She stretched her arms up high as she fumbled with the rough cord that bound her hair. "Once the physical is mastered, we train the mind. Meditation, purification, focused prayer—all take many hours, many months."

Her hair finally slipped free, the weight on her head released as she arched in purring delight. The long strands slid down her back, the edges brushing sensuously across her skin. She burrowed her hands across her scalp, scratching and lifting, opening and—most of all—relishing this simple pleasure while in her mind's eye she saw the trailing ends of her hair playing with the tigress tail. Then she looked back down. He was watching her with dazed awe, and she smiled. Men did not understand. They had no idea that the simple act of releasing hair could be a tigress act of devotion. It was all in the thoughts and attitude.

When she gloried in the present, when she felt every sensation of hair on skin, of coarse fabric against the tops of her feet and the captain's hard bones beneath her shins—all of that was devotion. She relished every sensation without judgment. She experienced her body and her life without worry or thought or fear. That was devotion, and she did it too rarely.

She shifted her shoulders to set her breasts to dancing. The jiggle of her flesh in front mimicked the wave of hair behind, and she grinned as Jonas's breath caught in his throat. Men did not understand what a tigress did, but they felt the effects nonetheless.

"It takes years of study, white captain, and only then are we ready for the examination."

She leaned forward, pleased when the full weight of her hair slipped across her shoulder to tickle his chest and chin. He responded, but not with words. His forearms flexed beneath her legs, and he released a low possessive growl. It was a sound that came from deep within his yang center, and she knew from the rumbling tenor that his health was returning.

"Only after we have passed the examination are we marked with a tigress."

"What is it?" His voice came from the same place—the deepest part of his energy—and so she was surprised that he was capable of speech. Truly he was an amazing man.

"What is what?"

"The test. What . . . ?" Words had deserted him, but she understood.

"We try to attain Heaven without touch or stimulation. With only the power of our minds, we stretch for the holy place and try to become Immortal."

He frowned. She had spoken in euphemism, in words deliberately vague so no outsider could follow. Men hated to be thought stupid, so he would never push for more details. Except that this captain was not like other men.

"Show me," he said. Again, yang energy throbbed in his words.

Her laughter was deep and throaty, but no less real. "I am not your slave to be commanded. I am a—"

"A tigress. So you have said." His eyes were bright in this dark room, and she was startled by the challenge that flowed from him. "Show me this reach to Heaven."

"Why?"

"So I will believe in your Immortality."

She shrugged, surprised to realize her nipples had tightened again. "I care not if you believe, Captain Jonas. I require only—"

"Money?"

She shook her head. "I have spoken with your first mate, Seth. You have no money to offer."

"I have men." He lifted his head slightly to push his yang thoughts on her.

"I need no—"

"To guard the house."

She frowned. "They are already guarding the house."

"Not if I send them away. Not if—"

"You would not do that." She said the words, but she wasn't so sure. Ghost people were moved by the wind. Everyone said so. If his mood of the moment was to send his men away, then what would become of her and the Tan house? The servants were already scarce, frightened by his possible death. If his people were gone as well, then she would be defenseless.

He was silent, watching her closely, no doubt reading

her fears off her body. A Chinese man would not notice. He would order her to comply and assume it was done. But Captain Jonas was white, and his eyes were piercingly direct. He knew she wavered.

"My men follow orders." His voice was growing stronger. His increased yang was flowing outward to all parts of his personality. "If you show me this thing, then they will stay for as long as you need."

"You will change your mind."

His body tensed beneath her. "I have never gone back on my word. *Never!*" His outrage was real. And even if it wasn't, she knew that Master Tan trusted this man. She believed he would not betray her. But . . .

"It is a sacred act. Not something to be done—"

"I wish to see it. I wish to know."

"Why?"

His eyebrows arched in challenge. "Does it matter?"

"Yes."

He hesitated, then abruptly his expression shifted to casual disdain. It was a pretense. She could tell his thoughts bothered him, but she had no understanding beyond his next words: "I wish to prove to you that it is not possible. One does not go to Heaven from sex."

She jerked in reaction. He understood what she'd meant! But how was that possible? She had spoken in vague phrases. She could have been speaking of a garden of delights or succulent morsels of tender meat. The sacred texts were filled with such euphemisms such that only the initiated could understand. And yet—

"I know of tigresses," he said, obviously reading her thoughts. "I know what your test is. Kui Yu spoke of it, and we both wondered." He shook his head. "But what happens is no miracle. It is simply biology—science. There is no God at work in a woman's orgasm."

She stared at him, stunned that he knew these words. Stunned, too, that Master Tan would have shared these things with him. But who knew what men said amidst their drinks and tobacco? And could a white man be trusted with such knowledge?

She didn't know, and she wasn't given time to sort it out. He had shifted his hands to caress the back of her ankles. He could barely touch her; she still held his forearms pinned with her shins. Truthfully, her legs were beginning to strain from the position, and yet she had no wish to move from her place of dominance. But when his fingertips stroked the edge of her ankle, she became fully aware of his thick dragon, poised beneath her cinnabar cave. She smelled his yang scent in the air and tasted the sweet dew of yin moisture in her mouth.

"Show me," he urged. "Show me this once, and I will protect you."

It was a good offer. In one night's work, she could ensure her safety for as long as she needed it. And yet . . . "It is not something to be done without thought. It is—"

"Sacred devotion. So you have said. But you passed this test long ago—"

"Over four years ago."

"Then it should be simple. You are a tigress. You have the tattoo. . . ."

She bit her lip, undecided. "I am tired and my thoughts are scattered."

"You are afraid," he mocked. "Surely a tigress like you could perform your test with ease."

"Don't try your male games on me," she snapped. "I am not a boy who must prove my manliness with every breath." She straightened to her full height above him. "If I do this, I do it for what you offer, not because you have insulted my pride."

"I apologize. I forgot myself."

She pressed her lips together, cutting off a curse. Then, because her legs were aching, she abruptly pushed off of him. She tottered as her feet sought purchase on the ground. She would have fallen if he had not anticipated her shaky legs and lifted an arm to brace her. A moment later, she was able to face him with her legs closed and her body full and tall.

"I will do this thing for you." She could see surprise light in his eyes. In truth, he echoed the sentiment deep inside her heart. She had not attempted an examination since her initial test; she was not at all sure she could perform it now. "You swear you will leave your men at my discretion? For as long as I need them?"

"I cannot promise more than a month. We will have to set sail."

She nodded. A month was a good bargain. "It will take time for me to prepare. And once begun, I must not be interrupted. You must be silent."

"Agreed. As long as I see it all. Tonight."

"Agreed." Then she frowned. His dragon was no less small. But perhaps there were other things he needed. He had slept a long time. "Are there things you need first? Food, water, the pot?"

He was raising up, slowly pushing himself upright with a loud groan. When she moved forward to help him, he waved her away. "Make your preparations. I am strong enough for this."

She was not so sure, but she would not insult his pride. Besides, she needed to settle her thoughts. Normally, an examination took a week of cleansing herbs, three days of special bathing rituals, and a day's meditation. She had perhaps a half hour. Could she do it?

She could for a month's protection from bill collectors. She could because . . . Her thoughts stumbled and her belly stilled. She would do this thing, she realized. She would sit on the floor beside a white man and meditate herself into orgasm. Then she would allow him to examine the truth of her action. She would do these things not because he promised her protection, but because she wanted him to see. She suddenly wanted him to believe, and she wanted to be the one to convert him.

She refused to push deeper into her motivations than that.

March 21, 1888

Dearest Albert,

Or should I call you Father Bert? A priest soon to have his own parish—a change so fast that I scarce learned of your plan before I found it effected. Did you intend this for a long time? You must have, to have completed your studies so quickly.

I will tell you the truth, Albert. I did not expect this of you. I am your brother, and I knew nothing of your plans until I made port and heard that you were in seminary. Your letter found me much later.

Did you think I would be ashamed? To have a man of the cloth as a brother is a great thing, a blessed thing. I hope that you will soon preside over my wedding to sweet Annie. But I cannot understand why it was done in secret, why you told me nothing of your thoughts.

Albert, we must rely on each other in this life. There are no others. How could you do this without a word to me?

—Jonas

*To make rice dough correctly, the water must be boiling; the
hot water cooks the rice flour and gives the dough the proper
consistency. Be careful as you begin to work the mixture
because it is hot enough to burn your hands. This means that
you will only be able to work the mixture for a few seconds at
a time. Do not let this prevent you from working the dough
while it is still hot; if you let it cool, the dough will not work.*

Chapter Seven

Little Pearl sat naked on the floor. Her mind was cluttered, her body exhausted, and yet her spine was
straight, her yin center already wet despite being exposed to the air. At the moment, she rested on her knees,
but when she began, she would lie back with her legs
spread. She would not be allowed to touch herself, but
the examiner could. At any point, he had the right to slip
his fingers inside her to check her progress.

She opened her eyes. She should be concentrating on
the task at hand, but she could not stop herself from following the white man's movements. The man was
washing himself, and not just his hands and face. He
used his good arm to rub a cloth slowly all over his entire body despite the pain it obviously gave him. He
even unwound his bandages and changed his own
dressings with the cloths set beside the bed for that
purpose.

She had not expected a man to be so fastidious, much
less a white man, but Captain Jonas clearly wanted to be

clean. And rather than demand she bathe him, he performed all the actions himself despite his injuries. Even more bizarre, the man was obviously embarrassed by his nudity. He kept slanting glances in her direction and his face heated to a dull red. But he was a white man, akin to a monkey, according to the Empress Dowager. Why would an animal be so anxious about his dress? But he was, and so to ease his discomfort, she offered him a gentle smile.

"Would you feel better if I meditated outside until you are ready?" She felt anxious about leaving him alone when he was so clearly weak. Normally, she had little patience with other people's sensibilities. One could not be a tigress and still be nervous about another's opinion. And yet, he seemed so anxious about his undress that she headed for the door even before he answered.

"You're naked!" he gasped, clearly horrified.

"There is no one in the hallway."

"But what if one of my men—"

She smiled. "They already think this place a brothel. My nakedness would not surprise them."

He dropped the cloth into the bowl as he spun toward her, but the twist pulled at his broken ribs and he gasped then braced himself against the wall. She crossed to his side to help him, but he waved her away, pushing out words between clenched teeth. "If they see you . . . They're rough men. . . . I cannot . . . I'm not strong enough . . ."

He was trying to protect her? The thought quickened her heart and heated her yin center. "Return to the bed, Captain Jonas. You are hurting yourself."

He shook his head. "Stay here." His breath was evening out, the pain obviously receding. Yet his expression remained tight, his eyes fierce. "Do not go outside."

She smiled. "I am perfectly safe."

"Not from my men—"

"Sit, Captain." Then she sighed, strangely disappointed. "You are too weak for the examination tonight. You need to rest."

He shook his head, his jaw clenching as he shuffled to the cot. "The bargain . . . is for tonight."

He half sat, half collapsed on the bed. She stood before him, watching him carefully. Droplets of water still clung to the dark hair on his chest. She'd been surprised to see that his hair didn't completely cover him like fur. It was more sculpted than she'd expected, with light curls shading his body in some places, and darker, denser lines drawing the eye down his belly toward his proud, full sex. In truth, she found it quite attractive, as though a painter had brushed skillful ink strokes about his body to emphasize his muscular form and yang prowess.

"Stop staring," he grumbled.

She frowned. "I am evaluating your health. You need to rest."

He lifted his gaze. "I am injured, not sleepy. And I will not release you from our bargain."

"Tomorrow will be soon—"

"Now," he snapped. "Or not at all."

She remained silent, watching his dark expression. Something lay beneath his order. Something beyond lurid curiosity or simple lust. Did she dare press him for an answer?

"Now, tigress," he snapped. "Or I order my men to return to the ship."

It was an empty threat. He hadn't the strength to find the men surrounding the Tan compound. And yet she bowed to him, acceding to his demand. "This will take much time," she warned. "Especially since I am tired. You should lie back—"

"I will stay awake. I will know if you fake it."

She paused, realizing he did not understand his rights. She need not tell him the truth. . . . "I will lie on the floor right beside your bed," she rushed. Nothing defeated a tigress's purpose faster than lies. "As examiner you can touch me as you wish to check the strength of the yin tide."

He stared at her a moment, then his eyes abruptly widened.

She lifted her chin. "I will not lie to you. In this or in any other aspect of my practice."

He swallowed and nodded. She stood a moment longer, swaying delicately on her tiny feet. Then she could not delay any longer and she folded herself toward the floor.

"On the bed," he suddenly said. "I cannot . . . I cannot examine you down there."

She froze in a half crouch. The bed was large enough for two. In truth, it would easily accommodate three. This was, after all, a practice room. But to lie beside him seemed so intimate. A ridiculous thought, given that she was about to show him something no man had ever witnessed. Even the jade dragons were denied this aspect of the practice. She still did not fully comprehend why she had agreed so easily.

But she had, and the examiner had the right to demand the location and manner of the test. So she nodded and slowly settled a knee on the bed. "Where should I lay my head?"

It was a simple question, but one that completely confused him. Did she place her face next to his where they might lie like lovers? Or did she reverse their positions such that he could see her cinnabar cave with absolute ease?

"Lie that way." He pointed at the foot of his bed. "A woman's face can lie."

The pleasure grotto could lie as well, but he did not know that. It didn't matter, though, because a tigress was always honest with her yin center. Liars did not attain immortality. So she arranged herself as he indicated, her head at his feet, her body lax and open near his hand. She closed her eyes, moderated her breath, and waited.

And waited.

Then she lifted her head to stare at him. He watched her with a cynical air, one brow arched as she frowned at him. It took her a moment to realize that he did not know the next step. "You must begin the test now," she prompted. "You must verify my yin state before I start."

He didn't understand. His expression was blank, his brows drawn together in confusion.

"You must touch me, Captain Jonas. The examiner adjusts my legs and touches the yin petals. She usually pushes inside the cinnabar cave to verify the thinness of the walls. It is to prove that I am not already aroused."

She watched as comprehension dawned on his face. His brows shot upward and his mouth slipped open. He meant to say something, she guessed, but no words formed. Then his gaze dropped to her pleasure grotto and back to her face.

She said nothing, but waited for his decision. Still, she could not deny the thrill it gave her to see him shocked into immobility. "I had not thought you squeamish, Captain Jonas."

He pulled back, his mouth abruptly snapping closed. "I'm just getting ready," he said. Then he reached behind himself to adjust the pillows. This was a practice room with five large perfumed cushions available for use. He took his time arranging them such that his back was braced, his arms comfortable and well supported.

She did not offer to help him though she flinched

every time his breath caught in pain. She was already in place for the examination. She was not allowed to move once she lay down. Besides, she wondered how long he would delay touching her.

Not long. In the end, he settled into a semi-recline, like a Mandarin among silk cushions. The image was disconcerting, especially since he was so very white. Who would ever have thought a ghost man could look like a rich Chinese aristocrat? She closed her eyes, not wanting to hold so unsettling an image. But then he grabbed her leg and unceremoniously pulled it across his chest. She gasped at the unexpected contact, breaking the rules by raising her head in surprise.

"What are you doing?" she gasped. He grunted as he moved her, obviously straining his shoulder and ribs, but his purpose was absolutely clear. He wanted her to lie half on top of him. Her head was at his feet, but one leg was stretched over his naked body such that he could see right up her legs. Worse, she could feel the subtle scratch of the hair on his legs against her hip and arm. She knew his every shift and tensing of corded thighs and bony hip. In truth, she believed she could feel his breath as his chest lifted and lowered though there was no logical reason for her to think that.

And all the while, she was wide open to his dark gaze. Her entire pleasure grotto was within casual distance of both his hands. She was a tigress who had once been a whore. She had experienced and done far worse than this. And yet, she felt chilled all the way up her spine. For the first time this evening, she feared that she would not be able to make the smallest start to this examination. She would be . . .

She wasn't. As he settled his large hands on the inside of her thighs, she realized that her yin cloud was thick and wet. The heat from his body made her yin perfume stronger, spicier, and all the more potent. And still she stared at him, her mind struggling to grasp the situation. Which was when he made one last shift. He adjusted her leg such that the base of his dragon and its twin pearls rested against her thigh. His full organ was no warmer than his hands, and yet she felt his yang heat like a brand. Searing, it coiled fire into her blood, though his touch was only the merest tickle against her skin.

"You cannot expect me to lie in such a way!" To her shame, her voice trembled as she spoke. But perhaps it was for the best, she realized. If she appeared disturbed, then perhaps he would relent.

She looked to his face, and her hopes died. His expression was dark, his face set. She saw no cruelty in him, only a coiled determination. It made no sense. He was clearly aroused, and yet this was not simple titillation. She heard anger in his voice, and yet there was no hatred in his eyes. What did he seek to gain from this?

His hands tightened on her thighs. Not painfully, just enough to imprint the texture and shape of his fingers onto her mind. Then he slid his good arm forward. With no warning at all, he pushed one calloused finger inside her.

She gasped. His finger was thick and dark from the sun. To watch it disappear into her was intensely erotic, and yet she was so wet, she barely felt it all. Without even thinking, she clenched her lowest internal muscles to intensify his presence.

He must have understood. He must have known what she wished because without another word, he extended his middle finger, slowly and firmly working it inside her.

Her neck was beginning to strain from her position. She wanted to lie back and rest her chest, but she could not stop herself from watching. Two thick fingers burrowed deep inside her. Over her lifetime, many men had rutted there. Larger men, thicker men, crueler men. But it had been a decade since that time, and she had spent much of her practice restoring smallness to her cinnabar cave. At the moment, his two fingers felt like a huge presence, an overwhelming intrusion into her body. She could not wait for him to remove it even as her back arched to deepen his thrust.

"I thought you weren't supposed to move," he said. The rumble of his voice vibrated into her from the myriad places where they touched, and she stilled to better appreciate the sensation.

"I have not begun," she answered as her chest and belly finally gave out. She dropped backward onto the mattress and stared at the shadowed ceiling. But she didn't see the old wood or the scorch of soot across the beams. Her mind was completely consumed by the image of his hand cupping her grotto. His thumb and last two fingers stroked her tattooed tigress spine and belly while the other two burrowed deep into its fur.

"So begin," he said.

"I am waiting for you to finish the initial examination." How odd that she spoke so calmly. Her voice sounded flat while inside all was a jumble.

She felt him shift his hips beneath her. "I am done," he said.

"But—"

"I cannot sit up, Little Pearl." He spoke in an equally flat tone. "I cannot watch well, so I must feel."

He lied. From his position he could see everything. But it was an examiner's right to choose the time and manner of inspection. She had just not expected this; not thought he would be there, the whole time. "But . . ." she began, though she had no idea what she wished to say.

"Begin!" His order came as a sharp crack, lightning within a storm. There was no denying the power in his command or the surge of yang that pulsed straight into her from his fingers.

She took a deep breath. She pulled the air into her lungs and, while she was at it, she drew in his yang as well. He wanted to remain inside her? Then he would pay the price. She would take every dram of yang energy he had. . . .

Yet, he was ill. She could not take from him. Not when he was sick. She sighed, releasing both her breath and her mental hold on his energy, his body, his . . . presence. But he would not leave her thoughts. His fingers were large and thick, a solid presence between her thighs. Worse, she was lying across his body, her back forced into an arch, her legs heated from his body and the hot brand of his dragon. He was *here* in every sense of the word, and she could not distance herself from him.

What a tigress could not escape, she had to accept. With humility and a yielding gentleness of spirit, she became so thin—like wine with too much water—that she became transparent and disappeared. These words were not in the sacred texts, but they existed for Little Pearl nonetheless. And as always, she turned her humiliation on her ancestors.

This is what I do. . . . Her anger faded. She had no wish to bring the ancestors into this holy act. Even with the white man here, she was still performing the examination—the proof that she was a tigress. This she did for herself. They had no part in it.

Which left what? Herself and him. She closed her eyes.

In her mind's eye, a man touched her. He kissed her breasts, tugged at her nipples with his teeth, rubbed the rough texture of his beard against her skin. The man was clearly Captain Jonas. No matter how much she wanted to bring a fantasy lover into her thoughts, *he* was there now. He touched her in truth, and so his was the body that caressed her in her thoughts.

The more she accepted that, the more her nipples tightened and her breasts became heavy with yin. Her chest began to tingle. It was an early stage of opening. In a slowly expanding circle above her heart, a tingling prickle of current danced. Like oil in a heating pot, it simmered and hissed, and soon it popped.

The oil fire added to the yin flame. With increased breath it soon glowed, encompassing her chest all the way to the hot spice points of her nipples. She was tired. Her body drooped with fatigue, and yet none of it seemed to matter. In her mind, Captain Jonas's beard teased her nipples, her breasts, her heart.

In truth, she longed for the physical touch of hand and lips. She wanted the brush of calloused fingers and the enveloping strength of a man who took hold of her as if he would never let go. But that wasn't what the examination was about. She was here to prove independence and personal skill.

She breathed and focused on her fantasies. The tingling expanded, her breasts ached, and the hot oil of yin rain slid down her belly into her womb. Her back tensed, deepening her arch, pressing a little harder against his hand. If this were her real test, such a movement would be severely reprimanded. But if this were a real examination, his fingers would not be inside her. His hips and legs would not be burning against her back. And his dragon would not be bobbing beside her thigh.

This was different than a real examination. This was a bargain for protection from bill collectors. And it was Captain Jonas inside her, making her lotus petals swell with his yang. She wondered if she could make him move, make his fingers shift and stroke in reaction.

She clenched her inner muscles. His fingers stiffened and his dragon reared. She smiled, enjoying the tiny movements. It was not enough. She wanted deeper penetration, harsher power, fuller strokes. With her yin moisture, every little sensation was dulled. And yet, she could feel his energy. He was inside her in more ways than just his hand.

In her thoughts, Captain Jonas was a healthy man, prowling over her then plunging inside. Over and over he thrust into her while their yin and yang rolled together in the churning cauldron of her cinnabar cave. Her breaths became shorter, the circulation of air vital to the coiling power of their union. She began making the noises of love, the tigress growl that came with stalking her prey. The gasping pounce of union. The high keen of yang absorption. And then . . .

And then . . .

Nothing. She strained, but could not reach the goal. She tried again: stalk, pounce, absorb, fly . . .

In her mind, she joined with Captain Jonas over and over. In her thoughts, the cauldron bubbled and boiled. The steam rose, her body tensed, but . . .

His hand shifted. It twisted and moved. *What?* She lifted her head to see his face dark with yang flush. His dragon pushed and reared against her inner thigh. And his hand, wet with her desire, wiggled and pushed a third finger inside.

Yes. Oh yes. She arched into the pressure. She fell backward and closed her eyes to better feel his penetration. Her legs were spread wide, her belly quivering. And with the addition of another finger, she felt another thrust of yang coiling into her. Deeper. Fuller. A trembling in her womb. Soon. Soon.

The image in her mind shifted. Suddenly, she no longer thought of his dragon roaring inside her. Instead, she saw the captain's face—dark and intense, rugged and . . . tender. He kissed her: the softest brush of his lips against hers. She actually felt it. Gentle, muted, the merest whisper. It could have been a current of air or the tingle of yin, now expanded all the way to her mouth. It didn't matter. In her mind, it was his lips on hers. His kiss.

Completion! Her womb contracted, her breath suspended, and the cauldron of energy surged upward through her entire body. She flew!

Where?

Little Pearl tiptoed daintily through an enveloping darkness. She paused, tasting warmth, smelling safety, stretching her body and her thoughts in luxurious sweetness.

Was this Heaven?

No. The answer shivered through her awareness with ugly finality. And yet . . .

Yes. She was safe and happy. Her tummy was full and her legs curled sweetly around her body. How could it not be Heaven?

She felt another presence. A man? Up here? No man should be here yet. Not until . . .

She tumbled away. She lost her footing on her tiny bound feet, and she fell down, down past the upper story railing to the hard floor below. Any moment she would feel the impact. Her body would shatter, her bones would break, her head would split open like a melon. The pain would be awful. The agony . . .

She gasped and opened her eyes. The impact had not come, and yet, she felt the ache in every part of her body. Her head pounded and her hips felt split open in the cold air. She shuddered and yet her body was too broken to move. Too broken, or too heavy?

She struggled, trying to sort image from reality, spirit from body. It was her spirit that shivered. Her body lay slack. Her spirit trembled and sobbed. Her body did nothing at all.

Then she heard a grunt. A man's groan that became a grunt mixed with a rumble. In truth it was simply sound issuing forth from a body just waking. The body that was beneath hers. The man's body.

Captain Jonas. And she was stretched out on top of him while he was flattened beneath her. For a moment her thoughts were confused. She thought he had caught her as she fell. She thought he had surrounded her and protected her from disaster.

Then she remembered. She felt his fingers still inside her and she knew what had happened. But just in case she was wrong, she lifted her head. She stretched it upward and looked down at her feet.

She saw herself sprawled open and his fingers pushed inside her. She saw his flaccid dragon and his spent seed across her thigh. And she saw him with his eyes wide open, his mouth slightly ajar in shock.

She knew she echoed his expression even as her mind categorized and reasoned out exactly what had happened. She had performed the examination. She had meditated herself into a state of orgasmic excitement strong enough to launch her to Heaven.

She had gone to Heaven! The thought was incredible and amazing. Never had she flown from her body as she had then. Though she taught meditation and body control, though she instructed tigresses on the practice and had long since earned her own tattoo, she had never even approached the hallowed land of the Immortals. It had been her secret shame that she taught but could not perform.

But now she had! She had soared as never before. But not to Heaven. She had flown to some strange, horrible place. Why?

She glared at the white man beneath her. He had polluted her energies. His presence inside her had poured white man's yang into her pure yin essence. He had corrupted her path, shifted her energies, and sent her reeling to . . . where? Not Heaven. The afterlife? Feng Du, village of the underworld? She didn't know. Whatever the place, it had absolutely not been Heaven. And the fault for that wrong destination lay squarely at his feet.

She pushed backward, pulling away from his hand, his body, his very presence. It was extraordinarily hard. Her body was heavy, her limbs uncooperative. She was stretched across him, her hips lifted in an ungainly manner. She had to dig her feet into the mattress and push up such that her hips lifted even higher. That meant her head had to drop back as she shoved with her tiny feet. But there was no purchase on the sheets, and she slipped back down, her foot slamming into his . . . ribs?

He grunted as she dropped and she knew she had hurt him, but she didn't care. "Go away!" she cried, her voice a strange high mixture of sound. The words didn't even make sense to her, but the strangled cat noise of terror hissed through her teeth. "Go away!"

He wasn't speaking. She could tell from his breath that he was in a great deal of pain. Fortunately, that gave her time to try again. She pushed once more, shoving her hips backward and away. His fingers slipped free and she shuddered—in both body and spirit this time. Was it loss or revulsion? Fear or abandonment?

Emotions spun through, too fast to identify. With enough of her hips on the mattress, she was able to roll away. She turned, dragging her far foot across his hips, narrowly missing his dragon, to land—

Nowhere. He grabbed her ankle in midair, stopping her momentum and holding her in place half on, half off the bed.

"No!" she cried.

He held on tighter. She heard noises, sounds that were clearly speech, but she could not make sense of his accent just then. She could not understand—

"Stop!" One word finally penetrated her panic. "Stop.

Please." He was speaking through clenched teeth. His breath continued to rasp as he fought the pain. And yet he would not release her. She dug her elbows into the mattress, scooting even further backward, but he would not let go. He held her foot in a mighty fist.

She whimpered, but he did not relent. She tried to twist and his grip tightened. There was no pain. He held her ankle most tightly where it would not hurt. And yet the feel of his fingers around her toes, curving around the tips near her coiled sole, made her gasp at the intimacy. No one touched her there. No man—

"Don't go," he gasped. "Promise. Don't leave."

"Let go."

"Promise."

"Let go!"

His fingers tightened again, and a single finger slipped past her heel to burrow against her sole. She froze. She did not think he meant it to be sexual. He was merely holding her any way he could. And yet she felt his penetration as deeply as before.

"I promise," she whispered. "Let go."

"Swear?" His voice was still labored, but she understood.

"Yes."

He released her. She escaped to the base of the bed. She curled her feet up against her bottom, her knees against her chest, but she was still naked. She reached beside his feet to the clumped sheets. The blanket was there, too, shoved to one side and trapped within the damp linen.

She freed it with a hasty grab. She tore it from the bed and wrapped it tightly about her. She didn't stop until she was buried beneath two full circles of blanket that covered her from chin to beneath her feet as she scooted back against the wall. Then she stilled. She licked her dry lips, closed her eyes, and steadied her breath to a slowly lengthening pant. And all the while, the captain watched her. His face was pale from pain, but his eyes were dark and terrifyingly intense. She hunched, drawing the blanket up around her ears. He watched her, his breath at last steadying as the pinched look of pain left his face.

"What did you do?" he rasped. "What did you do to me?"

"Me?" she cried. "You poisoned me!"

"Don't be ridiculous!"

"You sent me to Feng Du. You killed me and sent me to the underworld." She knew she wasn't making sense. He had no way to understand what she meant or even what Feng Du was. She shut her eyes tight. "You sent me to judgment," she whispered.

He didn't answer. Instead, she felt the mattress shift. Her eyes flew open to see him tug at the sheets. He wanted to cover himself but she was sitting on the linen. Even with one arm, he tugged hard enough that she tilted on the bed.

Cursing him under her breath, she straightened her legs enough to shift. In the end, she had to lift up on her knees for him to gain enough sheet to pull over his thighs, groin, and chest. Not enough to hide his bandaged shoulder or even his flat right nipple, but it was apparently enough for him because he soon quieted.

Then they stared at each other, dark accusation thickening the air.

What had the witch done to him? His body felt heavy and yet it still tingled. It was an all-over prickling, like he stood in the silent center of a storm. His hair was on end, his skin itchy, and his mouth was so damned dry he wanted to swallow an entire river. But he didn't move. He didn't dare take his eyes off the witch. She was sending him to Hell. He knew that. There was no other explanation for the events of the last moments. Black magic, demon lust—these were the stepping stones to the underworld. Soon he would see hellfire and brimstone.

How easily he had fallen. She had a perverse religion. He knew that, and yet he was still curious. Kui Yu had explained the basics to him. The practitioner used sexual stimulation to excite the spirit. Add the power of the mind, and soon the spirit launched to Heaven to commune with angels.

Interesting concept. His Christian faith told him that sex was the way to damnation, and anything involving such perversion could only lead to Hell. But he was a tolerant person. He would not condemn any man—or woman—for their religion. In truth, he was more than a little curious to see the beliefs that drove other cultures. Did they, could they, have an answer lacking in Christianity?

Thus, he had wished to see her examination. And his base lust had thrilled to have a naked woman sprawled across his belly. What harm would it do? he'd wondered even as the devil inside him made it as perverse as possible.

God, how long had it been since he'd pushed any part of himself into a wet and willing woman? She was tight and hot, sweet enough to seduce a priest. He had pushed his hand into her while his John Thomas had wept in hunger. And he'd lain still, his hand dripping with her honey while he heard her gasp and moan. He'd felt her back arch and her belly tense. But when she'd started convulsing around his fingers, the devil had made his own lust roar free, spewing his seed all over himself and her.

Then he was well and truly trapped. Lust had softened his will, and black magic had dragged him straight to Hell. While he was still writhing in animal desires, Little Pearl had worked her spell and he had found himself in another place, another time. Nothing of Earth surrounded him. All was mysterious and evil.

He'd seen it as a dark place, a house of many levels. Not Heaven, that was certain. Not Christian Heaven in any event. Instead, he had stood in a second-floor hallway looking down at a Chinese man and woman in heated argument. He had felt Little Pearl's terror beside him and the horrible emotions that poisoned the entire house. And yet it had felt right, as well. As if he belonged there, as if he had brought himself to that satanic place.

In short, he deserved punishment. His transgressions had taken him to Hell because that was where he belonged. And God, in His merciful forgiveness, had given Jonas this chance, had shown him the future as clearly as an open window. If Jonas continued on this path of sin, he would end up in that house of judgment. He would be damned forever, his soul trapped in fire and brimstone for eternity. All because of the witch Little Pearl.

He didn't stop to question his logic. Why did Hell look like a Chinese home? Where was Satan? How could it feel both horribly wrong and yet terribly right? As soon as the questions surfaced, he pushed them aside.

He shivered as icy fear slashed through his soul. Then he winced at the pain the motion released in his shoulder and ribs. Fear, pain, then nausea—he experienced them all—God's clear warnings to a soul descending to Hell. And yet . . .

It had felt wonderful. Part of that feeling still clung to his heart and mind. It had been wonderful despite the ugliness. He could not reconcile the two thoughts—the two overwhelmingly powerful impressions. So he turned on Little Pearl with all his anger and uncertainty, searching for meaning from her.

She huddled in the corner of the bed, as small a lump as she could possibly make herself. Buried under the blanket, hunched against the wall, she glared at him through the tiny pinpoints of black that were her eyes. He could barely see the yellow cast to her skin or the almond slant of her eyes, but he was deeply aware of her alienness.

"Poison," she hissed. "You are poison, ghost man."

He shook his head, feeling lethargy grip him. More magic? Or just the normal aftereffects of sex? "What did you do? What was that place?"

"Feng Du," she whispered. "The underworld." Horror underlay her words.

His head twisted on his pillow as he struggled through his befuddled thoughts. She was clearly as terrified as he. Could she simply be another lost soul on the path to destruction? Not an agent of evil, but another person seduced into Hell? Her horror seemed sincere, but he had been deceived before.

"I can't think," he muttered. "I don't understand."

Her gaze dropped to his crotch. He had not bothered to clean up—hadn't the strength—but they both knew he had exploded into the air like a randy schoolboy. "You will die now," she said, her voice heavy with doom. "I told you not to release your seed. You have weakened yourself too much. And now, ghost man, you will die." She abruptly straightened, and the blanket slipped enough that he could see the slender arch of her neck. "You will die, but you will not take me. I will resist you!"

He blinked, his thoughts fogging with her every word. "I am not dying," he said firmly, willing it to be so. "And I'm not going anywhere with you, witch." Her skin glowed in the candlelight. Damn, she was beautiful.

"I will leave you now. If you die, it is your own fault. You must not haunt me. I told you not to waste your yang. I told you. You cannot haunt me."

"I'm not dying!" he growled, his thoughts clearing enough for that.

"I have fulfilled my promise to you," she pressed. "I

promised to wait to talk to you. We have talked. I have fulfilled my promise."

"I am not dying!"

"Swear you will not haunt me, ghost man."

He felt his hands clench at his sides. He felt stronger. His body was tired, but there was no new injury. He wasn't about to die. And yet she was so certain, it made him doubt.

"Swear!" Her voice was high with panic.

"I'm not going to haunt you! I'm not dying!" He lifted up enough to glare at her, but it was too late. By the time he had gathered enough strength to shift on the bed, she had already scrambled away. "Little Pearl!"

No effect. He saw one last flash of blanket and pearly white skin. Then he listened in frustration as the rapid tattoo of her footsteps faded away.

"Little Pearl!" he bellowed, not really expecting a response. Who else was around? "Seth! Thompson! Anyone?"

No one answered. He let his head drop back in defeat, his eyes slipping closed. He had enough strength to stand. He could probably search for someone, if he was careful and went slow. But why? What would he say? *I'm afraid I'm going to die tonight? I'm too scared to close my eyes or sleep alone?* As if another body in the room would make the transition easier. As if a guard could defend him from death. He might as well face it like a man. The Grim Reaper would not find him cowering in the corner like a terrified dog.

"Seth?" He tried again. "Anyone?"

Silence. Even the crickets had stopped chirping.

"Bloody hell." He closed his eyes on the curse, resolved to face his future with stoic and rational calm. Then he realized what he'd just said. Bloody Hell.

"Mary, mother of God, Jesus Christ, savior of all . . ." He didn't know the right words but was making them up from fragments he could remember. "Save me from the folly of my own lusts and the stupidity of my mouth. Forgive me my sins. Shield me from temptation. . . ."

May 30, 1888

Father Albert—
   As a man, your choices are your own. I had no right to question them. I am so long gone from your side that I still think of you as that scrawny eight-year-old that used to spit in Mum's water and kick me in the head. If you are content in your lot, then so am I.

—Jonas

P.S. Do not look forward to my wedding, brother. I will take no bride.

Mung bean soup is a hon leung *soup that cools the body of heat inflammations. In China, women often stop drinking mung bean soup after they are in their forties, because the soup is reputed to have such a strong cooling energy that it may cause them to faint.*

Chapter Eight

Number One Slave crawled forward and pressed his forehead to the floor, remaining there until Master Su saw fit to acknowledge him. This was not their usual morning meeting, but the situation had changed enough that Number One risked interrupting an evening's practice.

Number Eight Slave grunted and released his seed. He crouched behind Master Su, who had his eyes closed in the ecstasy of absorption. The padded ceremonial bench had shifted somewhat beneath the master's arms. Number Eight was always more vigorous than prudent, but Master Su seemed to value that. Exuberance indicated extra potency.

Number Eight Slave withdrew his organ and staggered backward. He grabbed a silk cloth from a basket beside the bench and gently wiped Master Su's backside clean. Then he bowed out, forgetting to crawl backward on his knees. He would be whipped for that. The young needed to be reminded of their place.

Meanwhile, Master Su sighed and signaled his attention. Number One lifted up enough to tap his forehead on the floor one more time before he straightened his arms. He kept his head lowered, observing his master in only the topmost part of his peripheral vision. He had no wish to disrespect the sanctity of the yang chamber.

"You may speak."

There was no time to compose poetry. Besides, mornings demanded eloquence; interruptions in the yang chamber demanded brevity. "Customs Official Chen Wan Li has confiscated the entire cargo and refuses to see reason."

"Has Captain Jonas discovered his cargo's location?"

"First Mate Seth learned of it tonight."

Master Su lowered himself into the first meditation pose—legs tucked beneath his rear, calves rolled outward, and the largest toes barely touching. He bowed his head as he spoke. "Customs Official Chen Wan Li will consume a bottle of the whiskey," Master Su finally pronounced. "Unfortunately, it will be poisoned. White cargo so often curses the unwary."

"Yes, Master," Number One agreed.

"All Shanghai should know of the tragedy by morning," Master Su ordered. "And poor Captain Jonas will be reunited with his cargo only to discover that none wish to buy it."

"Most wise," Number One intoned as he began crawling backward out the door. Master Su rarely tolerated useless flattery, but his spirit was generally softer in this chamber. It never hurt to slip in a little praise, especially when it was heartfelt.

Meanwhile, he had a poisoning to plan and a cargo to blame before sunrise—a potentially difficult puzzle given how well Customs Official Chen protected his storehouse. Still, it would be done. And if nothing else, it kept Number One's own yang out of his master's chamber.

He waited until the door closed completely in front of

him before straightening to his full height. With a quick tilt of his head, he sent Slave Number Seven into the chamber. The man went slowly, his old bones creaking as he moved, but his yang was wizened and therefore highly prized.

Then Number One grabbed his coat and headed outside to arrange for the poisoning. He was so focused he nearly forgot to order the whipping of Number Eight. Fortunately, the purveyor of poisons also sold the best whips. He could drive a harder bargain for the poison if he also purchased a new studded lash.

Heaven truly smiled on his endeavors when two goals could be met at once.

Little Pearl's back ached. Hunched over the oxtail soup, her spine cramped with every stir. Oddly enough, her feet felt better. She had not brought the bindings with her when she fled Captain Jonas's room. She had slept totally naked in the other practice building, her toes exposed to the chill night air.

This morning, she'd woken with feet that didn't itch or smell. She even used her fingers to spread her toes and move them around in unaccustomed freedom. But when it came time to dress, she'd discovered her ankles had swollen. The bindings would not tighten well, which meant her dainty shoes pinched no matter how loosely she tied the ribbons. Thank heaven she did not need to go to market this morning. She doubted she could stand it.

Balance. All of life was a balance. Happy feet, angry back. Swollen ankles, no market trip. She sighed in relief as she straightened up from over the soup pot. Good food, white guest.

She scanned the kitchen, sniffing the air. The mung bean soup was perfect, a gentle rolling boil thickening the air with the earthy scent of bok choy and fish stock.

Sweet rice steamed nearby, tended by her only help today—a girl no more than eight years old. There was no meat in the wads of rice, so the only fear was from scorching. Even an eight-year-old could watch for that. Otherwise, the place was clean, the fires well stoked. Nothing demanded her attention.

Which meant she could delay no longer. She had to go discover Captain Jonas's corpse. She would send someone else, but no Chinese would venture near the man's room. She could make one of his sailors go. She could give First Mate Seth a tray for his captain and allow the whites to deal with death according to their own customs.

But she was loath to push off her burden on the young sailors. They would be lost without their captain's direction and she had no wish to traumatize them further. She had no explanation for her strange maternal thoughts for the white men. None except that they praised her cooking, teased smiles out of her young kitchen servant, and kept the bill collectors away. Which meant that the discovery of the body was left to her. She sighed again as she stripped off her kitchen apron.

"Watch the soup, too," she ordered the girl. "I will go . . . I am going to . . ." She swallowed, startled to realize her eyes were watering. "I will be back."

Then she left, her steps heavy as she walked to the main practice building. It ate at her that she had left a man to die alone. White captain or not, no one deserved that. But she had been so frightened. He might haunt her. And no Chinese would do such a thing for a white man.

A thousand excuses crowded into her thoughts, but they were merely noise. It had been a cold, thoughtless thing for her to do, and she was ashamed. Worse, she kept remembering moments—flashes of memory—of other times the captain had visited. He ate with passion and laughed often. Even when he was angry, he never

raised his hand in violence. His yang flowed strong and
his eyes crinkled when he smiled. All these things
weighed upon her, clogging her qi and darkening her
heart. Worse, her shame was hers alone. She could not
even blame this on her ancestors. She had acted of her
own free will and so had left a good man to suffer.

"Forgive me," she whispered to his ghost. "I am a silly
woman with too much fear."

She climbed the stairs slowly. The steps were slick
from morning dew, so she had to move carefully. Bound
feet required careful balance on the heels and she had to
dig her hand into the wall to find security. She was nearly
at the top when she looked up. There was no surprise in
what she saw, simply a dark sense of the inevitable.

Of course Captain Jonas was dead. Of course his ghost
would haunt her. Of course he would appear before her
at the moment when she was perched most precariously
on the slick steps. His eyes were dark hollows, his skin
was equally haggard, and he made sounds that indicated
his soul's torment. She stared at him, her own breath
caught in horror. Then she simply let go.

She released her handhold. Without that brace pulling
her forward, her weight carried her backward. She felt her
heels lose purchase as her bottom began to sink. Above
her, the ghost released a cry of agony and reached for her.
She responded instinctively. The sound was so compelling
that she stretched for him, but she was too far away.

Her tailbone connected with stone. She grunted as her
spine jarred all the way through her teeth. Then she fell
farther, bouncing down the last few steps until there was
nowhere for her to go. She slid on the stone, rolling backward as her lower back then shoulders collided with the
heavy path. Her head would hit next, she knew. She
would die then, perhaps. But she didn't hit stone as she
expected. Instead, she felt the thud of soft dirt and cush-

ioning hair. Pins dug painfully into her scalp, but not so hard that it pierced her skull.

Still alive then, she realized. She opened her eyes. Still haunted. Captain Jonas's ghost stumbled down the steps after her. His breath rasped through his clenched teeth. Normally, she would find his grimace frightening. On a live person, such an expression would terrify, but a ghost was supposed to be horrible. It seemed right and proper that his features were twisted into an expression of terror.

He reached her side and dropped to his knees, hovering just above her. She stared at him mutely, wondering what the ghost would do now. In truth, her heart beat painfully fast in her chest, and her body seemed chilled to ice. She knew she was terrified, but her mind had distanced herself into a casual observation. She couldn't stop what came. Resistence accomplished nothing. She would wait and let the ghost torment her. She closed her eyes, opened her tightened chest with a shallow breath, and felt even her legs relax open. The inevitable was upon her. As always happened when pain was near, her mind wandered off in another direction. Dinner. What would she eat if she had all the money in the world?

She felt hands on her shoulders and heard gasping sounds. Pork dumplings had always been her favorite, but the meat had to be seasoned just right.

Words filtered distantly through her consciousness. Strange ghost sounds in the white people's language. She would eat fresh mangoes, too. With clotted cream. Master Tan had developed quite a taste for English clotted cream.

Hands ran quickly down her body, touching lightly across face and breasts, hips and legs. The ugly would come now. The painful rutting, the horrible grunting breath. She once tasted an English fruit called a pear.

Quite delicate in flavor. A perfect complement to spicy hot shrimp.

Somewhere in her thoughts, her spirit paused. She was not in that other place. She was not about to be spread like a rag doll and raped over and over and over. And yet that was what came with pain. The ache from the beatings, the grasping hands, the rutting. But . . .

"Little Pearl! For God's sake, Little Pearl, wake up!"

The words came in a strange mixture of English and Shanghai dialect, and for a moment she was completely disoriented. The scent of the room was not stale with sweat and sex. She felt a breeze on her face and tasted sweet soy on the air. And she was fully dressed. Where was she?

She remembered before she opened her eyes. She was in the Tans' garden after falling off the stairs. She was being haunted by . . . Her eyes flew open. Captain Jonas's face was huge, directly above her own. His skin was gray and tight, but his hands were warm where they gripped her arms. He was real, she abruptly realized. He touched her like real flesh, like a living person. She swallowed and finally found her voice. "You are alive?"

"Are you?" he answered.

She frowned. "Yes. You?"

"Yes."

"Huh." She had no other thought beyond that simple expulsion of sound. Meanwhile, the captain straightened slightly, his hands gentling but not leaving her body.

"Where do you hurt?"

Not between her thighs. She didn't say that out loud, but surprise echoed through her system.

"Little Pearl? Don't pass out. You have to tell me what's wrong."

Her eyes snapped open again. "Pass out? Pass what? I don't understand."

He shook his head. "Never mind my Chinese. Where do you hurt?"

Sensations were finally penetrating her thoughts, dragging her back to full awareness. Her bottom, her shoulder, the back of her head—all held a throbbing agony. But it was a bearable pain, the ache of a beating, not the brutal rip and tear of the other. She sighed and forced herself to move. "I am fine, Captain Jonas."

"Be careful. Tell me if there is pain."

She slanted a glance at him. Did he understand that all life was pain? Especially for a woman? Apparently not, because he was excruciatingly tender as he helped her stand. She watched him closely, noting when his lips pressed tight. She could hear his breath as it flowed uneasily through his lips—shallow now, deeper next, hitching at odd moments.

"You are in pain," she said.

"Then we are a pair because you are not standing straight."

She knew she was hunched, but her entire backside ached. If she hadn't been gripping his arm, she wouldn't even have gotten this far—nearly vertical except for her shoulders and head.

"Where can we sit down?" he asked.

"Why are you out of bed?" She wanted to ask him why he wasn't dead, but knew that wasn't polite. Instead, she steered him toward the kitchen. The eight-year-old had been too long alone.

They walked slowly, hunched into each other like two old scholars arguing politics. The air was growing warmer as they moved, the spices tingling on her tongue as she finally straightened to her full height.

"You must be hungry," she said.

"For your food? Always!" He flashed her a grin, disconcertingly white amid the rough reddish texture of his face. He had not shaved since the mob attack. She would have to remember to send someone to . . . No Chinese would shave him. She would have to do it herself. She smiled, surprised that she looked forward to it.

They made it into the steaming room. She showed him to a work table made of large scarred wood. It was where the whores ate between classes, the servants choosing to sit outside beneath a rough canopy rather than associate with the women of the house. She pulled out a stool for him, but he shook his head.

"For you, my lady." She did not understand his suddenly formal tone, so he shrugged and pointed. "You should sit. I hurt less when I stand."

His ribs. Of course. "I will get food."

She moved quickly, the ache from her fall fading as she set about her tasks. She stirred the soup, turned the sweet rice, then inspected the delivery of vegetables. She instructed the girl in the cooking of congee, but the child was incompetent, of course. Little Pearl mixed the captain's breakfast.

Boiled rice with spices, a little meat for his strength, and vegetables for his water. A fine china bowl for his status as a guest, a spoon because he was white, and chopsticks because she knew he could manage them. All these she prepared while he watched with steady eyes and a slight smile on his face. Finally she served him, bowing as she set it before him. He didn't move in the slightest.

She froze, inspecting food and utensils with a quick glance. Then she looked at the captain. Was he not hungry?

"I am waiting for you," he said gently.

Of course. Many masters preferred to eat alone. She bowed again, though the pull in her hips made her eyes water. She began to back away, but he grabbed her sleeve.

"I am waiting for you to bring your food and join me."

A woman eat with a man not her husband? A Chinese woman with a white man? The thought was bizarre. She could not think of a time she had ever eaten with a man. Certainly the male servants came through the kitchen. They often stole fried dumplings or rice cakes, then loitered to gossip while they ate. She had also served men before, watching while they ate, even kept silent at food perversions that made her throat constrict with disgust. But her own meals had always been a rushed bite as she worked, a sweet rice ball while she watched an assistant chop or a cold dumpling between clients.

"Please," Jonas said as he pulled out the stool she'd set for him. "Eat with me." Then he glanced at the girl who watched them with openmouthed shock. "Can you bring food for your mistress, please?"

Little Pearl woke from her stupor. "No, no. I cannot—"

"Of course you can." He grabbed her arm and half guided, half pushed her onto the stool. His grip was strong, but not bruising. She stared at his hand on her sleeve, noting its width and the thick fingers. His nails were blunt, the skin rough. He even had a reddish black smattering of hair on the first joint of his fingers. She ought to be repulsed. Here was a white man forcing himself on her, insisting that she forgo Chinese custom in favor of his bizarre barbarian ideals.

She ought to be furious, except that she wasn't. His manner was exceedingly gracious. He looked different, he acted different, and she found herself forgiving his ignorance and appreciating his generosity of spirit. She could be equally generous, she decided. She could enjoy his foreign request, relax on the stool, and allow herself to eat with this strange man. She turned her head to nod at the young girl.

She needn't have bothered. The child had a surprising well of courage or a desperate need for food scraps.

Rather than run screaming from Captain Jonas's smile, she simply nodded and did as the man asked. She filled a porcelain bowl with congee, added vegetable, meat, and sauce, then brought it carefully forward to the table. She even set the table identically to the captain's, which meant Little Pearl had the best bowl and utensils in the house. If the other servants saw that, they would snicker at how she'd raised herself above her place.

But no one else was here. No one would snicker at her. No one would whisper snide remarks into Mistress Tan's ear. No one was here to distract her from the odd situation of eating breakfast with a white man.

Feeling bizarrely out of place in her own kitchen, Little Pearl stared at her bowl and kept her hands folded tightly before her. She would not touch her food before he did. Meanwhile, he grabbed a stool and gingerly settled onto it. Then he reached forward but abruptly froze, slowly drawing back. He looked at her expectantly. She looked back, confused. What did this man want? Why would he not eat?

His brow lowered and he glanced at first her food then his own. Flat on the table, his fingers twitched slightly, but he did not move. Little Pearl waited in silence. It was not for her to ask about his bizarre food customs, but he appeared to be waiting for something.

"Is something wrong with the food?" she asked.

"Hmm? No, no. Is yours prepared well?"

"Of course." She had made it, after all.

He stared at her, his hands still slack on the table. Her stomach suddenly growled, and she pressed her hand to her mouth in horror. He looked at her and laughed, the sound as full as the ocean. She thought at first he was making fun of her, pointing out the crass action, but a moment later, she realized he was genuinely happy.

"Shows that you're ready to eat." He leaned forward.

"Did you know that some people belch after a meal to show their appreciation of the food?"

"Belch?" she echoed. She did not know this English word.

He nodded. "You know. Belch. With your mouth." She still did not understand, so he leaned forward. "You will not think me crude?"

She wasn't sure what he meant to do, but she shook her head anyway. He was a white man. All of them were crass. But his eyes were alight with merriment, and she found his actions delightful in a forbidden kind of way.

"Very well," he said. "This is a belch." He leaned away from her, lifting his head slightly and squaring his shoulders. She glanced up, following his gaze, only to be startled by his deep and full-bodied belch. She gasped in shock, but then immediately began giggling, both hands pressed to her mouth this time as her shoulders shook.

"I knew it," he said. "Now you think me the coarsest kind of lout."

Another English word she did not know. But she understood his meaning, and so she shook her head barely daring to let her hands slip away from her smile. "'All must be sacrificed to learning,'" she quoted. Then when he did not understand, she explained. "My father believed that education was the greatest pursuit of a gentleman. All was sacrificed to that goal."

"Even polite manners?"

Her smile faded as she remembered all that had been sacrificed in the name of her father's education. Good manners were the least of it. She grew sober in memory until, a moment later, she felt his hand on hers.

"My deepest apologies, madam. I am a boorish ship captain and not versed in the niceties of polite society." His Chinese was awkward, the words badly phrased, but she understood and felt her cheeks heat at her stupidity.

"Your manners are excellent, Captain, especially for a

lowly cook. I only wish I could belch as you do. It would show that I can learn new ways, too."

He grinned, the expression lighting his entire face. "You are everything that is perfect." Then his gaze slipped back to her untouched bowl. "Is the food too hot?"

She shook her head. "Congee is best hot."

He nodded. And waited. Her stomach even growled again. Finally he turned to her.

"If I may ask, why do you not eat?"

She blinked. Did he understand nothing? "I would never eat before you. It would be . . ." She almost said crass, but that was not the right word. Finally she dipped her head, excruciatingly aware of her status as servant and cook. "It would be disrespectful."

He was silent as she sat, head bowed before him. But as the quiet stretched on, she grew restless and finally lifted her head. When she did, she was startled by his grin. She stiffened. Was he laughing at her? Then he spoke.

"It is considered rude for a white man to eat before the woman."

She blinked. "It is considered rude for a Chinese woman to eat before a man."

"Then perhaps we should make a bargain before we starve to death. Shall we eat at the same moment?" He fitted word to action, picking up his spoon and holding it above his bowl.

She responded in kind, raising her chopsticks. In one motion, they both dipped their utensils into the porridge, lifted up the food and put it in their mouths. Both chewed and swallowed. Both watched the other, their gazes locked as if they shared some great secret.

They didn't, of course, and yet Little Pearl experienced a moment of perfect harmony such as had not happened since the beginning days of her tigress practice. It was a brief few seconds when nothing else existed except what occurred right there and then. All other fears and thoughts were silenced. Everything settled into quiet stillness such that what happened right then occurred in absolute clarity. That it happened here in the kitchen and not the bedroom made no sense. That her partner was a white man using a spoon in his congee made even less sense. And yet in that heavenly moment, everything was exactly as it should be.

The moment stretched on through a second bite. And then she—the tigress Little Pearl—broke the connection. It shamed her that she could not sustain perfection, that a white man could remain in the moment longer than she, but it was the truth. The flow of qi between their locked gazes rapidly became too strong, the heat too much for her to manage. She dropped her eyes and even turned her shoulder so that his energy was blocked from her.

He didn't seem to notice. He continued to eat and smile in a contented way. He maintained a steady flow of food from bowl to mouth, but she did not. She paused too long at the bowl or rushed the chew and swallowed too fast, deliberately changing her rhythms from his. But chopsticks and congee required precise timing. In the end, she was the one who suffered, with drips of food on her lap and arm.

"How long have you been a chef?" The voice was mellow, like oyster sauce mixed with green onion—it tasted almost ordinary, but the longer it lingered on her tongue, the more she wanted it to stay. She added it to all kinds of meats and vegetables, splashed it into soups, and loved it in her morning congee. Jonas had that kind of voice and that kind of presence. Most disconcerting in a white man, but most perfect in a companion.

"Did I ask a bad question?"

She blinked. "Oh! I am sorry. I have been chef here for

years, but I have been watching cooks for far longer."

"Watching cooks?"

She glanced at his face, feeling her own flush. What was the matter with her? She had not blushed this much since . . . ever. "As a child, I was not supposed to be in the kitchen."

He propped his elbow on the table and set his chin in his palm. "But you went anyway."

"I loved it there. And my mother loved it that I was quiet when I ate. But it still wasn't an appropriate place for a lady."

He was silent, watching her. Too late, she realized what she had said: not an appropriate place for a lady. Was he smart enough to understand? Would he realize her family background was better than that of a common peasant? She stood up from her seat, feeling her chin lift in defiance. Let him know. Let them all know her ancestors' shame. She thought the words, but she still tried to distract him with trivialities. "You are tired. You should rest."

He shook his head. "I have no wish to return to that room." Then he looked around, his gaze seeming to touch everything in her kitchen. "May I stay here for a while? I'll be quiet as a mouse."

She frowned, confused by his odd phrasing. "Mice aren't welcome in my kitchen."

"A statue, then. I'll be quiet as a statue."

She stepped backward, more fully into the cooking area of the kitchen. "You will frighten the servants. They will think you a ghost."

"They are not frightened. Right?" His gaze caught the little girls who had been watching everything they did. Overwhelmed by the captain's qi, the girl did exactly as he wished. She shook her head slowly.

"No, Master," she intoned. Then she abruptly smiled. "I like you here. You make her nicer."

Little Pearl spun around, sharply rebuking the impertinent child. Few understood the need for discipline in all things. People—girls especially—needed to know their place. The world had no forgiveness for those who stepped out of line.

The girl responded appropriately, immediately returning to her task, hunching away in fear of a slap. But behind them, Captain Jonas was not so anxious. His laughter filled the room with genuine amusement.

Little Pearl slowed. Discipline was vital. As a ship's captain, surely he understood that. And yet, such warmth made her uncertain. How could he be amused when she had just been humiliated? Had not the girl just called her a shrew?

"I like that I have an effect on you, Little Pearl," he said behind her. His voice was low, pitched for her ears only. "Let me stay. Let me watch you."

She turned back to him, her mind at war with her spirit. She did not want him here in the place where she ruled. And yet, her spirit responded to his smile, her heart forgave him for undermining her discipline. How could anyone work around such an influence? It would be much too disruptive. And so she meant to tell him. Except, when she opened her mouth, different words came out. "I will make you tea."

He bowed his head in thanks, and the tension in her belly increased tenfold. She should not let him stay. She could not work with him here. She . . . She went about making tea as if there were no problem at all. Then she worked on the vegetables and the soup. She cooked and cleaned and instructed the girl in the chopping of loda cabbage. In short, she went about her day with the prickling awareness of Captain Jonas watching everything she did.

True to his word, the captain said nothing. But he was a man who filled a space with his presence, infusing everything with his qi. It upset her, this alien thing in her kitchen. And yet, she refreshed his tea when it emptied and even shared a cup when he insisted. He asked questions then, while they drank together, casual queries about fish and mushrooms. He wondered why noodles and not rice, why the red sauce and not the black. She answered as simply as possible, warming slowly to her topic as he continued to probe.

And over the course of hours, she became accustomed to his presence. Until the moment she turned around to see that his shoulders drooped and his eyes were hollow in his face. "You must go rest at once!" she cried, startled by the obvious weakness in his body.

He flashed her a self-conscious smile. "I am fine."

He was lying, and they both knew it. "Come," she ordered. "I will help you back to bed."

"And will you . . ." His voice trailed off as he glanced at the doorway. The girl was outside, tending the courtyard fire, so they were alone. Nevertheless, he lowered his voice, clearly nervous that someone might overhear. "Will you stay with me for a bit?"

"Are you afraid?" The thought was strange. He had not seemed like a man to fear solitude.

He shrugged. "I appreciate your company."

"Your men are outside. Perhaps I should send one of them. . . ."

He grabbed her hand, drawing her close. "You," he whispered. "I want you."

She almost nodded. Indeed, in her mind, she was already rearranging her cooking schedule so that she could sit with him. But then her mind scrambled to the truth. "You wish to have sex," she accused. She spoke crudely, not even dignifying the act with tigress words.

He stared at her a moment, then reared back. "No. Absolutely not." Then he sighed. "God knows I'm willing, but I don't think I'm up to it."

One glance down his body confirmed his words. At least for the moment, there was no sign of his dragon's strength. "Then why?" she pressed.

He shook his head. "I don't know." That was all. He didn't know. And strangely, she believed him. Worse, she understood. Their energies intertwined strangely. He both soothed her spirit and agitated her so that she wanted to attack something—anything. It made no sense, but that did not change the reality.

Without even realizing she'd agreed, they began walking to his bedroom. He dropped an arm around her shoulders while she wrapped a supporting arm about his waist. They moved across the garden and mounted the stairs with silent care. She helped him remove his clothing, then changed the bindings about his shoulder and ribs. There were myriad more details of sickroom care that they accomplished efficiently, as if they had established this rhythm after years of companionship.

"Join me," he urged from the bed, opening his arm so she could curl into his side. "You're tired, too. There's plenty of room."

"No." Things had changed between them this day. She could not specifically identify how, but she knew she would not sleep in this place—his place. And yet she was loath to leave. "I can strengthen your yang center, if you like."

He frowned, not understanding.

"It is what I did before against your dragon."

"The humming?"

She nodded.

"But I don't want . . . I'm not interested in . . . I mean—"

"This is not sex. It is healing with sound."

He struggled with the idea. "It's not necessary."

She bowed. "Then I will return to my kitchen."

"No!" He visibly swallowed. "Stay. It's fine. I . . . If you think it will help . . . I just don't understand."

She smiled, strangely pleased with his capitulation. "Healing does not require understanding." She adjusted the blankets such that he would stay warm even though his dragon was exposed. Then she paused a moment to slant him a stern look. "No yang expulsion. Your seed must stay inside you."

"Don't worry," he said, his voice settling into a gravelly rumble. "After last night, I doubt I have any left."

She looked down at his slowly thickening dragon. "You have a great deal," she grudgingly admitted.

Captain Jonas had no response. He remained silent as she set about her task. Excellent, she thought with a tiny smile. That meant now was the perfect time to experiment.

Jan. 5, 1890

Dear Jonas—

If you look at the date, you will see that you have just left on your newest voyage to China. I have just returned from the docks where I watched you weave your way on board clutching your head and your belly.

Brother, I fear for your very life. I know not what led you down this path of excess. In your drunkenness, you spoke often of Annie's refusal to wed the son of a whore. But it seems to me that debauchery is a way of life for a sailor on leave. You also spoke of a drugging smoke from China, of child whores and all manner of drink.

What happened to the boy who swore to never allow rum to touch his lips? Do you not recall the manner of our mother's death? Do you truthfully wish to walk down that path to damnation and ruin?

You have asked me why the priesthood. Today, Jonas, because of my great love for you, I will tell you how I made the choice. Do you recall our celebration of my six- teenth birthday? You introduced me to women and wine. Yes, I had drunk before, yes, I had seen women and tasted a few beautiful mouths, but never had I experienced a night such as you gave me. I remember your arm around me as a brother. I remember singing songs and leering at women. I felt glorious in my place at your side, I grinned to be your brother again, and I worked hard to drink as much as you, to whore as much as you, to do all that a man did.

And when you were gone, it was all stripped away. You were once again at sea, and I was once again nursemaid and protector to Mum. Did you understand my refusal to join you at sea? Did you know that without me, she would have died within a month? Did you know that she nearly did because I took the money you left and bought women instead of food, drink instead of coal? I longed for a return of that time, the joy of a day and a half celebrating that I can barely recall.

So I drank and I whored. More and more, Mother was left alone when her men came to call. I was more likely to drink her coin than squirrel it away for food. Then she died because I was in the Blind Pig. She was beaten and raped while I was whoring. I do not know if she woke and called for me. I do not know if she simply was too drunk to seek help for herself while I slipped into a drunken stupor. I know that by morning, her body was cold and covered in her own filth—blood, bile, and tears. The tears haunt me the most.

Do you not sicken of yourself in the morning, Jonas? Do you not clutch your head and think "never again"? What tempts you to return to the drink? What lures you into the fleshpots? I tell you, my dearest brother, if your arm leads you to sin, better to cut it off than let it take you to Satan. Better to be a one-armed man in Heaven than have two arms burning in Hell. The same, too, my brother, for your cock. Do not let women or the pleasures of the flesh destroy you.

I implore you. How much easier to find a good woman if you are not passed out drunk or ugly with disease? Annie is gone, but there are others. Please, let us talk more on this.

—Your loving brother, Albert

Raw chicken is chopped straight through the bone with a sharp meat cleaver into bite-sized pieces and then marinated. The breast is not difficult to chop, since the bone is quite soft. The drumstick, however, with its thick bones, requires perfect technique to chop into three bite-sized pieces. Cooking chicken on the bone makes it more juicy and succulent. In addition, it is the Chinese custom not to eat big pieces of meat.

Chapter Nine

Was there ever a more bizarre situation? wondered Jonas as Little Pearl lowered her cheek to his longjohn. She nuzzled it for a moment, and Jonas found his eyelids drooping in pleasure. The sensation—warm velvet, silken softness and sweet woman all rolled into one. And all this in the name of healing. He didn't really under- stand, but when her cheek rolled all the way up from base to tip, he didn't truly care. And that, of course, was the problem.

The situation was simple. He needed to get access to Kui Yu's office. The guard to that hallowed room, of course, was Little Pearl. So he had to remain around her, let her get to know him. Eventually, she would come to trust him. Eventually, they might even become friends. And if they repeated—

No. He cut off his thoughts. No part of his brain, rational or otherwise, wanted to think about last night. Instead, he had to focus on now. On getting her to trust him. On . . .

She was lengthening her chin, rolling her soft skin

over his, shimmying a bit such that he felt her caress on every part of his organ. She lay half off the bed, half on it. Now she was stretching herself across him so that her neck lay over his very hot, very insistent sex.

He knew he should stop her. Healing or not, this was becoming too pleasurable for him to resist. And with such hunger came desperation and total loss of focus. Other thoughts crept in as well. Emotions he had no desire to name. He could not let her continue. He reached down with his good arm, grabbing hold of her shoulder.

"Little Pearl," he said. She hummed. Pressed against her neck, he felt the vibrations as if they echoed through his entire body. Pleasure didn't even begin to describe the experience. Sex was too crude a term. This was seduction, pure and simple, and he was falling fast.

"Stop," he murmured. Then he found more strength. "Little Pearl, stop!" It was an order she ignored. She would not release her prey so easily. Time was running out. In moments he would do anything for her. His blood was coursing hot and hard through his body, his sex stretched with desire. He was too tired for this, and yet nothing was more important than that she continue. That she . . .

"Stop!" he bellowed. He gripped her shoulder and pulled. When she resisted, he put all his strength, all his will, into the action. It was pathetically weak, but she was a small woman and so he pulled her away. And she looked at him with eyes so beautifully wide, a face so fragile in her shock, that he almost relented. What was the harm?

But that way lay madness. He hardened his heart to her beauty. He labeled her actions manipulation and trickery. He remembered the bizarre experience of last night and the way she'd run from him in terror. He felt his resolve waver. Her fear had been real. Was she an innocent? Or a clever whore?

His grip relaxed on her arm, but he kept his voice strong. "You cannot control me through sex."

"This is not sex," she answered immediately, just as he knew she would. "It is—"

"Healing. Yes, so you say. The point is, every time I turn around, you are touching me, using your beauty against me. You are trying to seduce me," he accused.

She pulled away. "How can you think such a thing? I am a simple cook. I try to heal you—"

"You have healed me. You saved me from the mob and set my wounds. That is healing."

"Your yang center has been damaged. I can strengthen it." She made to move back to his groin, but he tightened his hold.

"No."

"You wish to die?"

Her certainty was chilling. Could it be true? No doctor healed in this manners. "I wish you to understand that I won't be controlled by my cock." He used the crude term on purpose. It reinforced the ugliness of what she was trying to do.

"I am trying to help," she repeated.

The way she said it, he could almost believe it. But he had seen his mother act the innocent as well, while she took hundreds of pounds from her victims. He knew better than to trust the honesty of a whore. And yet, try as he might, he could not make his accusations ring true. Something was different here—something he could not discover while lying in blissful stupidity.

"I will not be controlled that way, Little Pearl. You have to understand that."

She bowed her head and shuffled backward, the picture of a wounded girl unjustly accused. He caught her hand before she moved too far. "What do you want from me?" he asked. "You have my men as guards. I am no threat to you. Why do you spend so much time—"

"I am trying to heal you!" She practically spat the words, and part of him finally believed. She did think she was healing him. But there was another motive. There had to be.

"What do you want, Little Pearl? Just tell me. Maybe I can help without all the games. Without . . ." His voice faded as she ran away. Even with bound feet, she moved incredibly fast. She was out the door, and he was not strong enough to follow.

He would have to wait until she came to him. Unfortunately, he doubted he had much time before things became even more complicated.

He woke some hours later. The sunlight told him it was late afternoon, nearly dusk. His body told him that he was healing, but not fast enough.

He took a moment to simply breathe, to be glad he was still alive. To listen closely: no one was about. And to plan his next move . . . His mind was blank. Seth had reported this morning that he had found both Customs Official Chen and their cargo. Jonas should be out there applying pressure, talking to officials, doing some damn thing to stave off disaster. Instead, he groaned like an old man and rolled off the bed to find the chamber pot.

Once his immediate needs were taken care of, he washed his face and sniffed the air. Baked dumplings. Where? Outside his room on a tray on the floor. Little Pearl had run in fear from him, but she always remembered the food. He grimaced. She could not control him through lust, but his stomach was another matter entirely.

He leaned down to pick up the tray, then immediately froze, his ribs screaming. How exactly was he to get his dinner if he couldn't bend? He settled gingerly onto his knees, then lowered himself to the floor. Damned if he knew how he was going to get back up, but at least the food was now within reach.

Then he heard them: two voices, both Chinese. One was a man, his voice clipped and angry. The other was Little Pearl using a wheedling, begging tone that he had never heard. They were coming up the stairs.

"What does this mean, that you have bought my debt?" whined Little Pearl. "I have no debts—"

"I own this place now, Little Cook. The Tan house and everything in it."

"That cannot be true. The Tans are coming home—"

"The Tans are dead."

"You lie! They are not—" Her words were silenced by a loud slap. The sound was vicious; it echoed down the hallway, and Jonas struggled to his feet. The pain that lanced through his ribs was nothing compared to his fury.

"I am master now," the man hissed. "Be grateful to me, whore. Serve me well or I will throw you out on the street."

Jonas heard a sob from Little Pearl. He reacted without thought, grabbing simultaneously for the door and the water bowl. He might be weak, but he could certainly fight one abusive Chinaman. Especially if he had something large to throw and the element of surprise.

But the water bowl was heavier than he expected, and he had rushed his movement. His shoulder could not manage the weight, nor could his ribs recover when jerked upright. The pain was crippling, dropping him to his hands and knees, which further jarred his shoulder. He gasped, his eyes watering so that he couldn't even see. But he could still hear as the man and Little Pearl continued down the hallway.

"Do you want me to throw you out? To toss you to the ghost monkeys? You would like that, wouldn't you, whore?"

"You cannot—"

"Trust a woman to pollute a home with animals."

They were nearly at his door and Jonas hadn't even found his feet yet. Meanwhile, Little Pearl's voice rose even louder. "You cannot kill him! Swords have no place here!" She was trying to warn Jonas, making her words very loud, very clear. "Stop, Mr. Su!"

Another slap, louder this time because they were so close. Jonas tried to rise up like a man, but he could barely manage to breathe, much less fight. He was completely useless, and so damn vulnerable. . . .

He bit his lip, drawing blood. How many times had he been vulnerable—a small boy against a large adult foe? Hadn't he always overcome?

"Maybe I should order you to rut with the ape. Maybe your new master would watch you while—"

"No, Master Su!"

The door slammed open. Jonas didn't move from where he lay, slack-jawed and bloody in a pool of spilled water. Little Pearl gasped and cried out. "Jonas!"

He didn't move, though the urge was strong. He lay still, his good arm braced beneath him in such a way that he could push off with it, launching himself upward. It would probably pull hard at his ribs, but this was the only defensive opportunity he had. Offensively, he had a few other tricks up his sleeve—mostly a prayer that his men were a half breath away, about to storm to the rescue. He had to stall and hope. So while Little Pearl dropped to her knees beside him, Jonas began the rattling breath so common in the nearly dead.

"Oh no," she sobbed, abruptly backing away. "No."

Jonas slitted his eyes and moaned. Little Pearl looked pale, the only color in her face the bright red mark of a man's hand. His moan became more menacing.

Little Pearl was shoved aside as the villain stepped forward. Mr. Su, she had called him, and he looked . . . urbane. Austere face, dark clothing, thin build. He carried a slim Chinese dagger in one long-fingered hand. His other hand dragged Little Pearl away.

"Leave him alone!" she sobbed. "Let him die!"

Mr. Su ignored her. Stepping closer, he studied Jonas, his gaze thorough as he inspected every inch of both patient and room. He even sniffed the air and touched the fetid pool of water.

"I believe he wanted to eat and fell." Mr. Su's voice was softer as he puzzled out the situation. "Was he this sick before?"

Damn, damn! The man was smart. That increased the danger tenfold. Meanwhile, Little Pearl looked morose. "I thought he would die last night. The bill collectors were vicious. Terrible."

"Then you should be grateful that I am now master here."

Little Pearl's expression twisted into one of resentment and a sly fury. She was behind Mr. Su, so the only one who saw was Jonas. He had to speed things up. He needed to bring this to a head before she slipped and exposed herself as a possible threat to the man. He did not want her hurt.

Jonas tightened his throat muscles so that his breath rasped loudly then abruptly stopped. Little Pearl gasped and began scurrying backward out of the room, exactly as he'd wanted, but Mr. Su stopped her, using his long fingers to grab hold of her bun of hair, burrowing his nails deep into her scalp. He hauled her forward. She cried out and clawed at his wrist, but Mr. Su was relentless.

"Finish it," he ordered, and shoved his dagger at her. She reared back, sobbing and screaming like a fishwife.

Where were his men? Surely someone somewhere would hear her. But no one came, and when Little Pearl refused to take the dagger, Mr. Su turned the blade on her. He shoved the tip right up against her neck.

Jonas tensed, not knowing what to do. He didn't have the right angle, much less the strength to accomplish anything. But he was willing to try—until Little Pearl proved she had her own skills.

Most women would freeze in terror with a knife pressed to her neck. Not Little Pearl. Instead, she fell to her knees and descended into a truly awesome display of hysterics. Experienced as he was in such tricks, Jonas couldn't tell if hers was real or an act.

Whatever the truth, Mr. Su allowed none of it. He still had hold of her bun, and he hauled her back hard, exposing her throat. "Shut up, whore." There was no compromise in his voice. Little Pearl would be dead soon if she didn't settle down.

She did. Clearly, she understood the danger, because she quieted to a couple hiccups.

"Do you want to die?" Mr. Su asked softly. She didn't answer, and Jonas watched the man's eyes narrow—not in anger, but in thought.

Jonas tensed again, mentally judging the best line of attack. There was none. Little Pearl was too vulnerable. Much though his spirit burned with the strain, he had to remain still.

"Do it or die, whore," Mr. Su hissed.

Jonas watched Little Pearl's body shift. Instead of stiff-backed hysteria, her arms became more fluid as she reached for the dagger. She was still on her knees, her neck fully exposed, but her hips seemed to shift, drawing backward a bit to a more supported position. Mr. Su couldn't see. He was towering over Little Pearl and not at the right angle. But Jonas saw and immediately adjusted his thoughts. There was no time to stop it, much though he feared for her. He might as well give her the best chance.

Little Pearl took hold of the dagger with all appearance of reluctance. She was making little hiccuping sounds of fear, and Jonas had a moment to wonder if he was imagining her duplicity. What if she were exactly as she appeared?

Mr. Su did not surrender the dagger to her. Instead, he twisted the weapon—his hands surrounding hers—and leaned forward. "The fleshy underside of his chin. Push it up, as if he were a chicken on a spit."

Little Pearl wasn't going to get her chance. The bastard wasn't going to risk letting go of the dagger. It was time for Jonas to make his move or die.

He began to thrash. It had been hard to maintain the raspy, half breaths. Now he took deep gulps of air like a dying fish. He pretended to choke, convulsing. He had seen enough men die to know what it looked like. So, too, had Mr. Su.

Instead of drawing away in horror like Little Pearl was trying to do, Mr. Su pushed even closer. "Quick! He will die soon. Finish it!"

"Why?" whimpered Little Pearl. "Why not let him die naturally? Let his spirit go as it wants!"

"Because I command—"

Now! Jonas reached out with his good arm, latching onto the villain's calf. He continued to gasp, pretending the action was the mindless thrashing of a dying man, but he poured all his strength into that one hand. Every year of fighting full sails, every moment he'd tied ropes or hauled cargo, every ounce of that past went into his grip. He dug in his fingers until Mr. Su's leg was crippled with pain.

It took longer than expected. The man was highly resistant to pain, but eventually he grimaced, his leg buckling. As Mr. Su bent forward, his face dropping lower and lower, he tried to use his knife on Jonas. But Little Pearl was stronger. At that moment, she wrenched the dagger away, and Jonas at last launched himself upward.

He didn't need finesse. He used his body's weight and momentum to topple his assailant. He prayed Little Pearl was fast enough to slip clear.

She was. And as she darted backward, she managed to grab Jonas's other arm. She helped him rise upward and directed his weight onto Mr. Su, who could still not use his leg. Then Jonas added a head slam, crushing the man's jaw with his forehead. The impact brought stars to his vision. And he'd been prepared! How much worse for Mr. Su, whose head reared back and who stumbled and collapsed beneath Jonas's heavier bulk.

The man's head bounced hard on the wood floor, and his eyes rolled back into his head, but he wasn't unconscious. In truth, he struggled like a trained fighter. But he'd been caught off guard and Jonas outweighed him by two stone. The man was subdued within moments.

Now, for the final stroke. Jonas made his face into a hideous grimace, and moved within inches of the bastard. When he spoke, it was in a hiss meant to terrify. "Run, Mr. Su. Hide behind your doors and beneath your bed. Depart from Shanghai, flee to the farthest corners of this godforsaken country, Mr. Su. Because when I die, my ghost will haunt you. I will curdle your milk, steal your gold, and shriek night after night whenever you close your eyes. This I swear, Mr. Su. I will haunt you if I can find you."

He waited a moment, feeling the man struggle for breath beneath his bulk. He watched the villain's eyes narrow in fury, then slowly give way to wide-eyed terror. Then he felt the final choking gasp of surrender. Mr. Su was terrified. He had the usual Chinese superstitions. He would run far away from Shanghai and never bother Little Pearl again.

Grunting in satisfaction, Jonas slowly rolled backward. He paused long enough to whisper one last threat: "White ghosts can kill, too, if they wish."

Mr. Su rasped an acknowledgment, a strange rattle low in his throat. Jonas lifted off him. The man would run like a frightened child. Now he would . . .

The body shuddered and exhaled. Mr. Su's eyes rolled back into his head. It took a moment for Jonas to realize the truth: Mr. Su was dead.

Jonas stared in shock. Even when the waves of his own pain finally penetrated his distraction, he still couldn't move. Mr. Su was dead?

From the side of his vision he saw Little Pearl. Removing a bloody dagger from Mr. Su's side, she straightened in a huff and wiped it on the man's elegantly tailored jacket. Her next words were delivered with a chilling finality.

"*That* is how a tigress spits a chicken, Mr. Su."

July 10, 1890

Father Bert—

Save your sermonizing for your parish, brother. I am not of your flock. A ship's life is hard. On leave, we celebrate. I have no diseases, and my hands are steady. Unlike you, I have not slept with or near our mother since I was ten. How dare you preach to me, Little Runt?

—Jonas

Sweetened Red Bean Soup (Hoong Dul Sah) *is
recommended in the winter, when the weather is cold, to
warm the body. The soup is reminiscent of lentil soup in
texture. The brown candy* (peen tong) *must always be added
when the soup is at a rolling boil, or it is believed the sugar
can cause fainting.*

Chapter Ten

Number One Slave gasped out an order as he launched
himself into the rickshaw. If he wasn't back in ten minutes with more men, he would be slowly bled from his
genitals until dead. All was going wrong.

The plan had been gloriously simple. Master Su had
walked straight in the front gate, demanding an audience with Little Pearl. Number One had stationed himself near enough to hear most of the conversation
without being seen. The cook had few servants to protect
her, fewer still who could withstand Master Su's forceful
presence. Within moments, the master was inside.

Then Number One waited five hundred heartbeats before setting his men to attack the sailors. It was to be a
silent assault, quietly removing the white guards and re-
placing them with his own. But that was where Number
One had miscalculated.

Who knew that these sailors were so well trained?
And they took their duties seriously and weren't caught
off guard by the usual techniques. They did not accept

offers of liquor or the lures of women. Worse, they fought like demons.

Number One had brought six men for the initial attack. Two more had flanked Number One just in case. Given the example of all the other white sailors frequenting Shanghai, these should have died quickly and silently. They had not. The three had fought like demons and roared warnings to their compatriot—a fourth man who had been loitering in the kitchen. Number One sent his extra men but it was too late. The fourth sailor carried a gun.

Yes, all it had taken was one gunshot and one scream, and his men had turned tail and run. They would fight drunk sailors on command, but not ghost demons with guns. All had run in terror, leaving Number One to contemplate his own fate. He had failed in his task. His master would surely kill him. In fact, Master Su enjoyed finding creative ways of killing his Number One Slaves, and was probably sitting inside right now, drinking tea and planning.

Grabbing the whip, Number One lashed the rickshaw runner and ordered him to greater speed. Ten minutes. He had to be back in ten minutes with at least fifty men or he would be dead. But who?

Inspiration came as they rounded a corner past a brothel and one of General Kang's soldiers stumbled out. Soldiers! They would fight well against four annoying sailors. And best of all, he could have a whole company here in ten minutes.

Little Pearl stared at the dagger in her hand, feeling the metal grow cold and heavy. She wiped the blood from the blade, but some of it still coated her hand, drying sticky and thick. She felt herself grow still, the exultation of the moment fading. What she'd felt had been a dark joy, drugging in its own way, but it had left a stain behind, a thick, greasy film that now seemed to coat her spirit.

Captain Jonas was speaking, but his words made little sense. He reached out and gently removed the knife from her hand. She didn't acknowledge his movement, but her spirit breathed easier. Jonas's words finally penetrated her distraction.

"You didn't need to kill him, Little Pearl. He would have left you alone. He was frightened of me—"

"No." She didn't know where she found the breath to speak, but her words were strong despite her confusion. "He was not a man to be afraid of ghosts."

"But—"

"It had to be done!" she snapped. "He would not have stopped."

"You don't know that!"

She turned to look him in the eye. "I knew this man. I felt his anger and tasted his yang." She straightened to her full height. "He would not have stopped."

She watched the captain deflate—not in the way of a man accepting the truth, but because his strength gave out. He must be in a great deal of pain, she realized. His attack had saved her life, but it had also likely reinjured his ribs and shoulder.

"Come to bed. I will tend to—"

He shook his head, his breath ragged. "We have to call the police. The body—"

"No police! No Manchu!"

He looked at her, his eyes wide. "Don't fear for me. I . . ." He swallowed. "I understood the risks when I came here. I will take my punishment."

She blinked, not understanding. Then she gasped, suddenly following his thoughts. He was a white man in Chinese Shanghai. She had gotten so used to his presence that she no longer thought it odd to see him or his men here. But the authorities would not—

"Where the hell is Seth?" he growled.

She leaned down and helped him stand. He acknowledged her with a grateful nod, but his attention was on the hallway. She felt him stiffen against her, and though she urged him to the bed, he turned to the door instead.

Only then did she hear the noise: footsteps—two pairs—running up the stairs. She gasped, abruptly terrified. Would she have to face more of Mr. Su's men? Her hands began to tremble.

Jonas shifted his weight in front of her, the dagger gripped in his hand. Coward that she was, she didn't stop him. He was injured, she was whole. She should face the threat, but she could not force herself to move before the running feet pounded into the room. Instead, gratitude for his courage filled her heart.

Two men, white sailors. They had blood on their clothing and dark bruises on their faces. Little Pearl recognized them as Tom and Scott, gangly young men with bottomless stomachs. They spoke in rapid English that she couldn't understand, but Jonas slumped in relief. She thought he would cross to the bed then—she could see the tight lines of pain in his face and body—but he stayed on his feet and spoke in a commanding tone. The boys responded smartly, their replies recognizable even though English. Yes, sir. No, sir. Immediately, sir. Then they made to leave, and Little Pearl stopped them.

"No! No police!" She didn't know if that was their intent, but she couldn't take the risk.

Jonas turned to her. "I won't put you at risk," he began.

"No police. No Manchu."

"But—"

She gripped his arm. "It is not because you are here. They have already arrested the Tans. To add a murder would doom us all. They will not ask questions. I will be executed—"

"I will tell them that I killed—"

"It does not matter! You should not be here. Your men have been fighting! Mr. Su is powerful. He will see that we all die! Then he will come and take over the Tan home anyway."

Jonas touched her arm with his empty hand, his caress gentle as he cupped her elbow, guiding her to sit on the bed. Only then did she realize how terribly she shook. "Little Pearl," he said. "Mr. Su is dead. He cannot take over anything."

"His men! He is powerful."

"There—"

"No police!" she repeated. "You do not understand China. No police!"

He sighed. He seemed to be studying her, or perhaps just waiting. Whatever the reason, she had time to calm herself. She gripped her hands together and concentrated on evening out her breath. Eventually, he spoke, his deep voice soothing.

"Tell me everything about Mr. Su. How long have you known him?"

She tried to remember. "He came here the day the Tans disappeared. He said he was partners with Master Tan, and that he wants the list."

"What list?" Jonas pressed.

She lifted her chin. "The same one you look for. With the names and addresses."

Jonas grimaced. Turning to his men, he issued orders in quick English. Tom and Scott ran out, their footsteps amazingly silent. Little Pearl rose to run after them, but Jonas held her still. "They are only going to protect the house. We can call the police—"

"No!"

"—later if we need to. For now, they just guard the compound." He sighed as he awkwardly maneuvered to sit beside her.

She tried to help him, but right then he was stronger than she. He sat down with a grimace, but his energy flowed clear, surrounding her with power. She could breathe easier when he was beside her. Her thoughts became clearer as well.

"You think Su's men are coming back," she said.

Jonas shrugged. "I don't know for sure, but there's no point in taking a risk. The attack was coordinated. We were lucky that Tom was scrounging in the kitchen."

"He likes steamed bao."

Jonas smiled. "He likes anything he can get. Tell me more about Mr. Su. Had you ever seen him before Kui Yu's arrest?"

"No. Never." She tried not to look at the body on the floor, the slow seep of dark red blood that greased the floor. She should cover him. She should mop the floor. She . . .

"You said you've tasted his yang," Jonas continued. There was an edge to his voice, an anger at what she had done and she felt shame bite hard at her spirit.

"He insisted. Payment for his warnings. He said the creditors would come, and they did. He said I would need money, and—"

"So you serviced him for the money." Jonas's voice was low and dark.

"He likes to humiliate, and he practices what we teach here." She frowned at her hands. She was babbling. "It seemed prudent to keep him happy. He knows the teaching, but he has twisted it for power, not enlightenment."

Jonas shrugged. His gaze went to the body. "He doesn't practice anything anymore."

Little Pearl said nothing. She stared at Master Su and began thinking stupid little things. The body was probably cold now, but it had been burning hot as he gripped her. Only two days ago, she had wrestled him as a tigress wrestles a dragon—each fighting for the release of qi that empowers those who understand it. He had felt warm then, too, though he preferred tepid tea. She would serve him soups designed to cool the temper . . . if he would eat. But of course, he would not eat now because he was dead.

Her thoughts ran in useless circles as she stared at the expanding pool of blood. Jonas reached behind him to pull the very large blanket off the bed. He tossed it on the ground beside the body, right on top of the blood. Then, with slow, ponderous movements, he pushed off the bed and onto his knees.

"What are you doing?"

"Swabbing the deck," he answered. She didn't understand his words until he began to use the blanket to wipe up the gore. Then he glanced over his shoulder at her face. "What will happen when Mr. Su doesn't return?"

She blinked. "He didn't intend to return home. He meant to stay here."

"But his men," Jonas pressed. "What will his men do?"

She didn't answer. Her vision was caught by the thought of a dead man with servants. Master Su—with his glossy black hair and thin mouth still open in shock—had slaves and business partners and at least one home. She had thought her problems abolished with Master Su's death, but she had not killed his network. She had not removed his power.

"Little Pearl? Little Pearl!"

She heard Jonas's words but couldn't manage to respond. Not until he flipped the corner of the blanket over Master Su's face. It was coarse fabric, designed for warmth not pleasure, and all she could think was that Master Su probably didn't like it on his face.

"Little Pearl!"

She jumped, her gaze drawn to Jonas's face. "Yes?"

"What will his men do when he doesn't return?"

She shook her head. "I don't know." Then she blinked. "Should I go cook something?"

"What?"

"Should I cook something for your men? They looked

hurt." She meant to stand, but couldn't seem to make herself move. "I should cook some soup for them. It might get cold tonight. And maybe a salve. For their injuries." She nodded and finally made herself stand. "I should be in the kitchen."

Jonas watched her closely. She could feel his gaze on her face, but could not meet his eyes. "An excellent idea," he finally said. "But first, are there any other servants in the house? Anyone but you, me, and my men?"

She nodded. "Yes. There's . . ." She could not remember their names.

"Do you trust them?"

She nodded. "Of course. No. Don't trust them at all. They burn the rice."

"Send them to me, Little Pearl. Send them all to me, then go make soup. Make a lot of soup. It will be very helpful."

She nodded. She could make tea. "Beans? Do you think you will want bean soup?"

"Of course. You can make that without leaving the house, right?"

"Yes, yes. I will stay in the kitchen. I will cook food for your men. And mix salve."

"Excellent, but send all the servants to me. Anyone in the compound."

She forced a smile. "I will send them right away." She took a few steps. Her balance was precarious as she stepped around the body, but eventually steadied near the door. Then she stopped, turning back to look at Jonas. How solid he appeared. How thankful she was that he was here. She bit her lip in guilt. "You are hurt. I should be helping you."

He smiled, and the lines of weariness eased. "You are helping, Little Pearl. Food is the most important task right now."

He was lying, of course. He was getting her out of the way while he dealt with the body and . . . and whatever else needed to be done. She wished she were stronger. She wished it for his sake, because no man wanted a useless wife. Then she bit her lip and looked away. What an idiot she was. He was a white man and she'd once been a whore. No marriage was to be had in such circumstances.

She blinked in shock. She must be very unsettled to think about such things, but once she had dreamed of a strong man—a good man—to protect her. What a surprise to wish for such a thing again.

"I will make tea, too," she said. "A black tea with special herbs for strength."

"An excellent idea," he repeated.

She bit her lip. "I am so sorry," she whispered, not even knowing what she meant. Perhaps she apologized for once being a whore, and that he was white. If things were different . . . She cut off her thoughts. Things were *not* different. "I will go make tea," she said again. Then she turned and ran away.

Jonas groaned as he wrapped Mr. Su tightly in the blanket. Thankfully the man was small and Jonas had been strong before his injuries. Also, he had wrapped many a sail around a body in his life. This procedure was simply a variation.

He eyed the blanket as he worked. He judged it to be an everyday kind of blanket, with no identifying marks and large enough for two. It was simple, useful, and the kind of thing any man—rich or poor—might have. Perfect for this task.

Time rode him hard. He feared being caught by the wrong person at the wrong time, so he moved as quickly as possible, dragging the body down the hall. He wanted to roll it down the stairs. He had little reverence for the dead, and even less for the man who'd held a knife to Little Pearl's throat. But he could not risk the sound or undoing the wrap.

So with a grimace, he continued to drag.

Fortune smiled on him. The stairs descended near the gardener's shed. Jonas found a small wheelbarrow inside, large enough to hold Mr. Su but small enough to be maneuverable. He quickly lifted the man inside, wincing but making sure the blanket stayed tight while watching the darkness for surprises. He greatly feared this villain would not leave much to chance. That meant that somewhere, somehow, there would be consequences for this murder. The only hope was to delay discovery.

Jonas pulled on a gardener's shirt, worn thin in places but still comfortably clean and not too small. With the addition of some dirt and the small Chinese hat called a watermelon cap, his white skin suddenly became much less obvious. He grabbed the wheelbarrow—an amazingly light wood construction—and headed for the back gate. It took a moment to locate Tom hiding in the shadow of an ornamental bush. The boy was a genius at disappearing; he rose when the wheelbarrow came close, but Jonas gestured him to stay in position as he hurried past.

The compound opened onto a back alley between houses. It looked strangely English, in that all the houses crowded close together. He supposed the rich in any city struggled with the same problems of tight quarters; they built high wood houses and planted trees to hide the fact that their neighbors lived a handsbreadth away. He saw the front street had gates of distinctly Chinese design—round portals, black lacquered in intricate shapes—but the back dumped into an alleyway between fences. He wended and maneuvered his way, looking for a solution. Ten minutes later, he found it: an open ditch cluttered with garbage. It was wide and foul-smelling, and likely used by all the houses throughout the neighborhood.

With a great sense of justice, Jonas tossed Master Su—blanket shroud and all—on the nearest pile, then turned and headed back. Unfortunately, activity had taken its toll. He struggled to move, and he used the wheelbarrow for support more than he pushed it. He was pathetically winded, and had to stop to catch his breath a house away from Kui Yu's home. But as his ribs finally settled into a dull agony, Jonas's mind cleared enough for him to hear two men talking outside the gate.

It was late evening—not an unusual time for men to be outside smoking—but something about their tone indicated these weren't on a casual stroll. Abandoning his wheelbarrow, Jonas sneaked forward, trying to understand their Chinese. He couldn't. It wasn't the Shanghai dialect he knew. Risking even more, he crept around a corner, holding tight to a wall. His every breath burned like fire, and he fought to keep his vision clear. The stone wall felt gritty against his hand, but it kept him grounded and upright as he crept along.

There. Two soldiers laughed as they guarded the back gate. Chinese soldiers? Where was Tom? Surely he'd heard the men. Likely Tom would be crouched down, a knife in his hand, ready to gut whoever dared cross the threshold. If only there was a way to tell the boy not to slit the soldiers' throats. Jonas was perfectly willing to kill any number of Su's thieves, but soldiers were a different matter. His few men could not possibly hold out in Chinese Shanghai against the Imperial army.

Sliding backward, Jonas decided to risk sending a stand-down order. He took a steadying breath, knowing he would have to move quickly once he started. He wasn't at all sure he was up to the task, but he wouldn't let either Little Pearl or his men down. When he was ready, he whistled long and loud. Tom was sure to hear it and understand. He wouldn't put away his knife, but he wouldn't attack either. Unfortunately, the soldiers heard it as well. Their conversation abruptly stopped. A split second later, they rushed in his direction.

Jonas didn't wait. He wasn't near quiet enough nor

fast enough, but he was running and they were follow-ing. Apparently none of them knew the area well. But they were two to his one. Given his injuries, he would end up trapped like a rat in a cage.

Fortunately, he was smarter. Soldiers weren't sailors, so they didn't think about rigging or sails or all those marvelous places a man could hide above his enemies. Even one-handed, Jonas found places to climb, hand-holds to grip, and thin branches that supported just enough to get him to a roof. He was scraped bloody in places, his ribs might never recover, but he was alive. And he'd lost the landlubbers.

Doubling back, he slipped over the wall to land with a bone-jarring thud. Tom was beside him in a moment, knife at the ready.

"We got soldiers, Cap. A whole fat load of them."

Jonas didn't have the breath to respond. Instead, he gestured weakly with one hand: *Where?*

"Front door. With a rat-faced Chinese slave, bald as my arse and dressed like an undertaker."

Had to be Su's slaves. Only slaves had shaved heads and the clothing sounded like Su's choice of uniform. And here were those consequences. When the first attack failed, Su likely had a fallback plan in place, like a slave poised to bring in the army. General Kang had already arrested Kui Yu; they'd probably jump at the chance to inspect the house again. Then, if any white man was found here in Chinese Shanghai, the entire Tan household was cooked for sure. The army would kill the white men, arrest Little Pearl, and likely leave the compound in the care of Mr. Su.

"Little Pearl?" he whispered.

Tom shrugged. "Up front with the soldiers."

The thought of Little Pearl with any of those men gave him renewed strength. He'd be damned if he left her alone to face that. But first he had to take care of his men. "Tell everyone to hide. Get outside if you can manage it."

"But what about the soldiers?"

Jonas shook his head. "Can't kill all the soldiers in Shanghai." Much though he wanted to. "Hide. Or die." He added the last two words as warning; his men knew he wouldn't say such unless their lives truly did hang in the balance. "Go."

"But what about you—"

"Go!" He could hear the two soldiers coming back, their curses as loud as their pounding feet. Tom heard it as well, and disappeared faster than Jonas could see. Then it was his turn. Fortunately, it wasn't hard. Kui Yu's garden was designed for beauty, with wandering paths through ornamental plants. The large area had dozens of hidey-holes and thousands of shadows. Hell, some of the pathways narrowed to a point where only a woman with bound feet could wander without stepping into mud.

While the soldiers clamored in from the back gate, Jonas slipped around behind them, following as they stomped forward and called for their commanding officer. Right on cue, a group of people erupted from the front receiving area: three men and Little Pearl.

Jonas focused on her. Little Pearl didn't seem to be hurt, but she wrung her hands and limped in distress. He narrowed his eyes. Was it feigned, or was she truly so upset that she couldn't think straight? No way to tell. If only he could get closer.

He looked at the men. Two had uniforms. Jonas didn't know the Chinese military, but from the relative youth of the group, he figured he was looking at a lieutenant and several privates, raw recruits barely a month away from Mama. Generally they wouldn't be a problem if he could confront them eye to eye, but he was in hiding and Little Pearl was the one being bullied. No rifles, at least. Still, the boy had a sword that he probably knew how to use, at least against a small woman with bound feet.

The third man interested him the most, the smaller

rat-faced Chinese with the bald head. Definitely Su's slave. He had to be. He hovered in the background—close enough to hear and interject if necessary—but quiet enough that one might tend to forget he was there. Who paid attention to slaves anyway?

The soldiers were reporting. Jonas crept as close as he dared, near enough to hear the words clearly. Unfortunately, the men still spoke in their northern dialect. Then one of the soldiers whistled. Not a bad imitation of the stand-down order. Jonas smiled. If any of his men hadn't heard his earlier whistle, they did now. Unfortunately, it was a dead giveaway that something was rotten in Denmark. The lieutenant stared hard at the open, unguarded back gate, and barked a series of commands. The two idiot soldiers blanched, then took off at a run to cover it.

Good luck, Jonas thought with silent glee. His men would be gone by now, slipping outside the gate to hide in the nearby trees or rooftops—far enough away from the compound to disappear, near enough to come running if Jonas gave the signal. Plus, knowing Tom, one of the men would already be halfway to the ship where he would report everything to Seth.

That left Jonas and Little Pearl as the only ones in danger. Keeping that in mind, Jonas crept even closer—right into Little Pearl's line of sight. She didn't see him at first. Not until he grinned at her, flashing his white teeth in the moonlight.

That got her attention. Her eyes widened and her mouth gaped. She raised her hand, probably to gesture him backward, but then froze, her eyes darting between him and the lieutenant. Wrong worry, he thought with a frown. Soldier boy isn't the problem. Look at Rat Face, Jonas silently urged.

The lieutenant issued orders to the remaining soldier, who dashed to the front. Rat Face was looking smug, while Little Pearl began rapidly demanding answers and sobbing. "Aie, aie, aie!" She was providing a distraction, giving Jonas time to hide. He obliged by scooting deeper into the shadows, but he'd be damned if he left her alone. Meanwhile, the lieutenant began answering Little Pearl's questions in Shanghai dialect.

"My men heard a signal, the kind that white devils use."

"White devils!" Little Pearl cried in terror. "Oh no! Not here, no white devils! Aie!"

The rat-faced man pushed forward. "They must have killed him! They must have attacked Master Su and killed him!"

"Aie! Aie! Murder! Oh no!"

The lieutenant did his best to hush them both, but Little Pearl was in rare form. If Jonas feared she'd lost her wits, he soon realized his mistake. The moment the lieutenant began showing signs of irritability, she settled, wiping her eyes.

"I am so upset. White devils here? With the master away? No. No. I need some tea. Would you like some tea, Mr. Lieutenant?"

The man sighed in relief. "An excellent suggestion. We can have some tea while my men search—"

"No! No! There are no devils here."

"Master Su—," interjected Rat Face, but Little Pearl thundered at him like a tiny summer storm.

"I told you and told you! Master and Mistress are away! This is a house of women, and so I told your Mr. Su. He left, as well he should. He is not here!"

"But he was here—"

"He left! Now go away! Go away, ugly slave!" With a quick flick of her wrist, she knocked the man's small watermelon cap away, revealing a short stubby queue. So, he wasn't really bald. The man's hair had been shaved off some months ago and was only now regrowing.

"See!" Little Pearl continued to the soldier. "He is a

shamed slave. Probably because he likes to make trouble for good people. Make him go away!"

Rat Face was purple with anger, but Little Pearl's drama had been effective. The lieutenant pushed him aside.

"Go home. We will look for your master. If we find him, we will contact you."

"He was here! The white devils killed him!" sniveled the slave, but it was no use. The lieutenant had him by the arm and pushed him toward the front gate.

"My men will search the grounds thoroughly. If we find any signs of the white devils—"

"Aie!"

"—then we will protect you."

Little Pearl paused, her face blanched. To her credit, she didn't slant a look Jonas's way, but she spoke loudly, making sure he heard. "Are you sure? You must search here?"

"I am sure."

Little Pearl bit her lip, looking for all the world like a lost and frightened waif. "Very well," she said. "Thank you for your help. I will rely on you." Then she abruptly straightened. "And tell your men: I am the best cook in all of Shanghai. I will cook for them now. As soon as they are done, I will have red bean bao and my special soup for them. Famous in all of Shanghai is my soup. And the red beans—most sweet, most excellent. I will give them to your soldiers as soon as they are done looking, yes?" She gripped the lieutenant's arm. "You send the nasty slave away while I make special soup for you."

The lieutenant was boyish enough to grin. "That sounds excellent," he said. It sounded great to Jonas, too, especially as at least one of the privates had heard the offer. The moment the lieutenant disappeared into the kitchen, the younger men would rush through the search, doing only the most cursory inspection before running to the kitchen to eat.

Little Pearl hurried the lieutenant and Su's slave forward to the front gate. The rat-faced man tried one last time to push the search for Mr. Su, but he was no match for the lure of Little Pearl's food, and the look of pure hatred that crossed the slave's face struck Jonas. That man was dangerous, and his venom was directed at Little Pearl.

Jonas grimaced. There was nothing he could do about it now. Besides, it was time for him to move, before one of the other soldier boys stumbled over him in their haste to find the kitchen. Not so easy a task. Hunched and still as he'd been, his muscles had stiffened. It was no small thing to slink through the shadows again, moving without groaning or passing out from pain. He needed to find a hiding place near the kitchen, and he had to get there now, before the lieutenant finished tossing out the slave. Unfortunately, he couldn't move so fast.

He looked carefully around. No soldiers. He made his dash, creeping as low as possible. He rounded a corner, hugged the wall, then slid into the hallway just before the kitchen. He could still hear Little Pearl in the receiving room. She kept up a steady patter of nonsense with the lieutenant.

Damn, the woman was good. Nearly hysterical one moment; the next, coolly saving his life again. He grinned, turned the next corner and ran straight into a solid body; one with faster reflexes than his.

Feb. 19, 1892

Dearest Jonas,
  I write to tell you of my marriage to Beth Tanner. She is a most excellent and godly woman. It is my hope that you will adore her nearly as well as I do. My parish is in Yorkshire where she has lived nearly all her life. She has a cousin as well, one who is as beautiful as she is reserved.

*You once said you liked a quiet woman beyond all else.
Come visit us, brother. Meet my new bride and see what
glories await a good man at home. There is much work
that a strong man can do here. Good pay and a good life.*
                    —Your brother in blood and in Christ, Albert

There are many different kinds of pork dumplings, and siu mai *are one of the most popular, typically served in dim sum restaurants. When homemade, these dumplings are unsurpassed if they are made with an equal amount of fresh water chestnuts to ground pork, Chinese mushrooms, cilantro, and scallions.*

Chapter Eleven

Little Pearl patted a soldier's hand as she dropped another dumpling onto his plate. It was clear the boy missed his mother, and his grin showed adoration. She smiled back, awed as usual that such a simple thing as food could inspire love.

She turned back to stir the soup, trying not to let her worry show. The soldiers had swept the compound and found no sign of white devils. She had simpered and laughed, just as an idiot woman would, but in her heart, she worried. What had happened to Captain Jonas? He was injured and vulnerable. Was he now breathing his last in a ditch somewhere?

The need to find out made her stir the soup too vigorously, spilling the thick red mixture. Looking down, she forced herself to calm, reaching for her tigress teachings to separate herself from chaotic feelings. No good. There was too much noise, too much commotion in her kitchen for her to find calm.

"Hai!" The male cry exploded through the room, silencing everyone. Little Pearl spun around too fast, barely catching herself before she fell. Unfortunately, her flailing movement brought her hand down on the hot iron stove, burning her palm. It was a small accident, too common to count, but she cursed nonetheless, her crude word echoing loudly in the sudden silence.

The lieutenant glanced apologetically toward her, but then his attention riveted on the last reporting soldier. The newcomer was excited and rushed his words. Any prayer of understanding his northern dialect was lost in a fury of high-pitched, excited sounds. But everyone else understood. To a man, the soldier boys bolted to their feet and ran from the room. Little Pearl watched them go, an eerie sense of childishness souring her stomach. Here she was, a girl sucking her burned hand, while the men scurried about on important tasks. Dropping her hand from her mouth, she turned back to the soup pot. She would hold her tongue though the anger and hurt coiled inside.

"Mistress," the lieutenant said, his voice thick with self-importance. "We have found him."

She looked up, schooling her face into wide-eyed innocence. "Found who?"

"Mr. Su."

She gasped, preparing to break into wails of agony. He would tell her that Mr. Su was dead, murdered on her very street, and she would be expected to descend into very feminine hysterics. But first she had to pretend he was alive. "Bring him here," she said as calmly as possible. "I have enough soup for all—"

"He has been stabbed."

"Stabbed?" Men always liked it when you echoed their thoughts. The next step was to ask a ridiculous question that encouraged them to speak importantly to you. "What do you mean?"

He shook his head. "I do not know, except that he was

gravely injured and thrown in a ditch. We require bandages and hot water."

She frowned, not following. "What? Why?"

"I have told my men to bring him here. You have rooms and supplies." He gestured vaguely to the storeroom. "Surely you know how to care for an injured man."

"He is injured?" she echoed again, her mind unable to follow.

"He has been stabbed."

"Oh no!" she wailed, not needing to pretend. "Not dead?"

"Not yet. We are bringing him here. I sent for a doctor."

"Aie, aie, aieeeee!" She wailed because she didn't know what else to do.

"Please. Where should we take him?"

"His home! Master Su has—"

"No. He could die. Should I put him on the table?"

Little Pearl reared back in horror. A dying man on her kitchen table? "What if he dies? His ghost will haunt me!" She couldn't think. She could barely breathe. What if he woke up? What if he opened his eyes and pointed at her and told the lieutenant that she had killed him? She would be shot for sure! "Aie!" she moaned.

"Calm yourself!" the lieutenant snapped, and Little Pearl glared at the boy. Resentment seethed inside her, but she suppressed it, especially since he was right. She needed to think. She needed Jonas.

"Where can we take him?" the officer pressed.

"I will show you." She spoke, her mind still reeling. She had no idea what to do. There was only one place to take the injured Master Su: a practice room. Not the same one as Jonas used, of course, but nearby. Five doors down the hallway. Would the two men murder each other in the night? "I do not want him here," she moaned to herself.

"There is no other place," the lieutenant answered. At

his gesture, they all left the kitchen and headed for the
practice rooms.

"He has servants. Where is that terrible slave?" She was
whining, acting like a spoiled child, but what could she
do? If Shi Po were here, then none of this would be happening. If either of the Tans were here, she could be sleeping right now, thinking of nothing more than tomorrow's
lunch. She didn't want to be mistress of a large house. She
didn't want to care for a man she'd tried to murder.

But a woman's life was to serve men. Though she hated
it and pouted, the soldier would not likely change his
mind and no amount of food or wheedling would save her.
Mr. Su would reside here under her care. "I cannot take
care of a sick man," she sulked. "I haven't the servants."

"I will send someone for that slave. He can—"

"No!" she cried. "I do not want him here. *You* must
stay. You must—"

"I cannot remain. I have responsibilities."

"Then Mr. Su cannot stay!" She folded her arms and
tried to look just like Shi Po: regal, important, unshakable.

The lieutenant was silent for a moment, considering.
Then he nodded, and Little Pearl had a moment of hope.

"You will take Mr. Su away?" she asked.

"I will leave a man to watch for the white devils and to
help you with Mr. Su." Then he turned and gestured behind him to four soldiers carrying a bloody blanket. It
took a moment before Little Pearl dared look at the body
inside. Mr. Su was wrapped tight, but his gray face was
clear even in the dim lantern light. Blood smeared his
pasty skin, and she couldn't truly believe he was alive.

"But he is dead," she said softly.

"Not yet," the lieutenant responded. "Which room?"

"Aie," Little Pearl moaned. "Not the one on the right.
Not . . ." She swallowed, trying to think. Why couldn't
she think? "The last one! The last one on the left."

The lieutenant spoke to his men, who began climbing

the stairs. Then he turned back to Little Pearl. "Watch for the doctor."

She almost complied. She almost allowed him to send her away. She could simply grab her things right then— the few things she had stashed away—and run. She could leave everyone behind and start again. She could do that. She could become a whore again. What was it but more yang to take her to Heaven? She could . . .

Tears began coursing down her cheeks, and her breath caught on a sob. Her knees buckled and she found herself scrabbling in the dirt. Her burned hand scraped on a pebble and broke open. She cried out at the pain and immediately cradled the hand, watching as blood smeared the dirt there. It was merely a burn mixed with dirt and blood—nothing significant, and yet it looked like a diseased sore. It looked like the pussed and chafed skin of the beggar women outside the market. It looked . . . *She* looked like them.

"Mistress?" the lieutenant called. "Mistress?"

"I am not a whore," she whispered. "I am not a whore to accept any man with dirty hands. I am not a whore."

"I never said—"

"And I will not be a bitch, a dog in the street licking its sores and whimpering when kicked."

"Mistress, the doctor—"

She looked up, her eyes blazing in fury. "I am not a whore!"

His eyes widened and he stared at her, slowly backing away.

"I won't live like a dog!" she spat again, her fury giving her enough strength to push to her feet. "I am a woman! A rich woman with bound feet, and I cook!"

The soldier nodded, backing away as fast as he could. "Of course, Mistress. Of course—"

"*You* find the doctor, soldier boy. You watch Mr. Su. You do it! I am not a whore!"

"I—I—"

"You do it or I will find General Kang. I will tell him what you make good women do! I will tell him and he will whip you! I will—"

"I will find the doctor," the lieutenant babbled. "I will go now!" He looked back over his shoulder at his men who had made it to the top of the stairs. "I will take care of this, Mistress. I will do it." Then he spun on his heel and ran up the stairs after the others.

Little Pearl started to follow. Her hands were clenched and her fury was riding her to pursue him, to bellow, to attack. But her legs were too wobbly and her hands clammy. She could hear the soldiers bumping around upstairs as they settled Mr. Su—the man who was not dead. She couldn't think. She didn't want to feel. She wanted . . . She wanted to wash her hands. She shifted her gaze to her kitchen, trying to gather the strength to move. She fell on her bottom instead. She fell down in the dirt like the dog she was. And then she began to sob.

In the back of her mind she was aware of myriad things. The soldiers would return in a moment, and she didn't want to be here squatting on the ground. The doctor would arrive soon, too. And over on the edge of the garden, the little kitchen girl was trying to get her attention. These things filtered through her consciousness, but she could not manage to do anything about them. She could not do anything.

Until she heard his voice. It slipped into her mind a fraction of a second before she felt him. Jonas. His voice was low, his touch the lightest feather of a breeze. But she heard him and knew he caressed her arm and coaxed her away.

"Come on, little one. Let me help you. Little Pearl, I will help. I promise."

His hand was warm on her arm, his caress growing stronger. She opened her eyes and saw his face. It was unquestionably white: pale, weathered, and with round eyes that wrinkled. He looked familiar to her in the way of a favorite tapestry so much a part of her daily life that she no longer truly saw it. And yet she did notice it now.

She saw where a rippled scar cut through the dark reddish black dots of his beard. She saw that his eyebrows bristled every which way. They were closer together than Chinese eyebrows, but she found she didn't mind the extra weight on his face. His eyes were dark, but she could read his expression in the lift of his cheeks and the curve of his dry lips.

"Come along, little one," he continued to croon. "I will help you."

She didn't believe him. No one could help her. She was alone in her misery. And yet, he was here. His hands helped her stand. His touch kept her warm.

"I want to wash my hands," she said.

"There's a basin in the kitchen," he answered.

She knew that. And yet, it felt nice to have him say it. He wrapped an arm around her. "Are you hurt?" he asked.

"No."

"Tired then?"

"Yes." She spoke because he asked.

"It's been a hard day," he said.

They made it to the edge of the garden where the little kitchen girl hovered. Jonas didn't slow his pace, so neither did Little Pearl. The girl quickly slipped in beside her, speaking in an urgent whisper. "He wouldn't leave you," she said. "I hid him in the storeroom, but he wouldn't leave you."

Little Pearl nodded. She was able to hear more things now. With Jonas beside her, she was beginning to process the noise of soldiers talking as they headed down the stairs on the opposite side of the garden. Sound carried well here, but the plants obscured the view. "The soldiers are coming," she said, proving to herself that she could speak. "The doctor, too."

"For Mr. Su. Yes, I heard."

She shuddered at the villain's name. She remembered slipping the knife between his ribs and the flow of blood across her hand. She had tried to cut then—slash downward—but the resistance had been too strong. Stupid of her. She had cut meat before. She knew how useless it was to bury a knife all the way in. You couldn't carve that way, only poked holes in good meat.

"We need to go to the kitchen," she said. To wash her hands.

"We're almost there."

They made it to the edge of the garden and slipped into the back hall that led to the storeroom. And as they stepped into that familiar place, she felt the cool brush of air on her face and smelled the pungent scent of vinegar and ground bean sauce.

"There's water here." He led her to a bowl on the floor, as if for a cat or dog. But with his help she knelt on the floor, and he guided her hands into the water.

She closed her eyes as he washed her. There was no cloth, merely the slight abrasion of calloused hands around her own. She watched his larger hands and felt his arm around her back. She was not a big woman. Most men were larger than her; many women, too. And yet she had not felt this surrounded by a person since she was a little girl.

She snuggled tighter into his embrace. He grunted as she bumped his ribs, and at that moment she remembered his pain. "I'm sorry—," she began, but he cut her off.

"I'm fine, Little Pearl. How do you feel?"

She took a breath. His hands continued to work on hers; gently easing the dirt away, cleaning out the cut, soothing the burn. She felt it all as when he touched the sole of her foot, with excruciating clarity and a bit of excitement as well. "Little Pearl?"

She turned and kissed his cheek. It was an impulsive

act, the touch of a little girl. But as the dirt and pain were washed away, she felt her actions maturing, her thoughts turning to other acts, and she fought the change. "I am not a whore," she said to his rough cheek.

His hands stilled on hers, but he didn't speak. She felt her chest constrict. He didn't believe her. Or he didn't understand.

"A tigress isn't a whore," she said. "And I haven't had a partner since Ken Jin. That was years ago. I just teach classes now. And cook."

Her hands were clean. The skin felt raw and abused, but it was a good feeling—a healing pain that she welcomed. He lifted her hands out of the water and wrapped them in a cloth draped nearby. Little Pearl noticed that the kitchen girl was gone. She and Jonas were alone. He took his time drying each finger, then carefully dabbed at her palm.

"I am the Tans' chef," she said firmly, forcing pride into her voice. "I was raised for better, but . . ." She shrugged. "I like cooking. I am—"

"My mother was a whore," he interrupted. His voice was gentle, but it still boomed through the storeroom. She imagined the rice grains trembling at his words, and she felt a stillness inside as she listened to him. "We lived near the docks. She would service anyone who could pay. She wasn't even expensive." He grimaced. "Just a whore like a dozen others."

"Did her parents sell her?" She hadn't meant to speak, but the words slipped out. Jonas's eyes leaped from her hands to her face, and she felt her skin heat from a blush.

"No," he answered. "She just grew up a whore, I think. Her mother was one and probably her mother before her. They must have died before I was born."

She frowned. "But you're a ship captain. You own a ship."

"One of her johns liked me." At her confused look, he

explained. "I would entertain her customers while she got ready. He thought I was smart, knew I'd be loyal, and asked me if I'd like to sail on a ship." He flashed a quick smile. "He was good to me. Taught me everything there is to know about the ocean."

She realized she was smiling back. "Are white whores treated . . ." She swallowed, not knowing how to ask. "Are they important in your country?"

He shook his head. "Whores are despised everywhere in the world." He looked down at her hands, then carefully released her. "And sons of whores are no more important—"

"You're a ship captain. You do business with Master Tan. You—"

"I'm the son of a whore and no better than I should be."

She didn't understand his awkward phrase, but before she could speak, they heard a noise in the kitchen. It was one of the soldiers calling for her, and the softer answers of the kitchen girl. Little Pearl closed her eyes, the weight of the day returning.

"You don't have to go out," Jonas said, but she was already moving for the door.

"Hide," she whispered. "I am feeling better now." And she was. Her hands were clean and she wasn't alone. Jonas was right here, settling down behind an urn of fine flour.

"I can hear everything from here," he whispered. "If you're afraid, just say . . . rice petals."

She frowned. "Rice petals? That makes no sense."

He shrugged. "Pick whatever you want—"

"Rice petals is fine." She wanted to say more, but she was needed in the kitchen. She needed to keep the soldier from coming in here. She needed to be a hundred miles away, safe from Mr. Su and General Kang. Instead, she hesitated by the doorway and stared at the dark shadow that was Jonas. No words came.

"I am right here. If you're afraid, I'm right here."

She smiled, at last finding her voice. "I am not afraid of ghost devils anymore." Then she left, bracing herself to face the devils of her own people. Two steps out the door and she realized it was not a soldier who waited for her. It was someone much worse.

Master Su's slave stood in her kitchen, sniffing her food and curling his lip at the little girl he had obviously made cry.

"Thank you, Mei Wan," Little Pearl intoned. "It's late. Why don't you go to bed?" The girl gaped at her, wiping her tears across her sleeve, but she didn't speak. "You have done very well today," she said with unaccustomed graciousness. "Go sleep in the practice room—the first at the top of the stairs."

Mei Wan's eyes widened. She knew Little Pearl was asking her to sleep in Jonas's bed. It was a convenient excuse for the disheveled sheets and obviously used room. But would the girl be too afraid to rest in a bed used by a ghost devil?

Little Pearl waited, her breath suspended, then got an idea. Sometimes people needed a full belly to face their fears. She crossed to the last of the soup—cold now, but still tasty. She dished out a bowl and handed it to the girl. Then, on impulse, she handed over a sweet bean pastry, too. "Go and sleep. Tomorrow will come soon enough."

The lure of the pastry overcame the child's fears. Mei Wan grabbed the food and disappeared, already cramming her tiny mouth full. Which left Little Pearl alone with Mr. Su's man. On impulse, she offered another pastry to the slave. Normally she would not think to do that, but she was tired and hungry. She could not eat and ignore him. That would be cruel.

And yet, she did not wish to eat with him as she had

with Jonas. So she offered him the pastry and did not serve herself, only belatedly realizing what she had done. She was serving a slave as if he were an honored guest.

The man was as disconcerted as she by the offer. He glared at the food as if he suspected poison. But in the end, he reached out and took the dumpling from her hand. But he didn't eat it. He cradled it close to his chest as if it were precious, and then he began speaking, his voice a low whisper. "I know the white devils are here. I know they tried to kill my master, and I know you are terribly afraid. I can help you. My master will be very grateful. Let us protect you."

She said nothing, her thoughts on her feet and her stomach. Both ached, but with different concerns. She dished up the last of the soup thinking she would take it to Jonas.

"The white captain's cargo has been released. He will leave you soon. Then who will protect you?"

Her hand froze and she nearly glanced at the storeroom, stopping herself just in time. But there were no such restrictions on her thoughts. Was it true? Would Jonas leave? She bit her lip, frightened now where she had not been before.

"Customs Official Chen is dead," continued the slave. "Poisoned by the white's cargo."

Little Pearl swung around, spilling the soup. She cursed under her breath, already reaching for a cloth.

"That is what happens with the white devils. They have a ghost miasma that poisons the air. It seeps into everything around them." Rat Face leaned closer. "Customs Official Chen didn't know that. He didn't understand the danger until his breath became blood. He lost control of his bowels and vomited. Then he choked to death on his own swollen tongue."

Little Pearl shuddered. It wasn't so much the words

used, but the way he said them. His voice was a low hiss of horror, and his eyes seemed to bulge out toward her.

"Mr. Su is powerful," he continued. "You have felt his yang, you know his qi. I am his slave. I have seen his secrets. He can save you from the white poison."

She said nothing as she set the bowl of soup aside. Then she grabbed the heavy pot and put it to the side to be cleaned—or so she tried. But when she lifted the pot, she pressed against the open sore on her palm. She cried out, letting go with her hurt hand. The pot tilted, banging hard against the stove.

The slave leaped backward and moaned. "See! It has already begun! Spilled soup and broken hands!"

She glared at him as she awkwardly righted the pot and set it on the floor. "I burned my hand, nothing more!"

He shook his head. "Idiot. Your luck has been poisoned. Can you not see it? Your master commerces with white devils and is now in jail, probably dead. You accept protection from them, and now your hand is burnt, your pot broken."

"The pot is not broken!"

"Are you sure? Sometimes the cracks are very tiny. But they grow until the food spills everywhere."

She didn't answer, only peered down at the pot. She liked the pot. It was sturdy with well-formed handles perfect for her hands. She would be very angry if it broke.

"Mr. Su has magics to save your luck."

"Mr. Su has a slave who speaks nonsense. Get out. Leave before I call the soldiers to beat you."

He nodded, scurrying backward as he went. He bowed, hunching over his pastry even as his eyes stayed trained on her. "We only seek to help. Ask Mr. Su. He will tell you of the ghost devils." He made it to the door, his bottom pushing it open as he slipped backward into the shadows. "Better yet, ask Custom Official Chen's widow."

The door swung shut, leaving Little Pearl alone with her pot. She didn't believe a word the slave had said. Superstitious nonsense! She was a tigress who understood energy. She had felt Jonas's yang. She knew he did not poison.

And yet, she went to the pot, inspecting it inside and out. She found the crack on the third pass. Her rational mind admitted that it could have been there for years. It wasn't really a crack, but an irregularity in the metal. She knew it couldn't possibly be because white people had poisoned her luck. And yet, she still wondered, and her heart beat triple fast with nervousness. Whites were strangers, newly come to China. No one knew for sure what effect their presence had on a person's qi.

"I have not hurt your pot," Jonas said.

She started in surprise. No, she mentally corrected herself; she had felt the subtle shift of energy in the room and had known when he came in. Her jump had not been due to surprise, but guilt.

"It is fear," he continued. "Simple fear and superstition make you think I have such power." He walked forward, gently taking the pot from her hands to set it on the ground. "I am just a man like any other. I don't have the power to poison luck or hurt pots or anything else. I—"

"You are not just a man." She bit her lip, her gaze sliding away from his face. "You are not like any other man I know."

He sighed, as if she confirmed what he had long suspected. "You have not known very nice men."

"There was one," she said, more to herself than to him. "There was one who was like you."

"What happened?" She heard an odd note in his voice, but didn't understand it. She looked at him and, when she didn't speak, he took her hands in his, drawing them to his lips. "I will not damn you, you know. I am a whore's son. I know what goes on. . . ." Then he shrugged. "Besides, I am not so holy that I can judge you or anyone else."

She believed him. A deep sadness resonated in his voice. "His name was Ken Jin."

"I know him. Kui Yu's adopted son."

"He was my first partner." She broke away and retrieved the pot to put it in its proper place for cleaning. "He was like you."

"Like me how?"

She didn't know. She wasn't sure exactly what she meant. "Kind."

She could tell he didn't understand. Except, maybe he did, because when she looked at him, he did not seem confused. Resigned, perhaps. With eyes that were soft with . . . pity?

"I tossed him aside!" she snapped. "I was cruel to him, and greedy, and I hate him!"

"Are you warning me?" Jonas asked, his eyes growing colder. "Are you cruel to every man who is nice to you?"

Yes. "Perhaps."

He nodded. "Then perhaps I will not be kind to you."

She laughed. It was not a nice sound. "You will not be able to stop yourself." And as she said the words, she knew they were true. Captain Jonas was a kind man. At heart, he was gentle and forgiving. And in return, she would poison him.

She stared once again at the pot, the horrible truth hitting her with enough force to make her eyes water. Sweet Buddha, it was not Jonas or any of his men who had warped this pot. It was herself—her luck and her qi. She was the poisoner. It was her fault that the Tans had been arrested. Her fault that Jonas had been beaten by the mob and that Master Su now slept inside the compound. She was responsible for all of it.

The realization stole her breath with its clarity, and yet somehow she had known all along. Why else would she have been sent away as a child? And only then had her family's fortunes prospered.

"Little Pearl? Little Pearl!"

She didn't respond to the panic in his voice. She didn't speak until she felt his hands touch her arms and his body slide close to hers.

She jerked away. "No! No touching!"

He froze, his hands lax enough that she could escape. She did, but reluctantly. "I wasn't looking for anything," he said gently. "You looked sick. I thought you might fall."

"I am a tigress. I do not fall unless I want to." It was an obvious lie. She had fallen many times this day and she had wished for none of it. "The soldiers will look for me soon."

"I will be nearby—"

"You will hide. If they find you, *I* will pay the price."

He folded his arms across his chest. There was no hesitation in his movement, but she was excruciatingly aware that he had to be at the end of his strength.

"There is a room next to the stillroom," she said. "Rest there."

He didn't respond. She knew he would not leave her. She could see it in his eyes and in his stance.

"You will hurt yourself," she warned. *I will hurt you.*

Still no answer. And then the soldiers came.

Sept. 2, 1892

To Father Bert,
    So, you have selected a reserved beauty for my bride? And we are to live in hallowed Yorkshire. You misun-

derstood my tastes. *A quiet woman spreads her thighs faster. I have no use of a good life on land. I am not finished with the sea.*

                            —CAPTAIN *Jonas*

P.S. I have a wedding gift of the most beautiful silk for your excellent bride, but I was so drunk, I forgot where I left it. Perhaps next time I am on leave.

A well-seasoned cast-iron or carbon-steel wok is a Chinese chef's most treasured utensil, for the more you use it, the more it becomes like a nonstick pan, requiring less and less oil for stir-frying. Be sure never to use a well-seasoned wok for steaming, as the water will strip the wok of its seasoning.

Chapter Twelve

Jonas closed his eyes in relief. The doctor was finally gone, all but one soldier had departed, and Little Pearl had set out the signal—an ornamental plant on a rock—that said there would be no classes tomorrow. He glanced at the sky. One bell before morning.

He watched her leave the front reception hall. He'd stayed near her all night long. He'd stayed and he'd watched and he'd been singularly useless. He wasn't in fighting condition. Hell, he was barely in watching condition. He was sitting on his ass in the dirt. If something happened in the front hallway, it would have taken two long minutes before he was near enough to do anything. In a battle, two minutes was an eternity.

Fortunately, Little Pearl hadn't needed his protection. She was strong and resilient and so damn afraid of believing in anything good that she had become a hardened shell of hostility that not even Mr. Su could break. Jones had seen it before. Whores often went one of two ways: so hard it took an ocean of love and an eon of pa-

tience to break through to them; or the way of his
mother, falling in and out of love with every breath,
every john, until the shifting emotional winds became
too much. She'd ended up dying of drink. It was a hard
life for those who sold their flesh—in China or in England. One he had escaped when he'd stepped on his
first clipper ship. He had no wish to enter into it again.
And yet . . .

His eyes drifted to where Little Pearl maneuvered
across the bizarre Chinese doorway. Who put a huge
board nearly knee-high in front of a person's feet? The
Chinese did, forcing every person to step over the obsta-
cle to enter or leave a building.

He knew the reason why. The Chinese believed that
ghosts hovered very low to the ground and the board
blocked them. To add to the stupidity, the Chinese believed that feet smaller than a nail were the height of
feminine beauty. So they crippled their women and
forced them to step over huge obstacles while hobbling
from room to room. Add a tight skirt, and daily life settled into farce.

Such was the life of a Chinese woman, and yet looking
at Little Pearl, he saw how strong these abused females
could be. Despite all obstacles, she moved with grace.
Her every act was poetry, even when she hauled about a
heavy cooking pot or shoved closed the massive front
door. She was stunningly beautiful even with her hard,
frightened soul.

He forced himself to stand, biting back a groan of
pain. His chest felt banded in agony and his shoulder
burned like the devil. How much worse was it for her on
her tiny feet? He narrowed his eyes, watching as she
turned away from the garden. She was going to the
kitchen, the place where she felt most in control. She
would putter there for a while, trying to decide what to
say to him. That gave him a little time. He would make it

to her bedroom before her. He'd found it earlier, made it his business to learn every room in this place even from his sickbed. Thankfully, sailors had lots of experience in finding hidey-holes and women's bedrooms. His men had reported everything accurately.

He pushed himself to move quicker. He wanted to at least glance into the kitchen to make sure it was secure. He slipped into the warm room and scanned it. No one about. Then he turned to leave—too late. She stepped into the room. They stared at each other across the kitchen, then she dropped her eyes and spoke to the floor. "All is safe now. You can rest."

"You, too."

She nodded. "I am very weary." Then she glanced up. "Have you found your bed? Do you need—"

"I found it. I'll be fine."

"Are you hungry? I can cook—"

"You need to rest, Little Pearl. I'm going to bed now."

She nodded but didn't move. "I just have to clean the pot first."

He knew it would be useless to argue. She didn't really want to clean the pot. That was a task for the kitchen girl. But she probably felt too anxious to sleep just then, too crowded by people and demands to quiet easily. He understood the feeling.

He bowed in his awkward English way. "I will leave you to it then." He turned for the door, but hesitated before going through. "Don't stay awake too long. You need sleep to keep your mind sharp."

He could tell she didn't understand his English phrasing. It didn't matter though, she was smart enough to decipher his meaning. Better yet, she was Chinese enough not to argue. She simply lowered her head in acknowledgment and lifted the pot to carry it outside to wash.

He nearly left then. He hadn't intended to stay when

he thought the pot was an excuse. But now he saw she truly intended to clean it. His gentlemanly spirit wouldn't let him leave her to it alone. Besides, who knew what might happen while she was out there sweating over her damned pot?

With a groan, he followed her outside. Water and soap for cleaning were all out there. She was halfway to the pump when he lifted the heavy iron from her hands. She gasped but said nothing. Then together they washed and scrubbed until the damn thing gleamed. After much too long, she determined their work acceptable. He didn't speak aloud as they brought the pot back inside, but he was able to arch a brow in question. *Time for bed?* he silently asked.

She dipped her head. *Yes.*

He held the door open for her. She maneuvered her way through. Then began a silent jostle for position; he kept trying to walk beside her, even extended his arm in a courtly gesture, but she just looked blankly at him. He sighed and let it drop to his side. But she would not walk beside him either, dropping behind as he stepped ahead.

These were tiny things between a man and a woman, he realized. Tiny customs of everyday life that reminded him how alien she was. No, he amended in his thoughts, he was the foreigner. She was in her own country. He walked past his room toward hers.

"No, Captain Jonas," she called from behind him. "Your room is—"

"I will make sure all is fine in your room before I rest."

"I will sleep nearby. There is no reason to fear...." Her voice trailed away as he climbed the stairs to her bedchamber. "How do you know I sleep up there?"

"I know." It wasn't an answer, but sometimes women— especially Chinese women—didn't press for a full explanation.

She climbed the stairs. He extended a hand to help her, and she hesitated. For a moment, he thought she would disdain his touch, but then she put her hand in his and allowed him to help her climb. But her nearness came at a cost. When they achieved the top step, she refused to release his hand, gripping him tightly as she held him close.

"How do you know my bedchamber is up here?" she asked.

He looked into her eyes and said the truth in bold flat tones. "I sent my men to find it."

She blinked, but did not pull away. "Why?"

"Because I want to know everything about you."

This time she did rear back, but he held her close. "But why?" she whispered.

He could have bantered with her. If he weren't so exhausted, if her dewy soft skin weren't gray beneath her lashes, if any of a dozen tiny details were different, then he could have flirted with her. But they were both dead on their feet. So rather than argue with her further, he chose the most efficient method of getting to bed.

"Don't scream," he said. Then he leaned down and scooped her up. The pull on his ribs made him groan, though she weighed next to nothing. She gasped in shock but thankfully made no other sound. The last thing either of them needed was for the soldier to come running. Three strides later, he maneuvered her into her bedroom and gently deposited her on the bed.

It was tempting—so incredibly tempting—to settle down beside her, but he refrained. Instead, he stepped back and wearily dropped to the floor. He'd already set up a crude mass of blankets there. Enough to cushion his head and keep him from getting chilled. It took the last of his strength to pull off his boots before gingerly settling onto his back.

"What are you doing?" Little Pearl cried.

"Getting comfortable," he lied. He was actually reliving the feel of her in his arms. Her slender body had felt so delicate, so womanly in all the right ways.

"But what are you doing . . . there?"

He sighed, not relishing another argument. His eyes were closed to better remember the feel of her breast against his chest, but he cracked them open now, looking at her as if what he did was absolutely normal. "I will not leave you alone. Not with Su here."

"He's unconscious."

"Not with that soldier here or debtors coming to the door."

"You will be discovered!"

He frowned. He hadn't considered that she might have a lover. "Is someone coming?"

"No!"

"Then no one will find me."

Her eyes darted about the room. "But . . ."

"I'm not leaving, Little Pearl. And neither are you."

It took her a moment to realize what he had said. Then her gaze flew to her packed satchel, fully hidden behind the privacy screen. He had seen it when he set up his bed, when he had done a cursory search of her room and learned that she had pitiful few belongings, a couple of badly hidden stashes of Chinese coins, and a packed satchel ready for her to run.

She stared at him, her mouth slack with shock. A moment later, she snapped it shut and stiffened her spine. "You misunderstand, ghost ape."

He grinned, not in the least offended. Now that he was finally lying down, he found a little more energy to banter. "I'm not saying it's a bad idea, Little Pearl, but you can't run right now. You're too tired and I still need you."

"For what?" she challenged, but he heard genuine confusion in her tone. "If I leave, then you could get the list and leave, too."

"Su would gain control of the entire household."

She didn't respond. He twisted from his position on the floor and saw her face dark with sadness. She knew the cost of defection. Then she sighed. "His yang is very strong. I thought he was dead."

Jonas nodded. So had he. He'd checked for a pulse. There hadn't been one. But then again, he'd been rushed, Little Pearl had been in shock, and . . . "I don't know how he survived," he admitted.

"Strong yang," she said. "And a tight blanket. You bound his wounds."

He frowned. He'd saved the man's life? He didn't know what to think about that.

"But he will probably still die," she continued. "The doctor said so."

Jonas was silent, mulling over the implications but finding himself too tired to think clearly. Then he heard her sigh, irritation clear in her body language.

"Come up here. Sleep on my bed."

He tried not to grin. He'd been lying on the hard floor waiting—praying—for just that invitation. How long should he resist? "I am fine here."

"I will not nurse you through a chill."

"It is a little cold down here," he admitted.

"Come up here. I will check your wounds."

"Are you sure? I will not throw you out of your own bed."

She cursed him, and he knew he had pushed her far enough. He gingerly rose onto his knees and crawled into her bed. She would have left him then; she was scrambling backward as his larger bulk descended upon her bed. But he pretended to stumble and quickly grabbed her arm to stabilize his position. His gasp of pain wasn't faked, and she was immediately concerned.

"Careful! You must go slowly. Let me help you."

She was helping more than she knew. Touching her brought new life into his mind and body. She gripped his arm to support him just as he allowed himself to tumble down into the mattress, taking her with him. A moment later, she was wrapped in his arm and he was nuzzling her. In truth, he hadn't intended so intimate an action, but her neck was right there, and she smelled so wonderful— soy sauce and ginger—that he couldn't stop.

"Captain Jonas! You will harm yourself!"

He smiled. She sounded like a Chinese schoolteacher.

"Captain Jonas!" More alarm this time. He eased back reluctantly.

"Rest with me, Little Pearl. I swear I won't attack. I just sleep better with you beside me." It was a ridiculous statement. They had only shared a bed once, and he'd been half dead. But he knew it would be true. She settled his spirit.

She sighed, and his arms expanded with the shift in her rib cage. "It is my qi," she said. "A tigress spends years purifying her energy. You may not understand it, but you must feel my clarity."

He nodded, as if that made sense. "I need you beside me."

"You need to make sure I do not run."

He shook his head, relaxing his hold on her. "I won't stop you, Little Pearl."

She stilled. "You will let me leave?"

"Of course." He let her digest that for a moment, then hit her with the truth. "But you won't leave."

She twisted so that they lay face to face. "What do you mean?"

He smiled, liking the view. She was close enough that

he could see the contours of her short Chinese nose. One of his sailors joked that Chinese doctors were so stupid they slapped the babies' faces instead of their bottoms, making the poor kids flat-nosed and ugly. What Jonas saw now wasn't ugly or flat. Without the hard eye ridge, Little Pearl's face was smooth and delicate. Without the protruding Roman nose, she looked adorable in the way of a porcelain doll. And yet she was alive, her expression shifting in subtle ways, creating a mystery that he had to explore.

Right now, that mystery was glaring at him, annoyed by his silence. "Why do you say I won't go? I am packed. I—"

"You're too loyal to leave," he said simply.

She hissed with startling vehemence. "I spit upon Confucius and his grave."

He frowned, not following.

"Confucius says a woman must be beautiful and chaste and loyal." She lifted her chin. "I am beautiful. The rest is as dust to me."

Jonas was surprised. What a strong reaction against the father of Chinese education, and the one text all women were taught. "Don't care much for womanly virtues?"

"I spit upon them." She screwed up her face but didn't follow through. Then she blinked, narrowing her eyes to look closely at him. "You are not shocked?"

He grinned. "I despise womanly virtues, myself."

Her eyes widened in real surprise. "Truly? Why?"

He sobered, his memories still holding some power over him. "A long time ago I loved a woman. She was as chaste and beautiful and loyal as any good Confucian bride."

"And she hated you on sight."

He shook his head. "No. She loved me, and I loved her."

She shifted slightly, her mouth ajar with shock. "You are married!"

"No. We never married."

She pulled away even farther, her outrage obvious. "You took her virginity and then abandoned her!"

He tightened his hold on her so that she wouldn't escape. "No, Little Pearl. I could have, but I didn't."

"But—"

"I'm the son of a whore. She wouldn't marry me."

Understanding settled on her face in the same way a beautiful mask is peeled away to show imperfections underneath. Her eyes pinched a bit, and her cheeks puffed then settled unevenly. Even her lips thinned and became less red. "My family was very wealthy," she said. "They had already picked my husband. He had broken teeth and smelled like rotten pork."

"Did you love someone else?"

"Yes," she said firmly. "Myself. When they brought him to the house, I kicked him and ran away." She lifted her chin. "He was too old to catch me."

"A clever escape," he said lightly.

Her expression smoothed. She was putting her mask back on, hiding her thoughts from him. He could have fought it. He could have pestered her with questions about how she'd started as a wealthy daughter and ended up a whore, but she would not tell him. Not yet. So he held his curiosity inside and watched her closely as her eyes slipped shut. She would be asleep soon, and he as well. But there was one more thing he had to say.

"We're going to sleep now, Little Pearl," he whispered. "We're both really tired."

She didn't speak, but he saw agreement in her eyes.

"Then later—after we've rested—I'm going to kiss you. I'm going to start with your face, then I'm going to kiss your breasts. I'm going to touch you everywhere, and then I'm going to spread your legs and put my dragon inside you. And then we're going to mix, you and I. We're going to share our yin and yang together. Tomorrow morning."

He used her strange tigress phrases so there would be no misunderstanding. He intended to make love to her as soon as she was rested, because that was what a man did with a beautiful woman in his bed. He didn't allow himself to think beyond that. He only knew a primal need to claim her in the most basic of ways. In truth, the coupling had been inevitable since she fought an entire mob to save his life. Since she meditated herself to orgasm by his side. And most especially, since he had watched her juggle soldiers and sailors and slaves with amazing grace and skill.

The more she had grown in his esteem, the more his desire had multiplied. He wanted her for his own, and he would not deny himself. Not when she lay sweet and pliant in bed beside him. "I want you more than I want my next breath," he whispered, stunned that he spoke the truth.

Her face didn't change, but her mouth opened and soft words drifted out as if on a purr. "Tigresses don't allow dragons to sport in their caves."

"This dragon will."

Her eyelashes lowered. Their faces were too close together for her to see his thickening organ, but he had the feeling she was measuring it anyway. "Very well," she finally said.

He frowned, wondering at her response. "You will allow it?"

Her gaze leaped to his face. "I can refuse you?"

He swallowed, needing to be honest. "I do not know if I can stop myself, Little Pearl. I do not—"

"I can stop you." No doubt showed in her voice. "All whores know how to hurt a man."

"I am not using you as a whore. I am not a customer, you are not my cunt."

Confusion flickered in her eyes. He had used the English word—as crude as he could possibly be—because that was his intent. And yet, he hadn't wanted to say such a thing in her presence. He cursed under his breath. What was he trying to say? "I want to make love to you."

She shifted, lifting her fingers to his lips. She lingered there, a single delicate caress as she outlined his mouth. "The texts say a great deal about dragons and tigresses. They talk about all different states of arousal and release, about health and sickness, vital and impoverished. Never do they mention this 'making love'."

"It is what we English do, Little Pearl. We make love."

She shook her head. "I do not think all Englishmen do this—"

"It is what *I* do," he responded. "It is what *we* will do."

She was silent a moment longer, her thoughts reflected in her eyes, but not in any clear fashion. He didn't know what she was thinking, and he found himself increasingly nervous the longer she remained silent. Finally, she nodded. "I will explore this with you, Captain Jonas. I will make love with you."

He blinked, hardly daring to believe. "You will?"

"I will. And the loss of your yang will kill you, and it will be your own fault." Then she closed her eyes.

His lips curved into a smile. "I'm not going to die."

"You will," she said without opening her eyes. "I will poison your qi and you will die. I will not cry. Good night." Then she rolled onto her other side and went to sleep.

He watched her in silence, wondering at her words and her actions. He watched her breath settle into a rhythmic pattern, while his John Thomas stiffened at the press of her bottom against him. And in time, he realized the truth: he *was* going to make love, and to a whore. Not rut like an animal with her, not diddle with a woman for the sake of entertainment, not even explore the forbidden fruits of an exotic Chinese woman. He was going to make love with Little Pearl as he would a wife. Her words to the contrary, he knew very soon he would worship her, pleasure her, and express every aspect of a deeper emotion—as if he were in love with her.

He shouldn't have lied to her like that. He knew nothing about making love with a woman. He knew none of the tender emotions or how they could possibly relate to the sexual act. But women liked such false words of adoration. His mother had thrived on them. Could he treat Little Pearl this way merely to get between her thighs?

He could, because he was a weak man steeped in depravity long before he met Little Pearl. Yes, he would indeed lie to her. He would ease his organ inside her and feel the power of a tigress. And then, after he got what he needed from her, he would board his ship and leave. Little Pearl would be nothing more than a sweet memory to him. And she . . . she would go on to service other customers.

His thoughts settled badly, making him restless while Little Pearl slept peacefully in his arms. Damn, his ribs ached and his shoulder burned like hellfire. Maybe he wouldn't even be able to perform. Maybe his organ would remain shriveled and cold because of his injuries.

But, no. He'd been a great deal sicker yesterday, and he'd been ready to rut then. No injury would keep him from between her thighs. She was his. Nothing would keep them apart tomorrow, not even his guilty conscience. His eyes drifted shut. Nothing but God Himself . . .

Then the nightmare began.

Feb. 5, 1893

Dear Albert,
    I'm sorry, Little Runt. No matter how long you wear the collar, I will never be able to call you "father."

I have been thinking a great deal of you lately. Not your sermonizing, my brother, so don't sing any hallelujahs on my account. I will never join you on land, shackled to a plow or counting coins in a dingy room. Indeed, I am now a ship's captain in name and ownership. Old Hory has died and left me his fleet.

Two ships, little brother! I own two clippers, one as sweet and fast a runner as you could imagine, the other old enough to be scrapped, but mine nevertheless. I shall refit her soon and rename her The Auspicious Wind. *A strange name for a ship, I know, but my Chinaman partner recommended it. He has all sorts of heathen ideas, but he makes sound business decisions. Together we shall make a fortune on silks and whiskey. The Chinese have an abundance of one and a thirst for the other. And even if they didn't, the Englishmen in China certainly do. If one stays to the treaty ports— and why venture elsewhere when the greatest whores on Earth reside here?—then all is safe and easy. Riches, Little Runt. Enough to educate my nephew and namesake.*

And here we come full circle. I drink and debauch with the best of them. Brother, your letters are tedious sermons on the glories of sheep husbandry and accounting houses, of the church's blessing and Jesus's redemption. I have no need for your Heaven.

So why, brother, did you name your son Jonas? Do you try to replace the sad memory of me with a fresh baby boy? Do not so curse the child. Do not lay your tripe day after day on a child who has no need for your reproach and no wish for anything but your most wholesome love.

I fear this letter will arrive too late. You will have baptized the boy in water and lace, and already the biddies whisper in his ear: Do not turn out like your uncle. Do not grow to love the wind and the water, to carve a place in the world that is your own.

Why, Albert? Why would you curse your own son with such a fate? Ah well, you will do as you wish. You always have.

My mates and I have toasted young Jonas. And the sweet whore who eased my ache called my new nephew the luckiest child alive.

—Captain Jonas

According to ancient Chinese custom, every thought and deed at New Year's determines the outcome of the entire year. Optimism and a positive mood and demeanor ensure blessings, while anger and negativity obstruct the possibility of noteworthy aspirations.

Chapter Thirteen

Bodies, hot and sweaty. The wet slide that sends shivers up the spine, that encompasses the entire mind, that was and is and always will be completely wonderful; Jonas felt it and grinned, the sensations blurring into disconnected pieces that floated about his consciousness.

His hands fumbled with something—a breast, a leg, a cunny—he didn't know. He smelled musk and the sharp bite of pain. He tasted sweet and hot rasping breaths—bile, blood, woman? Nothing sharpened into focus, nothing upset the cloud of giggles and grunts, of bodies in movement.

Nothing upset it and nothing penetrated it—not grief, not loneliness, not even fear or hope or love. This was emptiness in the sweetest package, sensations devoid of meaning, bliss surrounded in muting emptiness.

He erupted, his sperm disgorging with a pleasure that saturated his body but not his soul. He screamed but heard giggles. He roared and tasted stale water. Smoke filtered through his thoughts and he gripped a woman's hips.

"Again," he said.

He moved, perhaps. Again came the slide of flesh that shivered through his skin. This time, it would be better. This time he would feel it. He *did* feel it. It felt yellow, dark, and black hot. The thought did not connect as logical, and he laughed because her hair was in his face. Pain bit from his backside, but the sensation floated away. Had he erupted again? Did he feel it? Hot smoke burnt his tongue. Something soft and spongy pressed against his hand. He tried to squeeze but his body didn't respond.

The fog thickened and he couldn't breathe.

Was this pleasure? Was there pain?

Hot. Wet.

Bodies slid. Again and again. Did he erupt? Did he care?

So hot.

Did he erupt?

He screamed.

Did he scream?

Why?

Little Pearl woke when Jonas's qi shifted. Sometime in the night she had twisted to face him. In the predawn darkness, she could see very little of his face, but she knew he was dreaming. She heard his breath shorten with panic, felt his hand twitch across her back, and knew his spirit was rippling with anxiety.

She remained quiet, putting her silence into her energy, using her stillness to ease his. She didn't dare wake him. She had no idea what would happen to a ghost person with an agitated spirit. Would startling him awake be enough to break the cord that bound ghost to body? That would kill him. So she put power into her qi and hoped it was enough.

It wasn't.

His yin and yang energies were at war, his qi convulsing with the fight. She extended her hand to touch the hot skin above his chest. Sometimes that helped. Not that she'd had any experience with energies this turbulent, but she had heard of such things. She felt his heart banging beneath her fingertips, the rapid pulse reminding her of a frightened puppy she'd held as a child. She wouldn't be able to restrain Jonas the way she had the dog. Did she need to leave his arms? Was she in danger?

Of course she was. Nothing involving a white man was safe, especially for a woman. But she didn't abandon him. He had stayed by her side all last night; she wouldn't run from him now. His breath was coming faster, a scream building in his chest. His legs moved restlessly, shifting over hers to pin her down. She didn't fight it, though her own breath shortened in fear.

"Jonas." She spoke softly. "Jonas, wake up."

His dragon was thick and heavy, she noticed. His yang churned hot against her thigh, but not with healthy power. His rod was not hard and the dragon head tilted to the left. His hips began to move against her, his dragon pushing and seeking, but with a disjointed tempo. One moment would be a hard push, then next was a weak sideways shift accompanied by a whimper. And still his eyes remained firmly shut.

"Jonas," she said louder. "You must wake. This is an unhealthy dream." Beneath her fingertips, his chest was growing chill, the skin slick with sweat. She slid her fingers to his shoulder and gripped him hard. "Jonas!"

He cried out, his voice high-pitched and keening. Then his eyes flew open, but they didn't focus. They rolled bizarrely in his head. No, his eyes didn't roll, but he did, and she with him. He came up on top of her, pressing her into the mattress while his dragon twisted between them. It was still only half-alive, but the heat was intense as it burned against her belly.

"Jonas!" She gasped, struggling to keep calm. Only a quiet heart could settle a spirit in turmoil. She knew that, but he was so heavy. Her breath caught in her throat as she bared her teeth. "Jonas, stop!"

He hadn't the strength to hurt her—not physically at least. She'd already worked her hand to his ribs and was ready to punch him there. A shove against his weak shoulder would topple him. And his dragon was not hard enough to penetrate her. She was safe. And yet, he frightened her. She had never felt energies so chaotic. They were infecting her, making her hands weak and her mind confused. This had to end. Now.

"Jonas!" she bellowed. "Wake up!"

He froze. She thought at first that she had killed him, that she'd startled his spirit away and now he was about to topple, a corpse on top of her. Tears blurred her vision. She raised her hand from his shoulder to touch his cheek to better feel the warmth as it left his body.

It was that caress that woke him. His eyes riveted to her arm, then slowly raised to her face. He frowned at her, and she felt his energy still—not in quietness but in a sudden cessation of war. All was frozen.

She knew the moment he recognized her. His eyes widened and his gaze took in her face, the bed, and his position so heavily atop her. Then his mouth opened and she expected a roar—a full-throated release of anger and fury—but nothing came out except the tiniest puff of air. It was hot and brief and cut off by a gasp.

In one lithe movement, he rolled off of her and curled into a ball. He pulled his knees in tight to his chest and gripped them with his arms. It had to strain his ribs and shoulder, but he made no sound. She watched as the corded tendons in his neck bulged, and his strength curled in against himself. She had never seen such a thing before. What man fought himself? Who allowed yin and yang to war within one's own spirit? "Jonas?"

"I'm sorry. I am so sorry." His words were mumbled, and she heard agony in his tone.

"I don't understand," she said.

"I hurt you."

He had coiled into the wall, pressing his knees and forehead against it with his back to her. She reached out to touch his shoulder, but he flinched away.

"You didn't hurt me, Jonas. You did nothing."

"I hurt you."

"No, Jonas. You didn't."

"I hurt . . ." His words stopped. Then he took a deep breath, his chest and body visibly expanding with the motion. His rational mind was gaining control, and she didn't know if that was for good or ill. Something important had happened and she did not want him to tuck it away before she understood what.

"We were sleeping, Jonas. And in sleep, my energy opened yours." She wasn't sure what she was saying. It had no basis in the sacred texts, but the words flowed anyway and she did not fight them. "Tell me what poisons your qi."

He shook his head. "I don't understand."

Neither did she, but she would not confess that to him. "What was your dream?"

He shuddered, and she knew his body was trying to throw off the evil energies. She let him shake, then settled her hand on his arm as soon as he was done. This time, he didn't fight her. Could be he couldn't feel it with his eyes squeezed shut and his body coiled so tight.

"Jonas?" she pressed when he didn't speak.

"A dream?" he asked.

"Yes—" she began, but he interrupted.

"A memory. A reminder." His body stiffened. "A vile horror." He turned and looked at her and hatred flowed from his body into hers. "China poisons me."

She didn't answer. There was nothing to say to such black qi except to let it escape. And yet there seemed to be no end to it as he turned from her to stare at the wall.

"It is not China that hurts you, Jonas. Tell me about the dream."

"It was not a dream!" he snapped, and then he growled at his knees.

She bit her lip, wondering what to do. Her training was no help. At best, all she could do was wrap her body around him and pray that her qi settled his.

"Don't touch me," he whispered. "I will hurt you."

"No," she said as she pressed her chest to his back. "No, you won't. Right now, I am stronger than you."

He laughed, the sound bitter and cold. But it faded as she worked her hand beneath his arm and around his chest. In her mind, she surrounded him with her energy, wrapping it around his entire body except for where his mouth was. She left that place open so that the ugliness could escape.

"What poisons you, Jonas?"

"Shanghai is an evil place, Little Pearl."

"Not everywhere. Not here."

He shrugged his shoulder, trying to shove her away. But it was his injured arm and he hissed in pain.

"You took in a poison, Jonas. It happened without your knowledge or consent, but it slipped inside and now sickens your spirit." She tightened her grip on him. "It set your energies at war within you. In time, it will kill you."

He fought her for a moment longer. She felt the struggle within him in the flickering, chaotic motion of his body. And then she felt him surrender, the blackness at last beginning to flow from his mouth.

"I knew, Little Pearl. I knew and I took it in anyway."

"What was it?"

"Opium. And rum. And whatever else the whores had with them. I took it and did it and I don't even remember any of it. But I knew then what I was doing, and I chose it anyway."

She nodded, having already come to that conclusion

herself. She knew of no white sailor who escaped the pleasure gardens. All succumbed to the lure of whores and their drugs at some point. "But that is not the root," she said. "It is merely a branch of the tree. What poison took root in your spirit, Jonas?"

He had no answer for her. The evil was embedded too deep for him to see. So it was up to her to find the truth. "Tell me about the dream, Jonas."

He closed his eyes, a shudder wracking his frame. "We went to the Palace of Sweet Blossoms for a New Year's celebration. It was many years ago. Kui Yu and I had just started working together, but he was busy and I was flush with cash." He released a harsh laugh. "We were celebrating New Year's, a good sale of cargo, and a full hold to take back to England—silks and paper fans to sell for a fortune."

She set her chin against his arm, resting there while he spoke. It was hard to concentrate on clearing his qi while hearing his words, and in the end she abandoned her tigress focus. She wanted to be with him, not work his energy. She rubbed her cheek lightly against his shoulder. "What happened?"

He sighed, his body slumping with defeat. "Everything. We ate. We drank. We whored. All of us."

"How many?"

He shook his head. "I don't remember. It was a large room. We paid the madame for the whole place, the whole night."

"But something happened. Something gave you the nightmare."

"I don't remember the night. Not really."

He curled away from her. She tightened her grip so he couldn't go. But he was stronger, and her hand slipped a little.

"Little Pearl," he said, his voice breaking. "I can't tell you."

She pressed a kiss into his shoulder. It was a bizarre gesture for her. She never kissed, and not like this; with no intent except because she wished to touch his skin with her lips. And while she was still mulling over her strange action, she whispered into him. "Whatever it is, Jonas, I have done worse. I have been worse. You cannot think to frighten me."

He twisted, turning in her arms to stare at her. They lay face to face and in his eyes she saw fathoms of darkness, a bleak emptiness that she recognized. It was another strange thought in a night of strangeness, but there it was. Something in her spirit knew the darkness in him.

"She was my mother," he whispered.

She blinked. "What?"

"The whore." He grimaced. "She wasn't truly my mother. She was a Chinese woman of about the same age, same build. But that morning when I woke . . . I was disoriented with a sore head and a putrid throat. I wasn't thinking. I just turned in my sleep, and I saw her: sagging breasts, weak legs, painted groin. I thought—for a moment—that I was looking at my mother. I thought . . ." He swallowed.

"You thought you had been with your mother."

He nodded, his expression horrified.

"But she wasn't your mother. She wasn't—"

"It doesn't matter. Don't you see? I was a john. I was one of those men who grunted like pigs between her thighs. Who sweated and growled and rooted at my mother's teats then left with a curse. I was one of them."

She looked at his face, seeing his agony but not fully understanding it. Her hand had slid to his elbow, but she drew it higher now, gently touching his face. She felt the coarse scrape of his beard, but also noted the cooling touch of his skin as his unnatural yang began to drain away. "You were a john," she finally said, knowing she spoke the English word awkwardly. "But that is the nature of men and . . . and yang donation."

He shook his head. "No. Not me. Not ever."

There she saw the root of what poisoned his soul. It stemmed from his mother, from the unhealthy atmosphere that pervaded the pleasure gardens and the nail shacks. He had traveled the length of the world to escape it, only to find the exact same places in Shanghai. It chained his spirit and destroyed his qi.

She closed her eyes, breathing deeply of his scent and his warmth. His yang still burned hot, but not blisteringly, and she smiled as she simply enjoyed his presence. But eventually she knew she had to speak. It was time for him to learn as she had.

"It was hard for me to leave the pleasure garden," she said. "I hated it there, but it was what I knew. I sweated and toiled everyday, hoarding my coins until I could buy my way free, and still it was hard for me to leave. I would still be there if it weren't for Mistress Tan."

"Tan Shi Po? Kui Yu's wife?" Surprise colored his words and opened up his body enough for her to burrow even deeper into his embrace.

"She taught me the way of the tigress, the way of sex that is not animals wallowing in the mud. The way of power that will lead to Heaven and Immortality."

He blinked, then his expression gentled into pity. "You don't really believe that, do you? This religion of yours is . . ." His words faded off in in embarrassment.

"You think it is a lie, a clever turn of phrase to hide a whorehouse."

He held her gaze, clearly reluctant to answer. But she allowed him no escape, and in the end he nodded. "Sex leads to despair, Little Pearl. It is nothing but emptiness." He paused and his hand caressed her arm. The movement was slow and intentional. He wanted to touch her, to stroke her. "When I see you . . . touch you, I . . ." His words faded on a sigh. "I forget, Little Pearl. I look at you and I want you, and I forget that sex leads to emptiness." He lifted his hand away from her. "I forgot before," he said firmly. "But now I remember."

She smiled, pulling on her role as a tigress instructor as she began her first speech to new cubs. She said what she always did with passion and strength, though inside her spirit trembled. Did he lie? Or did she?

"Sex such as you experienced is a draining of energy—yang spilled like precious milk upon the floor. But what if you could catch that milk, drink it up, and use it to power your spirit's flight? What if enough milk would give you wings to fly to Heaven?"

"Then we would have shrines to whores throughout the world."

She smiled and leaned forward, touching a kiss to his lips. She did so as a tigress, and yet she also felt a glimmer of something else: a hope that what she said was true. A prayer that this time, with this man, it would be different. Her own qi was unbalanced and had been for some time. That was the source of her poison that imprisoned the Tans, that blemished her pot, and set her to stab Mr. Su then have him recuperate inside her home. She was unbalanced and she desperately needed a partner to help her stabilize her energies. She thought perhaps this white man could do that for her, and she for him. "We can help each other, Jonas. We can balance one another as tigress and dragon."

"As a whore and her customer?"

Her spirit hardened in anger. "Do not call me a whore again."

He snapped his mouth shut and his gaze slid down to the sheet. "I apologize—"

"Hush. You speak in ignorance. Do you wish to learn?"

His gaze lifted to her face. "The way of the tigress?"

"The men are called dragons."

He frowned. "I thought the . . . That my . . ."

"That is also the name of your organ. Yes."

He laughed, and the sound was not as dark as before. "I will not be called by my cock. It does not define me."

"Have you touched a woman since that night? Have you sought release or attention since you woke and thought you saw your mother?"

He blanched, and a flash of anger sparked in his eyes. "You touched me!"

She nodded, unable to flee from his accusation. "Yes, I did. But have you sought a woman since then? Have you—"

"No! I will not become another piglet in search of a teat!"

"Then you are defined by your . . . cock." The English word felt harsh on her tongue, like a grunt released in anger.

He shook his head. "No. That's not—"

"Choose," she snapped. She had not intended to react so harshly, but his frustration angered her. "Ignorance or education, ghost man, which do you want?"

He stared at her, the darkness in his eyes boiling within him. She felt his yang surge—hot and ugly—and she instinctively retreated. But they were intimately entwined and he held her still before she could go far. "I told you we would make love this morning," he rasped.

"You lied."

He reared back, obviously stunned that she had read him so clearly.

"There is no love inside you. There is only poison poured into you from the moment your mother conceived you in commerce."

"You don't know that!" he bellowed.

She didn't answer out loud; she merely stared at him while mentally opening her energy to him. She knew what poison grew inside him. She understood the evils of sex in commerce. She lived every day to uproot the horror, to dig out the sickness.

They continued to stare at one another, and then slowly, gently, she reached up to touch his mouth. Her energy still surrounded him, still supported all but his mouth so that the unhealthy humors could escape. But now she touched his lips, trying to stroke her strength into him.

"I know," she whispered. "Will you learn what I can teach?"

"The way of the tigress?" He sneered.

"Yes." She frowned, trying to find the right words. "I know that since I became a tigress, the poison in my spirit lessens. I am not as angry as before. Not as afraid." She did not add that she felt the same things with him: less angry, less afraid. It was yet another reason she guessed that they should become partners. "The tigress practice calms the spirit. And when we exchange energy—your yang and my yin—all becomes balanced and whole."

"And we exchange this energy during sex?" His tone made it sound laughable.

"Can you think of a more intimate process? A better way to join two people, body and spirit, together?"

Silence grew in the room, filling the small space with all the ugly humors of yin/yang imbalance. She felt anger, frustration, hatred, even bone-deep sadness roil through the air and pulse in the room. Then it began to fade. Eventually the emotions cleared, the darkness quieted, leaving behind a man who quivered beneath her fingertips.

"You believe this?" he asked, his voice barely audible.

"I *hope* it is true."

She didn't know why she answered honestly, but the words escaped too fast for her to call them back.

"You don't know?"

She bit her lip. "Two people have found Immortality—one white woman and her Chinese dragon. And there are rumors of another pair—another white woman and her Imperial lover."

He grimaced. "Rumors."

"I believe them."

He stared hard at her, his gaze both searching and uncompromising. She understood why. He was both hopeful and afraid as well. Could he believe enough to set aside his pride to try? Could she?

"You are not certain," he accused.

She lifted her chin and forced faith into her heart. "I do believe. I am a tigress."

His lips curved in a slight smile. "Now that is very true. You are definitely a tigress."

She hesitated, unsure what he meant.

"Very well," he finally said. "I will try this path of the . . . the dragon." His lips lifted again, his smile growing wider and—perversely—more bitter. "After all, I'm already damned by my God. Why not try yours?"

"You must discard all your preconceptions. You cannot think of sex as you have known it before. Every action must be deliberate and absolutely different than it was before."

"Sex with intent." He shook his head. "That's not—"

"Not sex!" she snapped. "An exchange of energy. I give you my yin. You give me your yang. Together, we mix the energy in the cauldron of our spirit and . . ." She was losing him. Her words meant nothing to him, the imagery alien and distracting. "Never mind," she said. "We begin in this manner. Sit up and face me. Spread your legs so that our pleasure centers are near but do not touch."

She demonstrated the position, then helped him straighten. Because of his injuries, he would lean against the wall and she would face him. He began to move into position but she stopped him.

"You must be naked, Jonas."

He blinked, then flushed. She waited in silence to see if he would fully commit to this action. Many men refused to be that naked before a woman. But he merely shrugged, stripping out of his clothes with a sigh of relief. She mirrored his movements, quickly pulling off blouse and skirt, even unwrapping her foot bindings before she knelt on the bed.

"Like this?" he asked.

She nodded as she looked at him, his back pressed against the wall, his legs spread open in a narrow V. "Place a cushion behind your back. You must give me enough room to set my legs behind you."

He did as instructed, and she again mirrored his actions. She settled on the bed between his thighs, opening her legs wide, then draping them over and around him. Her cinnabar cave was chilled by the air, dry as a bone. Similarly, his dragon was small and weak, huddled back against its pearls. She straightened her back and faced him eye to eye.

"Now we begin."

June 9, 1893

Dear Pastor Bert—Albert,

My hand shakes as I write this. It was a simple thing, little brother. Load the cargo, then enjoy one last night in port. You would call it debauchery and tell me my soul is damned for it. For the first time, I think you are right.

My cargo is lost. All of it gone and for the stupidest reason of all. I did not supervise the loading. I wished to spend one last night . . . You know what I was doing. Indeed, all my crew, all sailors enjoy their leave. What else can you do when in port? We are here for so short a time, then gone. We work hard. We deserve our leisure. We deserve it.

Perhaps that is true of all sailors, but not for the captain. I did not supervise the loading of the cargo. I left it to my first mate who left it to another. It was stacked stupidly. The silk was on the bottom where it got fouled by seawater. The paper fans were on top where the netting was secured badly. Those crates fell, breaking the fragile wood and wetting the paper.

I have done what I can to salvage the voyage. I have rescued what little remains, have disciplined the sailors responsible, and spent hours teaching all on board the correct loading of cargo. But who will punish me? Who will see that I learn my lesson? You and God. And every sailor who will gain nothing from their months of labor at sea. There will be no shares from this voyage, no coin for any of us. So, Pastor Bert, I beg you, name my punishment and the means of atonement. I suffer without your guidance.

I will be at my usual rooms in London for at least two months. There is much work to do on the ship before she can sail again. Come see me if you can. I long to speak with you again.

—Captain Jonas

From the Chinese perspective, to be a whole person one must have a good start and a happy ending in all aspects of life, and eating a whole fish is the epitome of this sentiment. A whole chicken also symbolizes a proper beginning and end to the year and the wholeness of life on earth.

Chapter Fourteen

"We must excite our energies," Little Pearl said, wondering why her heart was beating so fast. She had done this dozens of times, alone or with a partner. This was no different. "We must touch one another," she lied. In truth, sometimes it worked better if each partner excited him or herself. But she did not want to do that with him. She wanted to feel his white hands on her breasts. She wanted to watch as his thick knuckles pressed into the folds of her pleasure grotto.

She glanced at his face, and guilt made her confess. Partners had to be honest with one another. "Unless you wish to stroke yourself. Sometimes it—"

"No! No. I . . . I will touch you." He lifted his hands but hesitated, his fingers hovering in the air before her. "Is there a special way? Like your circles the other—"

"However you will." Then she suited words to action, knowing he would not start before her. She extended her hand and touched the very tip of his dragon.

He jumped backward, knocking his head against the

wall. She pulled back, uncertain while his breath came in unsteady gasps. "Sorry," he mumbled. "I'm just not ready."

Her hands dropped to her lap. "One of us must start."

"Let me. I will begin. You . . . you wait."

"As you wish," she answered. She folded her hands quietly in her lap, knowing she covered her cinnabar cave with the motion. He would have to start with her breasts. Then she straightened her spine, closed her eyes, and attempted to slow the rapid tremble of her pulse. "I am ready," she lied.

She was excruciatingly aware of her breasts. She tried not to move, but that made her breath too shallow and she grew light-headed. When would he touch her? How would he—

His fingers brushed her lips. She started in reaction, her thoughts scattering.

He froze. "I . . ." he began. "Is this wrong? Should I—"

"There is no right or wrong," she snapped. "Just do it!"

"Sorry," he mumbled, and her eyes opened again.

"No, I am sorry. It seems I am a skittish tigress today."

His head tilted sideways, a strange light coming into his eyes. "Are you nervous? Is that unusual?"

She nodded. "Yes. And yes."

He grinned. "Good." He gave no more explanation, and she did not pursue it as he abruptly widened his fingers and burrowed deeply into her hair. She had few pins left there, so her loose bun quickly tumbled free. The strands fell to her back, and she arched into the tickle, loving the sensuous slide of hair across her shoulders and back.

Jonas didn't say a word, but she heard his breath quicken and, when she looked, she saw his gaze riveted to the sway of her hair. She accentuated the movement, lifting her breasts, letting her hair shimmer in the weak predawn light. He extended a hand and stroked his fin-

gers through the strands. Then he raised a handful only
to let it slip free. More minutes were spent in play as he
combed her hair, draped it around her shoulders, even
tried to pile it on top of her head, then laughed as it fell
back down.

When she thought he was gathering more hair, he
abruptly tugged her forward and pulled her lips to his.
She stiffened in shock, and he immediately froze. Embarrassed, she pushed forward toward him, but he
pulled back with a question.

"Something wrong?" he asked.

She shook her head. "I was just surprised. I haven't
kissed anyone—not on the mouth—in a very long time."

His lips curved into a pleased grin. "Tell me more
things that you haven't done."

She blinked, trying to think. "I haven't spent a morning outside the kitchen since I came to the Tan home."

He paused a moment. "You are sure no one will come?
No one will interrupt us?"

She shook her head. "None. Morning classes are can-
celled, the servants stay away until called, and the soldier sits with Mr. Su. Even the kitchen girl will sleep the
whole day if I let her."

"Excellent." Then he closed the last distance between
their lips.

White men's mouths were different. That was her
thought as they finally met. His lips were fuller, the texture rougher, and—most wonderful—they moved and
teased and brought her into full awareness of her mouth.
She began as usual, noticing his technique, analyzing
how he worked. But this was not work to him. He was
not a trained jade dragon, but an enthusiastic green one.
To him, this was all new and joyous, and his fascination
created hers.

He pressed closer, his mouth opened further, and his
tongue pushed through to meet hers. In practice, every

act was supposed to be deliberate, every caress a thoughtful step. But this was done in exuberance, and Little Pearl didn't want to change it. She opened to his assault and found herself meeting him with her own glee.

She knew what to do now. As a tigress, she had a multitude of techniques at her command: rhythmic sucking, pushing and pulling, swirling and biting. She must use them. They were too ingrained in her to avoid. But she lost the conscious decision aspect of this encounter. Her focus dissolved into enjoyment without distraction or control. *Presence.* That was the Buddhist term for it. She was fully and totally present for his lips, his mouth, his tongue. And long minutes were spent in the very wonder of it all.

He broke away to breathe. He lifted from her to drag in huge gulps of air, but his eyes remained trained on her. She met his gaze with a wide stare, only now realizing they no longer faced each other. She was draped across his lap, her hair caught against his arm. Her hands gripped his shoulders, lifting with his inhalations, rippling with the shift of his large muscles.

"My yin flows," she whispered, amazed at how quickly the cauldron had heated. Even her lips were hot and full. His yang flowed, too, she noticed, for his dragon stood proud.

"Do all tigresses kiss like that?"

She shook her head. "None. Is it because you are white? Do all—"

"No. Only you. Only now."

Her mind filtered through possible explanations. Was it an auspicious day for religious applications? Had she received blessing for service? Was this his luck that spilled onto her?

"I want to make love with you now," he rasped. And as he spoke, his hands dropped to her thighs. "And I want to kiss you again." His fingers twitched, narrowing around her hips.

She straightened, returning to her seated position, but her thoughts remained on the warmth of his hands, the pressure against her hip bones, and the way he skimmed across her belly now and up to her ribs. A bare breath farther and his hands would hold her breasts. But he stopped and she found herself unwilling to breathe because it would lift her nipples away from him.

She should direct him. He was looking at her breasts and farther down to her flushed tigress tattoo. He was clearly waiting for her instruction, but her mind was too blank to answer. She opened her mouth to speak, but no sound emerged. Then when he lifted his gaze, he made it no farther than her parted lips. He moved toward her and she met him without conscious volition. Their lips connected at the same moment his hands found her breasts.

"Circles," he gasped into her mouth. "Am I supposed to make circles?"

She answered by circling his tongue with hers. She heard his groan as he made an attempt with his hands. He narrowed his fingers and rubbed in a circle, but the movement was jerky, the pressure too firm, and his hands slipped open so that he moved her entire breasts in a circle. It was the wrong technique, wrong motion—and yet she sighed in delight.

She tried to help him, to show him the proper method. She dropped her hands to his chest but got distracted by the rough tickle of his hair. Soft, springy hair against her palms, it made her feather her fingers in delight, then burrow deeper to explore the quivering tension in his muscles beneath. What strength he had, not only in physical power, but also in the energy that pulsed through his body.

He pinched her nipples. She gasped as lightning sizzled through her chest straight down to her yin center. And all the while, their mouths were playing with each other. He thrust as she nipped. He caressed the roof of her mouth while she teased the underside of his tongue.

Then the tenor of his hold changed. Instead of twisting her nipples, he flattened his hands and pushed her sideways toward the mattress. She had shifted her own hands to run a nail over his nipples. As he tried to tug her down, she ran her hands around his sides. His chest hair ended and she felt smooth flesh and the occasional ridge of a scar.

"Lie down," he urged.

"You."

"What?"

She narrowed her hands against his ribs and pushed. "*You* lie down."

He paused a moment, pulling back far enough to look into her eyes. "Side by side, then."

She frowned, startled by his suggestion. She knew of no untrained Chinese man who would think of such a thing. "You are very strange," she said.

He grinned. "So are you." And then, with an abrupt push, he toppled her to the mattress. He followed a moment later so that they lay face to face, their legs entwined.

"Very nice," he said as he ducked his head to her breasts. He kept hold of her left one, his hand large enough to encompass the whole. The other breast was for his mouth, and he struggled to reach it from his position.

She felt his lips first, wonderfully mobile as he pressed the very, very tip. But he was not quite close enough, and she slipped free, the nipple rolling slightly as it escaped.

He tucked his head a little more and she felt the scrape of his beard. Then his mouth sought her nipple again, this time capturing the tightened bud but unable to draw it further inside. He rolled his jaw then, twisting her left and right while his tongue wetted her tip. And then he lost it again, and the sudden bite of cold air made her shiver in amazement.

Ten years as a tigress had made her breasts used to being handled. But this was different. This was fumbling and awkward and sent waves of sensation crashing through her chest. She tightened her legs and drew him closer, arching her back to offer him better access.

Still not far enough. She felt his tongue lap at her nipple, trying to coil around it, stretching to lift it to his hot mouth. But she constantly dropped away, creating an alternating caress of hot and cold, pull and release. The power of it echoed in her womb. Her yin center began to tighten, the pulse of blood and qi quickening.

"Stop." She gasped. "Stop!"

He pulled back, his body abruptly stiff with surprise. "Little Pearl?"

"The yin builds too fast. I . . . I . . ."

"You are losing control of the process," he said gently.

She blinked, startled by his perception. "It is supposed to be deliberate."

"Are you sure? Perhaps you just like to be on top."

She frowned, not understanding his phrase. "But we are side by side."

He grinned, as if she had made a joke. "Tell me what you need. We are exchanging energy, yes?"

She nodded. "Female yin and male yang."

"I have plenty of yang, but you—"

"My yin is ample and pure. It—" He plunged into her. His dragon thrust hard and deep into her cave when she hadn't even realized he was poised to strike. She cried out in shock. His girth was beyond what she knew. His length stretched her to her fullest. He was large, so large, and yet she clenched her internal cauldron to hold him tighter still.

"God, this is good," he moaned against her. Then he lifted his gaze to her. "Does it hurt?"

"No," she whispered. But there *was* pain. There was disappointment that the breast play was over, the tickle and caress of mouth and tongue finished. For a man, there was little beyond this point. The push and grunt, the withdrawal before another shove. And then the explosion of seed and yang into her womb. It was that last release that a tigress sought; to capture and use his power. It was what the men wanted as well, the glorious rush of release that eventually led to depletion of qi and death.

All in all, an equitable exchange. The man released, the tigress gathered. And yet, she had no wish to rush there with this man.

"Little Pearl?"

She forced herself to smile. "I am ready. You may ride to release."

He arched his brow. It was a strange gesture, one that the Chinese were adept at—the tiniest movement to convey a thousand different things. But on him, with his thick forehead and bushy eyebrow, it appeared more comical than practiced. He was not trying to convey a subtle meaning. He was merely startled—and amused—by her words.

She frowned. "You are laughing at me?"

"Never." He immediately sobered.

"Then why . . ." Her voice trailed away. She had no idea what she wanted to ask. Only that she had questions.

"I like being inside you, Little Pearl. It's tight and wet, and your legs grip me." He leaned forward and touched his tongue to the tip of her nose. "I like it too much to end it quickly."

She pulled back. "I don't understand."

"Kiss me."

"But the cauldron is below. Between my legs—"

"I know where it is, Little Pearl. Kiss me!"

She shook her head, wondering at herself. Why was she delaying? "Yin cools easily. If we are—"

His mouth was on hers, stopping the words. He thrust into her mouth, his tongue pushing against hers. The kiss was deep and forceful and she opened immediately beneath the onslaught. But the action was centered up high, on her mouth and not below where all was quiet. Why would he not move?

She tensed her inner muscles, gripping him in rhythmic succession, using first her shallow muscles, then rolling the pressure deeper inside. She did it once slowly, then a second time faster. By the third time he was growling deep in his throat, but he still didn't move his dragon.

Then his hands found her breasts again, held them. As she continued her pull on his dragon, he moved his hands. She milked his jade stem, and he drew on her breasts, pulling each nipple to a narrow point that he squeezed exquisitely before starting again at the base. And still his dragon remained quiet.

His tongue was moving more furiously now. It pushed and withdrew, it burrowed and pulled back. She added another incentive, sucking on his tongue as it thrust forward, narrowing her lips to slow his withdrawal. She felt the tension in his body grow, his thighs bunching between hers, but still, his dragon remained still.

Then a strange thing happened. She began to lose the rhythm of contraction. Her mind could not focus on so many things—her mouth, her breasts, her cave—all at once. They slipped from her control. Her belly contractions faltered first, the muscles settling into a quiver of reaction rather than the deep pull of before. Her breath changed. No longer able to manage a steady inhale and release, she gasped and panted as the yin river coursed through her body.

"I will not—can't ride—the tigress!" she gasped.

He pulled back from their kiss, his own breath unsteady. "Are we exchanging energies? Is that what we're doing?"

She nodded. She could feel his yang pouring into her through his dragon. It wasn't the torrid river of power that would come with his seed, but a steady flow that warmed her belly and maintained her yin rain. "But the mix must be careful. You stoke the fire too hot."

He lowered his mouth back to her face, using his lips to whisper across her skin. "*You* make it too hot, Little Pearl." He bared his teeth at her ear, nipping at the edges. She shivered in reaction. "It's so good," he murmured. His tongue lapped at her lobe. "Is it like this with all tigresses?"

She couldn't answer. How could he be so clear when she . . . ? His tongue delved inside. When she . . . ? He pinched her nipple. When she . . . ? He moved his pelvis, grinding down against her.

She arched against him—once, then again, then again—creating a pulse in her yin pearl. "Jonas. Help me." She didn't know what she was asking. Did she want more from him or less? The fire was too hot to control, and yet a little bit more pressure from him and she would . . .

Jonas pulled back, capturing her gaze with his. His dragon withdrew a half measure from her and she cried out in panic, wrapping her legs around his hips to keep him with her. She gripped him hard at the same moment he thrust. His body slammed against her just as she arched to receive him.

Twice he thrust, twice she met him, her hips raising off the mattress with the force of their movements. It was too soon, too hot. And yet . . .

He kissed her. No thrust, no grinding of hips, just a swift sudden invasion of her mouth.

The yin fire engulfed her. Her womb contracted in physical release, but her blood and mind went further. Every energy channel burst into light. His yang roared through her body until it reached her mind. Heart and spirit became engulfed in power.

She screamed in ecstasy, then all went dark.

July 30, 1893

Dearest brother Jonas,

    I cannot leave to visit you now, much though my heart longs for it. Beth is with child again, and I cannot abandon my flock. As for your atonement and God's forgiveness, your path is clear. Pay off your crew as if the voyage had been a complete success, then leave off all manner of sin for the rest of your days. No drink. No women except your lawfully wedded wife.

    This means you must leave the life of a sailor—leave it utterly. I do not say this lightly. Think a moment of your future. You must foreswear all manner of debauchery, but how resolute can you be when surrounded by the very life that drew you to sin in the first place? Every day as a sailor, you will be tempted by drink. Every moment on leave, your companions will strive to draw you back to loose women and heathen pleasures. You must leave your temptations. This is God's commandment to you.

    Will you allow your soul to perish? Sell your ship, give up all and come to me and Beth in Yorkshire. We will aid you. There are good women here, Jonas, and good employment for godly men. Come to us, Jonas, or suffer Satan's eternal damnation.

In earnest prayer,
Father Bert

Peanut Soup (Fa Sung Woo) is marginally a yun soup. When eaten in moderation, it is soothing to the system, but when eaten in excess, peanuts can cause yeet hay (excessive internal heat), as they are very rich. This soup has that incredible quality of tasting too delicious to be good for you, but the Chinese believe peanuts are a longevity food.

Chapter Fifteen

Little Pearl wedged herself backward under the hallway table. It was pitch black here, and at ten years old, she didn't fit as well as she once had. But this was the closest hiding place to the stairs and—more important—the best place to hear conversations from the library.

Her heart abruptly started beating with alarm. She was an adult. She was Little Pearl, cook at the Tan school for tigresses. She was not this little girl again. But the experience did not stop. She was here, wedged beneath a hallway table while her parents argued below.

She heard their voices, not raised in anger as so often happened, but quieter, harder to hear—and so sad it made the child cry. The adult in her, however, raged in fury. She spit curses and tried to crawl from her hidey-hole.

"See what you made me! See what I have become!"

But the dream continued as her mother's words shifted to sobs. There was another voice then drifting up the stairs. A man's voice that was not as ugly as the adult remembered. But it was coarse and cruel and even the child shied away from it.

The haggling took some time. It was her mother who argued, her father having no head for numbers. In between sobs, her mother bartered for a higher price.

The child didn't understand what was happening. The child merely knew fear and an icy cold that seeped into her body from the floor. But the adult knew. Within moments, they would come for her. Within moments, the child would scramble away, trying to run on bound feet. She would fail. The ugly man would catch her and drag her away while her parents whispered platitudes from below. Her brothers would tumble out of their shared bed to crowd in their doorway, watching with wide sleep-fogged eyes.

No one would help her. Her clothes would tear, her knees would get bloody in the struggle, and her nails would break where she clutched the table, dragging it down the hallway until the man broke her grip with a quick chop to her wrists. She would grow hoarse from screaming, and she would be muffled by a heavy rug thrown over her face.

The adult remembered and refused to live it again. The adult fought with all her strength to scramble away from the dream, away from the demon who had brought her here. She would wake. She would—

"—Pearl! Little Pearl!"

She felt something on her arms, a force that shook her tiny body roughly, and she struck out, fighting the restraint. But her arms wouldn't move, her body felt so heavy. She screamed in frustration but heard only the barest whimper.

"Oh God, Little Pearl. Are you all right? Can you hear me?"

It was Jonas, his voice shaky with panic. She blinked her eyes, trying to sort meaning from shadows. She saw his face, gray and slick with sweat, but his eyes were clear. They were dark and round and steady enough that she could focus on them while the rest of her mind settled.

"Jonas . . ." she whispered.

"Little Pearl." She felt the grip on her shoulders ease. "Are you all right? You had . . . You went completely still. It was like a fit or something. I couldn't wake you."

"Poison," she whispered.

"What?"

She blinked and forced her head to turn away. "Poison," she repeated more firmly. "Your yang is poison. It took me to a terrible place. To—"

"I didn't poison you! Little Pearl, you had a fit. A seizure of some kind—"

"No!" She reached out. The gesture was feeble, but he grabbed her hand to help. She pushed him away and used the leverage to roll sideways. "No," she repeated as she curled her knees to her forehead. "Your white yang poisons."

She heard him release his breath in a huff of frustration, and tears pricked at her eyelids. "I don't understand," he said. She didn't answer at first, but he set a hand on her arm. It was warm and gentle, and it made her tears burn.

"Your white yang," she hissed. "It is . . . powerful. But it's a ghost power. It took me to an evil place."

"An evil place," he echoed, and she could tell he was thinking hard, trying to make sense of her words. He would not be able to. Men never thought they could be poisonous to women. "You had a nightmare," he finally said.

She hissed and spun back to him, using all her strength to push him away. He did not move, of course. He was much too solid and she too weak. "It was not a nightmare! Do nightmares happen when you are not asleep? Do you refuse to wake when someone grabs you? This was no childish dream!"

He nodded, his eyes wide. Now that his panic had faded, his skin was less pasty, more ruddy. The sweat had dried, leaving behind nothing for her to focus on except his broad shoulders and his quiet energy. It tempted her: his qi. His body's size and his energy called to her, begging her to absorb his yang, to draw it into herself and become strong. But it was a lie! His yang took her to that awful place, so she hardened her heart and her fist, slamming it against him.

"You are poison, poison, poison! Get away!"

He caught her fists and held them away from her. His grip was not bruising, merely firm as he kept her still. She continued to rant at him. She called him names, she cursed his ancestry and his body parts. If she could have spat on his ship and all his gold, she would have. And through it all, he held her firmly, waiting in silence until she quieted. It made her angrier, more furious.

In time, her wind blew itself out. Her throat was raw and her arms ached from fighting him as she sputtered into a hiccupping silence. She tried one last time to jerk away, but he still did not release her. So she collapsed in on herself, her face pressed to her knees while tears trailed from her chin onto her thigh.

"That must have been some nightmare," he commented.

She lifted her head long enough to glare at him. He softened his expression with a self-conscious shrug. "I know. It wasn't a nightmare, but it was kind of like one. A waking dream. A waking, nasty dream."

His hands gentled on her wrists, opening enough to stroke her arms. She had no doubt he could manacle her again if she lunged at him; he was that fast. But she was too tired to fight anymore. And his voice was soothing:

"My mother had fits sometimes. She'd stare out the window like a statue. Then something—I don't know what, but something—would set her to screeching. It was like a lake storm, suddenly blowing up out of nowhere then fading just as quickly. That was my mother—a summer squall."

He twisted on the bed, grabbing the blanket with one hand while the other remained against her arm, a quiet source of warmth. With a quick flick, he settled the covering across her shoulders. It was a welcome weight. It shielded her nakedness and would eventually give some heat. But for the moment, all she cared about was his hand on her arm and the steady cadence of his words.

"Of all the things I escaped when I went to sea, that was the worst. A child wants to help his mother, but these fits would take her and there was nothing I could do."

"Her qi was unbalanced," Little Pearl said, surprised that she spoke at all. "A child cannot be expected to understand such things."

He shrugged, and the movement brought his other hand back in contact with her skin. It was her leg this time, just below her knee along the outside of her calf.

"I was just glad to escape. A ship made sense to me. It had rules and logic, an obvious chain of command. It made sense. For a while."

She narrowed her eyes, trying to read the contours of his face. "Something changed. Someone's qi became unbalanced."

His lips curved, but the gesture was not warm. "Yes. Mine." He was mocking himself, she realized. "I fell in love."

She flinched, his words chilling her though she had no reason to experience such a thing. Perhaps she was merely responding to his energy imbalance.

"She was young and beautiful, with blond ringlets and pure blue eyes. She liked my muscles and that I laughed loudly. We took walks by the cliffs in Dover and she listened for hours to my stories. I loved that her hands were soft and white, and I spent hours remembering just where she put them when we kissed."

"Where?" The word escaped her mouth on a whisper. She didn't truly want to know, but he wouldn't keep talking unless she prompted him.

He looked at her in surprise, then smiled, his expression wistful. "One hand here on my cheek." His hand left her side to touch his chin. "The other over my heart, here." He shifted to touch his chest.

Key energy points—the mouth and the heart. She'd probably been drawing off his yang, though neither of them knew it.

"She is the one who refused you. Because your mother was a whore." Her voice felt rough in her throat.

"Yes."

She nodded, knowing most Chinese girls would have the same reaction. "I am surprised her parents let you visit her."

"They didn't. We met in secret."

She grimaced. Secret loves were at the core of most Chinese love poems. They always ended in death.

"My fits began just after we left for sea."

She blinked, startled equally by his statement and that he would admit it so readily to her. "What kind of fits?"

"Just like my mother. I would stare at the ocean, thinking and thinking without moving. Then the smallest thing would set me to screaming." He looked down at her hand on his arm. "I didn't sob, but I bellowed orders. I was cruel to my sailors. I . . ." He shook his head. "I had fits of fury. And . . . other things."

"She drained too much yang from you. You had to recover it somehow. Anger is based in yang. You were merely replenishing your empty stores." She paused a moment, guessing at what other things he did. "Men will often have strong lusts at this time, too—for money, drink, or even women."

He stared at her. "I don't understand anything of what you just said."

She smiled, both sad and pleased. "It doesn't matter. You recovered. Your qi is more balanced now."

"Maybe." His gaze tightened on her face. "I don't think about Annie much anymore. But then . . . I would wake in a sweat from a nightmare I couldn't even remember. Then I'd pick a fight with someone if I was on board, or drink myself into a stupor if I wasn't."

She frowned as she tried to remember him from the very first time he came to the Tan home. She recalled a balanced man, a lover of food without any appetite for women. "How did you restore your yang?" Anger and lust were symptoms of a problem, not solutions.

He shook his head. "I don't know. One day I woke up disgusted with all of it."

She straightened, unable to believe it could be so simple. "Yang does not balance on its own. Surely something happened to restore the harmony in your spirit."

He was quiet, unable to answer her questions. And while she struggled with all she knew about energy, puzzling out possible explanations for his change, he sat silent, his eyes and his attention growing more intense the longer they stared at one another. Finally, she could stand it no longer.

"What are you thinking?" she snapped.

"I am wondering what happened to you. What set *your* energies into such fury?"

She recoiled from him, her anger surging. Without even realizing it, she raised her hands like claws, but he was there, gripping her arms and holding her still.

"How did you become a whore, Little Pearl?" he asked. "You were a daughter of privilege with bound feet and a future Mandarin husband. How do you come here?"

"They sold me!" she hissed. "They sold me to a man with large feet and a mole on his neck. And he sold me to the Palace."

He nodded as if he had guessed this, and yet he still

didn't understand. "Why, Little Pearl? Why would they do such a thing?"

She coiled in on herself, shifting to her knees when she could not get her feet beneath her. "For money," she spat. "To pay for my brother." She could tell he didn't understand. Neither did she, for all that it was common enough in the lower classes. "He advises a viceroy now! A Confucian scholar who runs all of Canton."

He blinked. "They sold you to pay for his education?"

She straightened to her full height. "For all their educations—my father and my three brothers. Even then I was a beautiful girl. And with bound feet, my sale price was very high."

"Of course it was," he said with absolute sincerity. "And if I were you, I would be furious, too. I would have fits and nightmares, and I would hurt anyone who came within my sphere just because I was so angry." He shook his head. "I would never sell a daughter. Never, even if my life depended upon it."

"So you say," she growled.

He looked her straight in the eye. "So I know." Truth throbbed in his words. She did not doubt he meant what he said. He would indeed sell himself long before he allowed such a thing to happen to his child. Her heart warmed to him for that alone: he would protect all his children—even the girls.

"Your ancestry is truer than mine," she whispered, stunned by the thought.

He didn't respond except to look at her, his expression and his grip gentling with every breath. He lifted a hand to touch her face, and she did not pull away. Even more bizarre, she closed her eyes and pressed a kiss into his hand. "How did you balance your qi?" she asked again. She needed to know.

He leaned forward and touched his lips to her forehead. "I don't know."

"It must be something in your ghost nature. It must be . . ."

He pushed upward on her chin, lifting her face to his. He met her lips, pressing his kiss onto her—into her—and she opened herself to his power. Poison or not, his qi was potent and she could not resist. She clung to him and he to her, their mouths fused together.

And in that moment of absolute silence, of mouth to mouth connection when their qi flowed together, a new possibility formed. Not thought, not even an idea, simply a presence like a tiny seed planted in her heart. She felt and feared it, but she could not pull away. It was too new, too strange, and too very, very present.

They broke apart only when a banging reverberated on her doorway, and little Mei Wan's voice cried out, "Mistress! Mistress! Mr. Su has awoken!"

Jonas turned to the door, but Little Pearl did not want the intrusion. The seed was too strong to ignore and so she reached up to his cheek, trying to draw him back to her lips. But he pulled away.

"You can't go see him. He'll have you kill—"

She surged forward, trying to connect their mouths again.

"Little Pearl," he gasped, catching her and holding her away.

"Mistress! Mistress!" Mei Wan cried from the door.

"I am in practice!" Little Pearl snapped, trying to focus on the seed. It needed his kiss to make it grow. She stretched up to meet him, but his face was turned toward the door as Mei Wan continued to bang.

"The soldier demands food and a messenger," the girl cried. "What should I tell them?"

"Soup," Little Pearl answered wearily. The seed had already withered away. It would not grow again. She would have to make another with him, and that would take more time than they had. "Heat the soup. I will come directly."

Jonas grabbed her arm, his eyes intense. "You can't see him."

Yesterday she would have pulled away, she would have pressed ahead and done what needed to be done without discussion. But something had changed during the turbulent night. Perhaps it was the seed that was not as dead as she thought. Perhaps it was simply that she had begun practice with this man and emotional ties were inevitable.

She knew his yang was poison to her, knew he was white and therefore barbarian. And yet, as of this moment, she trusted him. He would not hurt her. Indeed, he had already suffered a great deal of pain and difficulty in order to protect her.

Instead of pulling away, she pressed tighter into his embrace. "I will be safe with Mr. Su. Mei Wan will show you to Master Tan's office. The list is in a box beneath the floor just to the right of the door."

"Little Pearl—" he began, but she didn't let him speak.

"Mr. Su wants this list, too. If you control that, then we have something to bargain with." She felt an inner tremor that she was giving away her only bargaining chip, but again that seed must be influencing her. Bizarre though it was, she felt safer with this mysterious list in his hands.

She pressed a last kiss into his lips before hurriedly dressing. He dressed as well, though his movements were much slower. "I go to the kitchen," she said. "I will find you before I face Mr. Su." Then, with a nod, she slipped out the door.

How long had it been since she'd spent all morning in practice, not rising until after noon? Never. Certainly never since becoming the Tan cook. And never had she risen so reluctantly, aching in every bone not from exertion but because she desperately longed to return to her partner's side.

Was this attachment? Of course it was. But was it wrong? She wasn't sure, and worse, she wasn't sure she cared. She wanted to be with Jonas. Not just to practice with him, but cook for him, talk with him, even help him in his daily tasks so that they could sleep side by side at night. The thought was so disconcerting that she froze before entering the kitchen. She knew the moment she stepped through she would be focused on all the other tasks at hand. This was her only second to think of Jonas and her feelings for him.

Unfortunately, she came to no conclusions. He had some hold on her, some strange barbarian magic that made his yang strong enough to bewitch. Something in whites made their qi especially powerful. If only she could discover what it was, then she would be able to break Jonas's strange hold on her. But that was a task for another day. Right now, she had soup to prepare for a murdered man who was no longer murdered.

She entered her kitchen and began to work. First she sent Mei Wan to guide Jonas. They would both have to be very careful, but after last night, she had no doubt that Jonas could walk right in front of the soldiers and not be seen. That, too, appeared to be a white man's magic.

Soup, dumplings, rice, all those she set into motion, including the return of classes. She set out the plant that would tell all that the afternoon's work would be just as normal. It was not that she wished to teach, but because the more people milling about the compound, the more likely Jonas would fade into the background. And the less likely that Mr. Su could do something that she would not discover. All information flowed through the kitchen, and so she would know of his movements every second of the day.

She worked diligently, and then—abruptly—all was accomplished. It was time to bring food to Mr. Su. She made up two trays, one for Jonas and one for . . . the other one. But when she moved for the office, Mei Wan stopped her.

"He is in here," the girl said, gesturing to the storeroom just off the kitchen.

Little Pearl opened the door to find Jonas sitting on a sack of rice while a single candle at his elbow dripped wax onto a clay urn of rice flour. He looked up as the door pulled open, a smile on his face while he set aside a stack of papers that was in his lap.

"You have been here all this time?"

"I told you I would not leave you alone."

She stared a moment, feeling the warmth of his presence flood her. "I have food."

He grinned as he pushed to his feet, but she waved him back down and brought the tray to him. He ate quickly while she watched his face. The soup was not her best. The peanuts were not fresh enough and she feared that she had given him too much for his system. But he grinned as he swallowed, his enjoyment obvious.

"I have been listening to you work," he said between bites. "You could captain a ship the way you order the servants around."

She frowned, not understanding if he were complimenting her or not. His tone certainly sounded admiring, but . . . "They are servants. What else would I do?"

He shook his head with a smile. "Nothing. You just do it so very, very well. I'm impressed."

"You are exposed," she snapped, though her belly quivered happily at his words. "If the soldier comes—"

"You have dispatched servants to warn you of his movements. I heard you do it earlier."

"I must go—"

He wiped his face with a napkin. "I'm coming."

"But you cannot—"

"I will not leave you alone. Not with Su. Never."

"But—"

"Set up a meal for the guard. Have Mei Wan tell him that you will care for Su's wounds while—"

"While he eats. Then you and I will talk to Mr. Su."

"Yes. He already knows I'm here. And that way—"

"I will not be alone with him." She looked at Jonas, startled and a bit frightened by what had just happened. She'd understood what he meant even before he said it.

He grinned and lifted his bowl. "This should be washed before I leave."

She was already reaching. He released it to her, his hands caressing hers before he pulled on his coolie hat and slipped away. She watched him go, then ordered Mei Wan to call the soldier. The girl would stay with him while she and Jonas faced Su. And all the while, her belly quivered and her heart leaped in her chest. What was happening to her? What power did this white man have to so disquiet her? And how could their energies already be so aligned that they understood one another's thoughts?

She didn't have time to decide, for the soldier came stomping into her kitchen, his booted feet trailing dirt from the garden path onto her just-swept floor. Mei Wan set to serving the man, so Little Pearl bowed respectfully before leaving for the sickroom.

She didn't walk with Jonas through the garden. It would seem very strange for her to chat with a gardener. But she felt Jonas with her every breath, every shift of her wrapped foot on stone. He was nearby. He would not let her enter Mr. Su's room alone.

She climbed the stairs. She did not see Jonas until she stood before the evil man's door. The moment she set her hand to the knob, she felt Jonas step in behind her. She gave a silent nod. He returned it with a smile that warmed her chilled hand.

Then she opened the door.

Aug. 2, 1893

Dear Albert,
   I have paid my crew and am now penniless. I will arrive on your doorstep a week hence.

   —Jonas

Living up to the duties of a Chinese daughter can be especially trying at New Year's, a holiday steeped not only in tradition but superstition. Imagine the anxiety of feeling responsible—that the outcome of your relatives' New Year relates to your ability to make a perfect cake? Even if the family joked and dismissed my failure as unimportant, they would still be fearful of challenging the old ways.

Chapter Sixteen

Mr. Su's eyes opened the moment Little Pearl and Jonas stepped into the room. Looking at Su's shriveled form, Little Pearl could not help but compare the two men. Stepping into Jonas's sickroom had been like walking into a storm. Even slack-jawed in sleep, Jonas had a crackling qi that leaped from his bed to embrace her. Sometimes it teased the edge of her consciousness with power, sometimes it burst through her mind like lightning, but always there was raw energy that could not be denied.

Mr. Su's qi was like rancid oil. He looked like a shriveled stick on the bed, swathed in badly wrapped bandages as his breath rasped in his thin chest. Only his carved dragon bracelet looked healthy. But his qi was powerful. It coated everything in the room with dark fury, and Little Pearl instinctively recoiled.

She bumped into Jonas behind her. She closed her eyes, needing to feel the captain's cleanness, his strength that, like water, washed Mr. Su away. But of course, he could not wash their enemy away, and Mr. Su was speaking, drawing them both deeper into his foulness.

"So you finally come."

"So you're not dead," Jonas drawled.

Mr. Su's gaze barely flickered over him. His eyes were on Little Pearl, his attention concentrated fully on her. "Do you sleep with apes now, whore?"

Little Pearl felt Jonas stiffen behind her, but she grabbed his hand—low, beside her hip—and squeezed him into silence. In this way, she tethered herself to his power and strengthened her own flagging energy. "I am not arrested. The soldiers do not drag me away for your murder. What do you want?"

"They could still come. Perhaps I have told them to wait until—"

"Your wits are failing you. I am not arrested. Therefore you want something."

Mr. Su regarded her in silence. She thought for a moment that he was gathering his strength to speak, but soon realized that was merely an illusion. He was alert and stronger than he appeared. He was merely thinking, tempting her to underestimate him.

When she remained steadfastly silent, his eyes flickered to Jonas. "He has no money. His ships are lost, his cargo under my control."

"That's not true," Jonas responded. "My cargo has been returned." At her startled look he clarified in a low voice, "Seth sent the message this morning."

"Will any buy it?" snapped Mr. Su. "Your goods are poisoned. Customs Official Chen died horribly from your evil barbarian—"

"Enough!" cried Little Pearl, stunned how vehemently she hated Mr. Su. And not because of what he had done or said to her, but because he spread lies about Jonas. "You poisoned that man, you created the rumors. You, therefore, will buy the cargo. You will make Jonas a rich man or I will kill you now."

"No!" cried Jonas, his grip shifting from her hand to her wrist. "No."

Little Pearl's expression softened as she patted his hand. "Do not worry. I know subtle poisons that can be applied to his bandages or slipped into his food." Then she glanced significantly as Mr. Su's withered form. "Or I may not need to. His wound is severe. . . ."

Her words faded as Mr. Su began to laugh. It was a hideous sound—hot air slipping through oily lungs—and he waved long thin fingers at Jonas. "Tell her, ghost ape. Tell . . ." Mr. Su sputtered into silence.

Little Pearl turned to the captain to see that his face had become red with embarrassment. "He cannot have my cargo," Jonas said. "It's what he wants—a long-term partnership with me. That is why he poisoned Mr. Chen."

She frowned. "But what difference does it make? You will be paid."

"Five years," hissed Mr. Su from the bed. "We work together for five years at least, or you will be the one dying, little whore. In prison. After the solders use—"

"Oh, shut it," growled Jonas wearily. "That's not going to happen and you know it."

Little Pearl blinked. Of course it could happen. But the way Jonas grumbled his words made her feel as if he knew something she did not. As if she were truly safe and all of this negotiation was merely a game. As if . . .

She glanced back and forth at Mr. Su and Jonas, her thoughts whirling. This could not be true. Her whole last week, the difficulties with the Tans' disappearance, the mob and the missing money and . . . everything. It could not be simply a show in an elaborate negotiation between Jonas and Mr. Su. It could not be. And yet, looking at the two men, she wondered.

She abruptly twisted away, feeling her anger seethe inside her. "You planned this," she accused both men. "From the beginning, you planned on bargaining with each other. This was merely a game!" Though her words were aimed at both, the betrayal she felt was centered wholly on Jonas. How could he twist her emotions and her life? How could he—

"What?" Jonas snapped, and his voice was thunder. "Don't be ridiculous!"

"You did!" she began, but even as she said the words, she saw the bafflement on his face. The captain was not a subtle man. He was raw power. He had no need for subtle manipulations. What need had the ocean for caution?

She turned to Mr. Su and saw the glittering oil in his eyes. And in his smirk, she at last saw the truth. Mr. Su was the one who'd connived. He was the force behind all that had happened. Perhaps not the Tans' arrest, but everything since. Su was the manipulator. Jonas was simply a barbarian who needed Kui Yu to sell his goods. Why? Because a white man could not possibly understand the subtle currents of Chinese business.

She straightened. She understood business. She bargained with the best negotiators on Earth: the money-grubbing merchants of the food market. She had never fought over something as valuable as a whole ship's cargo, but the principles would be the same. She turned to Jonas, a slight smile on her face.

"You have your cargo but no buyer."

Jonas shook his head. "Kui Yu arranged for—"

She spun to Mr. Su. "You have made it so that others do not want his goods."

The man grinned. "They fear his white poison. No one will touch—"

"Therefore you must make an agreement, the two of you."

Beside her, Jonas released an angry sigh. "I told you, I will not sell to him."

"Of course not. But you will listen, yes? When he makes an offer?"

"No—"

"Jade," rasped Mr. Su. "I will give you rich blocks in all different colors. Carved, uncarved, you pick."

Little Pearl shook her head. "Imperial jade. Only that. And I will inspect each piece—"

"Are you mad, woman?" Mr. Su's color was rising, his health growing strong. "Only the emperor can sell—"

"You killed Custom's Official Chen. Do not pretend to worry about the emperor's men—"

Jonas stepped forward, pulling Little Pearl around. "Stop this now. I told you—"

"Imperial jade!" gasped Su from the bed. "But it cannot be carved."

Little Pearl twisted to glare over Jonas's shoulder at him. "Of course it must be carved. You think the barbarians have any skill with jade? Each piece will be inspected and then crated while I watch. There will be none of your thievery—"

"You call me a thief! I could have kept the precious cargo! I got that fool Chen to release it. I know the value of a returning customer. In five years we can both be richer than the most corrupt viceroy—"

"*I said no!*" roared Jonas, silencing them both.

Little Pearl gasped, pulling back in shock from his sudden black fury. On the bed, Mr. Su gurgled but said no more.

Jonas's brows were bunched together, the hair bristling on his face. His breath poured angrily through his nostrils. "No means no." He spoke with amazing gentleness, especially given how anger rolled from him in waves. "I will not sell my cargo to that man. Don't you understand? He wishes to replace Kui Yu. He wants to be my partner, to sell my goods to the Chinese."

Su straightened on the bed, his voice strong with his

dark qi. "I could have just taken your cargo, Captain Jonas, but I returned it to you. I will not deal falsely with you." He smiled. "I will even take a smaller share than Tan Kui Yu. We will work together well, I promise you."

Little Pearl stepped closer to Jonas. "And he will pay you a dragon fortune now to begin a prosperous alliance."

"No! Damn it, Little Pearl, I will not become partners with a murderer. He held a knife to your throat. He tried to make you kill me!"

She frowned. "He was negotiating. With you dead, your first mate would—"

"Negotiation by murder? Do you hear yourself?"

She sighed. Why was he so angry? "It is how Mr. Su does business. You may not understand, but this is how it is done by men of power in China." When Jonas opened his mouth to object, she rushed on. "It is how Mr. Su does business. Do not powerful whites ever kill one another?"

Jonas gaped at her. "And you call *us* barbarians."

She grimaced. "He is evil, yes. Heaven will punish him. But he is powerful in more than just his qi. He has men throughout Shanghai, and the Empress Dowager herself gave him his bracelet." She gestured to the five-toed dragon carved on the jade bracelet that perpetually hung on his wrist. "Such is the way here. Men of power kill without punishment. When he dies, the Feng-Du court will exact its revenge. Until then, his money spends just as well as an honest man's. Better, because he has more of it."

Jonas stared at her, his gaze darting between her and Mr. Su. "I hate this heathen land," he said. Then he shook his head and turned to leave.

Confused, she grabbed his arm, trying to draw him back. "Jonas, wait!"

He stopped, turning slightly, but he said nothing. He merely waited while she scrambled to find something to say.

"You truly will not sell to him? Just because he tried to murder you?"

"He held a knife to your throat, Little Pearl. He . . ." He pressed his lips together, stopping the flow of his grievances against Mr. Su. "You are correct," he said very slowly, each word enunciated with excruciating clarity. "I will not become partners with such a man. I would rather see my cargo at the bottom of the ocean." Then he turned on his heel and left.

Little Pearl looked at Mr. Su, who appeared as surprised as she. At her glance, he spat on the floor. "Barbarians. Who can understand the mind of an ape?"

The word "murderer" was poised on her tongue. She was more than capable of trading insults with the man, but she held back, knowing that she could not be so free with her speech. In China, all would be forgiven once a bargain was sealed. Murder, rape, deception—all these things were the price of doing business with a man of Mr. Su's standing. But an exorbitant price had been named and the transaction had been refused. Who knew what would happen now? Who knew what Su might do in spite?

"I will talk to him," she said. "Perhaps I can make him understand."

Mr. Su grunted. "Do so, whore, or suffer the consequences." Then he folded his arms—the one wearing the empress's bracelet lay on top—and closed his eyes. Knowing she was dismissed, Little Pearl withdrew.

She found Jonas immediately. He leaned against the outer wall, scowling at her. She smiled weakly at him, pleased that he would still wait for her even though he was angry. "Jonas . . ."

"Come with me," he said. Then he strode off, crossing the pathway to Tan Kui Yu's office in utter silence.

She scurried after him. She said nothing, her mind whirling as she tried to make sense of Jonas's attitude. Then they were at the office door. Little Pearl hesitated, looking into Master Tan's domain with typical nervousness. Jonas had no such qualms and stormed in, quickly crossing to the secret floor compartment. He squatted down, but didn't open it. He looked at her instead.

"Is there a problem?" His voice was like icy rain. It slid down her spine, stiffening her shoulders and straightening her stance. If he wanted to be angry, then so be it. She would not relish a partnership with Mr. Su, either, but if that were her only choice . . .

She stilled, her eyes taking in Master Tan's office. Of course! Jonas had the list now. That meant he had other buyers for his cargo. He would play Mr. Su, getting bids from his other buyers before coming back to bargain for a better price. Her face split into a smile, and she stepped into the room. Now she understood. "Do you need my help in finding the other buyers? You have the names now, yes? I know every corner of Shanghai. I will be a great—"

"Show me this list, Little Pearl," he interrupted. "Where is it?"

She frowned, her eyes going to the floorboards before his feet. Then she remembered that she had left the door open and quickly turned to close it. By the time she had accomplished it, he had the boards up and was lifting the box out.

She froze for a moment, jolted by a memory of her father's long thin fingers around a different box—an old puzzle box with black lacquer. It had been a gift to her great-great grandfather from some viceroy. She remembered her father's pale hand dropping grimy coins into it. More than a decade later, she still remembered the amount: seventy-two yuen. An impossible amount to her young eyes. Until she realized she had been sold. Her entire life for seventy-two yuen.

She swallowed, forcing herself back to the present. Jonas's hands were larger than her father's. His were not ink stained, but thick, calloused, and ruddy. The box he held was of hard metal and not beautiful; there was no craftsmanship in the thing, nor any ancient history. And yet, when he held it she felt a rightness in his actions. Business should not be transacted with family heirlooms.

Jonas straightened and offered the box to her. "Show me the list."

She stepped forward and carefully pulled out the rolled sheet of paper. She could tell that he had already looked at it; the curl was not as tight as before. Nevertheless, she did as he bade and opened the list, holding it out.

He glanced down at it. "Is that the list you meant?"

She nodded.

"You can't read English," he said, his words both a question and a statement. "So you saw this and guessed it was what I wanted."

Again she nodded, her heart sinking. She could tell by his tone that she had erred. "It is not the right one?"

He shook his head. "No."

She flipped the paper over, pointing at the Chinese symbols. "But these are prices and names. It—"

"Suppliers, Little Pearl," he said gently. "For one of Kui Yu's mercantiles."

She didn't understand the last word, spoken in English, but she grasped that he had not found what he needed. "But then where is the paper you wanted?"

He sighed and set down the box, his gaze traveling over Master Tan's extensive piles of books and papers. "Somewhere in here, I'd guess."

"But . . ." She looked down at the page in her hand. "This is not helpful at all?"

He set it aside with barely a glance. "Not at all." Then he crossed to the desk, sitting behind it just as Master Tan used to do.

"You will look for it now?" she asked, wondering why she was both angry and disoriented. The sight of him behind the desk looked right and yet so wrong at the same time. His unhappiness was a palpable thing, coiling throughout the room, and yet it was not directed at her. His last words had been almost gentle.

She took a step forward, wanting to both help him and lash out in fury. But he did not look up as she approached, his focus centered on Master Tan's papers. He reminded her of her father, who'd constantly stared at his books except when he cuffed her for venturing too close.

"Why are you being so stupid?" she suddenly cried, startling herself. "Make your deal with Mr. Su and be done with it!" Her fear had overwhelmed her.

His hands froze where they rifled through a stack of papers. He looked up, his eyes dark, his expression fierce. When he spoke, his tone was quiet, barely discernible. "Why do you insist that I work with the man who hurt you?"

"Pain is a part of life. You are childish if you think to do business and not spill blood."

He stared at her. "And you approve?"

"It is the way things are done!"

"Not by me." His words were flat and stark, and they shook her to the core. She bit her lip, wondering why she defended something she knew was wrong. Then he leaned forward, his voice low and intense. "My cargo is guns, Little Pearl. Winchester rifles. Do you know what a man like Su would do with something like that? Create his own personal army. Do you want a civil war here?"

Little Pearl reared back in shock. Guns? The thought of Mr. Su with rifles was horrific. And yet, Jonas was fooling himself if he believed Su did not already have a personal army. The Imperial army had stormed the Tan compound just on the word of one of Mr. Su's slaves.

Worse, the risks of defying Su were too great. The evil

man had restrained himself so far. Only one death—a corrupt customs official. Su wished to make a long-term arrangement with Captain Jonas; to refuse to negotiate would be an insult. With nothing to lose, Su would then simply kill them all, seize the cargo, and make what profits he could.

Tears blurred her vision at the thought of Jonas dead. "You are a fool!" she cried. "A fool to think you can change what has existed for generations."

He didn't answer, and she didn't move. Her mind raged that she should leave. She had no time for such a fool. And yet, she stood there gaping. His gaze dropped to the papers on the desk, then to the stacks of indecipherable books and notations on shelves on the wall. Then he looked at her and his face grew sad.

"Corruption is the same the world over, Little Pearl. In England, in China, the powerful take advantage of the weak and none stand against them."

"Because it is the only way to do business."

He shook his head. "Not the only way. Not for me."

She wanted to sob. "You will be crushed. Your guns will be taken from you, your ship destroyed, and then Su will murder you for daring to stand against him. He must or others will defy him."

Jonas's shoulders slumped, and she knew he finally understood. "Kui Yu never spoke of this."

"Why would he discuss Chinese business with you? Did you discuss the winds and the oceans with him?"

Jonas sighed, his attention returning to the desk.

Little Pearl dared to step forward. "You will talk with Mr. Su."

"No." He didn't even look up.

"No? No! Aie-yah," she cried, throwing up her hands as she cursed him long and fluently. When that didn't help, she switched to English, repeating words his sailors had taught the kitchen help.

He looked up, his mouth twisted with laughter. "Do you know what you just said?"

She didn't, nor did she care. Instead, she lunged forward and slammed her hands down on the desk. The sound was loud, and pain shot through her arms. "Don't you hear me? You must speak with Mr. Su or he will murder you!"

Jonas shook his head. "He will not murder me. I will leave long before he stirs from his sickbed."

An ugly coldness seeped into her spirit, an oily darkness that shriveled her qi. "You said you would stay a month. You said—"

"I am here, Little Pearl. And when I leave, you will still be protected. I will leave men—"

"You will be killed—a knife between your ribs in the middle of the night. Mr. Su will not allow the insult—"

"Perhaps, Little Pearl. But I will not partner with a murderer. It's stupid and dangerous. I have to be able to trust my partner."

"Pah! Then who will you do business with? The fish merchant? The coolies? Only the poor are honest."

"Kui Yu was honest. I did business with him."

"He is in prison!"

Jonas's jaw firmed as he spoke. "He had friends, honest associates. Good men."

"You know this for truth?" She couldn't stop the hope that sparked in her heart. But then that hope died as his gaze slid away.

"Yes," he said. But he obviously lied.

"You are a fool." There were no honest men. She knew how life worked in China. Had not her parents taught her? And if not their sale of her, then the daily commerce of life in the brothel.

She walked slowly around the desk, moving to kneel before Jonas with her head bowed, her eyes on the floor. She heard the paper shuffling cease. She waited in absolute silence as he twisted in his chair to look down at her.

"What are you doing, Little Pearl?"

"I come in all humility," she said in her most formal tone. "I am a tigress who has not begged for anything since I came to the Tan household. I come to beg a boon."

"Get up, Pearl. You don't have to—"

"I come to plead for your life, Captain Jonas. I beg you to reconsider as a favor to me. Do not embark upon this path. Do not throw away your life in the name of morality."

"Stop this."

"Allow me to barter a deal with Mr.—"

"Stop it now!"

"I beg you—" She gasped as he grabbed her arms and hauled her upward. He carefully set her on her feet, though she felt his fury tremble through his hands. She dared to lift her gaze and beheld his face contorted with such anger as to rob her of all breath. Never had she thought to see such darkness etched on his features. Not even when Su had tried to murder him. And yet, he still did not hurt her. His hands were firm but not bruising, his eyes cold but not violent as he set her away from him.

"Jonas—"

"I cannot sell guns to Mr. Su. I will not arm a murdering tyrant." There was no compromise in his tone.

"But—"

"Enough!" Qi power throbbed in his bellow, filling the room like thunder, echoing in the walls and in her skull. She squeaked in terror and ran. She ran as fast as her tiny feet could carry her, and she did not stop until she reached the kitchen. She cowered beneath the table there while the kitchen girl stared at her in horror. Then Mei Wan fled to someplace unknown. Little Pearl remained beneath the table, quaking in terror.

Her thoughts were ugly. She was being silly, she told herself; Jonas would not hurt her no matter how black his mood. And even if he were violent, squatting beneath a table was not safety. She was being childish and stupid, and she needed to crawl out right now. But her legs were shaking too much to move, and her heart fluttered in her throat so that she could not catch her breath. She would remain here with her head pressed into her knees just as she had done as a girl in her father's home. How ridiculous it was. Cowering like this had not helped then, and it would not serve now. Yet she still could not make herself move.

He was such a stupid, stupid man. Any idiot would know the truth. This was China, not some barbarian paradise. No one wanted him here. She should laugh and make four-happiness pork when he died.

She dug her knees into her eyes, furious to realize tears soaked her skirt. Crying had not helped her in the brothel, nor had it made any difference with her father. Even her brothers had laughed when she sobbed at not joining them with the tutor. How stupid she was then, crying because she wasn't allowed to sit for hours on end staring at scrolls. She should stop acting like a useless girl baby.

It was all Jonas's fault. Everything had been fine before he came. Everything was fine before the whites invaded China, pushing their ridiculous ideas on people who knew better. Any fool could see they were doomed barbarians who knew nothing. Nothing!

She had to get up; she had work to do. Let Jonas search through the master's papers. She hoped he didn't find anything. She hoped he crawled to her on his knees, banging his head on the floor in a kowtow, begging her for help. She would laugh at him and send him to Mr. Su. His deal would be terrible then. Mr. Su would have the upper hand, and Jonas would be given almost nothing.

And then, days later, when Jonas was leaving for his boat, Mr. Su would strike. A lackey, probably that slave who had been here earlier, would stick a knife in Jonas's ribs, quick and quiet like gutting a fish. The captain would be dead before his face hit the dirt. Then there would be political outcry, retribution and demands from the barbarians. General Kang's soldiers would come back and who would they blame? Herself. And the Tans. She would be locked in prison to die there from rats, or executed and eaten by Manchu dogs. All because Jonas was stupid, stupid, stupid.

She hated him. She hated all barbarians! She wanted them dead and gone. Jonas would deserve what he got. As did all the hateful whites.

Her thoughts continued to boil for another hour, but at the end of that time she'd finally found an answer. By the time she crawled on all fours out from under the table, she had done as she always did: pressed her hurt deep inside. She had converted those wilting yin energies into a tiny knot inside her spirit. A new seed grew inside her, one that was as familiar as it was strong.

It was hatred. And it searched for a white victim.

When it is so hot in Shanghai that you stick to the furniture, Herbal Winter Melon Soup is drunk to quench thirst and to cool you down. Unlike the Western practice of drinking iced beverages to cool the body, hot soups are often drunk in the summer in China. Meat is deliberately not used, as the Chinese believe fatty foods prevent the body from being cleansed.

Chapter Seventeen

Little Pearl was chopping vegetables when news of the visitor came. Ken Jin's white woman was at the door. What was her name? Charlotte. Little Pearl was about to refuse to see her; she had no interest in playing her old partner's games. But when she learned the white woman was alone, her interest grew. What could the white woman want badly enough to venture alone into Chinese Shanghai?

A plan began to form in the time it took for Little Pearl to change her clothes. She had dumplings and tea—a special mixture that would work nicely—but would this Charlotte meet her requirements?

She walked to the reception hall and peeked through a tear in the papered window. Ken Jin's woman paced the front courtyard with clear agitation. Her reddish yellow hair flew about her face, and her skin was flushed with color. What could possibly have happened to cause such anxiety? Little Pearl had some guesses, but decided to learn the truth. Plus, Little Pearl had been practicing her English. She would use that to help put the woman at ease.

Little Pearl stepped out, intentionally startling the woman with harsh words and tone. "And what does Ken Jin's newest pet want with me?"

Charlotte spun, clearly flustered. "I . . . I need to know how to stimulate Ken Jin's yang." Then she gasped and pressed her hand to her mouth. That obviously had not been what she'd intended to say.

Little Pearl sneered. "So, he has thrown you over for someone else, and you want him back."

"No, of course not!"

Little Pearl sighed, losing interest. It was cruel to abuse the weak. The kindest thing she could do right now was to throw the woman out, force her to move on without Ken Jin in her life. "Go home, ghost girl," she growled, turning back to the house.

But the white woman followed her, throwing out words in a desperate attempt to hold Little Pearl's attention. She said nothing interesting, nothing that didn't make Little Pearl grind her teeth and long to escape. Until . . .

"I have gone to the Chamber. The one with swinging lights."

Little Pearl froze. No! It wasn't possible. Even she, after years of study, had only heard of the Antechamber to Heaven. This white girl could not possibly have attained such a state. She turned slowly and studied the girl. "I do not believe you."

Charlotte reared back, insulted. "I have been there!"

"Describe it."

The woman did so, but in confusing terms. Her words were jumbled, her expression perplexed. Her hands fluttered chaotically about her face. And yet Charlotte's totally incoherent description of Heaven absolutely echoed the words of everyone else who had gone. In short, Little Pearl believed the girl had made it to Heaven's door.

Fury roared through her. Clearly, these whites possessed a secret. Jonas, now Charlotte, and before them, Lydia Smith—all had some ability that even they did not understand. It took them to Heaven, it gave them their warlike powers, it completely confounded everything a civilized Chinese knew. They did not deserve such good fortune. They were animals; cold-hearted, idiotic. A litany of insults scrolled through her mind, growing uglier in meaning and vehemence until Little Pearl completely enfolded herself in their blackness.

No, she did not understand these horrible creatures, but it was past time she learned their secret. The words were out before she could stop herself. She acted without restraint, focusing completely on executing her purpose without allowing herself to reason. "Come inside." And when the girl balked, Little Pearl continued most forcefully. "Ghost woman! Come inside!"

Charlotte hesitated, but in the end followed docilely enough. Little Pearl was able to implement her plan: sticky rice, drugging tea, incense to inflame the mind and body.

The girl was not stupid. She quickly grew suspicious, but by that time it was too late; Little Pearl had her partially naked and tied spread-eagle in the darkened teaching room. Charlotte's hands and feet were bound with leather straps, and her blouse was torn.

All around, the tapestries trembled. Often students watched from behind peepholes torn in the heavy fabric, and classes were in session. Little Pearl had no idea if any had come inside to watch, but if even one tigress-to-be hid behind the heavy curtains, then whatever happened would shortly become legend within the school.

All of the students had explored with another woman before. It was part of the initial training, and one of the best ways to learn about one's own anatomy. But no tigress had ever tasted a white woman or learned barbarian secrets. No one had ever dared. Little Pearl would. She would bring this girl to orgasm; she would taste the essence of the white yin and then watch and analyze the barbarian magic.

This was the only way, she reminded herself. And though the thought was distasteful to her, so be it. This was the path she had chosen, the life of a tigress, and it was what her ancestors deserved for reducing her to an existence spent among whores and barbarians. If her ancestors had protected her as they should, she would be married to a rich Mandarin now and would know nothing of whites and their bizarre nature.

"I will taste you now," she growled, feeling her hate surround her, infusing everything she did, everything she was.

Charlotte screamed and fought, and part of Little Pearl drew back in horror. What was she doing? Why was her spirit so black that it cherished every scream, gloried in the humiliation she inflicted? Her hand hesitated, and the blade of the knife she'd taken up trembled against the woman's white skin.

Little Pearl thought of the way she had knelt before Jonas to no avail. How she had humbled herself before him as she had not done with anyone since becoming a tigress. She had begged him to save his own life. But he had spurned her, bellowing in fury while she ran in terror. And she remembered begging her parents, pleading with them and so many others: *Don't sell me, don't touch me, don't—*

She bared her teeth and leaned forward, wielding her knife with careful precision. She began at the girl's ankle, pressing the back of the blade against the girl's white, white skin. Then she slowly drew the blade up, slitting cloth as she went. With the restraints in place, there was little the girl could do beyond scream. Let the white girl bellow; Little Pearl would have her answers.

The door burst open, slamming noisily against the wall. Little Pearl turned, expecting to see Jonas coming for her. Instead she saw Ken Jin, his gaze hateful as he wrenched the knife from her hand.

She fought, but she had no chance against the man's fury. He threw her aside in order to rescue his pet. He ripped away the white girl's arm bindings, and she wrapped herself around him, sobbing in fear and pain.

"Are you insane?" Ken Jin roared. "Have you lost all sense of reality?"

Little Pearl tried to answer calmly, tried to explain her reasoning. "I did what was necessary," she said through clenched teeth. She added more, but it made little sense. All she could see was a man saving a woman, and suddenly her pain was too much to contain.

Why did this white woman deserve a rescuer? What magic did she possess to win so powerful a protector when Little Pearl had nothing? Little Pearl had been a Chinese princess, and yet no one had come when she screamed. Why did a white bitch deserve more than she?

The questions churned within her until she couldn't contain it anymore. She launched herself at the couple, using nails and teeth and an animal fury to destroy everything around her. She heard a tapestry rip away, students running in terror. She felt her fingers dig into an arm, a face—or maybe just fabric. She didn't know anything beyond her attack—and that she was helpless against Ken Jin. He had her pinned against the wall within moments, harmless and without hope.

She'd drawn blood. She saw the damage she'd done with surprise, but his face was implacable, his grip even more so. "Shi Po is gone, Little Pearl," he said. "I have begged and bribed and railed, but General Kang will not give her up. That means you lead this temple now."

Little Pearl roared, leaped away like a tigress and soared to Heaven where none would touch her ever again—or so she wished. Her body and mind remained right there, pinned against the wall while Ken Jin's words weighted down her spirit.

"You shame us all," he spat. Then he pushed away, leaving her to crumple. He reached for his white woman and cradled her in his arms. Then, wrapped together as one, they left the dark room.

Little Pearl couldn't move. Ken Jin's words echoed in head. *You shame us all.* She pulled her lips back in a parody of a smile, mentally seeing her parents and their parents and their parents all lined up before the ancestral altar. In her mind, she threw her shame at their feet and they drew back in horror.

This is your *shame!* she spat at them. *You made me such!*

But things had changed; the image brought her no comfort. She continued to rail, tore her hair and spat upon their forms.

A voice interrupted her hysteria. A deep male barbarian voice, and the real reason she had begun all this. "Do you even know why you do the things you do?" Jonas asked. "Or is it just habit to be cruel?"

She had succeeded. She had brought him to her side! And yet the victory tasted like bile. "Go away!" she screeched.

"No."

"Goawaygoawaygoaway!" She launched herself at him, trying to fight as she had before. She was a tigress. Her hands were claws, her mouth a ripping jaw. But her feet were nothing more than bound stumps, and she could not go far from her place on the floor.

He caught her easily, restrained her as if she were a

child. She kicked him, she scratched him, and she aimed for the injuries she had once tended so carefully. He could not avoid all her blows, but he could knock her feet out from under her. He spun her around and pinned her arms from behind. He even dragged her backward a bit so that she could not kick him, and then pulled her down to the ground.

She fought, but he was too strong. She screeched with as much vehemence as an angry child, but he was deaf to it. He simply held her. And in time her fury turned to agony, her hatred to an overwhelming despair.

She began to cry. Or perhaps she had already been sobbing. Her hands tightened into fists, but then she gripped his arm instead. She drew her legs up to kick, then curled herself into her knees.

He wrapped his arms tighter around her, pulling her backward against his chest and murmuring into her hair. She didn't hear what he said, but she felt the vibration of his words. There was no anger in his tone. If there were, she would have thrown it back at him. But he gave her gentleness while she muttered abuse. He gave her peace while she still managed an occasional pinch or shove. He gave her nothing but kindness, and guilt made her hate him even more.

"You will be dead soon," she spat. "Su will have you killed, and I will laugh at your ugly corpse."

"Habit, then," he responded without rancor.

She frowned, confused. "You are a stupid animal who makes no sense."

"You are capable of kindness, but you spoil it with cruelty. I don't understand why."

"You are stupid! A stupid barbarian, a hairy ape!"

"And what are you? A bitter shrew? A vicious whore?"

"A tigress! I am a *tigress!*" She had already grabbed his arm, but now she shook it and him. She would have done worse—tried—but he held her too tightly. At best she could only slam her head backward into him, but he caught her beneath his chin and held fast. "I am a tigress," she whimpered.

"So tigresses drug women, tie them up and assault them?"

"Don't be ridiculous," she snapped. "I had to do that!"

He didn't respond; he just held her still. She didn't push backward anymore. There was no point, since whatever pressure she exerted he converted into a gentle rocking motion. In truth, she found it soothing, and wondered if this was what it felt like to be on a boat at sea. No wonder he was a ship captain. The feeling was so subtle and yet so powerful.

"She said she went to Heaven," she murmured. "I had to do it."

"Why?"

There was no accusation in his tone. She knew he was asking for a simple explanation, but she bristled nonetheless. "Because I had to!"

"So you've said."

She twisted and felt him grunt in pain. His ribs. His chest must be hurting, and yet he stayed wrapped around her though it could only make his pain worse. Pain always got worse. She grimaced, her thoughts a jumble. "Go away," she muttered. "Go back to your papers and lists. Go away."

"I'm exactly where I want to be," he said.

"Well, I don't want you here."

He didn't answer for a long time. Then he sighed, his breath warm and gentle across her cheek. "My mother played these games, Little Pearl. 'Go away. Stay. I hate you. I love you.'" He shook his head, his chin rubbing against her forehead. "I won't play them. They're endless and exhausting. If you tell me to leave, I will."

She spoke clearly and calmly. And with childish petulance. "Go away."

He sighed. "I will, Little Pearl. I have to trust you. If you tell me to leave, I have to do what you say. I have to believe it's what you want. I won't play games." He twisted to look at her more fully, but he didn't get up.

She stared at him, trying to remain firm. She was a tigress, not a child. She had no need of him except for yang. She knew this, and yet everything changed when she looked at his eyes. It made no sense. His skin was mottled and leathery around those eyes, not smooth or well-shaped like a Chinese. His eye color wasn't a normal brown, but a changeable green and brown and gold. She couldn't see what they looked like now—it was too dark here—but she knew they weren't like hers. Nothing about him was like her.

"I don't understand anything you say," she growled. But she did understand at least one part. She knew if she sent him away, he would leave. But he was going anyway. He was a sailor, and that's what sailors did. That's what *people* did.

He waited a moment, then sighed again. The sound was loud, and his body seemed to sag. "I love you, Little Pearl. I'm a fool for it, but the winds blow where they blow, and there's not a damn thing I can do."

She stared at him, her torso clenched. Her insides were sizzling like hot oil, and she fought to control her pain. She dared not speak or she'd explode.

He stared back at her, his expression infinitely sad. He lifted his hand and touched her face with excruciating tenderness. A single calloused fingertip pressed against the skin beneath her left eye, then followed her cheekbone up and away. It was only after he pulled his hand back that she felt a long trail of cold wet. He had wiped away a tear.

She had been crying?

Of course she had been crying. She had been in a rage when she launched herself at Ken Jin. She had screeched and attacked Jonas. She had released loud, messy sobs that clogged her nose and dirtied her clothing. But she'd thought she had stopped. She'd thought the fit had passed.

He wiped away another tear, this time from her right eye.

"My mother would cry like you," he said. "All screaming fury one moment; then later, in silence—one tear after another while she stared at nothing. I didn't understand then." His cheek lifted in a short laugh. "I still don't understand, but I know she was hurting. A hurt so deep she couldn't stop it, and it leaked free whenever she was quiet." He leaned forward, his face thoughtful in the gloom. "You and me, we're the lost people. Whore or son of a whore—it doesn't matter what we do in our lives, we are branded by that beginning. And only we can help each other. I know pain, Little Pearl, and anger, and a deep ache that nothing eases. There is no salvation for either of us unless we turn to each other." He held out his hand to her in hope.

She stared at it, the possibility he offered too much to bear.

"You are stupid." The words leaped out. Little Pearl's throat was clogged, her spine rigid, and her mind both empty and cluttered at the same time. And yet even with all that, the words sprang free to wound him.

"Aye-aye, Captain," he drawled in English. Then his hand dropped away as he stood up. "I'll leave you alone now," he said in Chinese. "Let me know if you need me for anything."

Her lips curled in a sneer. "You want to rut?"

"Like I want you to be happy." He shook his head.

"You don't trust, Little Pearl, but sometimes it's worth it. Whatever you need, tell me, and I'll get it or do it. *Whatever you need*."

She stared at him, shock sending ripples of anguish through her body. "Why would you say such a thing?" she asked. "Do you offer your money? Your ship? You want to be my slave?"

He winced at her words but didn't deny them. "I need you to survive, Little Pearl. I need you to be happy."

"Why?" The word escaped despite her intention.

"Because you are strong and smart and so damn beautiful it sometimes hurts to look at you. If you can't make it, then what hope is there for me? If you can't move beyond a bad beginning, then I am doomed as well."

She squinted through the darkness, wondering if he lied. Why would a man tie his fortunes to hers? Why would he think his happiness depended upon hers? She had given up such thoughts long ago, and here he was making her think again. Making her believe such things were possible again.

"You are crazy insane," she said. Then she shoved him as hard as she could. He had been standing, but she hit him so hard he staggered and sat back down with a groan. "Crazy insane barbarian!"

"Don't forget stupid and hairy."

"Stupid! Hairy!"

"Foolish ape."

"Foolish! Ape!"

"Who loves you."

"*Idiot! Idiot!*" She leaped upon him and began beating at his chest.

He held her off. By the time she stopped, her breath was coming in strained gasps and he was cursing in English. She did not understand his words, but she knew the sounds, knew she had pushed him to his limit. Some part of her knew that she was driving him away for good, but it was a small part with no sway over her actions.

"I am going back to Kui Yu's office now because you told me to leave. All you have to do is ask me to stay and I will. No games. Just ask—"

She spat out words in Chinese, insulting his ancestry, cursing his genitals and pitying his descendants. He simply waited for her to finish.

As if she hadn't interrupted, he said, "I know you want me to stay. I know that this is a game you play—to insult me, curse me, and hit me. By staying and waiting patiently, I prove that I won't leave you. I am supposed to wait through your abuse to prove that I care." He shook his head. "That is a game for children, Little Pearl, and I played much too long with my mother."

"I am not your diseased whore of a mother!" she screamed.

He winced, but she was past caring. If he would release her hands, she would hit him. If she could, she would yank his tongue out of his mouth. All she could do was spit in his face.

He abruptly spun her to the ground and rolled atop her. She felt the cold wood floor against her face, smelled the dust, and tasted the copper of blood from a cut in her mouth. She knew what was coming, knew in some part of her mind that this was where she had driven Captain Jonas. She even felt her legs relax in acceptance.

She felt the pressure of his chest on her back. Her arms were pinned beneath her so that she couldn't push up or away. She was caught now, whatever he wanted to do. She absently realized that he would rip her dress, and she mourned it as her last decent gown. But he was a kind man unused to being pushed to such lengths. She guessed he would feel guilty later and would buy her a new dress.

She accepted his weight, knowing that he fumbled

with his pants. Soon he would spread her legs with his knees and shove himself inside her. It would be harsh and brutal and no more than she deserved.

She choked on her sobs, and yet a stillness settled inside her. This, at least, she understood. She knew what was to happen, and that comforted her. She closed her eyes and accepted that she had at last come to the center of Captain Jonas: he was a man like any other. She relaxed and accepted because she understood what was coming.

Except, he did not tear her dress. He did not fumble with his clothing or even seem to have a thickened dragon. He simply held her down with his weight, his breath coming in angry huffs against her cheek.

She frowned in confusion. Was he hurt? Had she hurt him? Despite her anger and her actions, she did not want him to die. She twisted as much as she could, but she couldn't see. She couldn't see anything beyond the torn tapestry on the floor and the table legs farther away.

"Captain Jonas? Are you hurt?"

"No, I am not hurt." He sighed. "I am lonely, Little Pearl. I never realized how much until you."

She frowned. If he was lonely, why wasn't he rutting with her now? Why didn't he take his ease as all men did? Her chest began to tighten as she struggled with her thoughts.

"I want a woman who isn't afraid to be with me. Or with herself." She felt his weight shift as he pulled away from her. She wondered if he were going to pull off his pants now, but his next words were too sad for that to be likely. "I thought you might be that person, Little Pearl, but you're . . ." His hand trailed across her back then withdrew. "I don't know. What happened to make you like this?"

A hot denial sprang to her lips, but he stopped it with a hand against her mouth.

"Think before you speak. Don't answer out of habit. Really think. What has happened? What do you want for yourself in the future?"

She didn't know how to answer, didn't want to think. Her chest was nearly too tight for her to breathe, and her insides still sizzled. "You make me think too much!" she accused. When he let her go, she rolled onto her side and scrambled backward and away. He watched with weary eyes.

"I have a crew to worry about and cargo to move. I have responsibilities, Little Pearl. But I will set them all aside to be with you. If you want me."

She didn't answer, just stared at him as she fought for clarity in her jumbled thoughts. And while she watched, he walked wearily to the door.

"What would we do?" she whispered. He didn't hear her, and she had no breath to speak louder. But she had her qi energy, and she used it to strengthen her voice. "Jonas."

He stopped and turned, his large body filling the doorway. "Little Pearl?"

She swallowed, forcing herself upright. She would not lie on the ground like a dog. "What would we do if you stayed?" Her voice was still weak, but he was listening.

"We would talk." Then he shook his head. "You would tell me why you are so hurt."

"I'm not hurt!" she began. Then she bit her lip, barely stopping herself from snarling. He waited less patiently than before as she climbed to her feet, but she wanted to face him eye to eye. When she felt enough in control, she spoke with clarity and intent. "I want to talk about habit." She tightened her hands, angry with herself for needing to speak when she should have just let him leave. Instead, she kept talking. "Do you get angry and . . ." She swallowed, forcing herself to admit the truth. "And you don't even know why?"

"Yes, I used to. All the time." He smiled, and the tenderness in his expression dislodged some of the weight in her chest.

"How did you stop?"

He shrugged. "I gave up everything. I put my ships up for sale, sold everything I owned, and moved to Yorkshire to raise sheep."

She stared at him. His expression was infinitely open and sad. What he said was absolute truth.

"I gave up everything, Little Pearl," he continued. "And tried to build a new life."

"As a shepherd?"

He released a short burst of laughter. "I tried everything—sheep farming, shop keeping, bean counting." He lifted his eyes to her face. "There were even a few lovely women who wanted to share such a life with me. Good, wholesome, God-fearing women."

She could not speak. She could not even breathe as she waited for the rest of his story.

"It didn't fit, Little Pearl. I was born to sail the seas. Still, it taught me something." His gaze focused on her. "It taught me I had a choice. I could choose to be a ship captain—or not. I could choose to drink and whore—or not." He took a step back into the room. "And I could choose to be angry or not."

She grimaced, already shaking her head. Did he not understand? The anger came from deep inside. It welled up without restraint and she had no control over it.

"I know it's not easy," he continued. "It was the hardest damn thing I've ever done. I had to think before I spoke, every moment of the day, and to always ask myself, 'Why am I doing this? Why am I acting this way?' I'm still not perfect at it."

"I get angry because I am thinking," she said.

"About what?"

She shook her head. "I don't know," she lied. But in her heart she knew the answer—at least a partial answer. Lately, she became angry whenever she thought about him.

He stepped back into the room, closing the door behind him. Then he lit several candles. "Lately," he said without rancor, "I get angry when I think about you, too."

She couldn't stifle her gasp. How could he know her thoughts so exactly? "You make me angry," she said to cover her confusion.

His smile turned rakish. "I know. So, I guess that makes us well matched."

She frowned. "I don't understand." He had spoken in Chinese, but the words made no sense.

He adjusted the cushions on the table and sat down, extending his leg such that it was well supported. It took a moment for her to remember that he had an ugly bruise on that thigh and probably needed to ease the strain.

She moved forward. "You are hurt. You should rest."

"I am exactly where I want to be." But he patted the other side of the table. "Sit down. We're talking, remember?"

"Stupid ape," she said without heat. "Of course I remember."

"Snooty cook," he returned with clear humor. "You remember, but you don't talk."

She couldn't stop her smile. It felt so strange to banter with him. She didn't even understand his English words, but she felt her breath flow more smoothly as she settled beside him. "At least you didn't call me a whore."

He shook his head. "You are a chef, Little Pearl. It is what you have made yourself, it is how you have thought and acted. Other people forced you into the other life. You chose—"

"I am a tigress," she interrupted. It was important to correct him, but how to explain what she meant? "Years ago, Shi Po came to the whorehouse to teach classes."

"Classes in whoring?"

She glanced up. "Of course. Only nail shack whores spread their legs without thought. Men pay more to be seduced. Girls need teaching for that."

"I suppose that makes sense."

"Shi Po showed us ways to seduce, but she also told us about yin and yang, about a woman's energies combining with a man's—"

"To reach Heaven," he drawled.

She nodded, despite his disdain. "It *is* possible. That white woman who was here went to Heaven. Ken Jin saw it."

Jonas reared back. "Ken Jin saw it? But how . . . ? What did he see?"

Little Pearl shook her head. "I don't know. He left too quickly." She swallowed, shame making her look at her feet. "I didn't have time to ask."

He stared at her for a moment, then slowly reached forward to touch her hand. She glanced up in surprise only to be caught by his gaze. "Why did you tie her up, Little Pearl? What were you doing?"

She sighed. "The texts say that when you become an Immortal, things change—your energy, your body, everything is different. If that is true, and if Miss Charlotte Wicks did ascend, then I would know."

He frowned. "Know? Know how?"

She swallowed, nervous about her next words. Many men found the thought distasteful. Then again, many men did not. "I would be able to taste it—taste the difference."

He took a moment to understand. "Oh. Of course." There was no horror in his words nor any excitement. His head tilted to one side. "But surely there is another way to know."

She shrugged, lifting her hands with a sigh. "I do not

know of one." Her gaze dropped to the restraints that dangled from the corners of the table. "I had to restrain her," she murmured. "The girl would not have allowed it otherwise. I thought the drugs would make her want it."

"You did not think at all," he growled. "She is not an animal to be used like that." He leaned forward, his grip on her hand tightening when she would have drawn away. "Whites are not animals."

She nodded. It was hard to do when her belly was taut with fear. Anger was so close to the surface at moments like this, but she held her tongue with an act of will. Then she lifted her gaze to his. "You are not animals," she agreed. "But you are not like us."

His eyebrows lifted. "Is that so bad? To be different?"

"Yes!"

"Why?"

She frowned. She'd known he would ask, but she had no answer. "Different is . . . bad."

She was staring at his hand on hers, so she was not surprised when he lifted it. Still, she had to hold herself statue-still when he touched her cheek, gently encouraging her to look at him. "I like different. You're different, and I—"

She slapped him, hard, her palm cracking across his cheek with a force that stunned her. Her hand was numb with the shock, and she gasped at her sudden violence. Especially as his eyes narrowed with fury.

She drew back her hand and bowed her head, waiting for the inevitable. She didn't even brace for the blow, knowing that men enjoyed seeing women sprawl. And since she deserved this, she would give him what he wanted.

"You do not want me to say you are different," he said through clenched teeth.

She glanced up, her chest tight again, forcing out the hot denial. "I am *not* different! You are different. I am not!"

His eyes narrowed. "Why? What happens to those who are different?" He grabbed her wrists and held her. "Answer. And know this: You attack me again, and I won't stay no matter what you do."

She almost wept. Why did she keep striking out at him? She didn't even mean to.

"I am tired of the abuse, Little Pearl. Stay rational or I'm done."

Curses sprang to her lips, but she held them back. And the conflict within her came out as a low growl.

"See?" he said gently. "You can control yourself. You can hold back the . . . the anger habit."

The struggle inside her grew, making Little Pearl's growl build in her throat. Finally she shoved away and spat out the greatest insult she could think of. "You are the most . . . *different* man I have ever known!"

He stared at her, watching quietly as she got up to prowl the room. The candle flames flickered as she passed, but she did not put them out. She liked the light too much for that. At last she returned to her seat on the table.

"So," he drawled. "Different is bad. Why?"

"I am not different," she repeated. "You are." Then she pulled her knees up to her chest, curling into herself and pressing her forehead into her knees.

His arms surrounded her. His hands flowed around her back and across her arms until she was enfolded in his embrace just as Charlotte had been enfolded by Ken Jin. The sensation was warm and full. It was quiet and powerful. It was everything she had ever imagined. And yet, it was not enough.

"I am not different," she repeated to her knees.

"You are the best," he murmured in her ear.

She nodded. "I am the best tigress ever." It was a lie, and yet it was also true. Little Pearl had spent many hours studying the sacred scrolls. She knew them better than anyone. She had the most skill at drawing out even the most reluctant yang. For years now, her entire life had revolved around two things: food and tigress practice.

And yet, for all her study she could not help but think she'd missed something, that she was wholly inadequate, flawed in some fundamental way. "Different is bad," she said. How strange that a ghost barbarian understood these things. She looked up, twisting so that she could meet his eyes. "And I *am* different," she confessed.

He had no answer. She saw the struggle in his eyes as he tried to form a response. "Different or the same, I don't care. I like you, Little Pearl, whatever you are. Just as you are."

She swallowed, stunned by the tears that blurred her vision. She did not want to cry again.

He smiled and leaned forward. "I *love* you," he whispered. "This love I have is different than I have ever known." He spoke low in her ear, his tone conversational. "When I loved Annie, it was with a sweetness and all the earnestness of youth. But with you, my eyes are open, Little Pearl. I see your faults—your anger and your pain—and I feel a kinship with you because of it. And then I see what you have done with your life, how you are a cook, a teacher, and so strong it surprises me. I admire you." He sighed. "I don't know when that admiration became love, but there it is. My heart longs for your happiness, and I will risk everything—my crew, my livelihood, even my sanity—to be with you."

He fell silent, and she twisted enough to look at him. He was close enough to kiss her. He wanted to kiss her. She could see it in his posture, his look, his very presence. He wanted her, and yet he was waiting and silently asking. Would she kiss him?

She frowned. What man asked such a thing? It compelled her. She pushed forward to press her mouth to his. At the last moment, he pulled back.

"We're going to do this my way, Little Pearl. No tigress

nonsense. No seduction or plan or pain. Just a man and a woman. Making normal love."

She pulled back, annoyed and bizarrely intrigued. "What do you mean—normal?"

He smiled. "Not different. Normal."

"But—"

"Don't worry," he cut her off. "I'll teach you."

The translation of won ton is "cloud swallow." If made correctly, won tons should be heavenly morsels, sweet from the shrimp and mushrooms, crisp with fresh water chestnuts.

Chapter Eighteen

Little Pearl did not like Jonas's "normal." She knew what normal was for a man. It was simple rutting, with him on top, her sweetly open and receiving beneath. She had done "normal" hundreds of times by the time she'd turned fourteen.

But this was what he wanted, and so she would give it to him. She would play the game. It would be her thanks for his insane kindness. She ducked her head, pretending to be shy so that he could coax her head up to his. He did, his touch exquisitely tender, and a smile trembled on her lips. He leaned in to kiss her and she offered her mouth with a sweet sigh.

Their lips touched. He extended his tongue, teasing her mouth open before pressing inside. She released a gasp that seemed to fire his blood. He delved boldly inside and she widened to give him access.

He plunged and plundered. She moaned, wondering all the time if Mei Wan would remember which mushrooms to put in the soup. He tilted her head, his hands surging into her hair. She arched back, letting the tendrils slip free of its knot. Mei Wan would singe the ginger. She always did. His hands found her breasts, lifting and squeezing in the clumsy way of all men. She wondered how many students had left, or if they would stay around, expecting food. She bit off a moan. This encounter would have to happen fast if she needed to cook for an additional twenty people. She had to remember who had paid for their classes and who hadn't; the temple could no longer afford to feed people who were behind on payment.

Jonas's hands lifted away. He had been pushing her down toward the table, but he stopped. She continued the motion because that was the next step. But he did not follow. Instead, he sat up and stared at her.

"Jonas?" she asked, making sure her voice was breathy. Should she resist more? Did he need to overpower her?

"Where were you just now?"

She frowned. "I am right here."

"Your body was. What were you thinking?"

She let her gaze slide away. "That I . . . That you are so large. That sometimes you frighten me with your strength."

"Do you think me an idiot?"

Her gaze jumped back to his face. "What?"

"Do you think me so stupid as to not know when . . . when . . ."

She slowly pushed herself upright. "When what?"

"What were you really thinking?"

"About you."

"Look at me!"

"I am!"

"Not now," he growled. "During."

He needed her to look at him? "Very well."

"No. Not just look at me. You have to *really* look at me. You have to be here with me."

"I am."

"No. You're off cooking or something. I can tell, Little Pearl."

She stared at him, her insides growing cold. He couldn't possibly know that. She was good at what she did. She was a tigress. How could he possibly know that she substituted technique for passion, education for interest? He couldn't know. And yet, he obviously did.

He gripped her chin, holding her face so that she stared directly into his eyes. "When was the last time you enjoyed sex? When did you last gasp out in ecstasy, in total joy?"

She jerked her chin out of his hand. "I experienced the yin tide this morning, with you."

"The yin tide. This morning."

She nodded. "Of course."

His mouth tightened. "Are we 'practicing' now?"

She reared back. "Of course not."

"Then what are we doing?"

She threw up her hands in disgust. "You know what we are doing."

"Tell me, Little Pearl. What?"

"We are doing what you wanted to do! Normal. No practice, you said. Normal."

He nodded, his body slumping. "Yes. Of course. This is normal to you. Sex without feeling. It's all an act." He leaned forward. "Feeling good without feeling anything at all."

She frowned, hearing an echo of deeper meaning in his words. "Jonas?"

"I know that is normal for you. Hell, it's normal for me." He shook his head. "But I'm tired of that. Aren't you? Wouldn't you rather just be cooking than do that again?"

How to answer? How to tell a man that his touch meant less than nothing, was a way to pass the time before dinner? And yet, even as she thought the words to herself, she knew she lied. Jonas meant more. He always had. His touch created more yin, aroused more interest than anyone else ever had. He'd even taken her to Heaven's door. But she didn't want to admit that.

"We are not practicing now," she said simply.

"We're not making love, either."

She stared at him, mute. What did he want her to say?

He reached out and touched her cheek. "Tell me what you are thinking."

She frowned. "I am thinking that you are the strangest man I have ever known."

"You've already said that. Tell me what you are feeling."

"Angry."

He nodded. "Yes. Of course. But let's see if we can get you to feel something else." His hand opened to caress her cheek, then slowly trailed down her jaw to her neck. "Now?"

"I . . . I am not sure," she simpered.

His hand froze, then drew away. "The truth, Little Pearl!"

She glared at him. What was this game? "I feel . . ." She studied his face—bushy eyebrows, large nose, ruddy white skin—and wondered just what he wanted her to say.

"Don't think about me. What are you feeling?"

"Cornered!" She said the word in Chinese, believing he would not understand.

But apparently he did, because he pulled back and gestured to the door. "You are not trapped, Little Pearl. You have complete freedom."

She stared at him, then the door. He was right; she could leave. She turned back to him, at last realizing what he wanted. She shrunk back in horror. "But this is not practice," she said.

"No."

No, it wasn't practice, and he still wanted her complete attention. He wanted her to be with him, to experience all that he did, not to stimulate act as she did with a customer. He wanted her with him as a man and woman in love. The thought was terrifying, for she had never considered it.

"I do not love you," she said.

He flinched. Then he leaned forward, his expression shifting from hurt to challenge. "Are you sure?"

An angry retort sprang to her lips, but she stopped its escape. Or maybe her mouth was just frozen shut. She turned away. "The Chinese do not talk about love."

"Of course they do," he returned. "You have poetry and songs. Aren't they about love?"

"*Whores* do not talk about love."

He laughed, a loud rumble of sound that echoed in the room. "Whores talk about love all the time. They just don't mean it. But that matters not. You're a tigress, not a whore."

"I am weary of this." She pushed off the table, only to be stopped by his hand on her arm.

"Do you want me, Little Pearl? As a woman wants a man? Look deep."

Her eyes widened and her heartbeat accelerated. Her chest tightened and her legs tensed, but she did not run. She stood rooted in place, not by him but by herself. Did she want him? Could she love him?

She had never thought of these things. Certainly she had dreamed of them when she was a child. Before . . . But afterward, her life had been a struggle for survival and sanity. The tigress training had saved her, but that teaching was not about love. It was about sensuality and energy, and about ways to remove oneself from Earth to become an Immortal. Love was a human attachment, and therefore to be avoided.

And yet, what if it was possible? What if she could fall in

love and marry and have children just like other people? As if she were respectable. What if that were possible?

She looked at Jonas, seeing his angular face, his white skin and his bushy eyebrows. She could not marry him and be respectable. She could not have children with him and have any hope that those children would have a future. Half-breeds were despised. And yet, the possibility drew her. Hope sparked within her. Desire flared as it never had.

"I could love you," she whispered, awed by the thought. "Can you really love me?"

He stroked the outline of her lips with his fingertip. "I already do. I don't really understand how that happened, but there it is."

The world changed. Yin/yang fire burned in a fiery trail wherever he touched. She sighed.

"Stay with me, Little Pearl. Be here with me," he said. Then he leaned toward her and pressed his mouth to hers. It was a quiet kiss, tender and filled with longing. "What are you feeling?" he whispered.

A mouth on fire. A heart beating faster than a terrified rabbit. Hands slick with sweat. "You," she whispered. "I feel *you*."

He thrust his tongue deep inside her mouth and she nearly choked on the shock of it all. Intimate, intrusive, and terrifyingly real. What was wrong with her? Hundreds of men had kissed her like this. Men, women, even children had all done this at one time or another. Why was this different? Why was it so powerful in what it made her feel?

He went slowly. He touched her tongue, he stroked the roof of her mouth, he even outlined her teeth while she clutched his arms and held herself still. She didn't know what to do. Her training had deserted her. She knew she should stroke him back, should suck on his tongue, should do all the things a tigress did, but she remained frozen and terrified.

He broke the kiss, not to pull away, but to push his head forward, rubbing his cheek against hers. She heard him inhale deeply and felt the fire spread from her mouth to her cheek to the entire left side of her face. Beneath her fingers, his qi surged through his tense forearms, and she moaned.

"You already love me, Little Pearl," he whispered. "I know you do."

"No!" she gasped.

"It's all right," he soothed, and continued to caress her cheek. She felt the rough scratch of his beard on her skin and lifted her chin to feel the sensation more fully. She even adjusted her shoulders to expose her neck.

"You don't have to say anything," he continued. "Just allow yourself to feel the possibility."

She swallowed. She wanted to speak but her throat was too tight. The fire had reached her neck, steadily progressing to her chest. She knew he would touch her there soon. Her yin was already flowing strong. And while part of her still tried to shift to technique, another part— the stronger part—kept her right where she was. *Feeling.*

His thumbs skimmed across her belly. She hadn't even realized that her blouse had lifted from her skirt, but his hands were beneath the fabric and she gasped at the sudden electric feel just above her womb. It was too much. She closed her eyes. She thought about dinner and vegetables and when she would go to the market. Except she couldn't really think about that. He had said he loved her, really loved her. And for the first time, she actually believed it. The belief shimmered in her spirit stronger than any yin tide, more amazing than the strongest qi. This man—this very good man—loved her.

Her entire body shivered with awe. He pulled off her

blouse while she continued to tremble in shock. He loved her. And perhaps . . . yes, maybe . . . she might love him, too.

"What are you thinking?" he rumbled into her neck.

Her hands were frozen on his upper arms. She felt the muscles thick and bulging. The image of Ken Jin holding Charlotte flashed through her mind. He had been helping her stand, cradling her in his arms as she found her footing. "Are you strong enough to hold me? To . . . pick me up?"

She felt his mouth curl into a smile. "Of course. You weigh less than nothing." He immediately shifted, slipping his arm beneath her legs and drawing her up. She rested totally in his power, which effortlessly buoyed her up. "Where would you like to go?"

She smiled and ducked her head, both embarrassed and pleased at the same time. "Nowhere," she confessed. "I just wanted to feel this." She was completely surrounded by his love.

"Wrap your arms around my neck."

She did. How quickly she followed his commands now. She pulled herself higher in his arms, drawing her face back to his, her cheek against his.

He murmured something. Appreciation, hunger, she wasn't sure what. It was half purr, half thunder, and she smiled at the sound. Especially as he shifted her a little more, untying her undergarment from behind and pulling it off of her. She was naked from the waist up. Her body itched in the most incredible way, and a tingle crawled all the way up her spine into her jaw.

Then he lifted her higher, raising her up such that he could taste her breasts. His arms were filled with her, so he could only use his mouth. His beard abraded the outside of her breast, then his tongue swirled and touched, obviously seeking a target. He found it: her nipple, which he immediately coiled around and sucked into his mouth.

She gasped at the sudden pull, and she tightened her hold around his neck. But that only lifted her higher, and soon his mouth engulfed her breast, pulling and tugging while her body dipped and swayed with his motion. It was sloppy work, he was not a dragon, and yet she quivered with his power—*their* power, for his yang made hers sing. Her chest still felt tight, her breath came in halting gasps.

He bit her nipple, softly, and she shuddered. A long tremble began at her womb and radiated outward until it shook her entire body. He paused, drawing back enough to look at her in worry.

"Little Pearl?"

She shook her head, uncertain how to answer. She felt like a tiny animal shaking water out of her fur. The image made no sense, and yet it felt so right. She was stepping out of something terrible, shaking clean, and feeling completely naked and alone.

"I'm here," he whispered. He began dropping kisses on her skin. "Don't be afraid."

He set her carefully back down on the table. She tightened her arms around him, keeping him close. As her feet, then her bottom set down, she relaxed enough to let him draw his face higher up her body. Soon they were again cheek to cheek.

"I want you, Little Pearl," he whispered. "But I want this to go slow, to help you understand—"

"I am ready." Her yin rain had soaked to her skirt, and her legs ached with desire. It was a powerful new sensation.

"Not yet. Not . . ." He swallowed. "I want to taste you. I want you to feel every moment."

She nodded. If he wished to do this, so be it. And yet, she still tightened with anxiety. Though she had experienced the Polishing of the Mirror many times by both men and women alike, with Jonas everything was different.

"Take off your clothes," she ordered. She needed him as naked as she was.

He nodded, stripping off everything with quick motions. Then he paused. "Should I take off your skirt?"

She blushed, confused. He was nude, his powerful body arrayed before her. She had seen it before. She knew the puckered scars of his wounds, the bristly hair on his chest, the broad set to his shoulders and the narrow cast to his waist and buttocks. She also had experienced the thickened glory of his dragon. And yet as she looked at him, all seemed new. She had never been loved before.

Soon he would touch her, taste her, then rut in her with that body. *No,* she mentally corrected herself. They would make love. What did that mean?

She quickly shucked her skirt. Excitement shimmered in her blood, heating her face and making her fingers unsteady. This was a glorious man with a beautiful body. She was a tigress who should understand exactly what was happening. And yet, it was all new, all breathlessly exciting, and anticipation bubbled inside her.

She ducked her head, feeling awkward. He lifted her chin, searching her face. "You are not a shy woman, Little Pearl."

She nodded.

"But you are nervous now?"

She kissed him. She knew she rushed forward, using the contact to silence his questions, but the action also stopped her thoughts. She became swamped in his yang power, and he swam in her yin essence. He tasted her mouth, then began moving down her body. He laved her breasts and her belly. She caressed whatever she could reach—the hollow just before his collarbone, the thick muscles that defined his broad shoulders, the soft curls of hair that coiled about his ears and the top of his head.

Then his tongue delved into the secrets of her cinnabar

cave. The shock burst through her body like lightning. His hands were on her knees, spreading her open, while his tongue found her pleasure grotto and burrowed along her tattooed tigress. She cried out, arching off the table in pleasure. This was not practice, so her mind had not been prepared for the firestorm of energy that came with the yin tide. Physically it was nothing more than muscle contractions, quivering thighs, tightened buttocks, an explosion of qi that she couldn't direct or control. Wasted qi power to no purpose. And yet, it was also like being in the center of a thundercloud with lightning flashes all around. Winds buffeted her with pleasure and a warming heat filled her with joy.

She laughed and felt the cool caress of tears on her cheeks. He was kissing the inside of her thighs, murmuring nonsense words against her body. She felt the arch in her spine ease and the flex in her legs release. The yin tide still washed through her, but the contractions were weaker. She looked down, her body languid as she reached for him. She could see the yang dragon had grabbed hold of him. His eyes were fierce and his muscles tight with restraint.

Her knees slipped open wider as he climbed onto the table. He was poised on all fours above her, and she realized with new shock how very large a man he was. What a big frame, thick muscles, strong body! Would he smother her? This man who loved her, would he destroy her?

He dropped onto his elbows, framing her face with his arms. Then he kissed her deeply, passionately, and with such intensity that she knew the yang flame seared him. His control could not hold long.

He broke the kiss, pulling back and glancing worriedly down at her. "Do you want to be on top?" he rasped.

"What?" She didn't understand.

"Do you want to switch positions? You're so tiny. I don't want to hurt you."

She smiled in relief and nodded. Her body was so lax that it was hard for her to move quickly, but she managed it with his help, and soon he was on his back while she prowled above him. His hands found her breasts even before she straddled him. He thumbed her nipples and kneaded her breasts. There was no skill in his movements, and she knew that what he did loosened the flesh there rather than tightened it. She didn't care. His hands were large, his touch firm, and she found she gloried in his command even as she found and gripped his dragon with her hands.

She meant to stroke him, to bring him to fullness this way, but she also wanted more. She wanted him inside her body though it was contrary to her tigress practice. She wanted him to open her floodgates wide; and so without any preamble, she pushed down on him.

He groaned in delight. His hands slipped from her breasts to her hips, clenching and unclenching rhythmically, though he allowed her to set the pace of their joining. She was a tigress, so she knew how to best prolong his pleasure. As wet as she was, he slipped easily in and out, in and out, and she clenched her tigress muscles to intensify his stimulation or dull it depending on what she thought was best. She began the series of long and short strokes according to pattern, and soon her mind slipped into expert handling.

His fingers dug tight into her sides, holding her still. "Little Pearl!" he gasped.

She blinked and focused on his face. His skin was flushed, his nostrils flared, and yet he controlled his breath as well as any dragon master holding back his yang. "Jonas?"

"Say you love me. Admit it. If you believe."

Her mouth went dry. She opened her mouth to speak pat lies learned in her first month as a prostitute, but no sound came out. She couldn't lie to him. Not now, not with him planted so deeply within her and his eyes so intense on her.

"Say it," he whispered. "Please."

She swallowed. If she said it to him, she would have to mean it. She tried to move her hips, tried to distract him, but his fingers bore down hard to keep her still.

"Do you?" he rasped. "Do you love me?"

Did she? Could she?

"Try. Try to love me. Will you at least promise to try?"

She nodded. She couldn't say the words, but she could move. She would try.

"Say it!" His yang dragon was roaring. He would not last more than a moment longer. All she had to do was hold out for a breath or two, and it would be too late. He would have his fulfillment, maybe even forget he'd asked anything of her. If she only waited . . .

"Yes," she rushed out. "Yes, I will try!"

His dragon released its yang. With an exclamation of power, Jonas thrust deep inside her and erupted, his body's convulsions bringing on her own. Her conscious contractions became unconscious, the yin tide surged, mixing with his yang fire, and she cried out in joy.

Only to realize that there was more. . . .

The importance of the fish derives from a play on words. The word for fish, yu, sounds like the word for wish. Thus, the Cantonese feel it is auspicious to eat fish to insure your wishes for the new year come true. It goes with the old Cantonese saying, Yu yuen yee sheung, *or,* May your wishes be fulfilled.

Chapter Nineteen

Little Pearl felt the darkness close in around her. It was a familiar place by now. She knew this was where her yin and Jonas's yang brought her. Not to Heaven. Immortals ascended to Heaven; she went to this small, dark, enclosed space beneath a table.

She folded into herself. She tucked her knees up to her chest and let her tears wet her silk skirt. She was wearing what had once been her least favorite outfit—a blue silk skirt that was too tight to take large steps—but was now nicer than anything she owned. If only she could take this dress from her dream into the daylight. She'd sell it for enough to buy a good, fat fish.

But dream dresses stayed in dreams. And all too soon it would be torn to shreds as the Ugly Man came to drag her away.

"Back here again, huh?"

Little Pearl looked up to see Jonas standing clear as the sun beside her table. She had to crane her neck forward and around to look up at him. "You don't belong here."

He shrugged, his gaze narrowing as he took in the hallway and the whole upper floor. "We didn't stay long last time. This is a Chinese house." He looked down at her. "Your house? When you were a child?"

She nodded, shrinking back against the wall. The space felt smaller than before, as if she had grown or the table had shrunk. "Go away." She didn't want him to see what came next.

"No." He wandered forward, his feet growing smaller in her view as he looked over the railing at the lower floor. He would see a traditional Confucian entryway with a vase of flowers for welcome and a mirror to ward off evil spirits. It didn't work: The Ugly Man had come anyway. But perhaps evil spirits weren't frightened off when invited in by her parents.

She whimpered and tried to become even smaller.

"Well, that's not what I expected," he drawled.

She glanced up, intrigued by the tone of his voice. It was both dry and horrified at the same time. She craned her neck to see, but her view was restricted to the hall-way floor.

"It's just my family," she snapped. And the Ugly Man.

"No," Jonas answered. "No, it's not. It's mine."

She looked up, startled enough that she banged her head on the table, then ducked back down. "Don't be ridiculous," she groused. "What would your parents be doing in my house?"

"I don't know," he murmured. Then he turned back to her. "Come out and see."

She shrank back and tucked herself tighter. She would soon be dragged out by her hair. Why would she come out willingly?

"Suit yourself." He stepped back to the edge to watch

and didn't move for a bit. She saw his body tighten as he watched. He abruptly burst into laughter.

Laughing? She was being sold into prostitution and he was laughing? "How dare you!"

He glanced back, startled. "What? Bertie was being funny."

"Bertie? Who's Bertie?"

"My brother. He's trying to juggle a loaf of bread, an apple, and a bracelet. Actually, he's not bad for an eight-year-old, but that apple will be mush by the time he's done." His gaze returned to the scene below. "He always had a way of making us laugh. I'd forgotten that."

She frowned. "What are you talking about?"

He gestured down to the main floor. "I told you. It's my mother, brother, and me just before I went to sea for the first time." His lips curved into a smile. "This was a good day. One of the best."

She shook her head. "This is an awful day. This is . . ." She closed her eyes. She could almost hear the argument, the clink of the coins, and the Ugly Man's heavy steps. Her throat was already raw from her screams. Her hands wrapped around the table leg in preparation.

"Mum had been gifted that bracelet from . . . I don't know. Some man. A generous one that she loved—or pretended to love." He glanced back at her. "It made it easier for her, to pretend to be in love." His expression sobered. "It didn't last long, of course. We were broke again in a month. But right then, it was good. And later, there was another man, another gift. That was our cycle. I went away to sea to escape it, only to discover that sailing has its own rhythms."

She was staring at him, hearing his words but also the echo of laughter behind him. Boyish guffaws, feminine giggles. "But this is my house. How could you be here?"

He shrugged. "I'm here. Maybe this is my dream."

"It is my house!"

He didn't answer except to turn back to the scene below. "You're the tigress. You tell me." He said the words, but she could tell that his attention wasn't on her. It was on himself as a boy and his family.

She released her grip on the table leg to crawl forward. She wanted to see what he was watching. "Is she beautiful?" she asked.

"Who?"

"Your mother."

"When she laughed. I think that's why she attracted so many men. Her smile was mysterious, alluring, and beautiful, but her laughter was . . . pure joy. She felt everything so deeply—the joy and the pain." He glanced back at her. "In that way, you two are very alike."

She stretched her head a little further, trying to see. She couldn't. Not without leaving her table shelter. But the more he spoke, the more she could hear. His mother's laugh was indeed filled with lightness and sweet yin power. "I was never that free," she commented without thought. "Not even as a child."

"You have been," he returned. "I have heard it. And once heard . . ." His gaze returned to his family. "A man does everything he can to hear it again. Lord, look at us. Even as kids, we did everything to make her laugh." He shook his head, but there was fondness in his tone. "I can't believe I was ever that silly."

She had to see, even at the cost of her shelter. She was going to be dragged out from it anyway, and she would be fast enough to dive back under when the time came. What would it hurt to look now? She wanted to see Jonas acting silly.

She made it to the edge of the railing to look down. For a moment she saw what she expected to see—her front hallway, her parents with the Ugly Man. But then Jonas laughed—a full sound without constraint—and she desperately wanted to see what he did. With the wish came the result, and the scene abruptly changed.

A white woman appeared, one past her prime. She had dyed red hair, which was curled and bound close to her head to cover its thinness. She dressed in an ethereal white robe that hung limply on her thin frame as she reclined on a faded couch. Before her sat two sons, of obviously different fathers. The youngest was dark-haired and thick-boned. His skin was olive-toned, his dark eyes wide and beautiful in the way of all young animals. His face was split into a wide grin as he laughed at his brother.

The older—Jonas—looked solid next to his mother for all that he was a lanky ten-year-old. His curly reddish hair mimicked his mother's, only with natural beauty rather than her dyed glory. His face already held some of the angularity that would later chisel his features, but for now, he was still soft with childhood, his body moving with awkward jerks rather than the rolling grace of the sailor he would become. Jonas looked like a young sapling next to his bear cub of a younger brother. He was tall and bony where his brother was compact, long where his brother was round. But both were undeniably brothers, especially as they gazed rapturously at their mother.

Apparently the boys were taking turns entertaining the woman. The younger had juggled, scattering debris about the small living space. Right now, Jonas was poised on a low table, a well-worn book balanced on his nose as he tried to add something else on top. A shoe? Yes, it was his mother's slipper that he tried to balance on top of the book on top of his nose. He failed. He couldn't see, and as he tried to settle the shoe, he lost the backward arch of his spine. The slipper fell lightly onto his younger brother, and the book tumbled down onto Jonas's toes. He howled in exaggerated pain, rolling about the floor in silly fits of pretend agony while his mother clapped her hands in delight.

Little Pearl did not hear the echoes of rapture in the

woman's voice. She saw instead the way the boys brightened at her humor, exaggerating their antics just for her. And as they tumbled and rolled around like two puppies, the woman grew younger and happier.

Little Pearl pressed harder against the railing, hunger and jealousy eating at her. When had her family ever played like this? Her brothers certainly had tumbled about the ground like animals, but she was a girl. She'd had to stand beside them in a silk dress while she relearned how to walk because of her bound feet.

The scene shifted before her, and soon she was watching her brothers play catch with her doll. They laughed at her, but soon their game of keep-away became three boys tumbling on the ground. Her doll was forgotten. She was, too, as she sat on the floor and sobbed. It hurt to press her feet to the ground, so she had to crawl to her doll. There was never any question that she might jump or run with her brothers; she was useless for anything but sitting and crying, and they told her so whenever they taunted her.

"You were the youngest?"

She glanced up, seeing Jonas's sober face. He was no longer looking at his happy mother, but at herself clutching a ragged doll and her brothers in riotous play. "Youngest by less than year," she answered. "But different by much more."

He nodded, his eyes sad. He watched her, not the scene below. "How young were you when they bound your feet?"

"Four, almost five."

"Old enough to remember?"

She nodded, and he turned back to the scene.

"It's a cruel thing to do to a child. I don't know how you could stand it."

She didn't answer except to look back at her hiding place. There was much that was cruel in China.

Below, she heard her parents storm into the hallway, bellowing at the boys. The children straightened immediately, but it was too late. Each was smacked soundly across the face, then given a bucket of water and a thick sponge brush. In a mulish line, they went outside to practice calligraphy with water on the brick walk. Their father went with them to pace behind their squatting backsides. He held a thick stick in his hand, always ready to strike again if their strokes erred. The child Little Pearl remained on the floor below, shrunken against another table. When all the hall was silent, she crawled to the window to watch her brothers and father. She would stand there for hours watching, completely alone as the boys were praised or beaten.

Closing her eyes to the memory, Little Pearl crawled back under the upstairs table, tucking her feet beneath her. "I was prized for my tiny feet," she said. "If I had married, my husband would have been envied." As a prostitute, she had made fortunes for the madame. She'd lost count of the number of men who'd wanted to play with her toes before they rutted between her legs. She looked out from beneath the table to see Jonas's gaze heavy on her.

"I care nothing for your feet, Little Pearl. Only your heart."

She tucked herself tighter against the wall. "You should go. They will come for me soon. I will not look so pretty to you then."

He squatted down to face her beneath the table. "Who will come, Little Pearl?"

"The Ugly Man!" Her voice was growing more childish by the second, but she was powerless to stop it. She could hear the voices now, clear as day. Jonas could, too, and he tilted his head to listen more closely. Turning away from her, he stepped to the railing and looked down.

"She is too loud!" her father snapped. "She will never marry well!"

"She is young and angry," her mother returned, equally loud. "All girls her age are. She will settle down with the right husband."

"We will all starve by then! We have three boys to educate. Three!"

"But—"

"One of us must pass the examinations," he said. "Or we will lose everything."

Jonas twisted back to look at her. "What are these exams?"

"To become an official. Many spend their entire lives trying to pass one level or another."

He glanced back to the floor. "Did your father pass?"

"I don't know!" she spat. "I only know that each level is expensive to take, expensive to study, and my father had no other skill."

Jonas sighed. "So he sold you to pay for his dream."

She didn't answer. She didn't need to; she could hear the dickering over her price begin. One glance at Jonas told her he was listening, too. Soon the Ugly Man would come—

"Why are we here?" Jonas asked. "Why are we seeing this?"

She ducked her head against the table leg. "It's where I go. Where your yang brings me."

"But why?"

She shrugged. "I don't know."

"Can we change it?"

She gaped at him. "One does not change Heaven."

He glanced around. "This doesn't look like Heaven to me. Can't we look at my memory instead?"

She didn't know how to answer; she didn't know if it were possible. As she stared at him, he decided to try. He turned and looked at the ground floor, his face tightening with concentration. She crawled out to see below. To her shock, she watched the scene change. One moment the Ugly Man was counting out coins. The next, she saw Jonas's mother doling out grapes to her sons.

"Much better," Jonas grunted.

Little Pearl felt her mouth open in shock. An irrational fury swept through her. "This is my home!" she screeched. "My home!"

Gripping the slats of the railing, she stared down. Before her eyes, the wall shifted and faded. Soon her parents appeared again. The Ugly Man pulled the last of his coins from his grubby purse. He would come for her now. She should scramble back under the table.

Except, she didn't move. She could hear the white boys' laughter on the other side of the ground floor. Jonas's memory existed alongside her own. His mother was playfully dropping grapes into their mouths, and their giggles jarred painfully with the sound of coins dropping into her family's heirloom box. How could both exist side by side?

"Why?" Jonas interrupted. "Why do you insist on seeing that?"

"This is my house!" she shot back. "My memory! My life!"

"But it's over," he pressed.

She glared at him. "So is yours. Where is your mother now?" She knew the answer: his mother had died in a drunken stupor. One of his sailors had told her.

As expected, his face grew sad, and she immediately felt remorse for her cruelty. Why did she always act this way?

"Yes, she's gone," he said sadly, and he turned back to his past. "That's why I like seeing her this way. It's a good memory of a good time." He shifted to pin her with his glare. "Why do you like seeing *that*?" He gestured to the floor. The Ugly Man was coming up the stairs. She could hear his heavy tread, smell the garlic and onion on his breath.

"No!" she screeched, and scrambled back under the

table. "No!" she cried again as she clutched the table leg. She knew it was a useless gesture. She was much too small to fight. Even as an adult, she would be too weak.

Jonas turned to face the Ugly Man. She saw him tense, saw him take a protective stance in front of her. Could he fight her memory? Was it possible? It wasn't the thought so much as the sight of him, fists ready, that penetrated her anger. And as he stood there waiting to face her nightmare, she felt her wall of irrational anger waver.

"Run," he said over his shoulder.

She blinked, the thought spinning in her head. "Where?" She had tried to run to her brothers, but the Ugly Man had caught her. Her parents blocked the only other exit.

"Go to my home—my memory."

She leaned out from beneath the table, craning her neck to see his family, but the stretch was too far; she had to come out from her hiding place. "It's not possible," she whispered back.

"Of course it is. Go!"

"I can't leave you here to fight for me. I can't." Even she wasn't so cruel as to leave him in her nightmare while she ran to his joy.

Jonas shifted and held out his hand. "We'll run together."

She instinctively shrank away from him, the intensity in his eyes too much. But he knelt down to face her directly, his back to the stairs.

"Stand up!" she cried. "The Ugly Man is coming!" Jonas's back was toward the stairs, leaving him unprotected.

"We'll leave. You're an adult now. Nothing is holding you here." He reached out to touch her arm, but she only tightened it around the table. Even her legs were wrapped around the solid wood.

"Come away, Little Pearl," Jonas coaxed. "There is nothing for you here."

She looked over his shoulder. She could see the Ugly Man topping the stairs. Behind him stood not only her parents, but every ancestor she had—every male name etched on the family altar, every remembered aunt and grandmother and cousin. They were all there, staring at her. At this point in her nightmare, she usually threw her shame at them. She screeched and cursed and cried that everything she did was their fault, their shame.

And yet, when she opened her mouth to damn them, she found herself interrupted. She heard the laughter of the two white boys, Jonas and his brother doing something silly. She twisted her head, wondering what it could be. She bit her lip and fought the tears. "I can't leave," she whispered.

"You can. Just let go."

"He'll get me."

"I'm right here," Jonas said. "We'll run together."

She closed her eyes, pressing her forehead against the wood. In her mind, she heard two things: the clink of coins and the boys' laughter. Which would she choose? "I'm afraid," she confessed.

"I'll keep you safe."

"But . . . what if you can't?"

He touched her cheek, stroking a tender caress across her face. "What if I can?"

She swallowed. Over Jonas's shoulder she could still see the Ugly Man, followed by her parents and her grandparents and all those ancestors. She had been cursing them every second of her life, starting from the night the Ugly Man first came. Could she just walk away? They were all she had.

Except, that wasn't true anymore, was it? Her gaze shifted back to Jonas. It was time to choose. It was time.

It took an act of will. She had to consciously decide to

release her grip on the table and crawl out. It was the scariest thing she'd ever done, and yet once decided, it happened so easily. Her hands opened; her legs relaxed. Jonas helped her crawl out. And then she jumped to her feet, grabbed his hand, and began to run. They went together, flying in the opposite direction.

In her family's house there was no stairway where they ran, and yet one appeared before them—one that led directly down to where his mother played with her sons. Grapes and bread crumbs were spread across the floor, and his mother clapped her hands in delight. They ran as fast as they could down those stairs.

When Little Pearl tried to look behind her, she slipped. She would have tumbled down the stairs, but Jonas held her upright, tucking her securely by his side.

"Don't look back. Focus ahead."

It was hard to obey, harder even than letting go in the first place. But she did. She willed it, and in time the urge faded.

"Focus on the laughter," he said.

She shook her head. She couldn't hear laughter anymore. She could only hear him—his breathing, his words. So she held on to that and to him. Without her even realizing it, the sounds of pursuing footsteps faded.

And then they hit the bottom step, turned a corner, and stepped into something completely new.

"This is not my memory," Jonas whispered.

"No," Little Pearl agreed, her breath filled with awe. "It's Heaven."

Every traditional Chinese household has a chuun hup, *a tray of togetherness, a teak or rosewood box with eight compartments filled with sweets that symbolize the sweetness of life. My parents fill their box with kumquats for golden luck; candied lotus seeds, symbolizing the wish for more sons; dragon eye for their sweetness and roundness; watermelon seeds for more children; chocolate gold coins for golden wealth; candied lotus root, symbolizing endless friendship; candied wintermelon, representing a continuous line of descendants like the vines of the melon plant; and coconut for good relationship between fathers and sons.*

Chapter Twenty

Jonas slowed his steps, his breath suspended in awe. This was Heaven? He saw so little, and yet what he did see filled his heart with joy. He heard sounds—a music that also had texture and taste and even a wonderful rich scent. His eyes feasted on colors that were so bright as to be white, and yet also much more. He could barely discern the palatial walls surrounding him, and yet he had the feeling that they were mere imagination. That if he willed it, he could also see trees or oceans, birds and sky—his choice, his delight.

"This is Heaven?" he breathed.

Beside him, Little Pearl nodded. "We are Immortals."

He glanced at her, feeling abruptly frightened. "Are we dead?"

"No, merely blessed. So blessed." Her eyes were huge, her stance reverent. Indeed, as he watched, she folded neatly upon herself, her knees falling to the ground, her head following in a deep kowtow. Only then did he notice that her attire had changed. Instead of a shimmering blue silk dress, she now wore a raiment too stunning to comprehend. He saw streams of light surrounding her like ribbons of glory, entwining and accenting her body, her face, her entire being. "Little Pearl," he whispered. "You are truly beautiful."

"As are you," she whispered.

At first he didn't know how he heard her with her face pressed to the floor, but then he realized that they had not been speaking with their mouths. Before, too—back in her parents' house—they had merely been thinking their words only to have the other person understand. Some part of him knew that he was thinking about logical things, stupid small things, because his surroundings were so much more than he could comprehend. He was a man in Heaven. He needed to try to understand. He might never get the chance again. So he lifted his gaze even as his knees bent in humility. Only to realize that he was face to face with an angel.

"Welcome, welcome!" the divine creature said with a laugh. She was as beautiful as everything here, not in form but in a brightness of spirit. And yet, he also saw a willowy body, flowing auburn hair, and arms spread lovingly wide in welcome. It was some moments before he realized she was achingly familiar.

Jonas blinked and blinked, but there was no need. He knew this angel, and his heart welled up at the truth. "Mum! Oh . . ." He embraced her without thought because he had always hugged his mother. She returned it in full measure, without either the reserve or the desperation he remembered of her earthly body. It was a wonder to him, and he was still in awe of her difference when they separated and she knelt before Little Pearl.

"Welcome, Little Sister," she said, her smile growing both brighter and gentler as she touched Little Pearl's shoulder.

Jonas began to tremble, his thoughts spinning with

the image before him. His mother and Little Pearl embracing like society matrons. And yet his mother wasn't an angel. She was a broken, wasted whore. In Heaven? It couldn't be.

He knew the thought was unworthy of this place, even felt the coldness of the idea weighing him down. "But how can you be here?" he gasped. "This is Chinese Heaven." Unless it was the place whores went after they died. Whores and their sons. And yet it was so beautiful, so incredible. His mind was reeling even as his thoughts continued to deaden his heart.

His angel mother kept smiling at Little Pearl, who was only now raising her head. "Everyone is welcome here when they are ready," she said to him. Then she gestured behind her to more beings clustered a short distance away. Jonas saw Little Pearl's parents and grandparents. Near them, he saw the old priest who used to walk the docks damning the unholy. He also saw sailors and prostitutes—all dead—standing beside an MP and a bishop. "Everyone," his mother repeated. "And now you are welcome, too."

Little Pearl's eyes never faltered; her gaze remained trained on his angel mother. Her mouth opened to speak, but no sound came out. Jonas could hear Little Pearl's thoughts, though, and knew what she wanted to say but couldn't. She was grateful. Where once had been a dark and cold anger was now a brilliant ocean of gratitude. She felt saved, forgiven, and so blessed that she couldn't even begin to express her joy.

Jonas himself could only stare, looking about him while his thoughts churned inside. His mother was in Heaven. He was so pleased for her, and yet the thought was impossible to understand. Because they stood so closely together, he could feel her spirit. He understood it in a way that wasn't possible on Earth. He knew that her past was still part of her. What she had done, what she had been, how she had hurt herself and others—all of that still shaped who she was. Her sins were not erased or washed clean. They were a part of her, and yet, she was welcomed joyously by the moral and the refined. She was stunningly beautiful, gloriously happy, and no better nor any worse than all the other angels in Heaven. She was completely equal even as she was uniquely herself.

But how could one be glorious and tainted all at once? She couldn't be. She wasn't. She was whole and divine no matter what she had done and how she had once been labeled. And he—a man who had prided himself on being open and accepting of all kinds—struggled to accept such total equality.

He reeled from the thought, and his heart grew colder and heavier the more he struggled. Then his wondrous mother turned to him and pressed a kiss to his cheek. "Come visit me again soon," she whispered.

He plummeted back to Earth.

Jonas woke with a slow groan. He was both cold and hot; his limbs chilled as they lay lax and immobile, his front hot where Little Pearl sprawled on top of him, equally still. He wasn't even sure she was breathing, and yet her body burned like the sun.

He blinked, but couldn't find the strength to do more. His thoughts felt heavy and slow, his body infinitely more so. He would have pushed Little Pearl from him, but he knew the weight that oppressed him came from himself, not her.

His mother was an angel in Heaven. He was stunned, and he was ashamed of his shock. He was pleased for her—really and truly pleased. He loved his mother and was glad she had made it into Heaven. He had been to church and read the Bible. He knew that belief in Jesus could wash away sins. And yet . . .

Perhaps in his heart he had never believed it. A whore was a whore and could never be anything else. Even those who gave up the life remained tainted in some fundamental way. Though he had prayed for a change, had been baptized in the hope that all sins could be washed away, even sought out and pushed Little Pearl to accept the hope of salvation . . . had he ever truly believed it? In his heart of hearts, had he ever really thought it possible?

He examined his own mind, the unconscious beliefs that wormed through his life without his knowledge. There he discovered the truth: He hadn't believed what he preached. At his core, he thought that one could love a whore, one could pray for her sanity, but the daily abuse of body and soul corrupted a woman until there was little left. He had seen it not only with his mother, but with countless other bawds who haunted docks the world over. They were lost forever. He had tried to help them—to help Little Pearl—but never truly believed it was possible. True forgiveness and salvation were real!

His gaze slid to Little Pearl. He felt her silky hair across his shoulder, knew the delicate curve of her bones and the sensuous caress of her hands. He knew her in every sense of the word, and yet in his unconscious mind she was a whore. He loved her; he knew that. But . . .

His mind balked as he lifted his head, looking down on her still form. She was still in Heaven, talking with his angelic mother, while he had been tossed out like so much rubbish. Jealousy stirred in his heart even though he knew it was unworthy. Little Pearl had lived a terrible life. As difficult as his own childhood had been, hers was infinitely worse. She deserved every moment of

Heaven she could get. He did not begrudge her that. And yet . . .

He closed his eyes, quietly longing for the soul-deep peace he'd experienced. Except, of course, it hadn't been simple peace that pervaded his spirit in Heaven; it had been love—a total, all-encompassing, all-accepting love. Love for himself, for Little Pearl, for the bawds and the priests, for all that had ever breathed or hurt or laughed. How he wished he were back there.

Little Pearl's breaths abruptly deepened. She inhaled enough for him to feel the press of her ribs and the delicate shudder that wracked her frame as she descended back to Earth. He raised his arms, gently wrapping them around her to ease her transition. Then he pressed a soft kiss to her temple, truly sad that she'd had to leave Heaven so soon. No wonder most people went to Heaven only after death. It was too hard to live on Earth after experiencing—even for a brief moment—the gloriousness of that place.

It took a long time for Little Pearl to return to her body. He held her throughout, sharing her every stuttering breath, her every reluctant moan. Without even realizing it, he began speaking to her, murmuring endearments against her temple. In time, he felt her eyelashes flutter against his neck.

"You left," she said, her voice a low croak.

"I wasn't worthy," he responded, surprised how easily the confession came. Then he pressed a kiss to her forehead. "I'm glad you could stay."

She shook her head. It was a slow, tiny movement, but they were pressed so closely together that he felt it. "All are worthy."

"I wasn't," he said, his failure cutting deep into his heart.

"No," she began, pushing up to face him more fully.

But at the moment she shifted, they both realized he was still deep inside her. She gasped in surprise while his mind was swamped by a wave of pleasure.

He gripped her hips, and their eyes locked. There was a great deal that he wanted to say to her. A great deal more he had to sort out before that. And yet, she was here—all sweet woman—and he was already lengthening inside her.

He extended a hand, touching her cheek as he saw both her physical body and the memory of her stunning beauty in heaven. "Little Pearl," he whispered. "I love you. More than I did before. I didn't understand; I didn't realize . . ." Why couldn't he find the right words? "I love you. Completely. Can you ever forgive me for being such an ass?"

She smiled the most honest smile he had ever seen on her face. There was no veneer of anger nor even the bright edge of fear. "We are forgiven spirits, you and I. Immortal and beloved." She grinned. "We are loved!" Then her grin shifted into something more personal and infinitely tender as she slowly, carefully, deliberately squeezed him with her inner muscles.

He groaned in response, all his thoughts washed away. Heaven had been overwhelming. This was something he understood, and he gratefully surrendered to it. He flexed his hips, grinning as she arched into his thrust and her breasts bounced in front of his eyes. She stretched out against him, lengthening her spine, teasing his lips with her nipples. He obliged, easily capturing a nub and drawing it into his mouth. He rolled the tip with his tongue and sucked in a rhythm to match the glorious things she did to him below.

"It's too soon to go back," she said. Her words came in stuttering pants. "We won't go back to Heaven."

"Good," he answered as he burrowed a thumb between them. He knew how to pleasure a woman, and he wanted this moment to be one of joy. She ground her hips against him. His thumb didn't have room to circle, but he could move it up and down over her while deep inside his organ thrust with a power all its own.

She lifted, her torso gloriously displayed before him. She was free with her actions, open with her pleasure, and absolutely beautiful in her excitement.

He felt a roar begin behind his eyes. It built to a thundering in his head and rolled through his body. Little Pearl's own shudders had already begun, adding power to his climax. He tried to hold off, but it was too late; his entire body compressed into a small dot before surging forward, erupting, pouring into her.

His vision darkened, his mind lost to wave after wave of release. He felt her still around him, somehow drawing whatever he had from him, but he willingly surrendered it to her. In an instant, he'd become wholly hers.

Little Pearl dozed peacefully on top of Jonas. Somewhere in the back of her mind she knew she had responsibilities: meals to cook, students to teach, servants to instruct. But all was lost in the wonder of resting quietly here.

Another part of her crowed that she was now an Immortal, a tigress who had walked in Heaven then returned to Earth. She smiled at that, allowing herself a moment of pride. Tigresses throughout China would now come to learn from her, to sit in her presence, to hear whatever wisdom she might impart. She had improved herself. She would have respect.

The thought was completely silly. She had no more wisdom today than she'd had yesterday. All she had was a suddenly quiet spirit, a heart released from anger and filled with love—Heaven's and a white man's love.

Never would she have thought this possible. But as she raised herself up off her lover, she knew that it all had happened, it all was true. Jonas was sleeping. He was an Immortal, too. Given his injuries, she was not surprised that he slept deeply and heavily. Ascension was exhausting. And yet, she remained awake, stunned by the lightness she felt. How had she not known that anger weighted the spirit, that love lifted and strengthened as nothing else could?

She gingerly moved her leg off of him, slipping to his side. But even this separation was too much, so she dipped forward to touch his lips with her own, to smell his scent, and to linger for just a moment more.

One moment. One more. One . . .

Stop! she told herself. It was time to return to reality and long-neglected duties. It was time to see if she could carry this joy through the rest of her days and nights, if life truly was different as an Immortal.

She slipped to the floor and lifted a blanket from the cupboard beneath the table. She gently covered Jonas's naked body, seeing not only how pale he was, but how beautiful. She smiled. Her big, hairy white lover was beautiful.

As she leaned down to grab her clothing, she abruptly froze with her skirt half tied on her hips. The door had opened and someone had slipped inside. She knew this from the sudden dark breeze. There had been little shift in light, so it must already be night. She turned to see whose energy so polluted this place.

Mr. Su. She made out his dark silhouette as he took shaky steps forward. He stepped into the candlelight, and she saw total determination in his face as he raised a long, wicked knife. She felt her mouth grow slack as the last of her spirit descended hard and fast to Earth. Unknown to her, part of her spirit had held on to Heaven, part of her had lingered in that place of total acceptance, total love. Mr. Su and his knife ended that link, and her spirit darkened accordingly.

His gaze flickered over her half-naked body. He was a dragon practitioner, she remembered, and he would sense her new status as an Immortal. Except, did he? She saw his lip curl in disgust at what he'd imagined happened here. Then his gaze shifted to Jonas on the table, and his mouth curved into a smile.

"Well done, whore," he said. "You will be rewarded for your sacrifice."

"We ascended to Heaven. We are Immortals."

He nodded, his knife lowering only slightly. "Agreed. You will be revered throughout China. Unfortunately, the experience was too much for the ape. He went insane and had to be killed. How fortunate I was here to save you."

It took a moment for her to understand. He didn't believe she'd ascended, simply was willing to support the fabrication in exchange for her help in killing Jonas. And in that moment, another truth hit her with enough force to cut the air from her lungs.

No one would believe she was an Immortal. Just as she herself hadn't believed Charlotte Wicks, no one would believe her. Unless, of course, someone like Mr. Su supported her claim. The word of a white man like Jonas would mean less than nothing.

In return for silence, Mr. Su was offering Little Pearl everything she had ever hoped for. She would become an Immortal in everyone else's eyes. He would reward her for her help, and she would suddenly have the protection of one of the most powerful men in Shanghai. She could lead this tigress temple if she chose, or he might even help her bring Shi Po and her husband home. She would receive the adulation she deserved and could have any earthly thing she wanted—if she switched allegiance from a stupid white ape to a powerful man of her own country and religion.

She swallowed, her thoughts still reeling. Her future

was so clear. It was more than she had ever hoped for, and the best that could possibly be for a whore in China. The alternative, of course, was a life of pain and ridicule as a white man's lover. And that was assuming Mr. Su didn't kill her.

All these things flashed through her mind as Mr. Su raised his knife, readying to plunge it into Jonas's chest. She made her decision in the space between one breath and the next. She closed her eyes; then, screaming with all the force in her lungs, she dove forward to land on top of Jonas. The knife plunged into her back— not straight down, but slicing sideways, as she might carve the side of a fish. Her scream became a screech of pain. Beneath her, Jonas started awake, his body moving even as she tried to hold him down, shielding him with her body.

Mr. Su cursed, his unsteady hands fumbling as he ripped the knife from her side. Beneath her, Jonas growled in fury. She felt a crippling pain that immobilized her, and yet Little Pearl's mind was a quiet place, at last serene.

Jonas was awake now. It would take a moment for Mr. Su to regrip the knife, long enough for Jonas to reorient and defend himself. Meanwhile, she stayed an effective shield.

She might die from this wound. Part of her accepted that. And the darker part of her mind knew a stabbing death was appropriate to a whore and she was already throwing that shame at her ancestors' feet. But she also would be ascending to Heaven for real. She would once again be accepted as a creature of light and love. A glorious future—one she was more than ready to embrace. And yet . . .

Mr. Su pushed at her, and she gasped as pain sliced across her consciousness. Jonas, too, was moving, sliding out from beneath the blanket, his widened eyes leaping from her to Mr. Su and back.

"Little Pearl!" he cried as the door opened and two men entered. She could not see them clearly except as large dark figures. Large, unfamiliar figures. Mr. Su's men.

"I'm fine," she lied. Except it wasn't totally a lie. If she died, she would go back to Heaven. She now knew it was a beautiful place.

Jonas was on his feet. How he had managed to gently set her on the table while maneuvering around Mr. Su, she hadn't a clue, but she was down and he was pacing carefully toward their attacker and the two large men flanking him.

"He came for you," she croaked. "He wants to kill you." She tried to shift position on the table, to gain her feet and help Jonas, but her pain was too severe. She couldn't move her arm, and blood was making the table slick. Besides, she realized with a sigh, what could she do? She was no fighter, and on bound feet, she would simply be a hindrance. And yet, there had to be something she could do.

The answer came to her. She might not be able to fight, but she could distract Mr. Su. She began speaking, her voice thick and coarse. But as her words started to flow, her voice grew stronger, her qi filling each sound with power.

"Do you know why I chose him over you, Mr. Su? Because he has more power. Because he has the loyalty of his men, where you only have slaves. Free men and women join their fortunes to this white man, while you . . . you are from old China. You are of a century of slaves and masters and hatred."

It worked. Mr. Su turned his attention to her. But he also gestured his two men forward to finish off Jonas. Little Pearl didn't stop. Using her good arm, she levered herself upright to face him.

"You will be betrayed, Mr. Su. I betrayed you. Your slaves betray you. We have all joined a white man against you."

Jonas lunged, intending to get between her and Mr. Su, but he was stopped as Su's cronies attacked. They had knives—long plain blades remarkable only because they looked very, very sharp. Jonas had nothing, not even clothing to cover himself, but he did not seem afraid.

Little Pearl took a breath, shifting to press the blanket against her wound. Mr. Su stepped forward, his hand growing steadier as he pointed his knife at her. How strange, that she did not fear it or him. She knew what waited in Heaven. And all the while her words kept flowing.

"You have nothing, Mr. Su. You *are* nothing but fear and hatred. I renounce you."

He sucked in his breath in a loud hiss, exposing teeth as if he were an animal. She grinned at him, knowing that she had at last found the key to Mr. Su. She knew his weakness. How much more wonderful that everything she said was absolutely true.

"Yes, Mr. Su, this dirty worthless whore dismisses you as unimportant." And she turned her back on him.

She wasn't stupid. She knew she had just sent the villain into a rage. But his breath was loud, his anger a palpable force. She didn't need to see him to avoid his attack. Without another word, she jumped off the table and staggered to the opposite wall. It was hard to balance with one hand pressed to her side.

Mr. Su's knife embedded itself deep into the blanket and the table where she had just been. She heard the fabric rip from the cut, and she tugged harder. To the side, Jonas was still fighting. He'd elbowed one man in the face while blocking the knife arm of the other. To her relief, she saw no wounds on him. The other two, however, looked wobbly. It looked like he might just finish them off.

She turned her attention back to Mr. Su just as the door opened one more time. More slaves come to help their master, she guessed. Could Jonas manage them all?

Mr. Su ripped his knife out of the table, and the sudden release of the blanket had her tumbling backward. She caught herself on a tapestry, but was unable to right herself before the man surged forward.

"Leave her alone!" Jonas bellowed, probably to distract Mr. Su. One glance to the side told her that Su's minions were not nearly as weak as they appeared. The first two had rallied, and were now pressing Jonas hard. She couldn't see the others.

"I'm fine," she shot back. "He is no threat." It was a lie, but it kept Mr. Su's attention firmly fixed on her.

Mr. Su roared in disgust, and Little Pearl realized his knife hand was steadier than any other part of his body. His steps were slow, but on her bound feet, she was slower. His breath rasped in his throat, but he would not die from suffocation anytime soon. Worse, he had full range of movement, able to come at her from all sides, while she was still hampered by clinging to the thick tapestry covering the walls.

Little Pearl glanced at Jonas and prayed he would be able to rescue her. No luck. The two thugs lunged together, and Jonas . . . She blinked. Jonas had dropped out of sight. They had gotten him. He was . . .

Bursting upward. Had he been crouching? Where there had been empty air a second before was now filled with Jonas and his heavy fists. He caught one man underneath the jaw, snapping the man's head back and knocking him senseless. The other was better protected. He blocked a blow with his upraised arm, but his chest was left wide open. Jonas slammed first one hand, then the other hard right above his heart. The brute's eyes bulged as his breath left him in a whoosh. Then Jonas grabbed the man's knife hand, twisting the weapon away while he slugged the man in the face. His second attacker dropped and suddenly the path to her was clear.

Too late. Mr. Su was lunging at her. Little Pearl tried to slide to the side, but knew she was too slow. Even if she avoided this cut, Mr. Su had her in a corner. Whatever path she took, she would end on his knife, spitted like a chicken.

"No," she whispered, shocked to realize she wanted to live. She still longed for the glories of Heaven, but even so, she wanted to stay on Earth a while longer. She wanted to stay here with Jonas. The past, as terrible as it had been, was nothing compared to the future she imagined. She reached out, searching for a weapon. She met only tapestry and hard wall on both sides. She grabbed a fistful of cloth, throwing it forward enough to deflect Su's blade. But she was now firmly pressed against the corner. There was nowhere for her to go.

Mr. Su grinned.

She heard a sound, but didn't quite understand it. Neither did Mr. Su, and for a moment he looked down, shock on his face. Following his gaze, Little Pearl saw the point of a knife protruding from his chest in an expanding circle of blood. She looked up to see Jonas grunt in satisfaction as he closed the distance between them. It took another moment before she understood. Jonas had thrown one of the men's knives. Even the most powerful qi would not save Mr. Su now. He would die of that wound.

But not yet. With a hiss of fury, the man raised his knife again. Little Pearl was trapped, her vision blurring from blood loss, her feet unstable on the slick floor.

But then Mr. Su was abruptly hauled backward and a

blade appeared across his throat. She thought it was
Jonas's, but he was moving in front of her, shielding her
with his body. So, who held Mr. Su?

The slave, Rat Face. Though short, he was still tall
enough to press a long blade against his master's throat.
"For my brother," he hissed. Then he pulled the edge
hard and fast across Mr. Su's throat. There wasn't even
time for a gurgle. His master dropped to the floor in a
wash of blood.

Little Pearl whimpered, trying to back away. Jonas
caught her. "I've got you," he said against her temple.
"You're safe now. I've got you."

She nodded and pressed her face into his shoulder. She
breathed deeply, absorbing his yang strength along with
his scent.

"I will see to this," said the slave. "He will stay dead
this time."

She felt Jonas pause. He faced the smaller man.
"Why?"

"Mr. Su is not dead," the man answered, wrapping the
body in a blanket. Mr. Su's head lolled back, the throat
open all the way to the spine. "He is recovering in his
room. I will manage all his business while he recuper-
ates."

Jonas shook his head. "You cannot maintain that for
long."

The slave shrugged. "Long enough. Mr. Su will die
of an infection in a week's time." Then he straightened. "You will find the list you want beneath Master
Tan's bed, hidden in the folds of the women's clothes
there."

Jonas recoiled in shock, but said nothing. The implica-
tion was simple. The slave had control of Mr. Su's business and money for a week, to bilk for as much coin as he
could. Jonas would sell his cargo and help maintain the
fiction of Mr. Su's recuperation. It would be difficult to

manage, but not impossible. And no one would involve the authorities or go to jail.

"Agreed?" the slave pressed.

"Agreed," Jonas answered.

"Agreed," whispered Little Pearl. Then she passed out.

In Chinese cooking, every ingredient and dish is imbued with its own brilliance and lore. This knowledge is passed on through a lifetime of meals, conversations, celebrations, and rituals. Every food has a story.

Chapter Twenty-one

Little Pearl woke slowly. She had been in a beautiful place where she was completely loved and totally accepted. Only after she woke was she able to label the place as Heaven. In her dream, she'd been home and could stay there forever if she so chose.

But she'd left home to return here, even knowing that this place would be hard and cruel. She'd left to come here because of one love. In Heaven, all were accepted openly, but one heart could get lost. Here, on Earth, one love—one man—could shine brighter because of the darkness around him. She would know his love completely before others drowned him out.

Yes, she'd left home to come here—to Earth—to be with Jonas in a dark and difficult place. And in this way, her love for him would also shine brighter than the sun.

She opened her eyes. He was beside her, as she knew he would be. He held her hand and bathed her face with cool water. He prayed over her fingertips, and pressed kisses into her palm. He was here with her, and so when she opened her eyes, his wide grin was the first thing she saw.

She smiled in her own greeting.

"Little Pearl!" he whispered. "How do you feel?"

She frowned, cataloguing her body. She felt dark and heavy with pain. In short, she felt as she had after first returning from Heaven. "Alive," she whispered. "I feel alive."

"You are that," he answered. "Though I had my doubts." He swallowed. "You've slept a long time."

"How long?"

"You've been in and out for a week. The fever was bad, Little Pearl, but you fought hard. It broke two nights ago. You've been sleeping since then."

She blinked, unable to comprehend the passage of time. In truth, she had difficulty understanding much beyond the present moment with Jonas at her side.

"Are you thirsty? I have soup here for you. Mei Wan made it. She says it will help you grow strong."

Little Pearl didn't have an answer. Her body was still too alien for her to discern one sensation from another. Was she hungry? Thirsty?

Jonas lifted her up, supporting her back with pillows. As he leaned over her, she felt the scrape of his beard across her face and smelled the not-too-unpleasant scent of white man. When he sat back, she mourned his distance.

"Is there a lot of pain?" he asked.

"No." It wasn't a lie. There was no more and no less pain than she'd expected. It was part of the bargain she'd made—that all made—when they chose to live on Earth for a while longer.

She frowned, wondering at that thought even as it

slipped away. She was an Immortal now, she realized again. And one of the things she remembered from the texts was that no Immortal remembered much of their time in Heaven. That was why the texts were steeped in imagery and vague phrases—no human could retain the fullness.

"Are you all right?" Jonas asked.

She nodded, smiling at him in reassurance. Only now did she see the dark circles under his eyes, the gray cast to his skin. He must have sat by her side day and night. She frowned, memories filtering back to her piece by piece, faster and faster, until she felt drowned in human reality.

"Mr. Su . . ."

"Gone to his home to recuperate. I have heard that he has caught an infection."

Mr. Su was dead, she remembered. There had been that agreement with the slave.

"Eat." Jonas held up a spoonful of soup to her lips. She obediently opened her mouth and swallowed, a grimace of distaste making her wrinkle her nose. "Too much ginger."

"You can tell Mei Wan that as soon as you get stronger."

She nodded in agreement, but her thoughts were elsewhere. Her gaze slipped to the sunny sky outside the window. Fair weather. And Jonas a sailor. But something had kept him here. . . .

"The list," she said between bites. "Your cargo."

His smile lightened his face. "It was exactly where that slave said it was. Everything's sold. We've loaded up a new cargo." He glanced at the window. "Seth is well out of port by now."

She frowned. "But you're here. . . ."

He nodded, and for the first time, his expression

turned hesitant. "I realized something, Little Pearl. I . . . when we went to Heaven . . . You remember, right? The day you—"

"I remember." At the moment, Heaven was clearer than Earth. "We met your mother."

He nodded as he set down the soup, then gathered her hand. "I should let you rest. You've had a rough time of it."

"Tell me about your mother." The beautiful angel was clear in her mind. She'd never thought of white people as angels before, but race made no difference up there. Neither did past or future, sins or blessings. All was different there, but only Earth had Jonas.

"You know I love you," he said slowly, his eyes on their intertwined hands. "I told you that before, but I never realized how much until then. And then that bastard stabbed you."

She frowned, searching her memory. Some things were still hazy.

"But that's not what I realized," Jonas continued, his words rushed. "I mean, I knew I loved you. I just didn't think about other things. About . . ." He swallowed. "You don't marry whores, you know. It's always a mess. They're damaged women, and even if they've renounced the life, it never works. I've seen men eaten alive by thinking of what was, of what could be, of . . ."

She didn't understand his words. "Jonas—," she began, but he cut her off.

"No, listen. For all my talk of love, I still thought of you as a whore."

"I *was* a whore. I have—"

"No. You haven't done that for a long time. You're a chef and a tigress. I know I said that before, but I don't think I ever believed it. Not truly."

She frowned at him, trying to sort through to his meaning. She couldn't find it. "Jonas, it's all right. I am what I am. I am at peace with it now."

He nodded. "That's what I'm trying to say. That I'm at peace with it, too. That it doesn't matter to me what's happened in the past. I know you, I know your spirit and your heart. And I realize that I love you. Completely."

He stopped speaking, his expression open and eager as he stared at her. She felt her chest heat and the pain fade from her consciousness just from the power of his smile. "I love you, too," she said. Amazing how easily the strange words flowed. "I love you, Captain Jonas."

He grinned, but when she leaned forward for his kiss, he tightened his grip on her hands holding her still. "You don't understand."

She sighed. Her heart and mind were becoming more centered on Earth the longer she spoke, but what was she missing? What—

"I want to marry you. I want us to marry. I mean . . ." He pulled her fingers to his lips. "Will you marry me?"

She stared at where his lips pressed into her knuckles. Was he crouching on the floor? On one knee? But why? "There's no need," she said. She had already chosen him over Heaven. A ceremony meant nothing to her; a binding vow made little difference when she had already chosen her path with him no matter where it went.

"There's every need," he returned. "I need to show you that I will stay with you, I will be with you no matter what happens or why. I want to bind my life to yours." He grinned. "And yours to mine."

"But we became Immortals together. We are already linked. . . ." Her voice faded away. It felt odd. She could see how important a ceremony was to him. And, in truth, she knew that the further she slipped from Heaven, the more important earthly events would become to her. Very soon, she would want this binding as much as he. So she smiled, lifting his hands to her lips. "Of course I will marry you. I love you."

He grinned and rushed forward to kiss her, only to stop before their lips touched. "There will be problems. I am still a white man. I know you want to stay here and teach. I can stay here and try and keep up with Kui Yu's investments until he returns. There's a great deal that needs attention. It will be hard—a white man living in Chinese Shanghai—but we could move. I will buy a place where I'm allowed. You could still come back here to teach. Or cook. Or whatever you like."

She shook her head. Not because what he said was wrong; he was probably right. It would likely be very difficult, but she saw determination in his face and body. He would make it work. Together they could make any of it work. She shook her head because it was too much for her to follow.

Teach? Cook? Live? Those were mundane details, the tiny management of life and body. What they shared—their love and their knowledge of Heaven—was all that mattered. So long as they were together, the rest would fall as it would.

"I love you," she said firmly. "I will go with you and be with you no matter where you choose to work."

He shook his head. "But you won't have to follow me, Little Pearl. That's what I'm saying. I'm staying in China with you. I want to be with you. Here."

She smiled, knowing soon she would understand the enormity of his sacrifice. But for now—right this moment—she had one thought on her mind. "I love you," she whispered. "And we are together. What else is there to know?"

He leaned forward, touching his forehead to hers.

"That *I* love *you*. And I will move Heaven and Earth to be with you forever."

"Agreed," she whispered.

"Agreed," he repeated. And then—finally—he kissed her. And at that moment, her earthly life truly began. A future of beauty and peace.

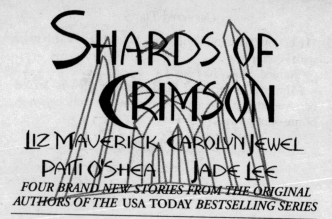

SHARDS OF CRIMSON

LIZ MAVERICK · CAROLYN JEWEL
PATTI O'SHEA · JADE LEE

FOUR BRAND NEW STORIES FROM THE ORIGINAL
AUTHORS OF THE USA TODAY BESTSELLING SERIES

It's been said there's no such thing as quiet here. Ever since the metropolis first became home to paranormals, discord was named queen. But who will be her king—vampires, werewolves, demons or men? One thing remains sure: This land is a battleground and conflict is eternal. Yet there are those who join together—strangers, enemies, lovers. Here, one silken caress can be deadlier than a bullet, but some still know joy. For darkness can become light, and in one sharp instant pain can become ecstasy, and hatred, love.

Dorchester Publishing Co., Inc.
P.O. Box 6640
Wayne, PA 19087-8640

_____52710-3
$7.99 US/$9.99 CAN

Please add $2.50 for shipping and handling for the first book and $.75 for each additional book. NY and PA residents, add appropriate sales tax. No cash, stamps, or CODs. Canadian orders require an extra $2.00 for shipping and handling and must be paid in U.S. dollars. Prices and availability subject to change. **Payment must accompany all orders.**

Name: _____

Address: _____

City: _____ State: _____ Zip: _____

E-mail: _____

I have enclosed $_____ in payment for the checked book(s).

CHECK OUT OUR WEBSITE! www.dorchesterpub.com
_____ Please send me a free catalog.

Desperate Tigress
JADE LEE

Shi Po has devoted her life to the Taoist ideal: enlightenment through ecstasy, through rigid control of the body and mind. The kiss, the caress, the bite, the scratch—these were the stairs to Immortality. But Heaven has been denied her. Shi Po, 19th-century Shanghai's most famous teacher and abbess, its greatest Tigress, has not been granted entrance into Heaven. And so it is time to die.

One man stands in her way: Tan Kui Yu. His fingers, his lips…his dragon. He swears he and Shi Po will attain Heaven even if he has to pleasure her every day—and night—for the rest of their lives. He has other ideas as well—ideas that have never occurred to the woman who has done it all. Perhaps, he says, it is not just about making love, but about feeling it.

Dorchester Publishing Co., Inc.
P.O. Box 6640   5505-8
Wayne, PA 19087-8640 $6.99 US/$8.99 CAN

Please add $2.50 for shipping and handling for the first book and $.75 for each additional book.
NY and PA residents, add appropriate sales tax. No cash, stamps, or CODs. Canadian orders
require an extra $2.00 for shipping and handling and must be paid in U.S. dollars. Prices and
availability subject to change. **Payment must accompany all orders.**

Name: _____

Address: _____

City: _____ State: _____ Zip: _____

E-mail: _____

I have enclosed $_____ in payment for the checked book(s).
CHECK OUT OUR WEBSITE! www.dorchesterpub.com
_____ Please send me a free catalog.

Burning Tigress

JADE LEE

Charlotte Wicks wants more. Running her parents' Shanghai household is necessary drudgery, but a true 19th-century woman deserves something deeper—her body cries out for it! Through a Taoist method, her friend Joanna Crane became a Tigress. Why should Charlotte be denied the same?

Her mother would call her wanton. She would label Charlotte's curiosity evil. Certainly the teacher Charlotte desires is fearsome. Glimpses of his body inspire flutters in her stomach and tingling in her core. The man had a reputation among the females of the city as a bringer of great pleasure. There is only one choice to make.

Dorchester Publishing Co., Inc.
P.O. Box 6640
Wayne, PA 19087-8640

_____5688-7
$6.99 US/$8.99 CAN

Please add $2.50 for shipping and handling for the first book and $.75 for each additional book. NY and PA residents, add appropriate sales tax. No cash, stamps, or CODs. Canadian orders require an extra $2.00 for shipping and handling and must be paid in U.S. dollars. Prices and availability subject to change. **Payment must accompany all orders.**

Name: _____

Address: _____

City: _____ State:_____ Zip: _____

E-mail: _____

I have enclosed $_____ in payment for the checked book(s).

CHECK OUT OUR WEBSITE! www.dorchesterpub.com
_____ Please send me a free catalog.